Val McDermid grew up in a Scottish mining community then read English at Oxford. She was a journalist for sixteen years, spending the last three years as Northern Bureau Chief of a national Sunday tabloid. Now a full-time writer, she divides her time between Cheshire and Northumberland.

Her novels have won international acclaim and a number of prestigious awards. *A Place of Execution* won both the Anthony Award for best novel and the *Los Angeles Times* 2001 Book of the Year Award (Mystery/Thriller category), while *The Mermaids Singing* took the 1995 Gold Dagger for best crime novel of the year.

www.valmcdermid.co.uk

VAL McDERMID

Crack Down
Star Struck

Grafton

HarperCollins*Publishers*
77-85 Fulham Palace Road
Hammersmith, London W6 8JB

The HarperCollins website address is:
www.harpercollins.co.uk

This omnibus edition published in 2004
by HarperCollins*Publishers*

ISBN 0 007 71194 8

Typeset in Meridien by Palimpsest Book Production Limited,
Polmont, Stirlingshire

Printed and bound in Great Britain by
Mackays of Chatham plc, Chatham, Kent

Crack Down

For my mother,
with love and thanks

ACKNOWLEDGEMENTS

I couldn't have written this book without help from several sources. In particular: Diana Cooper, Paula Tyler and Jai Penna all contributed invaluable legal expertise and background information; Lee D'Courcy was generous with specialist knowledge in several key areas; Alison Scott provided me with medical information; Sergeant Cross at the Court Detention Centre kept me on the straight and narrow; Geoff Hardman of Gordon Ford (Horwich) filled in the gaps in my knowledge of the motor trade; and Brigid Baillie provided constructive criticism and encouragement throughout. It would have been a lot less fun without the Wisdom of Julia, the G & R team and the four-legged friends – Dusty, Malone, Molly, Macky, Mutton and Licorice.

Although the book is identifiably set in Manchester and other Northern cities, and many of the locations will be familiar to those who know the patch, all the places and people involved in criminal activities are entirely fictitious. In particular, there is no post office in Brunswick Street, nor any club quite like the Delta. Any resemblance to reality is only in the minds of those with guilty consciences.

1

If slugs could smile, they'd have no trouble finding jobs as car salesmen. Darryl Day proved that. Oozing false sincerity as shiny as a slime trail, he'd followed us round the showroom. From the start, he'd made it clear that in his book, Richard was the one who counted. I was just the bimbo wife. Now Darryl sat, separated from the pair of us by a plastic desk, grinning maniacally with that instant, superficial matiness that separates sales people from the human race. He winked at me. 'And Mrs Barclay will love that leather upholstery,' he said suggestively.

Under normal circumstances, I'd have got a lot of pleasure out of telling him his tatty sexism had just cost him the commission on a twenty grand sale, but these circumstances were so far from normal, I was beginning to feel like Ground Control to Major Tom as far as my brain was concerned. So instead, I smiled, patted Richard's arm and said sweetly, 'Nothing's too good for my Dick.' Richard twitched. I reckon he knew instinctively that one way or another, he was going to pay for this.

'Now, let me just check that we're both clear what you're buying here. You've seen it in the showroom, we've taken it on the test drive of a lifetime, and you've decided on the Gemini turbo super coupé GLXi in midnight blue, with ABS, alloy wheels . . .' As Darryl ran through the luxury spec I'd instructed Richard to go for, my partner's eyes glazed over. I almost felt sorry for him. After all, Richard's car of choice is a clapped-out, customized hot pink Volkswagen Beetle convertible. He thinks BHP is that new high-quality tape system. And isn't ABS that dance band from Wythenshawe . . . ?

Darryl paused expectantly. I kicked Richard's ankle. Only gently, though. He'd done well so far. He jerked back to reality and said, 'Er, yeah, that sounds perfect. Sorry, I was just a bit carried away, thinking about what it's going to be like driving her.' Nice one, Richard.

'You're a very lucky man, if I may say so,' Darryl smarmed, eyeing the curve of my calf under the leopard skin leggings that I'd chosen as appropriate to my exciting new role as Mrs Richard Barclay. He tore his gaze away and shuffled his paperwork. 'Top of the range, that little beauty is. But now, I'm afraid, we come to the painful bit. You've already told me you don't want to part-ex, is that right?'

Richard nodded. ''S right. My last motor got nicked, so I've got the insurance payout to put

2

down as a deposit. Which leaves me looking for six grand. Should I sort out a bank loan or what?'

Darryl looked just like the Duke of Edinburgh when he gets a stag in his sights. He measured Richard up, then flicked a casual glance over me. 'The only problem with that, Richard, is that it's going to take you a few days to get your friendly bank manager in gear. Whereas, if we can sort it out here and now, you could be driving that tasty motor tomorrow tea time.' Classic sales ploy; take it off them.

Richard did his personal version of the Fry's Five Boys gamut, from disappointment to anticipation. 'So can we do that, then, Darryl?' he asked eagerly.

Darryl already had the forms prepared. He slid them across the desk to show Richard. 'As it happens, we have an arrangement with a finance company who offer a very competitive rate of interest. If you fill in the forms now, we can sort it with a phone call. Then, tomorrow, if you bring in a banker's draft for the balance, we'll be able to complete the paperwork and the car'll be all yours to drive away.'

I looked at the form, not so easy now Darryl had reclaimed it to fill in the remaining blanks. Richmond Credit Finance. Address and phone number in Accrington. It wasn't the first time I'd seen their footprints all over this investigation. I'd meant to check the company out, but I hadn't got round to it yet. I made a mental note to get on

3

to it as soon as I had a spare moment. I tuned back in at the bit where Darryl was asking Richard what he did for a living. This was always the best bit.

'I'm a freelance rock journalist,' Richard told him.

'Really?' Darryl asked. Interesting how his face opened up when he experienced a genuine emotion like excitement. 'Does that mean you interview all the top names and that? Like Whitney Houston and Beverley Craven?'

Richard nodded glumly. 'Sometimes.'

'God, what a great job! Hey, who's the most famous person you've ever interviewed? You ever met Madonna?'.

Richard squirmed. It's the question he hates most. There aren't that many rock stars he has much respect for, either as people or as musicians, and only a handful of them are names that most members of the public would identify as superstars. 'Depends what you mean by famous. Springsteen. Elton John. Clapton. Tina Turner. And yeah, I did meet Madonna once.'

'Wow! And is she really, you know, as, like, horny as she comes over?'

Richard forced a smile. 'Not in front of the wife, eh?' I was touched. He was really trying to make this work.

Darryl ran a hand through his neat dark hair and winked. In an adult, it would have been lewd. 'Gotcha, Richard. Now, your annual income. What would that be?'

I switched off again. Fiction, even the great stuff, is never as interesting when you're hearing it for the nth time. Darryl didn't hang about explaining little details like annual percentage interest rates to Richard, and within ten minutes, he was on to the finance company arranging our car loan. Thanks to the wonders of computer technology, credit companies can check out a punter and give the thumbs up or down almost instantaneously. Whatever Richmond Credit Finance pulled up on their computer, it convinced them that Richard was a sound bet for a loan. Of course, when you're relying on computers, it's important to remember that what you get out of them depends entirely on what someone else has put in.

Twenty minutes later, Richard and I were walking out of the showroom, the proud possessors, on paper at least, of the flashest set of wheels the Leo Motor Company puts on the road. 'I do all right, Mrs Barclay?' Richard asked eagerly, as we walked round the corner to where I'd parked the Peugeot 205 Mortensen and Brannigan had been leasing for the six months since my last company car had ended up looking like an installation from the Tate Gallery.

'You wish,' I snarled. 'Don't push your luck, Barclay. Let me tell you, the longer I spend pretending to be your wife, the more I understand why your first marriage didn't go the distance.'

I climbed in the car and started the engine. Richard stood on the pavement, looking hangdog, his tortoiseshell glasses slipping down his nose. Exasperated, I pushed the button that lowered the passenger window. 'Oh for God's sake, get in,' I said. 'You did really well in there. Thank you.'

He smiled and jumped in. 'You're right, you know.'

'I usually am,' I said, only half teasing, as I eased the car out into the busy stream of traffic on the Bolton to Blackburn road. 'About what in particular?'

'That being a private eye is ninety-five per cent boredom coupled with five per cent fear. The first time we did that routine, I was really scared. I thought, what if I forget what I'm supposed to say, and they suss that we're setting them up,' he said earnestly.

'It wouldn't have been the end of the world,' I said absently, keeping an eye on the road signs so I didn't miss the turn off for Manchester. 'We're not dealing with the Mafia here. They wouldn't have dragged you out kicking and screaming and kneecapped you.'

'No, but you might have,' Richard said. He was serious.

I laughed. 'No way. I'd have waited till I got you home.'

Richard looked worried for a moment. Then he decided I was joking. 'Anyway,' he said, 'now when we do it, I'm not nervous any more. The only danger is that it's so repetitious I'm afraid I'll blow it out of boredom.'

'Well, I'm hoping we won't have to go through it many more times,' I said, powering down the ramp on to the dual carriageway. The little Peugeot I chose has a 1.9 litre engine, but since I got the dealership to take the identifying badges off it, it looks as innocuous as a housewife's shopping trolley. I'd be sorry to see the back of it, but once I'd finished this job, I'd be in line for a brand new sporty Leo hatchback. Freemans.

'That's a shame, in some ways. I hate to admit it, Brannigan, but I've quite enjoyed working with you.'

Wild horses wouldn't have got me to admit it, but I'd enjoyed it too. In the two years that we'd been lovers, I'd never been reluctant to use Richard as a sounding board for my investigations. He's got one of those off-the-wall minds that sometimes come up with illuminating insights into the white collar crime that makes up the bulk of the work I do with my business partner Bill Mortensen. But the opportunity to get Richard to take a more active part had never arisen before this job. I'd only gone along with Bill's suggestion to involve him precisely because I felt so certain it was a no-risk job. How could I expose to danger a man who thinks discretion is a fragrance by Calvin Klein?

This job was what we call in the trade a straight up-and-downer. The only strange thing about it was the way we'd got the job in the first place. A two-operative agency in Manchester isn't the obvious choice for an international car giant like the Leo Motor Company when they've got a problem. We'd got lucky because the new head honcho at Accredited Leo Finance was the brother-in-law of a high-class Manchester jeweller. We'd not only installed Clive Abercrombie's security system, but we'd also cracked a major gang of counterfeiters who were giving the executive chronometer brigade serious migraine. As far as Clive was concerned, Mortensen and Brannigan were *the* people to go to when you wanted a slick, discreet job.

Of course, being an arm of a multi-national, ALF couldn't bring themselves to knock on the door and pitch us the straight way. It had all started at a reception hosted by the Manchester Olympic Bid organization. Remember the Olympic Bid? They were trying to screw dosh out of local businesses to support their attempt to kick off the new millennium by holding the Games in the Rainy City. Bill and I are such a small operation, we were a bit bewildered at being invited, but I'm a sucker for free smoked salmon, and besides, I reckoned it would do no harm to flash my smile round a few potentially lucrative new contacts, so I went off to fly the flag for Mortensen and Brannigan.

I was only halfway through my first glass of Australian fizz (as good a reason as any for awarding the Olympics to Sydney) when Clive appeared at my elbow with a strange man and a sickly grin. 'Kate,' he greeted me. 'What a lovely surprise.'

I was on my guard straight away. Clive and

I have never been buddies, probably because I can't bring myself to be anything more than professionally polite to social climbers. So when the Edmund Hillary of the Cheshire set accosted me so joyously, I knew at once we were in the realms of hidden agendas. I smiled politely, shook his hand, counted my fingers and said, 'Nice to see you too, Clive.'

'Kate, can I introduce my brother-in-law, Andrew Broderick? Andrew, this is Kate Brannigan, who's a partner in Manchester's best security company. Kate, Andrew's the MD and CEO of ALF.' I must have looked blank, for Clive added hurriedly, 'You know, Kate. Accredited Leo Finance. Leo Motor Company's credit arm.'

'Thanks, Tonto,' I said.

Clive looked baffled, but Andrew Broderick laughed. 'If I'm the loan arranger, you must be Tonto. Old joke,' he explained. Clive still didn't get it. Broderick and I shook hands and weighed each other up. He wasn't a lot taller than my five feet and three inches, but Andrew Broderick looked like a man who'd learned how to fight his battles in a rugby scrum rather than a boardroom. It was just as well he could afford to have his suits hand-stitched to measure; he'd never have found that chest measurement off the peg. His nose had been broken more than once and his ears were as close to being a pair as Danny De Vito and Arnold Schwarzenegger. But his shrewd grey eyes missed nothing. I felt his ten-second assessment of me had probably covered all the salient points.

We started off innocuously enough, discussing the Games. Then, casually enough, he asked what I drove in the course of business. I found myself telling him all about Bill's new Saab convertible, the workhorse Little Rascal van we use for surveillance, and the nearly fatal accident that had robbed me of the Nova. I was mildly surprised. I don't normally talk to strangers.

'No Leos?' he asked with a quirky smile.

'No Leos,' I agreed. 'But I'm open to persuasion.'

Broderick took my elbow, smiled dismissively at Clive and gently steered me into a quiet corner behind the buffet. 'I have a problem,' he said. 'It needs a specialist, and I'm told that your organization could fit my spec. Interested?'

Call me a slut, but when it comes to business, I'm always open to offers. 'I'm interested,' I said. 'Will it keep, or do you want to thrash it out now?'

It turned out that patience wasn't Andrew Broderick's long suit. Within five minutes, we were in the lounge of the Ramada, with drinks on their way. 'How much do you know about car financing?' he asked.

'They always end up costing more than you think,' I said ruefully.

'That much, eh?' he said. 'OK. Let me explain. My company, ALF, is a wholly owned subsidiary of the Leo Motor Company. Our job is to provide loans for people who want to buy Leo cars and haven't got enough cash. But Leo dealerships aren't obliged to channel all their customers through us, so we have to find ways to make ourselves sexy to the dealerships. One of the ways we do this is to offer them soft loans.'

I nodded, with him so far. 'And these low-interest loans are for what, exactly?'

'Dealerships have to pay up front when they take delivery of a car from Leo. ALF gives them a soft loan to cover the wholesale cost of the car for ninety days. After that, the interest rate rises weekly. When the car is sold, the soft loan is supposed to be paid off. That's in the contract.

'But if a dealership arranges loans for the Leos it sells via a different finance company, neither ALF nor Leo is aware that the car's been sold. The dealer can smack the money in a high-interest account for the remains of the ninety days and earn himself a tidy sum in interest before the loan has to be paid off.' The drinks arrived, as if on cue, giving me a few moments to digest what he'd said.

I tipped the bottle of grapefruit juice into my vodka, and swirled the ice cubes round in the glass to mix the drink. 'And you obviously hate this because you're cutting your own margins to supply the low-interest loans, but you're getting no benefit in return.'

Broderick nodded, taking a hefty swallow of his spritzer. 'Leo aren't crazy about it either because

11

it skews their market share figures, particularly in high turnover months like August,' he added.

'So where do I come in?' I asked.

'I've come up with an alternative distribution system,' he said simply. Now, all I know about the car business is what I've learned from my dad, an assembly line foreman with Rover in Oxford. But even that little is enough for me to realize that what Andrew Broderick had just said was on a par with the Prime Minister announcing he was going to abolish the Civil Service.

I swallowed hard. 'We don't do bodyguard jobs,' I said.

He laughed, which was the first time I'd doubted his sanity. 'It's so simple,' he said. 'Instead of having to fill their showrooms with cars they're then under pressure to sell asap, dealers would carry only one sample of the model. The customer would specify colour, engine size, petrol or diesel, optional extras, etc. The order would then be faxed to one of several regional holding centres where the specific model would be assembled from Leo's stock.'

'Don't tell me, let me guess. Leo are fighting it tooth and nail because it involves them in initial expenditure of more than threepence ha'penny,' I said resignedly.

'And that's where you come in, Ms Brannigan. I want to prove to Leo that my system would be of ultimate financial benefit to both of us. Now, if I can prove that at least one of our bigger chains of dealerships is committing this particular fraud, then I can maybe start to get it through Leo's corporate skulls that a helluva lot of cash that should be in our business is being siphoned off. And then maybe, just maybe, they'll accept that a revamped distribution service is worth every penny.'

Which is how Richard and I came to be playing happy newly-weds round the car showrooms of England. It seemed like a good idea at the time. Three weeks into the job, it still seemed like a good idea. Which only goes to show how wrong even I can be.

2

The following afternoon, I was in my office, putting the finishing touches to a routine report on a fraudulent personal accident claim I'd been investigating on behalf of a local insurance company. As I reached the end, I glanced at my watch. Twenty-five to three. Surprise, surprise, Richard was late. I saved the file to disc, then switched off my computer. I took the disc through to the outer office, where Shelley Carmichael was filling in a stationery supplies order form. If good office management got you on to the Honours List, Shelley would be up there with a life peerage. It's a toss-up who I treat with more respect – Shelley or the local pub's Rottweiler.

She glanced up as I came through. 'Late again, is he?' she asked. I nodded. 'Want me to give him an alarm call?'

'I don't think he's in,' I said. 'He mumbled something this morning about going to a bistro in Oldham where they do live rockabilly at lunch time. It sounded so improbable it has to be true. Did you check if today's draft has come through?'

Shelley nodded. Silly question, really. 'It's at the King Street branch,' she said.

'I'll pop out and get it now,' I said. 'If Boy Wonder shows up, tell him to wait for me. None of that "I'll just pop out to the Corner House for ten minutes to have a look at their new exhibition" routine.'

I gave the lift a miss and ran downstairs. It helps me maintain the illusion of fitness. As I walked briskly up Oxford Street, I felt at peace with the world. It was a bright, sunny day, though the temperature was as low as you'd expect the week before the spring bank holiday. It's a myth about it always raining in Manchester – we only make it up to irritate all those patronizing bastards in the South with their hose-pipe bans. I could hear the comic Thomas the Tank Engine hooting of the trams in the distance. The traffic was less clogged than usual, and some of my fellow pedestrians actually had smiles on their faces. More importantly, the ALF job had gone without a hitch, and with a bit of luck, this would be the last banker's draft I'd have to collect. It had been a pretty straightforward routine, once Bill and I had decided to bring Richard in to increase the credibility of the car buying operation. It must be the first time in his life he's ever been accused of enhancing the credibility of anything. Our major target had been a garage chain with fifteen branches throughout the North. Richard and I had hit eight of them, from Stafford to York, plus four independents that Andrew also suspected of being on the fiddle.

There was nothing complicated about it. Richard and I simply rolled up to the car dealers, pretending to be a married couple, and bought a car on the spot from the range in the showroom. Broderick had called in a few favours with his buddies in the credit rating agencies that lenders used to check on their victims' creditworthiness. So, when the car sales people got the finance companies to check the names and addresses Richard gave them, they discovered he had an excellent credit rating, a sheaf of credit cards and no outstanding debt except his mortgage. The granting of the loan was then a formality. The only hard bit was getting Richard to remember what his hooky names and addresses were.

The next day, we'd go to the bank and pick up the banker's draft that Broderick had arranged for us. Then it was on to the showroom, where Richard signed the rest of the paperwork so we could take the car home. Some time in the following couple of days, a little man from ALF arrived and took it away, presumably to be resold as an ex-demonstration model. Interestingly, Andrew Broderick had been right on the button. Not one of the dealers we'd bought cars from had offered us finance through ALF. The chain had pushed all our purchases through Richmond Credit Finance, while the independents had used a variety of lenders. Now, with a dozen cast-iron cases on the stocks, all Broderick had to do was sit back and wait till the dealers finally got round to admitting they'd flogged some metal. Then it would be gumshields time in the car showrooms.

While I was queueing at the bank, the schizophrenic weather had had a personality change. A wind had sprung up from nowhere, throwing needle-sharp rain into my face as I headed back towards the office. Luckily, I was wearing low-heeled ankle boots with my twill jodhpur-cut leggings, so I could jog back without risking serious injury either to any of my major joints or to my dignity. That was my first mistake of the day. There's nothing Richard likes better than a dishevelled Brannigan. Not because it's a turn-on; no, simply because it lets him indulge in a rare bit of one-upmanship.

When I got back to the office, damp, scarlet-cheeked and out of breath, my auburn hair in rats' tails, Richard was of course sitting comfortably in an armchair, sipping a glass of Shelley's herbal tea, immaculate in the Italian leather jacket I bought him on the last day of our winter break in Florence. His hazel eyes looked at me over the top of his glasses and I could see he was losing his battle not to smile.

'Don't say a word,' I warned him. 'Not unless you want your first trip in your brand new turbo coupé to end up at the infirmary.'

He grinned. 'I don't know how you put up with all this naked aggression, Shelley,' he said.

'Once you understand it's compensatory behaviour for her low self-esteem, it's easy.' Shelley did A Level psychology at evening classes. I'm just grateful she didn't pursue it to degree level.

Ignoring the pair of them, I marched through my office and into the cupboard that doubles as darkroom and ladies' loo. I towelled my hair as dry as I could get it, then applied the exaggerated amounts of mascara, eye shadow, blusher and lipstick that Mrs Barclay required. I stared critically at the stranger in the mirror. I couldn't imagine spending my whole life behind that much camouflage. But then, I've never wanted to be irresistible to car salesmen.

We hit the garage just after four. The gleaming, midnight blue Gemini turbo super coupé was standing in splendid isolation on the concrete apron at the side of the showroom. Darryl was beside himself with joy when he actually touched the bank draft. The motor trade's so far down in the doldrums these days that paying customers are regarded with more affection than the Queen Mum, especially ones who don't spend three days in a war of attrition trying to shave the price by yet another fifty quid. He was so overjoyed, he didn't even bother to lie. 'I'm delighted to see you drive off in this beautiful car,' he confessed, clutching the bank draft with both hands and staring at it. Then he remembered himself and gave us a greasy smile. 'Because, of course, it's our pleasure to give you pleasure.'

Richard opened the passenger door for me, and, smarting, I climbed in. 'Oh, this is real luxury,' I forced out for Darryl's benefit, as I stroked the charcoal grey leather. The last thing I wanted was for him to think I was anything other than brain-dead. Richard settled in next to me, closing the door with a solid clunk. He turned the key in the ignition, and pressed the button that lowered his window. 'Thanks, Darryl,' he said. 'It's been a pleasure doing the business.'

'Pleasure's all mine, Mr Barclay,' Darryl smarmed, shuffling sideways as Richard let out the clutch and glided slowly forward. 'Remember me when Mrs Barclay's ready for a new luxury vehicle?'

In response, Richard put his foot down. In ten seconds, Darryl Day was just a bad memory. 'Wow,' he exclaimed as he moved up and down through the gears in the busy Bolton traffic. 'This is some motor! Electric wing mirrors, electric sun roof, electric seat adjustment . . .'

'Shame about the clockwork driver,' I said.

By the time we got home, Richard was in love. Although the Gemini coupé was the twelfth Leo car we'd 'bought', this was the first example of the newly launched sporty superstar. We'd had to confine ourselves to what was actually available on the premises, and we'd tended to go for the executive saloons that had made Leo one of the major suppliers of fleet cars in the UK. As we arrived outside the pair of bungalows where we live. Richard was still raving about the Gemini.

'It's like driving a dream,' he enthused, pressing the remote control that locked the car and set the alarm.

'You said that already,' I muttered as I walked up the path to my house. 'Twice.'

'No, but really, Kate, it's like nothing I've ever driven before,' Richard said, walking backwards up the path.

'That's hardly surprising,' I said. 'Considering you've never driven anything designed after Porsche came up with the Beetle in 1936. Automotive technology has moved along a bit since then.'

He followed me into the house. 'Brannigan, until I drove that, I'd never wanted to.'

'Do I gather you want me to talk to Andrew Broderick about doing you a deal to buy the Gemini?' I asked, opening the fridge. I handed Richard a cold Jupiler and took out a bottle of freshly squeezed pink grapefruit juice.

He opened the drawer for the bottle opener and popped the cap off his beer, looking disconsolate. 'Thanks, but no thanks. Can't afford it, Brannigan.'

I didn't even think about trying to change the mind of a man with an ex-wife and a son to support. I never poke my nose into his finances, and the last thing that would ever make the short journey across his mind is curiosity about my bank balance. We never have to argue about money because of the way we organize our lives. We own adjacent houses, linked by a conservatory built across the back of both of them. That way, we have all the advantages of living together and almost none of the disadvantages.

I opened the freezer and took out a bottle of Polish vodka. It was so cold, the sobs of spirit on the inside of the bottle were sluggish as syrup. I poured an inch into the bottom of a highball glass and topped it up with juice. It tasted like nectar. I put down my glass and gave Richard a hug. He rubbed his chin affectionately on the top of my head and gently massaged my neck.

'Mmm,' I murmured. 'Any plans for tonight?'

''Fraid so. There's a benefit in town for the girlfriend of that guy who got blown away last month in Moss Side. You remember? The innocent bystander who got caught up in the drugs shoot-out outside the café? Well, she's four months pregnant, so the local bands have got together to put on a bit of a performance. Can't not show, sorry.'

'But you don't have to go for a while, do you?' I asked, running my fingers over his shoulder blades in a pattern that experience has demonstrated usually distracts him from minor things like work.

'Not for ages,' he responded, nuzzling my neck as planned. Nothing like exploiting a man's weaknesses, I thought.

I wasn't the only one into the exploitation game, though. As I grabbed my drink and we did a sideways shuffle towards the bedroom, Richard murmured, 'Any chance of me taking the Gemini with me tonight?'

I jerked awake with the staring-eyed shock that comes when you've not been asleep for long. The light was still on, and my arm hurt as I peeled it off the glossy computer gaming magazine I'd fallen asleep over. I reached for the trilling telephone and barked, 'Brannigan,' into it, simultaneously checking the time on the alarm clock. 00:43.

'Did I wake you?' Richard asked.

'What do you think?'

'Sorry. That kind of answers the question,' he said cryptically.

My brain wasn't up to it. 'What question, Richard?' I demanded. 'What question's so urgent it can't wait till morning?'

'I just wondered if you were at the wind-up, that's all. But you're obviously not, so I'd better come home and call the cops.'

I was no further forward. I massaged my fore-head with my spare hand, but before I could get any more sense out of him, the pips sounded and the line went dead. I contemplated going back to sleep, but I knew that was just the fantasy of a deranged mind. You don't become a private eye because you lack curiosity about the doings of your fellow man. Especially when they're as unpredict-able as the man next door. Whatever Richard was up to, I was involved now too. Heaving a sigh, I got out of bed and struggled into my dressing gown. I went through to my living-room, unlocked the patio doors and walked through the conservatory to Richard's house.

As usual, his living room looked like a teenager's idea of paradise. A Nintendo console lay on top of a pile of old newspapers by the sofa. Stacks of CDs teetered on every available surface that wasn't occupied by empty beer bottles and used coffee mugs. Rock videos were piled by the TV set. A couple of rock bands' promotional T-shirts and sweat shirts were thrown over an armchair, and a lump of draw sat neatly on a pack of Silk Cut, next to a packet of Rizlas on the coffee table. If vandals ransacked the place, Richard probably wouldn't notice for a fortnight. When we first got together, I used to tidy up. Now, I've trained myself not to notice.

Two steps down the hall, I knew what to expect in the kitchen. Every few weeks, Richard decides his kitchen is a health hazard, and he does his version of spring cleaning. This involves putting crockery, cutlery and chopsticks in the dishwasher. Everything else on the worktops goes into a black plastic bin liner. He buys a bottle of bleach, a pair of rubber gloves and a pack of scouring pads and scrubs down every surface, including the inside of the microwave. For two days, the place is spotless and smells like a public swimming pool. Then he comes home stoned with a Chinese takeaway and everything goes back to normal.

I opened the dishwasher and took out the jug from the coffee maker. I got the coffee from the fridge. Richard's fridge contains only four main food groups: his international beer collection, chocolate bars for the dope-induced raging munchies, ground coffee and a half-gallon container of milk. While I was waiting for the coffee to brew, I tried not to think about the logical reason why Richard was coming home to call the police.

I realized the nightmare was true when I heard the familiar clatter of a black hack's diesel engine in the close outside. I peeped through the blind. Sure enough, there was Richard paying off the cabbie. I had a horrible feeling that the reason he was in a cab rather than the Gemini had nothing to do with the amount of alcohol he had consumed. 'Oh shit,' I muttered as I took a second mug from the dishwasher and filled it with strong Java. I walked down the hall and proffered the coffee as Richard walked through the front door.

'You're not going to believe this,' he started, taking the mug from me. He gulped a huge mouthful. Luckily, he has an asbestos throat. 'Cheers.'

'Don't tell me, let me guess,' I said, following him through to the living room, where he grabbed the phone. 'You came out of the club, the car was gone.'

He shook his head in admiration. 'Ever thought of becoming a detective, Brannigan? You don't ring 999 for a car theft, do you?'

'Not unless they also ran you over.'

24

'When I realized the car was on the missing list, I wished they had,' he said. 'I thought, if Brannigan doesn't kill me, the money men will. Got a number for the Dibble?'

I recited the familiar number of Greater Manchester Police's main switchboard. Contrary to popular mythology about private eyes, Bill and I do have a good working relationship with the law. Well, most of the time. Let's face it, they're so over-worked these days that they're pathetically grate-ful to be handed a stack of evidence establishing a case that'll let them give some miserable criminal a good nicking.

Richard got through almost immediately. While he gave the brief details over the phone, I won-dered whether I should call Andrew Broderick and give him the bad news. I decided against it. It's bad enough to lose twenty grand's worth of merchandise without having a night's sleep wrecked as well. I must point that out to Richard some time.

3

Two nights later, it happened again. I was about to deal Kevin Costner a fatal blow in a game of Battle Chess when an electronic chirruping disturbed our joust. Costner dissolved in a blue haze as I struggled up from the dream, groping wildly for the phone. My arm felt as heavy as if I really was wearing the weighty medieval armour of a knight in a tournament. That'll teach me to play computer games at bedtime. 'Brannigan,' I grunted into the phone.

'Kate? Sorry to wake you.' The voice was familiar, but out of context it took me a few seconds to recognize it. The voice and I came up with the answer simultaneously. 'Ruth Hunter here.'

I propped myself up on one elbow and switched on the bedside lamp. 'Ruth. Give me a second, will you?' I dropped the phone and scrabbled for my bag. I pulled out a pad and pencil, and scribbled down the time on the clock. 02:13. For a criminal solicitor to wake me at this time of night it had to be serious. Whichever one of Mortensen and Brannigan's clients had decided my beauty sleep was less important than their needs was going to pay dear for the privilege. They weren't going to get so much as ten free seconds. I picked up the phone and said, 'OK. You have my undivided attention. What is it that won't keep?'

'Kate, there is no way of making this pleasant. I'm sorry. I've just had Longsight police station's custody sergeant on to me. They've arrested Richard.' Ruth's voice was apologetic, but she was right. There was no way of making that news pleasant.

'What's he done? Had a few too many and got caught up in somebody else's war?' I asked, knowing even as I did that I was being wildly optimistic. If that was all it was, Richard would have been more interested in getting his head down for a kip in the cells than in getting the cops to call Ruth out.

'I'm afraid not, Kate. It's drugs.'

'Is that all?' I almost burst out laughing. 'This is the 1990s, Ruth. How much can they give him for a lump of draw? He never carries more on him than the makings for a couple of joints.'

'Kate, it's not cannabis.' Ruth had that tone of voice that the actors on hospital dramas use when they're about to tell someone their nearest and dearest probably isn't going to make it. 'If it was cannabis, believe me, I wouldn't have bothered calling you.'

I heard the words, but I couldn't make sense of them. The only drug Richard ever uses is draw. In the two years we've been together, I've never known him drop so much as half a tab of E, in spite of the number of raves and gigs he routinely attends. 'It's got to be a plant, then,' I said confidently. 'Someone's had it in for him and they've slipped something into his pocket.'

'I don't think so, Kate. We're talking about two kilos of crack.'

Crack. Fiercely addictive, potentially lethal, crack cocaine is the drug everybody in narcotics prevention has the heebie-jeebies about. For a moment, I couldn't take it in. I know two kilos of crack isn't exactly bulky, but you'd have to notice you had it about your person. 'He was walking around with two *kilos* of crack on him? That can't be right, Ruth,' I managed.

'Not walking around. Driving. I don't have any details yet, but he was brought in by a couple of lads from traffic. I'm afraid it gets worse, Kate. Apparently the car he was in was stolen.'

I was out of bed, pulling knickers and tights out of the top drawer. 'Well, who was he with, then? He can't have known he was in a hot motor!'

My stomach knotted as Ruth replied, 'He was on his own. No passengers.'

'This is like a bad dream,' I said. 'You know what he's like. Can you see Richard as a major-league car thief and drug dealer? Where are you now, Ruth?' I asked.

'I'm on my way out the door. The sooner I get in to see him, the sooner we can get this business straightened out. You're right. Richard's no villain,' she said reassuringly.

'Too true. Look, Ruth, thanks for letting me know. I appreciate it.' I fastened my bra and moved over to the wardrobe door.

'I'll keep you posted,' she said. 'Speak to you soon.'

Sooner than you think, I told myself as I shrugged into a cream polo-neck knitted cotton top. I grabbed my favourite knock-'em-dead suit, a lightweight wool number in a grey and moss green weave. Of course, dressing on the run, my legs tangled in the trousers as I made for the hall and I ended up sprawled on the floor, face smacked up against the skirting board, forced to recognize that it was too long since I'd cleaned the house. Cursing in a fluent monotone, I made it as far as the porch and pulled a pair of flat loafers out of the shoe cupboard. On my way out of the door, I remembered the route I was planning to go down, and hurried back into the living room, where I picked up the slim black leather briefcase I use to impress prospective clients with my businesslike qualities.

As I started the car, I noticed Richard's Beetle wasn't in its usual parking space. What in God's name was going on? If he'd gone out in his own car, what was he doing driving round in the middle of the night in a stolen car with a parcel of heavy drugs? More to the point, did the owners of the drugs know who'd driven off with their merchandise? Because if they did, I didn't give much for Richard's chances of seeing his next birthday.

I pulled up in the visitors' car park at Longsight nick a couple of minutes later. There wasn't much competition for parking places that time of night. I knew I'd have at least fifteen minutes to kill, since Ruth had to drive all the way over from her house in Hale. Usually, I don't have much trouble keeping my mind occupied on stake-outs. Maybe that's because I don't have to do it too often, given the line of work Mortensen and Brannigan specialize in. A lot of private eyes have to make the bulk of their income doing mind-and-bum-numbing bread-and-butter surveillance work, but because we work mainly with computer crime and white-collar fraud, we spend a lot more of our backside-breaking hours in other people's offices than we do outside their houses. But tonight, the seventeen minutes I spent staring at the dirty red brick and tall blank windows of the rambling, mock-Gothic police station felt like hours. I suppose I was worried. I must be getting soft in my old age.

I spotted Ruth's car as soon as she turned into the car park. Her husband's in the rag trade, and he drives a white Bentley Mulsanne Turbo. When she gets dragged out of bed in the middle of the night, Ruth likes to drive the Bentley. It doesn't half get up the noses of the cops. Her regular clients love it to bits. As the dazzling headlights in my rear-view mirror dimmed to black, I was out of my car and waving to Ruth.

The driver's window slid down with an almost imperceptible hum. She didn't stick her head out; she waited for me to draw level. I grinned. Ruth didn't. 'You'll have a long wait, Kate,' she said, a warning in her voice.

I ignored the warning. 'Ruth, you and I both know you're the best criminal lawyer in the city. But we also both know that being an officer of the court means there is a whole raft of things you can't even think about doing. The kind of shit Richard seems to have got himself in, he needs someone out there ducking and diving, doing whatever it takes to dig up the information that'll get him off the hook with the cops and with the dealers. I'm the one who's going to have to do that, and the most efficient way for that process to get started is for me to sit in on your briefing.'

Give her her due, Ruth heard me out. She even paused for the count of five to create the impression she was giving some thought to my suggestion. Then she slowly shook her head. 'No way, Kate. I suspect you know the provisions of PACE as well as I do.'

I smiled ruefully. The Police and Criminal Evidence Act hadn't exactly been my bedtime reading when it became law, but I was reasonably familiar with its provisions. I knew perfectly well that the only person a suspect was entitled to have sitting in on their interview with the police was his or her solicitor. 'There is one way round it,' I said.

There's something about the mind of a criminal solicitor. They can't resist discovering any new wrinkle in the law. Dangle that as a carrot and they'll bite your arm off faster than a starving donkey. 'Go on,' Ruth said cautiously. I swear her eyes sparkled.

'Trainee solicitors who are just starting criminal work usually learn the ropes by bird-dogging a senior brief like yourself,' I said. 'And that includes sitting in on interviews in police stations.'

Ruth smiled sweetly. 'Not in the middle of the night. And you're not a trainee solicitor, Kate.'

'True, Ruth, but I did do two years of a law degree. And as you yourself pointed out not five minutes since, I do know my way around PACE. I'm not going to blow it out of ignorance of the procedures.' I couldn't remember the last time I'd had to be this persuasive. Before I knew where I was, I'd be down on my knees begging. This was going to be the most expensive night out Richard Barclay had ever had.

Ruth shook her head decisively. 'Kate, if we're going to quote each other, let me remind you of your opening speech. As an officer of the court, there are a whole lot of things I can't even think about doing. I'm afraid this is one of them.' As she spoke, the window rose again.

I stepped back to allow Ruth to open the door and get out of her living room on wheels. She let the door close with a soft, expensive click. She took a deep breath, considering. While I waited for her to say something, I couldn't help admiring her style. Ruth looked nothing like a woman whose sleep had been wrecked by the call that had dragged her out of bed. There was nothing slapdash about her understated make-up and her long blonde hair was pulled back in a neat scalp plait, the distinguished silver streaks at the temples glinting in the street lights. She was in her middle thirties, but the only giveaway was a faint cluster of laughter lines at the corners of her eyes. She wore a black frock coat over a cream silk shirt with a rolled neck, black leggings and black ankle boots with a high heel. The extra height disguised the fact that she had to be at least a size eighteen. We'd been friends ever since she'd been the guest speaker at my university Women In Law group, and I'd never seen her look anything other than immaculate. If I didn't like her so much, I'd hate her.

Now, she put a surprisingly slim hand on my arm. 'Kate, you know I sympathize. If that was Peter in there, I'd be moving heaven and earth to get him out. I have no doubt whatsoever that Richard's first demand will be that I get you on the case. And I'll back that one hundred per cent. But give me space to do what I'm best at. As soon as I'm through here, I'll come straight round and brief you, I promise.'

I shook my head. 'I hear what you're saying, but that's not enough, I'm sorry. If I'm going to do what *I'm* best at, there are questions I need to ask that won't necessarily have anything to do with what you need to know. Ruth, it's in your client's best interests.'

Ruth put an arm round my shoulder and hugged me. 'Nice try, Kate. You really should have stuck to the law, you know. You'd have made a great advocate. But the answer's still no. I'll see you later.'

She let me go and walked across the police car park towards the entrance, the heels of her boots clicking on the tarmac. 'You'd better believe it,' I said softly.

Time to exploit the irregular verb theory of life. In this case, the appropriate one seemed to be: I am creative, you exaggerate, he/she is a pathological liar. I gave Ruth ten minutes to get through the formalities. Then I walked across to the door and pressed the intercom buzzer. 'Hello?' the intercom crackled.

Giving my best impression of a panic-stricken, very junior gopher, I said, 'I'm with Hunter Butterworth. I was supposed to meet Ms Hunter here; I'm her trainee, you see, only, my car wouldn't start, and I got here late, and I saw her car outside already. Can you let me through? Only, I'm supposed to be learning how to conduct interviews by observing her, and when she rang me she said Mr Barclay's case sounded like one I could learn a lot from,' I gabbled without pause.

'Miss Hunter never said anything about expecting a trainee,' the distorted voice said.

'She's probably given up on me. I was supposed to meet her twenty minutes ago. Please, can you let me through? I'll be in enough trouble just for being so late. If she thinks I haven't showed up at all, my life won't be worth living. I've already had the "clients rely on us for their liberty, Ms Robinson' lecture once this week!'

I'd struck the right chord. The door buzzed and I pushed it open. I stepped inside and pushed open the barred gate. The custody sergeant grinned at me from behind his desk. 'I'm glad I'm not in your shoes,' he said. 'She can be a real tartar, your boss. I had a teacher like her once. Miss Gibson. Mind you, she got me through O Level French, which was no mean feat.'

He asked my name, and I claimed to be Kate Robinson. He made a note on the custody record, then led me down a well-lit corridor. I took care not to trip over the cracked vinyl floor tiles whose edges were starting to curl. It was hard to tell what colour they'd started out; I couldn't believe someone had actually *chosen* battleship grey mottled with khaki and bile green. Halfway along the corridor, he paused outside a door marked 'Interview 2' and knocked, opening the door before he got a reply. 'Your trainee's here, Miss Hunter,' he announced, stepping back to usher me in.

Like a true professional, Ruth didn't bat an eyelid. 'Thank you,' she said grimly. Typically, it was Richard who nearly gave the show away. His whole face lit up in that familiar smile that still sends my hormones into chaos.

He got as far as, 'What are you –' before Ruth interrupted.

'I hope you don't mind, Mr Barclay, but my colleague is a trainee who is supposed to be learning the tricks of the trade,' she said loudly. 'I'd like her to sit in on our consultation, unless you have any objections?'

'N-no,' Richard stammered, looking bewildered.

I stepped into the room and the sergeant closed the door firmly behind me.

Simultaneously, Richard said, 'I don't understand,' and Ruth growled softly, 'I should walk out of here right now and leave you to it.'

'I know. I'm sorry. I couldn't not. It's too important. But look on the bright side; if I can blag my way into the secure interview room of a police station, aren't you glad you've got me on the team?' I added an apologetic smile.

Before Ruth could find an answer for that particular bit of cheek, Richard said plaintively, 'But I don't understand what you're doing here, Brannigan.'

'I'm here because you need help, Richard. I know you spend most of your time on another planet, but here on earth, it's considered to be a pretty serious offence to drive around in a stolen car with enough crack to get half Manchester out of their heads,' I told him.

'Look, I know it sounds like I'm in deep shit. But it's not like that.' He ran a hand through his hair and frowned. 'I keep trying to tell everybody. It wasn't a stolen car. It was *our* car. The one we bought in Bolton on Tuesday.'

4

Before I could pick the bones out of that, Ruth interrupted. 'Let's just hold everything right there. Kate, you are here on sufferance. I, on the other hand, am here because Richard asked me to be. I've got a job to do and I intend to do it, in spite of your interference. So let me ask my questions, and then if there's anything we haven't covered, you can have your turn.'

It wasn't a suggestion, it was an instruction. I knew what I'd done was bang out of order. I'd taken a big risk on the strength of my friendship with Ruth, and I didn't want to risk damaging those bonds any further. Besides, I like watching people who are really good at what they do. 'That's absolutely fine with me,' I said.

'You mean she really isn't meant to be here?' Richard asked, his grin irrepressible even in the face of Ruth's frown.

'If you weren't facing such serious charges, I'd have bounced her out of the door. It didn't seem like a good time to generate even more suspicion on the part of the police. Now, Richard, let's get to it. I don't have all night.' Ruth picked up her pencil and started to write. 'Let's start at the beginning. What happened tonight?'

Richard looked uncertain. 'Well, the beginning isn't tonight. I mean, depending on what you mean, the beginning's either Tuesday night or three weeks ago.'

It was my turn to grin. I didn't envy Ruth her task. I love him dearly, but the only time Richard can tell a story in a straight line from beginning to end is when he's sat in front of a word processor with the prospect of a nice little earner at the end of the day.

Ruth squeezed the bridge of her nose. 'Maybe you could give me the short version, and I'll stop you when I don't understand something.'

'It's this job Kate's got on. I've been helping her out with it. We have to buy these cars, you see, and then we give them back to the car company.' Richard paused hopefully.

Ruth's grey eyes swivelled round and fixed on me. 'Perhaps you'd like to elaborate . . . ?'

I nodded. 'My clients are the finance arm of the Leo Motor Company. They suspect some dealerships of committing fraud. It's our job to provide them with evidence, so Richard and I have been posing as a married couple, buying cars with money supplied by Leo, who then take the cars back from us,' I said.

'Thanks. So, you've been buying these cars. What happened on Tuesday night?' she asked.

'We'd picked up this really ace motor, the Gemini turbo super coupé,' Richard said enthusiastically. 'Anyway, I had to go into town, and I decided to treat myself and drive the coupé, since we'd only got it for a day or two. Then when I came out of the club, the car was gone. So I came home and reported it stolen to the police.'

Ruth looked up from her pad. 'Did they send anyone round?'

'Yeah, a copper came round about an hour later and I gave him all the details,' Richard said.

'And I informed my client first thing on Wednesday morning, if that's any help,' I added.

This time Ruth didn't scowl at me. She just made another note and said, 'So what happened next?'

Richard took off his glasses and stared up at the ceiling. A line appeared between his brows as he focused his memory. 'I went into town about nine tonight. I had to meet a couple of women in the Paradise Factory. They're the singers in a jazz fusion band, and they've just signed their first record deal. I'm doing a piece on them for one of the glossies. It was too noisy in the Factory to hear ourselves talk, so we left and went round to Manto's.' Trust Richard to spend his evening in the trendiest café bar in the North West. Looking at his outfit, I was surprised the style police had let him in. 'We stayed till closing time,' he went on. 'The girls were going on to the Hacienda, but I didn't

40

fancy it, so I went off to get my car. I'd parked it off Portland Street, and I was walking past the gardens on Sackville Street when I saw the car.' He put his glasses back on and looked expectantly at Ruth.

'Which car, Richard?' Ruth asked patiently.

'The coupé,' he said, in the injured tones of someone who thinks they've already made themselves abundantly clear. Poor misguided soul.

'You saw the car that you had reported stolen in the early hours of Wednesday morning?'

'That's right,' he said. 'Only, I wasn't sure right away if it was the same one. It was the right model and the right colour. but I couldn't see if it was the right registration number. It had trade plates on, you see.'

'Trade plates,' Ruth repeated as she scribbled. I was intrigued. Any self-respecting car thief would have smacked fake plates on a stolen car right away. I couldn't for the life of me see why they'd use the red and white plates garages use to shift untaxed cars from one place to another. It was just asking to be noticed.

'Yeah, trade plates,' Richard said impatiently. 'Anyway, I went over to this car, and I lifted up the trade plate on the front, and it was the same reg as the one that got nicked on Tuesday night,' Richard said triumphantly. He put his glasses on and grinned nervously at both of us. 'It's going to be OK, isn't it?' he added.

Ruth nodded. 'We'll get it sorted out, Richard.

Now, are you absolutely certain that this was the same car?'

'I still had the keys on my key-ring,' he said. 'It had one of those little cardboard tags on it with the number of the car, so I wasn't just relying on my memory. It was the identical number. Besides, the key I had opened the car, and there was still one of my tapes in the cassette. Isn't that proof enough?'

'Somehow, I don't think the point at issue is going to be the car,' I muttered quietly. Ruth gave me a look that would have curdled a piña colada.

'Did you call the police and tell them you'd found the car?' Ruth asked.

'Well, I figured that if I wandered off to look for a phone, the guy that had nicked it could easily have had it away again while I was busy talking to the Dibble. So I thought I'd just repo it myself and call the cops when I got home,' Richard explained. It wasn't so unreasonable. Even I had to concede that.

'What did you do next?' Ruth said.

'Well, I did what any reasonable person would have done,' Richard said. My heart sank. 'I took the trade plates off and cobbed them in the gutter.'

'You cobbed them in the gutter?' Ruth and I chorused, neck and neck in the incredulity stakes.

'Of course I did. They didn't belong to me. I'm not a thief,' Richard said with a mixture of self-righteousness and naïvety that made my fingers itch with the desire to get round his throat.

'It didn't occur to you that they might be helpful

42

evidence for the police in catching the car thieves?'
Ruth said, all silky savagery.

'No, it didn't, I'm sorry. I'm not like you two. I
don't have a criminal sort of mind.'

Ruth looked like she wanted to join me in the
lynch mob. 'Go on,' she said, her voice icy. 'What
did you do after you disposed of your corrobor-
ation?'

'I got in the car and set off. I was nearly home
when I saw the flashing blue lights in my rear-view
mirror. I didn't even pull over at first, because I
wasn't speeding or anything. Anyway, they cut
me up at the lights on Upper Brook Street, and I
realized it was me they were after. So I stopped. I
opened the window a couple of inches, but before
I could say anything, one of the busies opened
the door and dragged me out of the motor. Next
thing I know, I'm spread-eagled over the bonnet
with a pair of handcuffs on and his oppo's got the
boot open.

'They kept on at me about the car being stolen,
and I kept telling them, yeah, I knew that, 'cos I
was the person it had been stolen off, but they just
wouldn't listen. Then the guy looking in the boot
came round with this Sainsbury's plastic bag, and
he's waving it in my face saying, "And I suppose
the villains that nicked your car decided to leave
you a little something for your trouble?" Well, I
had no idea what was in the boot, did I? So I told
them that, and they just laughed, and bundled me
into their car and brought me here. Next thing I

know is they're on at me about a parcel of crack. And that's when I thought, uh-oh, I need a brief.'

Richard sat back and looked at the two of us. 'It's an unexpected bonus, getting Brannigan as well,' he added. 'How soon can you get me out of this dump, Ruth?' he asked, gesturing round the shabby interview room.

'That depends on several things. Being absolutely honest, Richard, I'm not optimistic that I can avoid them charging you, which means you won't be going anywhere until I can get you in front of a magistrate and apply for bail, which we can probably manage tomorrow morning. I still have some questions, though. Have you at any time opened the boot of the coupé?'

Richard frowned. 'I don't think so,' he said hesitantly. 'No, I'm pretty sure I haven't. I mean, why would I?'

'You didn't check it out when you bought it? Look to see if there was a spare wheel and a jack?' Ruth asked.

'The salesman showed us when we took it for a test drive,' I interjected. 'I certainly don't remember Richard ever going near it.'

He managed a grin. 'We didn't have it long enough for Brannigan to take it shopping, so we didn't need the boot.'

'Good,' Ruth said. 'This carrier bag that they produced from the boot. Had you ever seen it before?'

Richard shrugged. 'Well, I don't know. It was just an ordinary Sainsbury's carrier bag. Brannigan's got a drawer full of them. There was nothing about it to make it any different from any other one. But it wasn't in the boot when that rattlesnake showed us the car on Monday. And I didn't put it there. So I guess it's fair to say I'd never seen it before.'

'Did you touch it at all?'

'How could I? I said, I'd never seen it before,' Richard said plaintively.

'The officer didn't throw it to you, or hand it to you?' Ruth persisted.

'He couldn't, could he? His oppo had me cuffed already,' Richard replied.

'Yes, I'm a little surprised at that. Had you put up a struggle? Or had you perhaps been a little over-energetic in the verbal department?' Ruth asked carefully.

'Well, I wasn't exactly thrilled at being bodily dragged out of what was, technically, my own motor when I hadn't even been speeding and I'd been on the Diet Coke all night. So I suppose I was a bit gobby,' Richard admitted. If my heart could have sunk any further, it would have done. Add resisting arrest to the list, I thought gloomily.

Ruth was clearly as cheered as I was by this news. 'But you didn't actually offer any physical violence?' she asked, the hope in her voice as obvious as a City supporter in a United bus.

'No,' Richard said indignantly. 'What do you take me for?'

Diplomatically, neither of us answered. 'The keys for this coupé – did you have both sets?'

45

Richard shook his head. 'No, Brannigan had the others.'

'Have you still got them?' she asked me.

I nodded. 'They're in the kitchen drawer. No one but the two of us has had access to them.'

'Good,' Ruth said. 'These two women you were with – can you give me their names and addresses? I'll need statements from them to show you were talking about their record contract, rather than sitting in some dark corner negotiating a drug deal.'

'You're not going to like this,' Richard predicted. Correctly, as it turned out. 'I only know their stage names. Lilith Annsdaughter and Eve Uhuru. I don't have any addresses for them, just a phone number. It's in my notebook, but the boys in blue have taken that off me. Sorry.' He tried a smile, but the magic didn't work on either of us.

Ruth showed her first real sign of tiredness. Her eyes closed momentarily and her shoulders dropped. 'Leave that with me,' she said, her voice little stronger than a sigh. Then she took a deep breath, straightened her shoulders and pulled a packet of extra-long menthol cigarettes out of her briefcase. She offered them round, but got no takers. 'Do you suppose this counts as Thursday's eleventh or Friday's first?' she asked. 'Either way, it's against the rules.' She lit the cigarette, surprisingly, with a match torn from a restaurant matchbook. I'd have had Ruth marked down as a Dunhill lighter.

'One more thing,' Ruth said. 'You've got a son, haven't you, Richard?'

46

Richard frowned, puzzled. 'Yeah. Davy. Why?'

'What does he look like?'

'Why do you want to know that?' Richard asked. I was glad he had; it saved me the bother.

'According to the custody sergeant, when the officers searched the car more thoroughly, they found a Polaroid photograph that had slid down the side of the rear seat. It shows a young boy.' Ruth took a deep breath. 'In a rather unpleasant pose. I think they're going to want to ask some questions about that too.'

'How do you mean, a rather unpleasant pose?' I demanded.

'He's stripped down to his underpants and hand-cuffed to a bed,' Ruth said.

Richard looked thunderstruck. I knew just how he felt. 'And you think that's got something to do with *me*?' he gasped, outraged.

'The police might,' Ruth said.

'It couldn't be anything to do with us,' I butted in. 'Neither of us has been in the back seat since we got the car. The only person who'd been in the back seat that I know of is the salesman, on the test drive.'

'OK, OK,' Ruth said. 'Calm down. All I was thinking is that the photograph might possibly have an innocent explanation, and that it might have been your son.'

'So what does this kid look like?' Richard said belligerently.

'I'd say about ten, dark wavy hair, skinny.'

Richard let out a sigh. 'Well, you can count Davy out. He's only eight, average size for his age, and his hair's straight like mine, and the same colour. Light brown.' The colour of butterscotch, to be precise.

'Fine. I'm glad we've cleared that up,' Ruth said. 'Any questions, Kate?'

I nodded. Not that I had any hopes of a useful answer. 'Richard, when you were in Manto's, did you see anyone you recognized from the club the other night? Anyone a bit flash, a bit hooky, the type that just might have nicked the motor?'

Richard screwed up his eyes in concentration. Then he shook his head. 'You know me, Brannigan. I don't go places to look at the punters,' he said apologetically.

'Did you do a number on anybody about the car?'

'I didn't mention it to a soul. I'd just have looked a dick-head next week, back with my usual wheels,' he said, with rare insight.

'I don't suppose you know who's doing the heavy-duty stuff round town these days?'

Richard leaned forward and stared into my eyes. I could feel his fear. 'I've got no interest,' he said, his face tense. 'I bend over backwards to avoid taking any interest. Look, you know how much time I spend in the Moss and Cheetham Hill with new bands. Everybody knows I'm a journo. If I showed the slightest interest in the gangs and the drugs, I'd be a dead man, blown away on the steps of some newspaper office as a warning to other hacks not to get any daft ideas in their heads about running a campaign to clean up Manchester. You ask Alexis. She's supposed to be the crime correspondent. You ask her the last time there was a heavy incident in Moss Side or Cheetham Hill where she did anything more than toddle along to the police press conference! Believe me, if I thought for one minute that the gang that owns these drugs knows it was me that drove off with them, I'd be begging for protective custody a long, long way from Manchester. No, Brannigan, I do not know who's doing the heavy stuff, and for the sake of both our healths, I suggest that you remain in the same blissful state.'

I shrugged. 'You want to walk away from this? The only way you're going to do that is if we give them a body to trade,' I turned to Ruth. 'Am I right?'

'Regardless of that, you're probably going to have to spend another few days in police custody,' Ruth warned him.

Richard's face fell. 'Is there no way you can get me out sooner? I've got to get out of here, double urgent,' he said.

'Richard, in my opinion, the police will charge you with possession of a Class A drug with intent to supply, which is not a charge on which magistrates are inclined to allow bail. I'll do my best, but the chances are heavily stacked against us. Sorry about that, but there we go.' Ruth paused to savour a last mouthful of smoke before regretfully stubbing out her cigarette.

'Oh, shit,' Richard said. He took off his glasses and carefully polished them on his paisley silk shirt. He sighed. 'I suppose I'll have to go for it. But there's one slight problem I haven't mentioned that Brannigan seems to have forgotten about,' he said sheepishly, looking short-sightedly in my direction.

My turn to sigh. 'Give,' I said.

'Davy's due on the seven o'clock shuttle tonight. Remember? Half-term?'

As his words sank in, I got to my feet, shaking my head. 'Oh no, no way. Not me.'

'Please,' Richard said. 'You know how much it means to me.'

'There isn't that much dosh in the world,' I said, panicking.

'Please, Kate. That bitch is just looking for an excuse to shut me out,' he pleaded.

'That's no way to talk about the woman you married, the mother of your child, the former joy of your existence and fire of your loins,' I said, slipping defensively into our routine banter. It was no use. I knew as I looked down at the poor sod that I'd already given in. A dozen years of efficient contraception, and what does it get you? Someone else's kid, that's what.

5

I had to sit through the whole tale a second time for the CID's preliminary taped interview with Richard. Ruth had instructed him to co-operate fully, in the hope that it might predispose them towards letting his bail application go through. Looking at their faces as they listened to Richard's admittedly unlikely story, I didn't rate his chances of seeing daylight for a while.

After the interview, Ruth and I went into a brief huddle. 'Look, Kate, realistically, he's not going to get bail tomorrow. The best chance we have of getting him out is if you can come up with evidence that supports his story and points to the real criminals.' I held my tongue; Ruth is one of the few people I allow to tell me how to suck eggs.

'The crucial thing, given the amount of drugs involved, is that we keep him out of the mainstream prison system so he's not in contact with criminals who have connections into the drug scene. What I'm going to suggest to the CID is that they use the excuse of the "stolen" car and the possibly pornographic photograph to exploit paragraph five of the Bail Act,' she went on.

I must have looked as blank as I felt, for she deigned to explain. 'If the suspect's been arrested for one offence and the police have evidence of his implication in another, they can ask for what we call a lie-down. In other words, he remains in police custody for up to three days for the other matters to be investigated. That'll give us a bit of leeway, since the meter doesn't start running till the day after the initial hearing. That gives us Saturday, Sunday, Monday and Tuesday. He'll appear in court again on Wednesday, by which time you might have made enough headway for me to be able to argue that he should be let out.'

'Oh whoopee,' I said. 'A schedule so tight I'll be singing soprano and an eight-year-old too. Go for it, Ruth.'

I left Ruth to her wheeling and dealing with the CID just after half past four and drove into the city centre. Chinatown was still lively, the late-night trade losing their shirts in the casinos and drunkenly scoffing Chinese meals after the clubs had closed. Less than a mile away, in the gay village round Chorlton Street bus station, the only sign of life was a few rent boys and hookers, hanging around the early-morning street corners in a triumph of hope over experience. I cruised slowly along Canal Street, the blank windows of Manto's reflecting nothing but my Peugeot. I didn't even spot anyone sleeping rough till I turned down Minshull Street towards UMIST.

The street was still. I pulled up in an empty parking meter bay. There were only three other cars in the street, one of them Richard's Beetle. I'd have to come back in the morning and collect it before some officious traffic warden had it ticketed and clamped. At least its presence supported Richard's story, if the police were inclined to check it out. I took my pocket Nikon out of my glove box, checked the date stamp was switched on and took a couple of shots of the Beetle as insurance.

Slowly, I walked round to Sackville Street, checking doorways and litter bins for the trade plates. I didn't hold out much hope. They were too good a prize for any passing criminal, never mind the guys who had stuck them on the coupé in the first place. As I'd expected, the streets were clear. On the off chance, I walked round into the little square of garden in Sackville Street and searched along the wall and in the bushes, being careful to avoid touching the unpleasant crop of used condoms. No joy. Stumbling with exhaustion, I walked back to my car and drove home. The prospect of having to take care of Davy weighed heavily on me, and I desperately wanted to crack on and make some progress towards clearing Richard. But the sensible part of me knew there was nothing I could do in the middle of the night. And if I didn't get some sleep soon, I wouldn't be fit to do what had to be done come daylight.

I set my alarm for half past eight, switched off the phones and turned down the volume on the answering machine. Unfortunately, I couldn't do the same thing with my brain. I tossed and turned, my head full of worries that wouldn't lie down and leave me in peace. I prayed Ruth's stratagem would work. While he was still in police custody, Richard was fairly safe. But as soon as he was charged and remanded to prison, the odds would turn against him. No matter how much the police tried to keep the lid on this business, it wouldn't take long in the leaky sieve of prison before the wrong people learned what he was in for. And if the drugs belonged to one of the Manchester gangs, some warlord somewhere would decide that Richard needed to be punished in ways the law has long since ceased to contemplate.

We'd both gone into this relationship with damage from past encounters. From the start, we'd been honest about our pain and our fears. As a result, we'd always kept it light, by tacit agreement. Somewhere round about dawn, I acknowledged that I couldn't live with myself if I let anything happen to him. It's a real bastard, love.

I was only dozing when the alarm went off. The first thing I did was check the answering machine. Its friendly red light was flashing, so I hit the replay button. 'Hello, Kate, it's Ruth.' Her voice was friendlier than I deserved. 'It's just before six, and I thought you'd be pleased to hear that I've manged to persuade the divisional superintendent that he has most chance of obtaining convictions from this situation if he keeps Richard's arrest under wraps. So he's agreed, very reluctantly, not to hold a press conference announcing a major drugs haul. He's not keen, but there we go. Was I put on earth to keep policemen happy? He's also receptive to the idea of a lie-down, but he wants to hang on till later in the day before he makes a final decision. Anyway, I hope you're managing some sleep, since working yourself to the point of exhaustion will not serve the interests of my client. Why don't you give me a call towards the end of the afternoon, by which time we both might have some information? Speak to you soon, darling. It'll be all right.' I wished I could share her breezy confidence.

As the coffee brewed, I called my local friendly mechanic and asked him to collect Richard's Beetle, promising to leave a set of keys under the kitchen window box. I also phoned in to the office and told Shelley what had happened. Of course, it was Richard who got the sympathy. Never mind that I'd been deprived of my sleep and landed with a task that might have caused even Clint Eastwood a few nervous moments. Oh no, that was my job, Shelley reminded me. 'You do what you've got to do to get that poor boy out of jail,' she said sternly. 'It makes me feel ill, just thinking of Richard locked up in a stinking cell with the dregs of humanity.'

'Yes, boss,' I muttered rebelliously. Shelley always

makes me feel like a bloody-minded teenager when she goes into Mother Hen mode. God knows what effect it has on her own two adolescents. 'Just tell Bill what I'm doing. I'll be on my mobile if you need me urgently,' I added.

I washed two thick slices of toast down with a couple of mugs of scalding coffee. The toast because I needed carbohydrate, the coffee because it was a more attractive option than surgery to get my eyes open. I pulled on jogging pants and a sweat shirt without showering and drove over to the Thai boxing gym in South Manchester where I punish my body on as regular a basis as my career in crime prevention allows. It might not be the Hilton, but it meets my needs. It's clean, it's cheap, the equipment is well maintained and it's mercifully free of muscle-bound macho men who think they've got the body and charm of Sylvester Stallone when in reality they don't even have the punch-drunk brains of Rocky.

I wasn't the only person working out on the weights that morning. The air was already heavy with the smell of sweat as half a dozen men and a couple of women struggled to keep time's winged chariot in the service bay. As I'd hoped, my old buddy Dennis O'Brien, burglar of this parish, was welded to the pec deck, moving more metal than the average Nissan Micra contains. He was barely breaking sweat. The bench next to him was free, so I picked up a set of dumbbells and lay back to do some tricep curls. 'Hiya, kid,' Dennis said on his next outgoing breath. 'What's the world been doing to you?'

'Don't ask. How about you?'

He grinned like a Disney wolf. 'Still doing the police's job for them,' he said. 'Got a real result last night.'

'Glad somebody did,' I said, enjoying the sensation of my flabby muscles tightening as I raised and lowered the weights.

'Fourteen grand I took off him,' Dennis told me. 'Now that's what I call a proper victim.'

He was clearly desperate to tell the tale, so I gave him the tiny spur of encouragement that was all he needed. 'Sounds like a good 'un. How d'you manage that?'

'I hear this firm from out of town are looking for a parcel of trainers. So I arrange to meet them, and I tell them I can lay my hands on an entire wagonload of Reeboks, don't I? A couple of nights later, we meet again and I show him a sample pair from this truck I'm supposed to have nicked, right? Only, I haven't nicked them, have I? I've just gone down the wholesaler's and bought them.' As he got into his story, Dennis paused in his work-out. He's physically incapable of telling a tale without his hands.

'So of course, they fall for it. Anyway, we arrange the meet for last night, out on the motorway services at Sandbach. My mate Andy and me, we get there a couple of hours before the meet and suss the place out. When these two bozos arrive, Andy's stood hiding behind a truck right the far side of the lorry park, and when the bozos park up beside my car, I make sure they see me giving him the signal, and he comes over to us, making out like he's just come out of the wagon, keys in his hand, the full monte.' Dennis was giggling between his sentences like a little lad outlining some playground scam.

I sat up and said, 'So what happens next?'

'I say to these two dummies, "Let's see the money, then. You hand over the money, and my mate'll hand over the keys to the wagon." And they do no more than hand over their fourteen grand like lambs. I'm counting the money, and when I've done, I give Andy the nod and he tosses them the keys. We jump into the motor and shoot straight off. I tell you, the last thing I see is the pair of them schmucks jumping up and down beside that wagon, their mouths opening and shutting like a pair of goldfish.' By the end of his tale, Dennis was doubled over with laughter. 'You should've seen them, Kate,' he wheezed. 'The Dennis O'Brien crime prevention programme scores another major success.'

The first time he said that to me, I'd been a bit baffled. I didn't see how ripping someone off to the tune of several grand could prevent crime. So Dennis had explained. The people he was cheating had a large sum of money that they were prepared to spend on stolen goods. So some thief would have to steal something for them to buy. But if Dennis relieved them of their wad, they wouldn't have any money to spend on stolen goods, therefore the robbery that would have had to take place was no longer necessary. Crime prevention, QED.

I moved over to a piece of equipment designed to build my quads and adjusted the weights. 'A lot of dosh, fourteen grand,' I said. 'Aren't you worried they're going to come after you?'

'Nah,' he said scornfully, returning to his exercise. 'They're from out of town. They don't know where I hang out, and nobody in Manchester would be daft enough to tell them where to find me. Besides, I was down Collar Di Salvo's car lot first thing this morning, trading the BMW in. They'll be looking for a guy in a red BM, not a silver Merc. Take a tip, Kate – don't buy a red BMW off Collar for the next few days. I don't want to see you in a case of mistaken identity!'

We both pumped iron in silence for a while. I moved around the machines, making sure I paid proper attention to the different muscle groups. By ten, I was sweating, Dennis was skipping and there were only the two of us left. I collapsed on to the mat, and enjoyed the complaints of my stomach muscles as I did some slow, warm-down exercises. 'I've got a problem,' I said in between Dennis's bounces.

Just saying that brought all the fear and misery right back. I stared hard at the off-white walls, trying to make a pattern out of the grimy handprints, black rubber skidmarks and chips from weights swung too enthusiastically. Dennis slowed to a halt and walked across to the shelves of thin towels that the management think are all we deserve. Like I said, it's cheap. I suppose it was their version of crime prevention; nobody in their right mind would steal those towels. Dennis picked up a couple, draped them over his big shoulders and sat down on the bench facing me. 'D'you want to talk about it?'

I sighed. 'To be honest, I'm not sure I can.' It wasn't that I didn't trust Dennis. Quite the opposite. I trusted his affection for me almost too much to tell him what had happened to Richard. There was no knowing what limits Dennis would go to in the attempt to take care of anyone threatening my happiness and wellbeing. Considering the different perspective we have on the law of the land, we find ourselves side by side facing in the same direction more often than not. For some reason that neither of us quite understands, we know we can rely on each other. And just as important, we like each other too.

Dennis patted my left ankle, the only part of me he could comfortably reach. 'You decide you want an ear, you let your Uncle Dennis know. What d'you need right now?'

'I'm not sure about that either.' I wiped the back of my hand over my mouth and upper lip and tasted the sharp salty sweat. 'Dennis. Why would you put trade plates on a stolen motor rather than false plates?'

'What kind of stolen motor? Joyrider material,

stolen to order, or just somebody stuck for a ride home?'

'A brand new Leo Gemini turbo super coupé. Less than a ton on the clock.'

He pondered for a moment. 'Temporary measure? To keep the busies off my back till I got it delivered where it was supposed to be going?'

'In this instance, we're talking a couple of days after the car was lifted. Plenty of time to have dropped it off with whoever, I'd have thought,' I said, shaking my head.

'In that case, you're probably talking right proper villainy,' he replied, rubbing the back of his neck with one of the towels.

'Run it past me,' I said.

Dennis pulled a packet of Bensons and a throwaway lighter out of the pocket of his sweat pants and lit up. 'They never have any bloody ashtrays in here,' he complained, looking round. The paradox clearly escaped him. 'Anyway, your professional car thief goes out on the job knowing exactly what motor he's going for. He doesn't do things on spec. He'd have a set of plates on him that he'd already matched up with another car of the same make and model, so that if some smart-arsed traffic cop put him through the computer he'd come up clean. So he wouldn't need trade plates. Your serious amateurs, they might use trade plates just to get it across town to their dealer. But they're not that easy to come by. OK so far?'

I got off the floor and squatted on a low bench.

'Clear as that Edinburgh crystal you offered me last month,' I said.

'Your loss, Kate,' he said. 'Now, on the other hand, if I wanted a fast car for a one-off job, I'd do exactly what the guy you're interested in has done. I'd nick a serious set of wheels, smack some trade plates on it from my local friendly hooky garage when I was actually using it, then dump it as soon as I'd finished the job.'

'When you say proper villainy, what exactly did you have in mind?' I asked.

'The kind of stuff I don't do. Major armed robbery, mainly. A hit, maybe.'

I began to wish I had the sense not to ask questions I wasn't going to like the answers to. 'What about drugs?'

He shrugged. 'Not the first thing that would spring to mind. But then, I don't hang out with scum like that, do I? At a guess, it'd only be worth doing if you were shifting a parcel of drugs a reasonable distance between two major players. Say, from London to Manchester. Otherwise there'd be so many cars running around with trade plates that even the coppers would notice. Also, trade plates are ten a penny on the motorway. Whereas brand new motors with or without trade plates stick out like a sore thumb on the council estates where most of the drugs get shifted. You want to get a pull these days, you just have to park up in Moss Side in anything that isn't old enough to need an MOT,' he added bitterly.

'What would you say if I told you there were a couple of kilos of crack in the boot of this car?'

Dennis got to his feet. 'Nice chatting to you, Kate. Be seeing you. That's what I'd say.'

I pulled a face and stood up too. 'Thanks, Dennis.'

Dennis put a warm hand on my wrist and gripped it tightly enough for me not to think about pulling away. 'I've never been more serious, Kate. Steer clear of them toerags. They'd eat *me* for breakfast. They wouldn't even notice you as they swallowed. Give this one the Spanish Archer.'

'The Spanish Archer?' This was a new one on me.

'El Bow.'

I smiled. 'I'll be careful. I promise.' I thought I'd grown out of promising what I can't deliver. Obviously I was wrong.

6

I walked into the office to find my partner Bill looming over Shelley like a scene from *The Jungle Book*. Bill is big, blond and shaggy, the antithesis of Shelley, petite, black and immaculately groomed right down to the tips of her perfectly plaited hair. He looked up and stopped speaking in midsentence, finger pointing at something on Shelley's screen.

'Kate, Kate, Kate,' he boomed, moving across the room to envelop me in the kind of hug that makes me feel like a little girl. Usually I fight my way out, but this morning it was good to feel safe for a moment, even if it was only an illusion. With one hand, Bill patted my back, with the other he rumpled my hair. Eventually, he released me. 'Shelley filled me in. I was just going to phone you,' he said, walking over to the coffee machine and busying himself making me a cappuccino. 'This business with Richard. What do you want me to do?'

On paper, Bill might be the senior partner of Mortensen and Brannigan. In practice, when either of us is involved in a major case and needs help from the other, there's never any question of the gopher role going to me just because I'm the junior. Whoever started the ball rolling stays the boss. And in this instance, since it was my lover who was in the shit, it was my case.

I took the frothy coffee he handed me and slumped into one of the clients' chairs. 'I don't know what you can do,' I said. 'We've got to find out who stole the car, who the drugs belong to and to make out a strong enough case against them for the police to realize they've made a cock-up. Otherwise Richard stays in the nick and we sit back and wait for the slaughter of the innocents.'

Bill sat down opposite me. 'Shelley,' he said over his shoulder, 'stick the answering machine on, grab yourself an espresso and come and give us the benefit of your thoughts. We need every brain we've got working on this one.'

Shelley didn't need telling twice. She sat down, the inevitable notepad on her knee. Bill leaned back and linked his hands behind his head. 'Right,' he said. 'First question. Accident or intent?'

'Accident,' I said instantly.

'Why are you so sure?' Bill asked.

I took a sip of coffee while I worked out the reasons I'd been so certain. 'OK,' I said. 'First, there are too many imponderables for it to be intentional. If someone was deliberately trying to set up Richard, or me, they wouldn't have bothered with the trade plates. They'd just have left it sitting there with its own plates, so obvious that he couldn't have missed it. Why bother with all of that when they could have planted the drugs in either of our cars at any time?'

Shelley nodded and said, 'The thing that strikes me is that it's an awful lot of drugs to plant. Surely they could have achieved the same result with a lot less crack than two kilos. I don't know much about big-time drug dealers, but I can't believe they'd waste drugs they could make money out of just to set somebody up.'

'Besides,' I added, 'why in God's name would anyone want to frame Richard? I know *I* sometimes feel like murdering him, but I'm a special case. Not even his ex-wife would want him to spend the next twenty years inside, never mind be willing to splash out – what, two hundred grand?'

Bill nodded. 'Near enough,' he said.

'Well, even she wouldn't spend that kind of dosh just to get her own back on him, always supposing he paid her enough maintenance for her to afford it. It's not as if he's an investigative journalist. The only people who take offence at what he writes are record company executives, and if any of them got their hands on two kilos of crack it would be up their noses, not in the boot of Richard's car.' My voice wobbled and I ran out of steam suddenly. I kept coming up against the horrible realization that this wasn't just another case. My life was going to be irrevocably affected by whatever I did over the next few days.

Thankfully, Bill didn't notice. I don't think I could have handled any more sympathy right then. 'OK. Accident. Synchronicity. What are the leads?'

'Why does somebody always have to ask the one question you don't have the answer to?' I said shakily.

'Has his solicitor got anything from the police yet?' Bill asked. 'Who's looking after him, by the way?'

'He's got Ruth. If the cops have got anything themselves yet, they've not passed it on. But she asked me to call her this afternoon.' I stirred the froth into the remains of my coffee and watched it change colour.

'So what have we got to go at?'

'Not a lot,' I admitted. 'Frankly, Bill, there aren't enough leads on this to keep one person busy, never mind the two of us.'

'What were you planning on doing?' he asked.

'I don't know anybody on the Drugs Squad well enough to pick their brains. So that leaves Della.'

Bill nodded. 'She'll be as keen to help as me and Shelley.'

'She should be,' I agreed. Not only did Detective Chief Inspector Della Prentice owe me a substantial professional favour in return for criminals translated into prisoners. Over the past few months, she'd also moved into that small group of women I count as friends. If I couldn't rely on her support, I'd better send my judgment back to the manufacturer for a major service. 'The only other thing I can think of is cruising the city centre tonight looking for another serious motor with trade plates on it.'

'The logic presumably being that if they've lost the car they were counting on, they'll need another one?' Bill asked. 'Even though the drugs have gone?'

'It's all I've got. I'm hoping that our man will be out and about, trying to find out who's got a parcel of crack they shouldn't have. But that's a one-person job, Bill. Look, leave me numbers where I can reach you, day or night. I promise, if I get anywhere and I need an extra pair of hands, I'll call you right away.'

'That's truly the only lead you've got? You're not holding out on me?' he asked suspiciously.

'Believe me, Bill, if I thought there was anything for you to do, I'd be on my hands and knees begging,' I said, only half joking.

'Well, let's see what Della has to say. Right, team, let's get some work done!' He strolled back over to Shelley's desk. 'This bit here, Shelley. Can we shift it further up the report, so all the frightening stuff hits them right at the beginning?'

Shelley rolled her eyes upwards and got to her feet, squeezing my arm supportively as she passed me on the way to her desk. 'Let me have a look,

Bill,' she said, settling into her chair.

As I headed for my own office, Bill looked up and smiled. I think it was meant to reassure me. It didn't. I closed my door and dropped into my chair like a stone. I put a hand out to switch on my computer, but there didn't seem a lot of point. I swivelled round and looked out of the window at the city skyline. The lemon geranium on the sill was drooping. Knowing my track record with plants, my best friend Alexis had given me the geranium, confidently predicting it was indestructible. I tried not to see its impending death as an omen and turned away. Time was slipping past, and I didn't seem to be able to take any decisive action to relieve the sense of frustration that was burning inside me like indigestion.

'Come *on*, Brannigan,' I urged myself, picking up the phone. At least I could get the worst job over with. When the phone was answered, I said, 'Andrew Broderick, please.'

Moments later, a familiar voice said, 'Broderick.'

'Andrew, it's Kate Brannigan. I have good news and bad news,' I said. 'The good news is that we've found the car, undamaged.'

'That's tremendous,' he said, his astonishment obvious. 'How did you manage that?'

'Pure chance, unfortunately,' I said. 'The bad news, however, is that the police have impounded it.'

'The police? But why?'

I sighed. 'It's a bit complicated, Andrew,' I said.

Brannigan's entry for the understatement of the year contest. When I'd finished explaining, I had an extremely unhappy client.

'This is simply not on,' he growled. 'What right have they got to hang on to a car that belongs to my company?'

'It's evidence in a major drugs case.'

'Jesus Christ,' he exploded. 'If I don't get that car back, this operation is going to cost me about as much as the scam. How the hell am I going to lose that in the books?'

I didn't have the answer. I made some placatory noises, and got off the line as fast as I could. Staring at the wall, I remembered a loose end that was hanging around from Broderick's job, so I rang my local friendly finance broker.

Josh Gilbert and I have an arrangement: he runs credit checks on dodgy punters for me and I buy him dinner a lot. Anything else he can help us with we pay through the nose for.

It turned out that Josh was out of town, but his assistant Julia was around. I explained what I wanted from her and she said, 'No problem. I can't promise I'll get to it today, but I'll definitely fax it to you by Tuesday lunch time. Is that OK?'

It would have to be. The one free favour Josh had ever done me was introducing me to Detective Chief Inspector Della Prentice. My next call was to her direct line. She answered on the second ring. 'DCI Prentice,' she said crisply.

'Della, it's Kate,' I said. Even to me, my voice sounded weary.

'Kate! Thanks for getting back to me,' she said.

'Sorry? I didn't know you'd been trying to get hold of me,' I replied, shuffling the papers on my desk in case I'd missed a message.

'I spoke to your machine an hour or so ago. When I heard what had happened to Richard,' Della said. 'I just wanted you to know that I don't believe a word of it.'

I felt a lump in my throat, so I swallowed hard and concentrated very hard on the jar of pencils by my phone. 'Me neither,' I said. 'Del, I know it's not your manor, but I need all the help I can get on this one.'

'Goes without saying, Kate. Look, it's not going to be easy for me to get access to the case information or any forensic evidence, but I'll do what I can,' she promised.

'I appreciate that. But don't put your own head in the noose in the process,' I added. No matter how much they spend on advertising to tell us different, anyone who has any contact with real live police officers know that The Job is still a white, patriarchal, rigidly hierarchical organization. That makes life especially hard for women who refuse to be shunted into the ghetto of community liaison and get stuck in at the sharp end of crime fighting.

'Don't worry about me. I'll find out who's on the team and see who I know. Meanwhile, is there anything specific I can help you with?'

'I need a general backgrounder on crack. How much there is of it around, where it's turning up, who they think is pushing the stuff, how it's being distributed. Anything there is, including gossip. Off the record, of course. Any chance?' I asked.

'Give me a few hours. Can you meet me around seven?'

I pulled a face. 'Only if you can get to the airport,' I said. 'I have a plane to meet.'

'No problem.'

'Oh yes it is. Richard's son's going to be on it. And the one thing he mustn't find out is that his dad's in the nick on drugs charges.'

'Ah,' Della said. It was a short, clipped exclamation.

'I take it that response means you don't want to share the child-minding?'

'Correct. Count me out. Look, I'll dig up all I can and meet you at Domestic Arrivals in Terminal I, at the coffee counter, just as you come in. Around quarter to seven, OK?'

I didn't want to wait that long, but Della wasn't the sort to hang around either. If quarter to seven was when she wanted to meet, then quarter to seven was the soonest she could see me with the information I needed. 'I'll see you then. Oh, one other thing. I don't think it's got anything to do with the drugs, but there was a Polaroid picture of a young kid in handcuffs, you know, bondage-style, in the car. Probably just dropped by one of the villains. But maybe you could ask around and see if there's anybody that Vice have in the frame for paedophilia who's also got form for drugs.'

'Can do.'

'And Della?'

'Mmm?'

'Thanks.'

'You know what they say. A friend in need . . .'

'Is a pain in the ass,' I finished. 'See you.' I put the phone down. At last I felt things were starting to move.

The conversation with Della had reminded me of the part of the problem I'd deliberately been ignoring. Davy. Not that he was in himself a problem. It's just that I wasn't very good at keeping eight-year-old boys happy when I was eight myself, and I haven't improved with age. According to Richard, Davy was the only good thing to come out of his three-year marriage, and his ex-wife Angie seemed more determined with each passing year to reduce his contact with the only child he was likely to have if he stayed with me. So it was imperative that Davy didn't go back from his half-term holiday with lurid tales of Daddy in the nick.

Which sounded simple if you said it very fast. Unless we could spring Richard in the next day or two, however, it was going to be extremely complicated. Richard and I had agreed an initial lie, which should hold the fort for a day or two. After that, it was going to get complicated. While Davy might just believe his dad had had to dash abroad on an urgent, chance-in-a-lifetime job, it wasn't going to be easy to explain why Richard couldn't get home again. There may be parts of the world where the transport isn't too reliable on account of wars and famine, but unfortunately most of them don't run to major rock venues. Either way, whether it took hours or days, I was going to need some assistant minders, if only to baby-sit while I rambled the city centre streets looking for fast cars with trade plates. And there aren't very many people I'd trust to do that.

I picked up the phone again and tapped in Alexis Lee's office number. '*Chronicle* crime desk,' a young man's voice informed me.

'Alexis, please.'

'Sh'not'ere,' came the snippy reply.

'I need to speak to her in a hurry. You wouldn't happen to know where I can get hold of her?' I asked, clinging to my manners by my fingernails. My Granny Brannigan always said politeness cost nothing. But then, she never had to face the humiliation of dealing with lads who still think a yuppie is something to aspire to.

''Zit'bout'story?' he demanded. 'You c'n tell me if it is.'

'Not as such,' I said through clenched teeth. I could hear my Oxford accent becoming more Gown than Town by the second. 'Not yet, anyway. Look, I know you're a very busy person, and I don't want to waste any of your precious time, but it's awfully important that I speak to Alexis. Do you know where she is?'

74

There's a whole generation of young lads who are either so badly educated or so thick skinned they don't even notice when they're being patronized. The guy on the phone could have featured in a sociology lecture as an exemplar of the type. 'Sh's a' lunch,' he gabbled.

'And do we know where?'

'Gone f'r a curry.'

That was all I needed to know. There might be three dozen curry restaurants strung out along the mile-long stretch of Wilmslow Road in Rusholme, but everybody has their favourite. Alexis's current choice was only too familiar. 'Thanks, sonny,' I said. 'I'll remember you in my letter to Santa.'

I was out of my seat before I'd put the phone back. I crossed my office in five strides and walked into the main office. 'Shelley, I'm off to the Golden Ganges. And before you ask how I can eat at a time like this, don't. Just don't.'

7

If the gods had struck me blind the moment I entered the Golden Ganges, I'd still have had no problem finding Alexis. That unmistakable Liverpudlian voice, a monument to Scotch and nicotine, almost drowned out the twanging sitar that was feebly trickling out of the restaurant's speakers, even though she was seated a long way from the door. The volume told me she wasn't working, just routinely showing off to her companion. When she's doing the business with one of her contacts, the sound level drops so low that even MI5 would have a job picking it up. I walked towards the table.

Alexis spotted me two steps into the room, though there was no pause in the flow of her narrative to indicate it. As I approached, she held up one finger to stop me in my tracks a few feet away, interrupting her story to say, 'Just a sec, Kate, crucial point in the anecdote.' She turned back to her companion and said, 'Thomas Wynn Ellis, a good Welsh name, you'd think you'd cracked it, yeah? I mean, she's not *crazy* about the Welsh, but at least you've got a fair chance that he's going to speak English, yeah? So she fills in all the forms to be taken on as a patient, then makes an appointment to see him about her back problem. She walks into the surgery, and what does she find? Straight from Karachi, Dr Thomas Wynn Ellis, product of the Christian orphanage, colour of a bottle of HP sauce! She was sick as a parrot!'

Alexis's companion giggled. I couldn't find a laugh, not just because I'd heard her ridicule the casual racism of her colleagues before. I sat down at the table. Luckily they'd progressed to the coffee. I don't think I could have sat at the same table as a curry, never mind eaten one. I didn't recognize the young woman sharing the table, but Alexis didn't leave me in the dark too long. 'Kate, this is Polly Patrick, she's about to take up a post at the university, doing research into psychological profiling of serial offenders. Polly, this is my best mate, Kate Brannigan, PI.'

Polly looked interested. I winced. I knew what was coming. 'You're a private investigator?' Polly asked.

'No,' Alexis butted in, unable to resist her joke of the month. 'She's Politically Incorrect!' She hooted in mirth. In anyone else, it would wind me up to some tune, but Alexis's humour is so innocently juvenile she somehow manages to be endearing, not infuriating.

This time, I managed to dredge up a smile. 'Actually, I am a private investigator. And I'd be fascinated to have a chat with you some time about what you do.'

'Ditto,' said Polly. Unusually for a psychologist, she had some people skills, for she took the barely indicated hint. 'But it'll have to be another time. I've got to dash. Perhaps the three of us could do lunch some time soon?'

We all made the appropriate farewell and let's-get-together-soon noises, and a few minutes later, Polly was just a memory. Alexis had ordered more coffee somewhere during the goodbyes, and I sat staring at the froth on mine as she lit a cigarette and settled into her seat. 'So, Sherlock,' she said. 'What's the problem?'

I reckoned I was about to ask her something that would test our friendship to the limits. But then, the last time she'd asked me a major favour, it had nearly got me killed, so I figured I didn't need to beat myself up about it too much. I took a deep breath and said, 'I need to talk to you about something important. It's personal, it's big and it's got to be off the record. Can you live with that?'

'We're friends, aren't we?'

'Yeah, and one good turn deserves the lion's share of the duvet.'

'Go on, girl, spill it,' Alexis said. She opened a shoulder bag only marginally smaller than mine and ostentatiously pressed the button that switched off her microcassette recorder. 'Your secret is safe with me.'

'Why d'you suppose that line terrifies me?' I said, in a weak attempt at our usual friendly banter.

Alexis ran a hand through her wild black hair. Coupled with her pale skin and the dark smudges under her eyes, I sometimes think she looks worryingly like one of Dracula's victims in the Francis Ford Coppola version. Luckily, her linguistic vigour usually dispels such ethereal notions pretty damn quick. 'Shit, KB, if that's the best you can do, there's clearly something serious going down here,' she said. 'C'mon, girl, spit it out.'

'Richard's been arrested,' I said. 'He was technically driving a stolen car that not-so-technically had two kilos of crack in the boot.'

Alexis just stared at me. She even ignored her burning cigarette. The woman who had heard it all could be shaken after all. 'You're at the wind-up,' she finally said.

I shook my head. 'I wish I was.' I gave her the full story. It didn't take long. Throughout, she kept shaking her head in disbelief, smoking so intensely it seemed to be all that was keeping her in one piece. When I'd brought her up to speed, she carried on smoking, head weaving like a Wimbledon spectator.

'It could only happen to Richard,' she finally said in tones of wonder. 'How does he do it? The poor sod!' Alexis and Richard play this game of cordially disliking each other. I'm not supposed to know it's a game; things must be bad if Alexis was letting me see she actually cared about the guy. 'I take it you want me to dig around, see what the goss is out on the streets?'

'I don't want you to take any chances,' I said, meaning it. 'You know as well as I do that most of the drug warlords in this city would blow you away at the slightest provocation. Don't tread on anybody's toes, please. I don't want you on my conscience as well as Richard. What I'm after is more practical.' I broke the news about Davy's imminent arrival.

'Sure, we'll help out. I like Davy. He's good fun. Besides, it gives me and Chris a great excuse to bunk off a weekend's labouring and have a giggle instead.' Alexis and her architect girlfriend Chris are members of a self-build scheme, which means they spend most of their spare daylight hours pushing wheelbarrows full of cement along precarious wooden planks. A dozen of them bought a piece of land, and Chris designed the houses in exchange for other people's skills in exotic areas like plumbing, wiring, bricklaying and roofing. It's my idea of hell, but they love it, though not so much that they're not glad of an excuse to give it the body swerve from time to time. I knew taking care of Davy fitted the bill perfectly; it had a high enough Goody Two Shoes element to assuage any guilt at skiving off the building site.

Hearing Alexis confirm my hopes almost brought

a genuine smile to my lips. 'So can you be at the house tonight about eight?'

Alexis frowned. 'Not tonight I can't. I'm having dinner with a contact.'

'No chance you can rearrange it?'

'Sorry. The guy's only in town for a few days.' She stubbed out her cigarette and washed the taste away with a swig of coffee. She must have felt the need to justify herself, for when I didn't respond, she carried on, 'I was at college with him, and we stayed in touch. He's one of your high-flyers, a whiz-kid with the Customs and Excise, if that's not a contradiction in terms. Anyway, he's in Manchester for a briefing session with the Vice Squad. Apparently, there's been a new range of kiddie porn mags and vids hitting the market, real hard-core stuff, and they think the source is some-where in the North West. Can you believe it, girl? We're actually exporting this shit to Amsterdam and Denmark, that's how heavy it is. So my mate Barney's up here to tell the blue boys what they should be looking for, and I've pitched him into letting me buy him dinner. Sorry, Kate, but I've already promised the editor a splash and a feature launching a campaign for Monday's paper.'

I shrugged. 'Don't worry about it. I'll get some-one else lined up for tonight, and you can weigh in when you're clear.'

'Don't do that. Chris'll see you right tonight, I'm sure she will. All she's got planned is a night in front of the soaps and a bottle of Muscadet in the bath. You got the talking brick with you?' Alexis held out her hand, and I passed her my mobile phone. I couldn't help thinking I'd be less than thrilled if Richard had offered me up for a night's baby-sitting when I'd got my heart set on a night in with *Coronation Street* and a Body Shop selection box.

'All right, darling?' Alexis began the conversation. 'Listen, Kate needs your body tonight . . . Girl, you should be so lucky. No, it's a bit of a crisis, you know? I'll fill you in later. She needs somebody she can trust to mind Davy round at Richard's . . . Eight, she said, is that OK? . . . Darlin', you'll get your reward in heaven. See you at home about six. Love you too.' Alexis pressed the 'end' button with a flourish. 'Sorted. I'll give her my keys for your house so she can let herself in.' She folded the phone closed and handed it back to me.

'I appreciate it,' I said. I meant it too. I hoped I wasn't going to run out of favours and friends before I managed to get Richard out of jail. 'One more thing – when you're chatting up your porn expert, can you ask him if there's any suggestion of a tie-in with drugs?'

'Why do you ask?' Alexis demanded, her brown eyes suddenly alert.

I groaned. 'It's not a story, trust me. It's just that there's an outside chance one of the people involved in this business of Richard's might be into paedophilia.'

'What makes you think that?' she asked, suspicious that she might be missing out on something that would plaster her by-line across the front pages of the *Chronicle*.

'It'd be cruel to tell you,' I said. 'You'd only be upset because you couldn't use it.'

Alexis shook her head, a rueful smile twitching the corners of her mouth. 'You know me too well, girl.'

I stood on the pavement outside the Golden Ganges, watching Alexis's car pull away from the kerb into a death-defying U-turn. The air was heavy with the fumes of traffic and curry spices, the sky bleak and overcast, the distant sounds of police and ambulance sirens mingling with the wail of a nearby car alarm. I turned the corner of the side-street where I'd left my car, and the ululations of the alarm increased dramatically. It took me a moment or two to realize that it was my car that was the focus of attention for the two black lads with the cordless hand-drill.

'Hey, shitheads,' I yelled in protest, breaking into a run without even thinking about it.

They looked up, uncertainty written all over their faces. It only took them seconds to weigh up the situation and decide to leg it. If it had been after dark, they probably would have brazened it out and tried to give me a good kicking for daring to challenge their right to my stereo. Shame, really. I had so much pent-up frustration in me that I'd have relished the chance to show them my Thai boxing skills weren't just for keeping fit.

By the time I reached the car, they were round the next corner. The mashed metal of the lock wasn't ever going to make sweet music with a key again. I pushed the control button that stopped the alarm shrieking. Sighing, I pulled the door open and climbed in. At least having the lock replaced would kill one of the hours I couldn't find a way to fill usefully. Before I started the engine, I called Handbrake the mechanic, checked he'd collected the Beetle without a hitch and told him I needed a new driver's door lock. That way, I wouldn't have to hang around answering his phone while he nipped out to collect the part.

I turned left on to Oxford Road and headed away from the city centre. I was clear of the curry zone in a few minutes, and straight into the heart of university residences and student bedsits. I pushed the eject button on the stereo. Goodbye Julia Fordham. Plangent and poignant was just what I didn't need right now. I raked through my cassettes and smacked the Pet Shop Boys' *Discography* into the slot. Perfect. A thrusting beat to drive me onwards and upwards, an emotional content somewhere below zero. At the Wilbraham Road lights, I cut across to Kingsway and over to Heaton Mersey where Handbrake operates out of a pair of lock-ups behind a down-at-heel block of flats. Handbrake is a mate of Dennis's who's been team mechanic to Mortensen and Brannigan for a few years now. And, for his sins, he also gets to play with Richard's Beetle. He's called Handbrake because he used to be a getaway driver for armed robbers, and he specialized in 180-degree handbrake turns when the pursuit got a bit too close for comfort. He did a six-stretch back in the early eighties, and he's gone straight ever since. Well, only a bit wobbly. Only now and again.

There was a Volkswagen Golf in one of Handbrake's two garages. As I pulled up, Handbrake emerged from under the bonnet. Anyone less likely to adopt the anonymous role of a getaway driver it would be hard to imagine. He's got flaming red curls as tight as a pensioner's perm and a face like a sad clown. He'd have no chance in an identity parade unless the cops brought in a busload of Ronald McDonalds. Handbrake wiped his hands on his overalls and gave me a smile that made him look like he was about to burst into tears.

'Gobshites get you?' he greeted me.

'Caught them in time to save the stereo,' I told him, leaving the door open behind me.

'That's saved you a few bob, then. The lad'll be back with the locks any minute,' Handbrake said, giving the door the judicious once-over. 'Nice clean job, really.'

'No problem with the Beetle?'

He shook his head. 'Nah. Piece of piss. I left it outside your house, stuck the keys back through the letter box. Mr Music out of town, is he?' I was saved from lying by the arrival of a young black kid on a mountain bike. 'All right, Dobbo?' Handbrake called out.

The lad hauled back on his handlebars to pull up in midwheelie. 'My man,' he affirmed. He shrugged out of a smart leather backpack and took a new set of locks for my Peugeot out of it. He handed it to Handbrake, quoted what seemed to be an interestingly low price and added on a tenner for delivery. Handbrake pulled a wad out of his back pocket and counted out the cash. The lad zipped it into his leather bum bag and cycled off. At the corner, he stopped and took out what looked like a mobile phone. He hadn't looked a day over fourteen.

'Don't take offence, Handbrake, but these parts aren't a little bit moody, are they?' I hate having to be such a prissy little madam, but I can't afford to be caught out with a car built from stolen spares.

Handbrake shook his head. 'Nah. Him and his mates have got a deal going with half the scrap yards in Manchester. Product of the recession. Not so much drugs around, not so much dosh to be made ferrying them round the town, so Dobbo and a couple of his mates spent some of their ill-gotten gains on a computer. One of them checks with the scrap yards every morning to see what new stock they've got in. Then when punters like me want a part, we ring in and the dispatcher works out where they can get it from and sends one of the bike boys off for it. Good game, huh?'

'You're not kidding.' I watched Handbrake pop

the remains of the lock out of my car door. 'Hand-brake? You know anybody on the drugs scene that moves their merchandise in stolen motors?'

Handbrake snorted. 'Ask me another. I try not to know anything about drugs in this town. Like the man said, a little learning is a dangerous thing.' Handbrake did A Level English while he was inside. Who says prison doesn't change a man?

'OK. How would someone get hold of a set of trade plates?'

'You mean if you're not a legitimate person?'

'Why would I be asking you about legitimate people?'

He snorted again. 'Well, you can't just cobble them together in a backstreet workshop. It's only the Department of Transport that makes them, and the numbers are die-stamped into the metal, not like your regular licence plates. You'd have to beg, borrow or steal. There's enough of them around. You could nick them off a garage or a motor in transit, though that way they'd be reported stolen and you wouldn't get a lot of mileage out of them. Beg or buy a loan of a set off a delivery driver. Best way is to borrow them off a slightly dodgy garage. Why, you need some?'

Handbrake likes to wind me up by pretending he's the innocent abroad and I'm the villain. But I wasn't in the mood for it right then. 'No,' I snarled. 'But I think I might be about to deprive someone of some.'

'Better be careful where you use them, then.'

'Why?'

''Cos you'll get a tug is why. The traffic cops always pull you if you're using trade plates. Not so much on the motorway, but defo if you're cruising round. If they so much as think you're using them for anything except demos, tuition or delivery, you've had it. So you better have a good cover story.'

I was glad of the tip. I didn't think this was the right weekend for a roadside chat with the traffic division.

8

I kicked my heels for the best part of an hour in Ruth's waiting room while she was dealing with a client. I'd have been better employed catching up on my sleep. After I'd stood on for a major bollocking for my outrageous behaviour at Longsight nick, we sat glumly staring at each other across her cluttered desk, depressed by the lack of information we had to trade. 'I suspect the officers actually working the case don't believe a word Richard's saying,' Ruth said. 'All I get is the condescending wink when I suggest that if they really want to make a major drugs bust they should be on the phone to every villain who's ever grassed in his life. Anything to get a lead on the car thieves. But of course, they don't really believe in the car thieves,' she added cynically. 'The one lucky break we have so far is that none of the police officers we've dealt with has made the connection between Richard and you. At least the superintendent is prepared to go along with the idea of a lie-down, even though he stressed that it was for his team's benefit and not mine.'

I got to my feet. 'I suppose it's a step in the right direction. I'll let you know as soon as I get anything,' I said grimly.

Out in the street, the city carried on as usual. I cut across Deansgate and through the Victorian glass-domed elegance of the Barton Arcade into the knots of serious shoppers bustling around the designer clothes shops of St Ann's Square. Nobody had told the buskers outside the Royal Exchange that this was not a day for celebration and their cheery country rock mocked me all the way across the square and into Cross Street. I'd abandoned the car on a single yellow line round the back of the Nat West bank, and to my astonishment, I didn't have a ticket. It was the first time all day that I'd got the benefit of an even break. I had to take it as an omen.

Back home, I checked Richard's answering machine and saved the handful of messages. I returned a couple of the more urgent calls, explaining he'd had to go out of town at a moment's notice and I wasn't sure when he'd be back. I also checked his diary, and cancelled a couple of interviews he'd arranged for the early part of the coming week. Luckily, he didn't have much planned, thanks to Davy's visit. God only knew how he was going to write this week's magazine column. Frankly, it was the least of my worries.

* * *

Manchester's rush hour seems to have developed middle-aged spread. When I first moved to the city, it lasted a clearly definable ninety minutes, morning and evening. Now, in the evening it seems to start at four and continue till half past seven. And on Fridays, it's especially grim. Even on the wide dual carriageway of Princess Parkway, it was a major challenge to get into third. It felt like a relief to be in the airport. That's how bad it was.

I was ten minutes early for our meeting, but Della was already sitting in the domestic terminal with a coffee. When the automatic doors hissed open to let me in, she glanced up from her *Evening Chronicle*. Even from that distance I could see the anxiety in her deep-set green eyes. She jumped to her feet and pulled me into a hug as soon as I got close enough. 'Poor you,' she said with feeling, steering me gently into a seat. The sympathy was too much. Seeing the tears in my eyes, Della patted me awkwardly on the shoulder and said, 'Give me a sec, I'll get you a coffee.'

By the time she returned, I was as hard-boiled as Philip Marlowe again. 'Like the hair,' I remarked. Her shining chestnut hair, normally controlled to within an inch of its life in a thick plait, was loose around her shoulders, held back from her face with a wide, sueded silk headband.

'Thanks.' She pulled a face. 'Think it'll impress a forty-year-old merchant banker?'

'Business or pleasure?'

'He thinks pleasure, I suspect business.' Detective Chief Inspector Della Prentice is the operational head of the Regional Crime Squad's fraud task force. She's a Cambridge graduate, with all the social graces that implies, which means that when she's got some bent businessman in her sights he's more likely to think this charming woman who's so fascinated by his work is a corporate headhunter rather than a copper. The problem is, as Della once explained with a sigh, the best con men are often the most charming.

'We never sleep, eh?' I teased.

'Not with people we suspect might have their hands in a rather interesting can of worms,' Della said. 'Even if he is buying me dinner at the Thirty-Nine Steps.' I felt a momentary pang of jealousy. Since Richard only ever wants to eat Chinese food, I don't often get the chance to eat at the best fish restaurant in Manchester. As if reading my thoughts, Della said, 'But enough of my problems. Any news on Richard?'

'Not a sausage. I feel so frustrated. I just haven't got any handles to get a hold of. I don't suppose you've got anything for me?' I asked morosely.

'We . . . ell, yes, and no,' Della said cautiously, lighting a cigarette with her battered old Zippo.

The ticket-free windscreen *had* been an omen. 'Yeah?' I demanded.

'The fingerprint SOCO who went over Richard's car did some work for me a while back when I was looking into forged insurance policies, and we got quite pally. So I bought her a butty at lunch time.'

'What did she find?' I asked.

'It's what she didn't find that's significant. She was being a bit cautious. Understandably, because she's not had time yet to analyse all the prints thoroughly. But it looks like Richard's fingerprints were on all the surfaces you'd expect – door handle, gear stick, steering wheel, the cassette in the stereo. But there were none of his prints on the boot, or the carrier bag or the plastic bags that the rocks were in. In fact, there were no prints at all on any of those. Just the kind of smudges you get from latex gloves. And Richard had no gloves on his person, nor were there any in the car.' Della gave a tentative smile, and I found myself reflecting it.

'D'you know, that's the first good news I've heard all day?'

Della looked apologetic. 'I know it's not much, but it's a start. If I hear any more on the grapevine, I'll let you know. Now, as to the other thing. You owe me, Kate – I thought when I left the West Yorkshire fraud squad that I'd never have to drink with another patronizing, sexist Yorkshireman. Today I discovered they actually get worse when they're in exile on the wrong side of the Pennines. According to DCI Geoff Turnbull of the Drugs Squad, it's understandable that a nice woman like me should be interested in drugs. After all, even if I didn't manage to fulfil my womanly role by reproducing myself before my divorce, I must have contemporaries whose kids are in their late teens and therefore at that dangerous age,' Della growled through clenched teeth.

'Oh dear,' I sympathized. 'And when exactly are they letting him out of intensive care? I know a choir that's short on sopranos.'

Della managed a twisted smile. 'Once he'd finished condescending, he did actually come up with some interesting information. Apparently, when crack first started to appear in this country, it was in relatively small amounts and in quite specific areas. The obvious inference was that there were only a handful of people involved in the importing and distribution of it, and while its presence was worrying, its level of penetration wasn't seriously disturbing. However, during the last few months, small quantities of crack have been turning up all over the country along with some unusual designer drugs. The really worrying thing is that these finds have been coming out of routine operations.' Della paused expectantly.

I didn't know what she was expecting. I said, 'Why is that so worrying?'

'It's turned up where they didn't expect to find it. The operations have been targeted at something else, say Ecstasy or heroin, and they've ended up producing a small but significant amount of crack as well. And it's not localized. It's dotted all over the shop.' Della looked serious. I could see why. If small finds were appearing unexpectedly, the chances were that they were only the tip of a very large iceberg.

'Any particular geographical distribution?' I asked.

'Virtually all over the country. But it's mostly confined to bandit country.'

'Meaning?' I asked.

'The sort of areas that are semi-no-go. Inner-city decayed housing, satellite council estates both in the cities and in bigger towns. The kind of traditional working-class areas where people used to leave school and go into the local industry, only there's no industry any more so they graduate straight to the dole queue, the drink and drugs habits and the petty crime that goes with them.' Della stubbed her cigarette out angrily.

'I bet your Yorkshire DCI didn't put it quite like that.'

'How did you guess?' Della said cynically. 'Anyway, the bottom line is that it looks like we've got a crack epidemic on our hands. And they suspect that whoever is dealing this crack has a very efficient distribution network.'

That ruled out the Post Office. 'And they think Richard is part of that?'

'I didn't ask. But they clearly think he's important enough to be worth sweating.' Della sighed. 'It doesn't look good, Kate, I'm bound to say.'

I nodded. She didn't have to tell me. 'Any suggestions as to where I might start looking?'

Della looked at me. Her green eyes were serious. 'You're not going to thank me for this, but I don't think you should be looking at all. These are very dangerous people. They will kill you if they think you're any kind of threat.'

'You think I don't know that? What option have I got, Della? If I can't get the real villains behind bars, they'll kill Richard. As soon as they find out just who drove off with their parcel of crack. You know they will. They can't afford not to, or every two-bit dealer in town'll think they can give them the run-around.' I swallowed the last of my coffee. I should have gone for camomile tea. The last thing I needed was to get even more hyped up.

'Did you get the chance to ask about the Polaroid?' Anything to avoid another unnerving gypsy warning.

'I spoke to a woman DS in Vice. She said she couldn't think of anyone off the top of her head, but she'd ask around. But the DCI running Richard's case doesn't seem particularly interested in it, probably because in itself it isn't technically obscene.' Della lit another cigarette, but before she could say more, bodies started flowing through the doors leading from Domestic Arrivals. Judging by the high proportion of men in suits clutching briefcases that seemed as heavy as anchors after a hard day's meetings, the London shuttle was down. I stood up. 'I think this is Davy's flight,' I said.

Della was at my side in a flash. She gave me a quick hug, threw a glance over her shoulder to make sure she wasn't about to be accosted by a small boy, and said, 'Stay in touch. I'll bell you if I hear anything.' And she was gone.

The first rush had subsided, leaving the stragglers who had had to wait for luggage from the hold. After what felt like a very long time, the double doors swung open on a woman in British Airways uniform, carrying a small holdall. By her side, Davy trotted, looking like he was auditioning for the moppet role in the next Spielberg film, hair flopping over his forehead in a slightly tousled fringe, big brown eyes eager. He was proudly wearing an outfit he'd chosen with his dad on his last visit, topped by the New York Mets jacket Richard had sent him from a recent trip to the States, still too baggy for his solid little frame. Then he saw me. All in a moment, he seemed puzzled, then disappointed. He looked around again, then realizing Richard really wasn't there, he waved uncertainly at me and half smiled. My heart sank. As far as Davy was concerned, I was clearly a poor substitute. As if I needed the confirmation.

It turned out a lot better than I expected. On the way to the car park, I told Davy the lie Richard and I had prearranged. Dad was in Bosnia; he'd had to fly off suddenly because he'd had an exclusive tip that Bob Geldof was out there organizing some sort of Bosnia Aid concert. I almost believed it myself by the time I'd finished the explanation. Davy took it very calmly. I suppose after eight years, he's grown accustomed to a dad who doesn't behave quite like other kids' fathers. At least he's not shy; that's one thing that being around Richard and his crazy buddies in rock and journalism has cured him of. 'You remember Chris and Alexis?' I asked him as we drove out of the airport towards the M56.

He nodded. 'Alexis is funny. And Chris is good at drawing and painting and building things with Lego. I like them.'

'Well, they're going to help me look after you, because I've got some work to do over the week-end.'

'Can't I come with you to work, Kate?' he wheedled. 'I want to be a private detective like you. I saw this film and it was in black and white and it had an American detective in it, Mum said he was called Humpty something, and he had a gun. Have you got a gun, Kate?'

I shook my head. Depressingly, he looked disappointed. 'I don't need one, Davy.'

'What about if you were fighting a bad man, and he had a gun? You'd need one then,' he said triumphantly.

'If I was fighting someone who had a gun, and he knew I had a gun, he'd have to shoot me to win the fight. But if he knows I haven't got a gun, he only has to hit me. That way I stay alive. And, on balance, I think I prefer being alive.'

Chris was waiting when we got home. I'd rung ahead to give her ten minutes' warning, so she was just assembling home-made cheeseburgers as we walked in. I could have kissed her. The three of us sat round the breakfast bar scoffing and telling the sort of jokes that eight-year-olds like. You know: why do bees hum? Because they've forgotten the words.

After we'd pigged out, I showed Davy the latest Commander Keen game I'd got for us both. I extracted a promise from him that he'd go to bed in half an hour when Chris told him to, and left him bouncing on his pixel pogo stick through Slug Village. Ten minutes split between the bathroom and the bedroom was enough to knock me into shape for the night. My lightweight walking boots; my ripped denim decorating jeans over multi-coloured leggings; a Bob Marley T-shirt I won at a rock charity dinner; and a baggy flannel shirt that belonged to my granddad that I keep for sentimental reasons. I tucked my auburn hair into a dayglo green baseball cap, and slapped on some make-up that made me look like an anaemic refugee from Transylvania. Grunge meets acid house. I found Chris in front of the television, watching the news. Bless her, she didn't turn a hair at the apparition. 'I really appreciate this. And believe me, Richard will need a bank loan to express his appreciation when all this is over. I take it Alexis filled you in?' I said quietly, perching on the arm of the sofa.

'She did, and it's horrifying. What's happening? Any progress?' That's probably the shortest contribution to any conversation I've ever heard Chris make.

'Not really. That's why I'm going out now. I've

got one or two leads to follow up. Are you OK to hang on here?'

Chris patted my knee. 'We're staying till this is all sorted out. I brought a bag with me, and I've moved us into Richard's room, I hope that's all right, but it seemed the most sensible thing, because then Davy can sleep in his usual bed in Richard's house so you can come and go as and when you please without worrying about waking any of us, and then we're on hand to take over the child minding as and when you need us.' I swear she's the only person I know who can talk and breathe at the same time.

I gave Chris a swift hug and stood up. 'Thanks. I'll see you in the morning then.' I walked out of the house, feeling a sense of purpose for the first time since I'd had Ruth's phone call.

9

I started off at the Delta, known to Richard and his cronies, for obvious reasons, as the 'Lousy Hand'. That's where he'd been the night the car was stolen. The Lousy Hand occupies a handful of railway arches in a narrow cul-de-sac between the GMEX exhibition centre and the Hacienda Club. Since it was only half past nine, there was no queue, so I sailed straight in.

The décor in the Lousy Hand has been scientifically designed to make you think you've dropped a tab of acid even when you're straight. God knows what it does to the kids who are really out of their heads. Everywhere I looked there were psychedelic fractals mingling at random with *trompe-l'œil* Bridget Riley-style monochrome pop art extravaganzas. There were only a few dozen punters in that early, but most of them were already on the dance floor, mindlessly happy as only those high on Ecstasy can be. The dancing was something else, too. Scarcely co-ordinated, the dancers looked like a motley assortment of marionettes jerked around by a five-year-old puppet master with all the elegance and skill of Skippy the bush kangaroo. The music had the irritating insistence of a bluebottle at a window, the heavy bass beat so loud it seemed to thump inside my chest. I'd have sold my soul to be back home with a nice restful video like *Terminator 2*.

Feeling about a hundred and five, I crossed to the bar. As well as the usual designer beers, the optics of spirits and the Tracy-and-Sharon specials like Malibu and Byzance, the Lousy Hand boasted possibly the best range of soft drinks outside Harrods Food Hall. From carrot juice to an obscure Peruvian mineral water, they had it all, and most of it was carbonated. No, officer, of course we don't have a drug problem here. None of our clients would dream of abusing illegal substances. And I am Marie of Rumania.

The bar staff looked like leftovers from the club's previous existence as a bog-standard eighties yuppie nightclub. The women and the men were dressed identically in open-necked, wing-collar white dress shirts and tight-fitting black dress trousers. The principal differences were that the men probably had marginally more gel, wax and mousse on their hair, and their earrings were more stylish. I leaned my elbows on the bar and waited. There weren't enough customers to occupy all the staff, but I still had to hang on for the obligatory thirty seconds. God forbid I should think they had nothing better to do than serve me.

The beautiful youth who halted opposite me raised his eyebrows. 'Just a Diet Coke, please,' I said. He looked disappointed to be asked for something so conventional. He swivelled on one toe, opened the door of a chill cabinet and lifted a can off the shelf, all in one graceful movement. I don't know why he bothered. I couldn't have looked less like a talent scout from MTV.

'Wanna glass?' he asked, dumping the can in front of me. I shook my head and paid him.

When he came back with my change, I said, 'You know the street outside? Is it safe to park there? Only, I'm parked right up near the dead end and there's no streetlights, and I wondered if a lot of cars get nicked from out there?'

He shrugged. 'Cars get nicked. Outside here's no worse than anywhere else in town. A thousand cars a week get stolen in Manchester, did you know that?' I shook my head. 'And two-thirds of them are never recovered. Bet you didn't know that.' Never mind the Mr Cool image, this guy had the soul of a train spotter in an anorak.

Ignoring him, I went on, 'Only, it's not really my car, it's my boyfriend's and he'd kill me if anything happened to it.'

'What kind is it?' he asked.

'Peugeot 205. Nothing fancy, just the standard one.'

'You're probably all right, then.' He leaned his

103

elbows on the bar and elegantly crossed his legs. I prepared myself for a lecture. 'Six months ago, you couldn't park a hot hatch anywhere between Stockport and Bury and expect to find it there when you went back to it. But with these new insurance weightings, the bottom's dropped out of the second-hand market for boy-racer cars. So the professionals gave up on the sports jobs and started nicking boring old family cars instead. Less risk as well. I mean, if you was the Old Bill, would you think the Nissan Sunny cruising past you was being driven by any self-respecting car thief?'

I giggled. Not because he was funny, but because he clearly expected it. 'Only,' I persisted, 'my boyfriend's mate had his car nicked from outside here the other night, and he was really pissed off because he'd only bought it that day. And it was a beauty. A brand new Leo Gemini turbo super coupé.'

'I heard about that,' he said, pushing himself upright again. 'That was the night they had the benefit, wasn't it?'

'I dunno.'

'Yeah, that's right. The gig was finished, because we'd shut up the bar and the lights were up. The guy came storming back in, ranting about his precious motor and demanding a phone.' So much for not mentioning the car to a soul. 'Mate of yours then, was he?' the barman asked.

I nodded. 'Mate of my boyfriend's. He reckoned

somebody saw him parking it up and coming in here. He said he thought they must have been coming to the club too, or else why would they be down the cul-de-sac?'

The barman grinned, unselfconscious for the first time. 'Well, he'd have plenty thieves to choose from that night. Half Moss Side was in here. Drug barons, car ringers, the lot. You name it, we had them.'

With a flick of his pony tail, he was gone to batter someone else's brain with his statistics. I swigged the Coke and looked around me. While I'd been standing at the bar, there had been a steady stream of punters arriving behind me. Already, the place looked a lot fuller than it had when I entered. If I was going to have a word with the bouncers before they had more important things to think about, I'd better make a move.

There were two of them in the foyer, flanking the narrow doorway that had been cut in the huge wooden door that filled the end of one of the arches occupied by the club. They both wore the bouncer's uniform: ill-fitting tux; ready-made velvet bow tie that had seen better days. As I approached, the older and bulkier one slipped through the door and into the street. Intrigued, I got my hand stamped with a pass-out and followed him. He walked about fifty yards up towards the dead end. I slipped into the shadows beyond the club and watched him. He looked around, then simply turned and walked back, carrying on past the club for another fifty yards or so before strolling back inside.

I stuck my head round the door and said, 'Where's the best place to park around here? Only, I don't want to get the car nicked. It's my boyfriend's.'

The smaller bouncer flashed a 'Right one we've got here' look at his oppo. 'Darling, you don't look like the kind of girl who'd have a boyfriend with a car worth nicking,' he said, smoothing back his hair with a smirk.

'Mind you don't wear out the rug,' I snarled back, pointing to his head. Although he was only in his early twenties, his dark hair was already thinning so it was a fair bet that would be a tender spot.

Right on the button. He scowled. 'Piss off,' he quipped wittily.

'Does the management know you're this helpful to customers who only want to avoid giving the club a worse name than it's already got?' I asked sweetly.

'Don't push it,' the bouncer with the wanderlust said coldly, glowering down at me. Now I could see him in the light, he seemed familiar, but I couldn't place him, which surprised me. I don't often forget guys that menacing. He was a couple of inches over six feet, thick dark hair cut in an almost military short back and sides. He wasn't bad looking if you ignored the thread-thin white scar that ran from the end of his left eyebrow to just underneath his ear lobe. But his eyes wrecked any illusion of attractiveness. They were cold and blank. They showed as much connection to the rest of humanity as a pair of camera lenses.

'Look, I just don't want to get my car nicked, OK?' I gabbled. 'It seems to happen a lot around here, that's all.'

The big bouncer nodded, satisfied I'd backed down. 'You want to be safe, leave it on one of the main drags where there's decent street-lighting.'

'You want to be really safe, don't bring the car into town. In fact, why don't you do us all a favour and leave yourself at home as well?' the balding Mr Charm sneered.

I winked and cocked one finger at him like a pistol. 'I might just take your advice.' I let the door bang shut behind me and walked back to my car. Even if anyone at the Lousy Hand knew anything about the coupé's disappearance, I couldn't see a way of getting them to talk to me. It had been a long shot anyway. Sighing, I climbed into the car and started cruising the city centre streets. There were plenty of clubs for the dedicated seeker of pleasure to choose from, and even more res-taurants catering to the late-night trade, which gave me plenty of kerbs to crawl. I prayed the Vice Squad weren't doing one of their occasional random trawls of the red-light zones. The last thing I needed was to have to explain to a copper why I was doing an impersonation of a dirty old man.

I drove systematically down the streets and back

alleys for a good couple of hours without spotting a single red-and-white trade plate. If I'd been working for a client, I'd have given up right then. But this was different. This was personal, and the man lying in a cell worrying about the charges he was facing was the man I'd chosen to share my life with. I might not be getting anywhere out on the streets, but I could no more jack it in and go home to bed than I could set Richard free with one mighty bound.

Just before midnight, I realized I was ravenous. I'd been so hyped up on adrenaline all evening that I was suddenly right on the edge of a low blood sugar collapse. I phoned an order through, then drove back through Chinatown, double parked outside the Yang Sing and picked up some salt and pepper ribs, paper wrapped prawns and pork dumplings. I couldn't help a pang of guilt, thinking about prison food and Richard's conviction that if it didn't come out of China or Burger King it can't be edible.

I drove back to the Lousy Hand. If the car thief plied a regular patch, I might just catch him at it. It was as good a place to eat my takeaway as any. I drove slowly up the culde-sac, looking for a space. Nothing. I turned round in the dead end and drove back down. I got lucky. Someone was pulling out just as I passed. I tucked the car in against the kerb and opened the sun roof so the smell of the Chinese wouldn't linger in the car for the next six months. I started on the prawns, wanting to polish them off before they became soggy.

I looked around as I ate. Nothing much was moving. There was a short queue outside the Lousy Hand, but it seemed to be static. The only car I could see worth stealing was a new Ford Escort Cosworth, but its ridiculous spoiler, like the tail of a blue whale, was so obvious that I couldn't imagine many thieves having the bottle to go for it. Besides, it was bright red and you know what they say about red cars and male sexual problems . . .

In my wing mirror, I noticed the man mountain bouncer emerging from the Lousy Hand again. Clearly time for another walkabout. As he rec-onnoitred the street, I thought he still looked nigglingly familiar, but I couldn't think where from, unless we'd had a brief encounter one night when I'd been on the town with Richard. After all, bouncers shift around the clubs about as fast as cocktail waitresses, and I wasn't always one hundred per cent *compos mentis* when we crawled out of clubs in the small hours.

He headed in my direction. Instinctively, I slid down in my seat till I was below window level. I heard his footsteps on the pavement, then, when he was level with me, he stopped. I held my breath. I don't know what I expected, but it wasn't the familiar bleating of a mobile phone being dialled. I inched carefully up till I could just see him. He had his back to me and a slimline phone to his ear.

'Hiya,' he said, his voice low. 'Ford Escort

Cosworth. Foxtrot alarm system. Been in about ten minutes . . . No problem.' The phone beeped once as he ended the call. I slid back down below eye level as he turned back towards the club. Valet parking I'd heard of. But valet stealing?

I watched in the wing mirror till he was safely back indoors, then I pulled off the dayglo cap and got out of the Peugeot, still clutching my Chinese. I melted into the shadows of one of the railway arches which had a deep door recess. I could hardly believe it wasn't already occupied by one of the city's cardboard-box kids. I didn't have long to wait. I still had half my spare ribs left when a black hack coughed up the cul-de-sac. It stopped outside the Lousy Hand, and a man got out. In the lights of the club entrance, I got a quick look. Thirtyish, medium height, slim build. He walked into the club, fast, like a man with a purpose other than a dance, a drink and a legover.

He was out again in seconds, carrying a small holdall. He walked briskly towards the Cosworth. As he came closer, I clocked a heavy thatch of dark hair, high cheekbones, hollow cheeks, surprisingly full lips, a double-breasted suit that hung like it was made to measure. He stopped a few feet away from the Cosworth, flashed a quick, penetrating glance around him then crouched down. Through the gap between cars, I could just see him take something out of the holdall. It looked a bit like an old-fashioned TV remote, bulky, with buttons. I couldn't see any details, but he seemed to be

110

hitting buttons and moving a slider switch on the side. This routine lasted the best part of a minute. Then, three sharp electronic exclamations came from the Cosworth, the hazard lights flashed twice and I heard the door locks shift to 'open'. He dropped the black box back into the holdall and took out a pair of trade plates.

The man stood up and gave that quick, frowning glance round again. Still clear, he thought. One plate went on the back of the car, hiding the existing number. He fastened the other over the front plate, then almost ran to the driver's door. He was in the car in seconds. It took less than a minute for the engine to roar into life. The car shot out of the parking space. Rather than drive to the end of the cul-de-sac and do a time-wasting three-point turn, as I'd expected, he simply shot back down the street in reverse.

Caught flat-footed, I leapt for the Peugeot. By the time he'd reversed on to the main drag and headed off towards Oxford Road, I was behind him, just far enough for him not to get twitchy. Interestingly, he didn't drive the Cosworth like a boy racer. If anything, he drove like my father, a man who has never had an accident in twenty-three years of driving. Mind you, he's seen dozens in his rear-view mirror . . . The speedo didn't rise above twenty-eight, he stopped on amber and he didn't even attempt any traffic-light grand prix stuff. We crossed Oxford Road and carried on sedately down Whitworth Street, into Aytoun Street and past

Piccadilly station. Then it was time for a quick whizz through the back doubles before he pulled up outside Sacha's nightclub and blasted the horn. Luckily I was far enough behind him to stay tucked away on the corner. I cut my lights and waited.

Not for long. If the speed of her response was anything to go by, patience wasn't her boyfriend's strong suit. Depressingly, she looked like she'd walked straight off the bottle-blonde production line. Expensive bimbo, but bimbo nevertheless. Bimbos are the last women in the world wearing crippling high heels and make-up that could camouflage a Chieftain tank. This one must have had enough hair spray on her carefully tumbled locks to lacquer a Chinese cabinet, since it didn't even move in the chill wind that had sprung up in the last hour.

She jumped into the waiting Cosworth and we were off again. He was still driving like a pursuer's dream. I dumped the Pet Shop Boys and let Annie Lennox entertain me instead. Round Piccadilly, down Portland Street, down to Deansgate, out along Regent Road. I had to hang well back now, because there wasn't a lot of traffic around, and the thief was driving so law-abidingly that any reasonable driver would have overtaken him long ago. At the end of the dual carriageway, instead of heading straight on down the motorway, he hung a left, heading towards Salford Quays. I can't say I was totally surprised. He looked the sort.

The Quays used to be, unromantically, Salford Docks. Then the eighties happened, and waterfronts suddenly became trendy. London, Liverpool, Glasgow, Newcastle, Manchester. They all discovered how easy it was to part fools and their money when you threw in a view of a bit of polluted waterway. Salford Quays was Manchester's version of greed chic. It's got it all: the multi-screen cinema, the identikit international hotel for jet-set business people, more saunas per head of population than Scandinavia, it's very own scaled-down World Trade Centre for scaled-down yuppie losers and more *Penthouses* than penthouses. The only thing it lacks is any kind of human ambience.

I noticed that the Cosworth was slowing. I pulled into the parking bay of a small block of flats and killed my lights just as he drew up. He'd stopped outside a long block of narrow three-storey town houses with integral garages on the ground floor.

He got out of the Cosworth, but I could see a whisper of exhaust in the cold night air that told me the engine was still running. He waved a hand in the direction of the garage door and it rose slowly to reveal a two-year-old black Toyota Supra. He swapped the cars over, leaving the Supra on the hard standing and the Cosworth tucked safely away inside the garage.

I watched for another twenty minutes or so as lights went on and off in various rooms. When the house went dark, I decided that if Richard's car thief was entitled to sleep, so was I.

I got home just after two. The house was silent, the bed chilly. If I didn't get him out of jail soon, I was going to have to buy a hot-water bottle.

10

I dreamed I was walking down a corridor filled with breakfast cereal, going snap, crackle and pop with every step. Cautiously, I opened one eye. It was only half a dream. Davy was sitting on the edge of the bed, tucking into a bowl of one of Richard's noisier cereals, a tumbler of orange juice on the bedside table next to him. He was watching me, and as he registered the rising eyelid, he smiled uncertainly.

'Did I wake you?' he asked. 'I didn't want to miss you.'

I propped myself up on one elbow and shook my head. 'Not really,' I lied. Things were bad enough without me giving Davy a bad time. I glanced at the clock. Five past seven. I couldn't even summon up the energy to groan.

'Have you got to work today?' he asked.

'I'm afraid so,' I said.

He looked crestfallen. 'Can't I come with you?' he asked wistfully. 'I could help.'

'Sorry, hon, not today. But I don't have to go out for a couple of hours yet, so we could play some computer games first, if you want?'

He didn't have to be asked twice. When Chris and Alexis stumbled through the conservatory just after half past eight looking like Beauty and the Beast, Davy and I were absorbed in a game of Lemmings. Alexis threatened to pull the plug out of the socket unless we reverted to normal English usage. Guess which one is the Beast?

I got up and said I had to go. Before Davy's disappointment could turn into a sulk, Alexis asked if he'd brought his trunks and if he fancied spending the afternoon at a fun pool. Nobody invited me, which is probably just as well, since the temptation of playing on the slides and surfing in the wave pool might just have proved too much.

Before the grown-ups could go into a huddle about how we were going to amuse him till lunch time, Davy solved the problem. 'Kate, is it all right if I go out and play this morning?' he asked.

'Who with?' I asked, trying to act like a responsible co-parent. Judging by the look on Davy's face, he was afraid I was turning into the wicked stepmother.

'Daniel and Wayne, from the estate. I *always* play with them when I come and see my dad.'

I didn't see a problem, and as soon as the deal was struck, Davy was gone. 'I've got to run too,' I said, heading for the shower.

'What's happening with Richard?' Alexis demanded,

following me down the hall as Chris disappeared into the kitchen and started brewing some more coffee.

'They've charged him with possession with intent to supply,' I shouted over the sound of the spray and the pump from my new power shower.

'Oh shit,' Alexis said.

'I'm hopeful we can keep the lid on it,' I said. 'Will there be any reporters in the magistrates' court this morning?'

'Well, if I don't go down, there won't be anyone from the *Chron*,' Alexis said. 'And with it being a bank holiday weekend, the court agency probably won't bother with cover either. You might just get away with it. If you do drop unlucky, there are two courts sitting. If there is a reporter kicking around, ask your solicitor to get the case called in one court while the reporter's in the other one. Shouldn't be a problem. I take it that Plan A is for you to find the evidence that will clear Richard before his next court appearance?'

'Got it in one,' I said. 'And unless you've got any bright ideas about how I'm going to do that, sod off and let me have my shower in peace.'

Alexis chuckled. 'OK. I'm going in to the office in a bit to write up my copy from dinner last night. That'll be my alibi for ignoring the mags. If anybody asks me, I'll say I checked it out with the clerk and there was nothing of any interest coming up. I'll be at my desk till lunch time if you need me for anything.'

'Thanks. I might just take you up on that. How did your evening go, by the way?'

Alexis pulled a face. 'That depends on whether you're asking the cold-hearted bastard journalist or the human being. As a journo, it was a major coup. There is definitely a big-time child porn ring operating somewhere in Greater Manchester, and I'm the only journo that knows about it. We're talking million-pound industry here. But Barney showed me some of their stock in trade. And as a human being, I have to say it was one of the nastiest experiences of my life. It made me fucking glad I don't have kids of my own to worry about.'

'I don't need child porn to make me feel like that,' I said gloomily. 'Temporary custody of Davy's quite enough. Did you ask him about any tie-ins with drugs?'

'I did, and if there are any, he doesn't know about them. Most likely, one of your drug dealers is a pervert. Which doesn't really help, does it?'

I love to start the day with the good news.

Saturday morning, Manchester Magistrates' Court. The one day of the week the marble corridors of the court don't resemble the supermarket chill cabinet – there's hardly a headless chicken in sight. The only cases dealt with at the Saturday court are the overnighters – breaches of the peace, drunk and disorderly, soliciting, the occasional assault. And Richard. Because his was such a major charge and he was arrested after midnight, the police hadn't been inclined to process the paperwork fast enough for him to appear at Friday's court, so he'd spilled over into Saturday. Although it probably didn't feel like it to Richard, that had its advantages. As Alexis had confirmed, the chances were good that it would escape press attention, so the people whose drugs Richard had driven off with wouldn't be picking up their *Evening Chronicle* and finding 'Rock journalist charged with massive drug haul' splashed all over the front page.

According to Ruth, Richard had been moved the night before from the nick at Longsight into the custom-built secure detention cells inside the magistrates' court building. As we'd arranged, I made my way to the duty solicitor's interview room on the fifth floor. Normally at quarter to ten on a court morning, the place is heaving with defendants, their families, their kids and their harassed lawyers. The air's usually thick with cigarette smoke and recriminations. Today, while it wasn't as silent as the executive floor lobby of a multinational, it was a lot quieter than weekdays.

I pushed open the glass door of the small office and sat on the far side of the round table, commanding a view of the entire length of the foyer outside the courtrooms. It was nearly ten when Ruth swept into sight, a nervous-looking man almost trotting to keep up with her. Ruth shoved the door open and subsided into the chair opposite me with a huge sigh. 'God, that holding area depresses the knickers off me,' she complained, lighting a cigarette. 'Kate,' she added through a mouthful of smoke, 'this is Norman Undercroft, the duty solicitor. Norman, this is Kate Brannigan, my client's partner.'

Norman ducked his head politely, looking up at me from under mousey brows. Close to, he looked a lot older than my first impression. His papery skin was covered in a network of fine lines, placing him in his late forties. He opened his mouth to speak, but Ruth beat him to it. 'Right, Kate. Listen very carefully, I only have time to run this past you once. This morning, Richard will be represented by Norman here. Norman will get up on his hind legs and tell the court that this is a complicated matter about which his client has not yet had the opportunity to consult his own solicitor fully. Therefore, Norman will be asking the court to remand Richard in custody for the weekend. The prosecution will leap to their feet indignantly and respond that Richard is a menace to society, and furthermore, the police are investigating other serious charges in relation to him. They'll ask for a lie-down so that these matters can be resolved. And the mags will smile sweetly and agree. Any questions?'

'When can I see him?' I asked.

'Between seven and nine in the evening. Any visit is at the discretion of the duty inspector, so don't be stroppy. You go round to the back entrance in Gartside Street opposite the car park.

120

That it? Sorry to be so abrupt, but I've got twenty for lunch and Peter has not got the knack of getting the caterers to do any work.' She got to her feet. 'Have you made any progress, by the way?'

'It's early days yet, but I think I might just be getting somewhere.'

'OK. Look, I've arranged to see Richard tomorrow morning. Why don't we meet afterwards? Say eleven, in the Ramada. You can buy me brunch.'

'Make it Salford Quays,' I called after her. 'I might need to be down there.'

'The Quays it is,' she tossed over her shoulder as she disappeared round the corner. The room seemed to double in size now only Norman and I were left. I gave him a friendly smile.

'Overwhelming,' I said.

'Mmm,' said Norman. 'Good, though. I'd choose her if I was ever charged with anything, especially if I'd done it.'

I hoped everyone else wouldn't assume Richard was guilty just because he'd hired the best criminal lawyer in town. Wearily, I followed Norman round to Court 9. There didn't seem to be a journalist in the court, unless the court reporting agency had taken to hiring elderly women who look one step away from bag ladies and have such excellent powers of recall that they don't need a note-book.

I sat on one of the flip-down seats at the back of the courtroom. There were two magistrates on the bench, a man and a woman, both middle-aged, both decidedly middle class. After two breaches of the peace and a soliciting, I decided she was a teacher and he owned his own small business. She had that unmistakable air of wanting to tell them all to behave, and he had the blunt style of the self-made man who has no conception of why everybody can't be like him.

Richard was the last case of the morning. Watching him walk into the dock, I realized just how hard it is for people to get justice. After thirty-six hours in custody wearing the same clothes, not having shaved or showered, he looked like a bad lad even to me, and I was on his side. The very structure of the court itself made the accused appear to be some sort of desperado. Richard stood in the reinforced dock, behind a barrier of heavy perspex slats, the door into the court locked to avoid any possibility of him escaping. Behind him stood an alert prison officer. The system made it clear who was the sinner here.

Although he was familiar enough with court procedures from his days as a local paper journalist, Richard looked around the court with all the bewilderment of an animal that went to sleep in the jungle and woke up in the zoo. His hair seemed to have gone lank and dead overnight, and he pushed it back from his forehead in a gesture I'd noticed hundreds of times when he was working. When he saw me, one corner of his mouth twitched in a half-smile. That was a half more than I could manage.

There was no chance for Richard even to protest his innocence. He was treated like a parcel that has to be processed. As Ruth had predicted, the magistrates made little difficulty about remanding Richard in custody. The prosecuting solicitor obligingly explained that not only were the police pursuing further inquiries but they were also keen that Richard be kept away from other prisoners to avoid any collusion with his alleged co-conspirators. They all looked as if the very idea of a bail application on a charge like this was the best joke they'd heard since Margaret Thatcher announced the National Health Service was safe in her hands. The whole thing took nine and a half minutes. As Richard's prison officer escort led him out of the dock, he turned his back to the bench, wiggled his fingers at me and blew a kiss. I could have wept.

Instead, I thanked Norman Undercroft politely for his efforts and walked briskly out into the fresh air. Since I was only round the corner from Alexis's office, I cut through Crown Square and entered the building via the underground car park. I had wheedled the door combination out of Alexis ages ago; you never know when you're going to need a bacon sandwich at four in the morning, and the motto of the canteen staff of the Manchester *Morning Sentinel* and *Evening Chronicle* is 'We never run out'.

I took the lift up to the editorial floor. Things were fairly peaceful. Most of the sports staff hadn't

123

come in yet, and Saturdays are such quiet news days that there's only ever a skeleton team in the newsroom. Alexis sat hunched over her keyboard in a quiet corner cut off from the rest of the room by a dense thicket of various interesting green things. I recognized the devil's ivy and the sweetheart plant. I've killed cuttings from both of them. I edged round the plants. Alexis flapped a hand at me, indicating I should sit down and shut up. I did.

With a flurry of fingers over the keyboard, Alexis reached the end of her train of thought, leaned back, narrowed her eyes and re-read her last paragraph, absently reaching out for the cigarette in her ashtray. It had already burned down to the tip, and she looked at it in astonishment. Only then did I merit any attention. 'All right?' she asked.

'As predicted. Remanded till Wednesday to allow for further police inquiries relating to other serious crimes. And unless the court agency has taken to hiring the Invisible Man for Saturday shifts, we're clear there too.'

'It's only a matter of time before somebody gets a whisper.' Alexis warned. 'It's too good a story for the Old Bill to sit on. It's not every day they capture a parcel that size.'

'So let's get a move on,' I said.

'What's with the "us"? Isn't unpaid childminding enough?'

'That's only the start. I need to look at your copy of the electoral roll.'

Alexis nodded and tipped back dangerously in

her chair till she could reach the filing cabinet behind her. She pulled out the bottom drawer. 'Help yourself,' she said. I don't know exactly where she gets it from, but Alexis always has an up-to-date copy of the city voters' list. She keeps it next to another interesting document which fell off the back of a British Telecom lorry, a list of Greater Manchester names and addresses sorted by phone number. In other words, if you've got the number, you can look up the address and name of the subscriber. Very handy, especially when you're dealing with the kind of dodgy customer Alexis and I are always running up against.

I looked up the relevant street in the electoral roll and discovered the occupant was listed as Terence Fitzgerald. The phone book revealed no listing for Terence Fitzgerald, but I checked Directory Inquiries on my mobile phone and discovered there was a mobile listed for him.

'Find what you wanted?' Alexis asked.

'Maybe,' I said. I had a way to go before I could be sure that the car thief and Terence Fitzgerald were one and the same. Thanks to the poll tax fiasco, the electoral roll has ceased to be an accurate guide to who actually lives at any particular address.

'Time for a coffee?' Alexis asked.

I shook my head. 'Places to go, people to see. Thanks all the same.'

For the briefest possible time, she looked concerned. 'Take care of yourself, KB.'

'I'll be fine,' I lied. I waved goodbye and headed for the lifts. As I drove out of the car park, I stared up at the grim concrete façade of the court building and tried not to think about Richard sitting in a windowless cell, nothing to do but stare at the walls and sweat with fear. I'd once been behind the heavy iron bars of the CDC, while I'd still thought that being a lawyer was a fit and proper job for a grown-up. A criminal solicitor friend had let me shadow him for a day's duty. I'd woken up sweating for weeks afterwards.

Luckily, fighting with the city traffic didn't give me much opportunity to brood. It was just after eleven when I tucked myself into the little parking bay that gave me a perfect view of Terence Fitzgerald's town house. The black Supra was still sitting on the drive, and the bedroom curtains were still shut.

I took my Nikon out of the glove box and fitted a stubby telephoto lens to it. Then I settled back to wait and watch. God knows, it was a thin enough lead. But it was all I had. I'd give it today and see what turned up. If nothing did, it looked like a bit of breaking and entering might be on the agenda.

11

I have friends who believe we can transmit psychic energy that reaches out and touches other people, impelling them to follow certain courses of action. They'd reckon their theory gained credibility when Terence Fitzgerald's bedroom curtains opened five minutes after I took up station outside his house. Me, I think it probably had more to do with Terence's alarm clock than the waves of anxiety and urgency I was generating.

Twenty minutes later, Terence emerged, hair still damp from the shower. He wore a chocolate leather blouson over baggy brown trousers, cream shirt and splashy tie. I banged off a couple of shots as he got into the car, then I started my engine. He passed me without a second glance, and I tucked into the traffic a couple of cars behind him as we hit the main road. He headed towards town, turning off at the big new Harry Ramsden's fish and chip shop at Castlefield, an area on the edge of the city centre which the powers that be are desperately trying to transform from post-industrial desert into tourist attraction. So far they've got the chippie, a couple of museums and Granadaland, Manchester's dusty answer to Disneyland and Universal Studios. And, of course, the expensive hotels that British tourists can't actually afford.

I pulled into the garage just beyond Harry Ramsden's and pretended to check my tyre pressures while I kept watch. He came out of the takeaway section a few minutes later with an open package which he carefully laid on the passenger seat as he got back into the car. Just the thought of the fish and chips had me salivating.

He shot back into the traffic again, and we were soon belting down the Hyde Road. No grandad driving today. The only time my speedo dropped below forty-five was at the traffic lights. I nearly lost him when he went through an amber as it turned to red but I put my foot down and caught him at the next set of lights, just before the motorway. It looked like we were heading over the Woodhead Pass to Sheffield. There was no chance to take in the magnificent scenery today. I was too busy concentrating on keeping the car on the road as I powered round the bends and up the long moorland inclines in the wake of the Supra. We hit the outskirts of Sheffield around one, and Terence slowed down, clearly less familiar with the steel city than he was with Manchester.

We skirted Hillsborough, driving more carefully

now since the police were already out in force for a Sheffield Wednesday home game. I can't understand how anybody can bear to go there to watch football these days. I know *I'll* never forget those newspaper photographs of dying Liverpool fans, nearly a hundred of them, crushed to death on a sunny spring afternoon just like this one. I tried to clear the morbid memories by focusing on the Supra's rear end, twitching now-you-see-it-now-you-don't round the next corner like a rabbit's tail.

We cut through backstreets lined with blank, silent buildings, monuments to an industry that once employed a city and made Sheffield steel world-famous. The captains of industry tell us that Sheffield produces more steel than ever before, and with a quarter of the old workforce. It just doesn't feel like it, driving through what appears to be an industrial graveyard.

Beyond the mills, we climbed steeply. Like Rome, Sheffield's a city built on seven hills. Difference is, you get better pizzas in Sheffield. Soon, we were engulfed by a sprawling council estate, sixties terraces and low-rise maisonette blocks as far as the eye could see. Terence seemed to know where he was now, for he speeded up again, scattering mongrels as he went. It was becoming more difficult to maintain an unobtrusive tail, since virtually every car in sight looked like it had at least one wheel in the grave.

The Supra signalled a right turn as it approached

a large asphalted area beside a low, square building. I carried straight on, turning into the first side-street. I gave it a few minutes, then I headed back the way I'd come. A couple of hundred yards from the building, I parked the car, made sure the alarm was on, and walked the rest of the way on foot. As I got closer, I could see a battered sign which told me that Suzane was a slag, that Wayne shags great and that Fairwood Community Centre had been opened in 1969. All the casual visitor needed to know, really.

There was a blackboard outside the centre, surrounded by a knot of teenagers who looked like Sheffield's entry for the Wasted Youth of the Year contest. I'd have felt threatened if I didn't know I could kick the feet out from under any of them. As it was, I was wary, avoiding eye contact as I glanced at the blackboard. On it was written in sprawling capitals, 'Q Here 4 Sale. 3pm and 6pm. Bargins Galore.' Stapled to the corner was a bundle of flyers. I detached one as I walked on by and stuffed it into my pocket.

I rounded the corner of the community centre to the sound of a wolf whistle and a couple of suggestions as to what the youth of Sheffield would like to do to me. In the car park, as well as the Supra, there was a Cavalier and a three-ton truck. The truck was reversed hard up against the hall, its doors opened back parallel with the wall. I crouched down to tie my shoelace and sneaked a look under the van. Beyond it, the double doors of what was obviously the hall's fire exit were open. Short of crawling under the truck and into the hall, there was no way I could see what was in either of them.

I was about to walk back to the car when my phone chirruped. I felt incredibly exposed, answering a mobile phone right there, so I hurried round to the far side of the truck. At least I was out of sight from the road now. Irritated with myself for not having the sense to remember to leave the phone in the car, I barked, 'Brannigan,' into the phone.

'Kate? Where are you? Are you near home?' It was Alexis, but Alexis as I'd never heard her before. Even in those few words, I could hear panic. And panic meant only one thing.

'Davy?' I said, my fear rising instantly to equal hers.

'Kate, can you get home? Now?'

'What's happened?' I was already skirting round the back of the community centre, crossing a scrubby playing field and heading back to the car. 'He's not . . . gone missing?' My immediate terror was that, somehow, someone had discovered who had driven off with the drugs and that Davy was either a hostage or the potential victim of a vicious reprisal.

'No, nothing like that. It's just . . .'

I could hear Chris's voice saying in the background, 'For God's sake, Alex, give me the phone, you're only winding her up.' Then Chris's voice replaced Alexis's. 'Don't panic,' she said. 'Davy's come back to the house and he's in a bit of a state, like he's high on something. I think he might have been given drugs or something, and I think we ought to take him to hospital. How long will it take you to get home?'

I was at the car, switching the alarm off, shoving the key in the ignition, all on automatic pilot while I digested what Chris was saying. I felt as if I'd been punched in the stomach. Taking Davy to hospital was the nightmare scenario. There was no way we could do it without everything coming on top. Angie would discover that not only was her ex-husband in jail but her son had been put at risk by said ex-husband's fancy woman and her lesbian friends. The chances of Richard ever seeing his son again without a social worker shrank to the size of a terrorist's conscience.

Chris cut into my racing thoughts. 'Hello? Kate? Are you still there?'

'Yeah, I'm here,' I said, powering down the street and heading back towards the Manchester road. 'Look, you can't take him to hospital. Oh shit, this is the worst possible thing . . . Give me a minute.' I thought furiously. On the other hand, if he was really ill, we couldn't *not* take him to hospital. The one thing Richard would never forgive was if I let anything happen to Davy. Come to that, I'd have a hard job forgiving myself. 'How bad is he?' I asked.

'One minute he's shivering, the next he's sweating. He keeps going off into crazy giggling fits and he keeps pointing at nothing really and giggling and then cuddling up to us,' Chris said. There was a note of desperation in her carefully controlled voice.

My brain had finally accessed the relevant information. 'Give me five minutes, Chris,' I said.

'I don't know,' she said. 'He's not at all well, Kate.'

'Please. Five minutes, max.' I cut off the connection before Chris could argue any more. I pulled up with a screech of rubber and the blast of a horn from the car behind. I flipped open my filofax and found the number I was looking for. I punched the number into the phone and moved back into the traffic. Sinful, I know, but getting to Davy was a greater imperative than the interests of other road users.

If anyone could help me, it was Dr Beth Taylor. Beth divides her time between an inner-city group practice and a part-time lectureship at the university in medical ethics. A few years ago, she had a fling with Bill which lasted about three months, which is probably a record for my business partner. Now, she's Mortensen and Brannigan's first port of call whenever we're investigating medical insurance claims. She also repairs broken bits of Brannigan from time to time.

The phone answered on the second ring. 'This is Beth,' the distant voice said. 'I'm not here right now, but if you want me to call you back you can leave a message after the tone. If it's urgent, you can try me on my mobile, which is . . .' I keyed the number into the phone as she recited it, then ended the call and dialled her mobile, praying to God she not only had it with her but was also in a decent reception area.

The phone rang once, twice, three times. 'Hello, Beth Taylor.' I'd never heard a more welcome sound.

'Beth? It's Kate Brannigan.'

'Hi, Kate! Long time no see. Which I suppose is a good thing, in your case. Is this a professional call? Only, I'm on my way to play hockey.'

I bit back the frustrated sigh. 'It's an emergency, Beth.'

'What have you done this time?' Underneath the warm humour in her voice, there was no mistaking the concern.

'It's not me. It's my partner's son. The friends who are looking after him think he might have been given drugs.'

'Then it's not me you want, Kate, it's the casualty department at MRI. You should know that.'

'Beth, I can't. Look, I can't explain now, not because I'm not prepared to, but because there isn't time. Please, Beth, I *need* this favour. I'm on my way back to my house now, and as soon as I get there, I'll tell you why I can't take him to hospital unless it's a matter of life and death,' I pleaded.

'If it's drugs, it could well be that,' Beth warned.

'I know, I know. But please, you're the only doctor I know well enough to trust with this.'

There was a moment's silence. 'I shouldn't do

this,' she said with a sigh. 'It's against all my better judgement.'

'You'll go?'

'I'll go. Where is he?'

'He's at my house. You remember it?'

'I remember,' Beth said. 'I'll be there in about ten minutes. Oh, and Kate?'

'Yeah?'

'You owe Crumpsall Ladies Hockey Club a round of drinks for every five minutes I'm late for the game.' The phone went dead before I could tell Beth it would be worth every penny.

I rang Chris straight back and told her Beth was on her way. The relief in her voice told me exactly how much fear she'd been hiding when she'd spoken to me before. 'Thank God!' she exclaimed. 'He's just been sick. We're really scared, Kate.'

'It's not your fault, Chris. This would have happened whether Richard had been there or not, believe me. Look, phone me if there's any change, OK? I'll be back as soon as I can.'

I might have broken all records driving to Sheffield. But I shattered them driving back.

I barrelled through my front door like the Incredible Hulk on speed. There wasn't a sound from anywhere, and it took me less than ten seconds to discover they weren't in the house. I ran through the conservatory and yanked open the patio doors leading to Richard's living room. Still no one. By now, I was convinced they'd had to rush him to hospital. All the way home, I'd been plagued by a vision of Davy lying in the subdued lighting of intensive care, more tubes than Central London coursing in and out of his little body.

I crossed the room in half a dozen strides and hauled the door open, cannoning into Chris, who stepped backwards into Beth, who continued the domino effect with Alexis. 'Ssh,' Beth said before I could say a word. I backed into the living room and the other three trooped behind me. Alexis shut the door.

'How is he? What's happening?' I demanded.

'Calm down,' Beth instructed. 'Three deep breaths.' I did what she told me. I even sat down. 'Davy's going to be fine. I've just given him a mild sedative and tranquillizer which have calmed him down and sent him to sleep. He'll probably be more or less zonked out till morning. He might feel a bit groggy tomorrow, but basically he'll be OK.'

'What was the matter? What happened?' I asked.

'He presented like someone who has absorbed a significant amount of an hallucinogenic drug,' Beth said. 'Nothing life-threatening, thank God.'

'But how? Where did he get it from? He only went out to play with a couple of other kids from the estate! Who'd feed drugs like that to kids?'

'I said "absorbed" advisedly,' Beth said. She ran a hand through her spiky blonde hair and frowned. 'You know those temporary tattoos that kids use? They wet the transfers and the pictures slide off on to their skin?'

136

I nodded impatiently. 'Yeah, yeah, Davy loves them. Some nights he gets in the bath looking like the Illustrated Man.'

'Did he have any transfers on his body this morning when he went out?'

'Not that I noticed,' I said. 'Did either of you notice last night?'

Chris and Alexis both shook their heads.

'He must have thirty or forty on his arms or chest now,' Beth said. 'And that's the source of the problem, I reckon. I've heard of a couple of cases like this, though I've not actually seen one before.'

'But I don't understand. It can't be something in the transfers, surely. He often has them covering the whole of his arms and his chest. He's crazy about them, like I said. He'll put on as many as Richard will buy for him.'

Beth sighed. 'You're right, it's not the transfers as such. It's what's been done to them. They've been doctored. They've been impregnated with a drug not unlike acid or Ecstasy, probably one that's been designed to provide a feeling of mild euphoria, general friendliness and energy. But taken in the dose Davy seems to have absorbed, it also produces hallucinations. We dumped him in the bath and washed them all off so he won't absorb any more, and luckily he seems to have had a pleasant trip rather than a terrifying one.'

Beth's words seemed to reverberate long after she'd finished speaking. None of us seemed able to come up with an adequate response. Finally, it was Alexis's journalistic instincts that hit the ground running ahead of my private investigator's. 'What do they look like, these transfers?' she asked.

'Some are geometric. Blue and gold stars, about the size of a 10p. Red and pink triangles, too. Others have pictures of clowns, cars, Batman and Superman logos and dinosaurs. The only difference between them and the straight ones is the packaging, so I've been told. Apparently the dodgy ones come in little foil packets, like those individual biscuits you get on aeroplanes. Sorry, I don't know any more than that.'

'I can't believe I've not heard about this on the grapevine,' Alexis said, outraged.

'She's a journo,' I explained to Beth.

'Why haven't there been any warnings about this?' Alexis continued. 'It's scandalous.'

'Presumably, the powers that be didn't want to start a panic,' Beth said. 'I can understand why, since it seems to be such a rarity.'

'Never mind the story, Alexis. What about Davy? Will he definitely be OK?' Chris demanded.

'He'll be absolutely fine, I promise you. In future, make sure he finds another bunch of friends to play with. Look, I've got to run. My hockey match starts in ten minutes. I'll swing by tomorrow morning, just to be on the safe side, but the best thing you can do is let him sleep it off in peace.'

Beth's departure left us in an awkward silence. Alexis broke it. 'It's nobody's fault,' she said.

'We're all going to beat ourselves up, we'll all be fighting each other to take the blame, but it's nobody's fault.'

'I know,' I said. I got to my feet. 'I just want to take a look at him.' I walked down the hall to the spare room and pushed the door open. Davy was lying on his back, arms above his head, legs in a tangle of kicked-off duvet. There was a smile on his sleeping face. I leaned over and pulled the cover up over him. He stirred slightly, grunting. I didn't know what else to do so, feeling awkward, I backed out of the room and closed the door behind me.

I went back through to the kitchen. Alexis was sitting on her own, rolling a modest joint from Richard's stash. 'Don't you think there's been enough drug-taking for one day around here?' I asked. I was teasing, but only just.

Alexis shrugged. 'The doctor says too much stress is bad for me. Chris is making a pot of coffee. You got time for a cup before you go back to wherever you were before you were so rudely interrupted?'

I raised my eyebrows. 'I wasn't planning on going back.'

'Why? Had you finished what you were doing?'

'Well, no,' I admitted.

'So get back on the road. There's nothing you can do here. Davy's zonko. Beth said he'd sleep till morning. Anybody can baby-sit a sleeping kid. But you're the only one that can get Dick out of jail.'

'Don't call him Dick,' I said automatically. 'You

know how it depresses me.' I looked at my watch and sighed. I had plenty of time to drive back to Sheffield and still be in time for the six o'clock sale. With luck, it would be over early enough for me to get back to Manchester in time to visit Richard. I got to my feet just as Chris came in with a tray of coffee.

'Aren't you stopping for a brew?' she asked.

I put on my FBI face. 'You expect me to drink coffee at a time like this?' I asked sternly. 'People, a girl's got to do what a girl's got to do.'

Chris giggled. Alexis guffawed. I don't know why it is that people just don't take me seriously.

12

Literary critics punt the theory that private eyes are society's outsiders. That might have been true in 1940s Los Angeles, but it's a joke in 1990s Britain. These days, if you want to last more than five minutes as a private investigator, you've got to have the instincts of a chameleon. Gumshoes that stand out in a crowd are as much use to the client as a chocolate chip pan. I've had to pass as everything from lawyer to temp, including high-class hooker and journalist, sometimes both on the same day. At least tonight I'd already cased the venue, which gave me a pretty substantial clue as to dress code.

I pulled the crumpled flyer out of my pocket and gave it the once-over. Whoever had put it together wasn't going to win any awards for grammar or graphic design. The one-day sale promised bargains of a lifetime – video recorders for £69.99, camcorders for £99.99, microwaves for £49.99, plus hundreds of other exclusive, unique, etc.

Already, and for free, we'd been presented with more exclamation marks than any reasonable person could use in a decade. With all this in mind, I dressed for the occasion. Tight faded Levis, a black Tina Turner *Simply the Best* sweat shirt (because black always makes me look like I have a major vitamin deficiency), and Richard's three-sizes-too-big Washington Red Sox jacket. I finished the ensemble with a pair of white stilettos with a two-inch heel, bought, I hasten to add, solely for professional purposes. I gathered my auburn hair into a top knot and held it in place with a gold lurex elasticated band. Never mind a million dollars, I looked about threepence halfpenny. I'd fit in like a flea in a cattery.

I was back in Shelfield for half past five. I dumped the car in a city-centre car park and found a cab to take me out to the council estate. I tipped the cabbie a fiver, which persuaded him to come back for me later. At quarter to six, I joined the queue snaking along the pavement outside the community centre. There were getting on for a hundred punters, and none of them looked like they'd be allowed to carry a donor card, never mind a gold card. I reckoned the youngest were under two, slumped slack-mouthed and sleeping in their pushchairs. The oldest were never going to see seventy again. The rest included harassed-looking women, middle-aged at twenty-five, to lads who looked fifteen till you clocked the eyes. I'd calculated well. Nobody gave me a second glance.

At ten to six, the doors opened and we streamed in. The hall was brightly lit, empty except for a raised dais in front of the Fire Exit sign. On the dais was a high counter, piled higher still with cardboard boxes claiming to be filled with microwaves, camcorders, videos and TVs. Other boxes had garish pictures of pan sets, dinner services, game consoles, canteens of cutlery, radio alarms, toasters, battery chargers and socket sets. It looked like a cut-price Aladdin's cave. Behind the stack of boxes I could see a burly man with a perm like a 1970s footballer. If his suit had been any sharper he'd have been arrested for possession of an offensive weapon. He fiddled with a mike, clipping it on to a tie so loud I expected a shriek of feedback. 'Ladies and gentlemen,' he cajoled, 'don't hang back. Come right down to the front where I can see you, and I mean that especially for you lovely ladies. I want to feast my eyes on your charms, because I have to tell you that even though I'm supposed to stand up here being scrupulously fair with you ladies and gentlemen, I'm only human. And I'd have to be more than human to resist some of the lovely ladies I can see in here tonight.' Unbelievable. Even more unbelievable, they obeyed. Like lemmings.

Sticking with the flow of the crowd, I moved forward, edging out towards the side of the hall. I looked around, searching for Terence. I spotted him after a few moments, one of several men flanking the dais. Their ages varied from late teens to early forties. I wouldn't have trusted one of them to hold the dog while I went for a pee. I reached the far wall and stopped about ten feet away from the platform. I took a good look round. The punters were eager, many of them patting the pockets that held their money, reassuring themselves it was still there. It wouldn't be for much longer, I suspected, and not because of pickpockets, either.

Now, most of the men by the platform, including Terence, were fanning out among the crowd, keeping one eye on the auctioneer as he 'entertained' the audience with a steady stream of patter consisting of *risqué* remarks, old jokes and jocular encouragement to the crowd to move forward and prepare to enjoy themselves. I tuned back in. 'I want you to promise me one thing tonight, ladies and gentlemen. I want you to promise me that you'll be good to yourselves. You're going to be offered the bargains of a lifetime here tonight, and I don't want to see you holding back because you don't think you deserve them. I am here tonight to treat you, and I want you to promise me you won't be afraid to treat yourselves. Is that a promise? Will you do that for me?'

'Yeah,' they roared back. I couldn't believe it. The guy looked like they'd minted the word 'spiv' just for him, yet the punters lapped it up like free beer.

'Now, who wants to start the ball rolling with me tonight? Who needs a cigarette lighter?' A few hands shot in the air. 'Who could use a pack of five blank cassettes?' A forest of hands joined them. 'And is there anyone out there who would like a pack of three brand-new video tapes?' I was probably the only person in the room not waving wildly. I buried my pride and stuck my hand up. The salesman grinned. 'Now if it was up to me, I'd be giving these items away, but unfortunately, the law of the land forbids me from exercising my natural generosity. So, you need to give me a token payment for these little tasters of what's to come.'

He paused for dramatic effect. The crowd hung on his words, rapt as a nineteenth-century congregation in thrall to some lunatic visionary minister. 'I'm going to be as fair as I can be. My team of lads are keeping a careful eye on you all, to see who qualifies. Now, I've got twenty of these disposable lighters here, and the first twenty to stick their hands in the air . . .' he paused again, and half a hundred arms flew wildly into the air. 'The first twenty to stick their hands in the air *after* I give the word, those lucky people can purchase a lighter for only one penny. Now, I can't say fairer than that, can I?'

The crowd obviously thought not. The salesman waved a ridiculous gavel in the air. 'Now, I'm going to bang me little hammer three times, and when I hit the counter the third time, that's the signal. Then the lucky twenty will be privileged to be allowed to buy a cigarette lighter for only one penny.' There was a pregnant pause. The hammer descended once, then twice. Half the hands in the room flailed in the air at the moment the hammer should have fallen the third time. Embarrassed, they dropped their hands again. 'Don't be greedy now,' the salesman admonished. 'I promise you, everybody who wants a bargain here tonight will get one.' As he ended his sentence, the hammer banged for the third time, and a thicket of hands straggled into the air. The salesman made a pretence of looking around to see who was first, nodding histrionically as he caught the eye of his henchmen scattered round the room. Twenty punters with waving hands were selected for the cigarette-lighter bargain. It looked to me as if they'd been chosen at random. As we progressed through the cassette tapes (fifty pence), the videos (one pound) and non-stick frying pans developed as a by-product of the American space programme (two pounds), the same arbitrary selections were made. The salesman's assistants only seemed interested in checking out the contents of people's wallets.

The salesman had them in the palm of his hand now. The initial loss leaders had convinced them that tonight they really were going to get bargains. The salesman tossed back his curls and fastened the top button of his jacket, as if to signal it was time to get down to serious business. 'Ladies and gentlemen, I'm not going to insult your intelligence here tonight. I bet you all watch *That's Life*. You know that there are unscrupulous people out there who want to part you and your money. Now, I'm not like that. So here's what I'll do. If you put your trust in me now, I will see to it that your trust does not go unrewarded. Ladies, this is something that will change your lives. Gentlemen, this is something that will change your luck. Every now and again, in the perfume laboratories of Paris, men in white coats come up with something that transforms the woman who wears it from the everyday to the absolutely sensational. With the right perfume, any housewife can make the man in her life feel like she's Liz Taylor, Joan Collins and Michelle Pfeiffer rolled into one. It's a scientific fact. They did it with Chanel No. 5. They did it with Giorgio. Now, they've done it with this!'

He brandished a box in the air. Candyfloss pink and silver stripes. It looked unlike anything I'd ever seen before. 'Here it is, ladies and gentlemen. My brother is in the import/export business, and he has secured a case of this unique Parisian perfume for my customers before it goes on general sale. This exclusive perfume, Eau d'Ego, will be the subject of a major advertising campaign right through the summer, ladies and gentlemen. It's going to be the hottest seller this Christmas, I promise you that. And tonight, you can be the very first people in Britain to own a bottle of Eau d'Ego.'

I struggled to keep a straight face. My French might not be up to much, but when Richard and I had spent a romantic weekend in Paris, we'd done a tour of the city sewers. I don't think

147

you'd find many chic Parisians wearing a perfume whose name sounds suspiciously like *eau d'égout* – sewage.

The salesman was still in full flow, however. 'Now, we have a massive selection of bargains here tonight. But inevitably, we don't have enough of our most popular items to go around. My boss puts limits on me. I mean, how many of you would like to buy a camcorder for under a hundred pounds?'

Nearly half the punters waved frantically at him. He gave a satisfied smirk. 'Exactly. Now, my boss would sack me if I was to sell more than three of our bargain camcorders in one evening. So I have to ration you. Now, I have fifty bottles of Eau d'Ego here on this platform tonight. If you trust me enough to buy a bottle of this exclusive Parisian fragrance, I will give you first refusal on the lots I'm selling here tonight. I'm not saying you *can't* buy a camcorder if you don't buy the perfume, because that would be illegal, ladies and gentlemen. What I am saying is that the people who trust me enough to become my customers now will be given priority when it comes to buying the lots where we have restricted numbers. Now, I think you'll agree, I can't say fairer than that.' His tone left no space for argument. It wasn't a particularly clever pitch, and he wasn't the world's greatest spieler, but they loved it.

'I warn you, ladies, if you get a taste for Eau d'Ego, you are never going to be called a cheap date again. When this marvellous perfume goes on sale in the shops, it will have a recommended retail price of forty-nine pounds ninety-five. Now, I'm not expecting you to pay forty-nine pounds ninety-five tonight. After all, you've not seen the advertising campaign, you've not read all the magazines raving about it, you've not seen the effect it has on me. All you've got is my word. And if I tell you that the wife helped herself to a bottle and I've gone home every night since, that should tell you something!' He winked. I winced.

'I'm not even asking you to pay half-price for the privilege of wearing this fragrance. Ten pounds, that's all. For only a tenner, you can be among the first women to wear a perfume that's destined to be the scent of the stars. Now, when my hammer falls for the third time, my assistants will have their eagle eyes peeled and the first fifty hands in the air will be given this exclusive opportunity.' This time, there was no pause. The hammer banged once, twice, three times. The audience proved Pavlov's theory of stimulus-response, the hands high above their heads as soon as the hammer hit.

All the assistants ran around distributing perfume and grabbing tenners. Terence seemed to be doing exactly the same as everyone else. At least, I couldn't see any difference. I began to wonder if I was wasting my time.

The salesman had moved on from the perfume.

Now, he was putting together bundles of items. I reckoned I could buy their equivalent down any high street in the land for less than they were asking. But common sense had died somewhere in the salesman's pitch, and he had stomped the corpse into the dust with his patter. They were *fighting* to be allowed to pay over the odds for crap that would explode, disintegrate, tarnish, break or all of the above within weeks.

The hysteria rose as he went through the charade of selling serious bargain lots to five hand-picked mug punters. I had to admire his style as he relieved them of between a hundred and fifty and three hundred pounds for bundles of goods they thought they'd bought at a huge discount. I wouldn't mind betting that at the end of the sale, they'd find that they hadn't been granted the special lots at all. All they'd get would be goods worth rather less than they'd paid, and a wide-eyed assurance that the parcel they'd 'bought' had been sold to that (non-existent) man standing right behind them . . . I was watching carefully, and *I'd* lost track of what was going on. The mug punters had no chance.

But the most extraordinary was yet to come. 'Have I been good to you tonight, or have I been good to you tonight?' the salesman demanded. He was greeted with a reasonably warm murmur. 'Do you think I'm someone you can trust? You, madam – would you trust me?' He went through half a dozen members of the audience, pinning them with his stare, demanding their loyalty. Every last one of them bleated a 'yeah' like so many sheep.

He smiled, revealing what he'd been doing with some of the profits. 'I told you about my brother earlier, didn't I? The one in import and export? Well, he knows how I love to treat you people, so he's always on the look-out for bargains that I can pass on to my customers. Now, a lot of these things come from outside the EEC, and according to EEC regulations, we can't display them in the same way. So what we do is we make them up into parcels. Even I don't know what's in these parcels, because we make them up at random. But I can guarantee that each of these parcels contains goods to a value well in excess of what I'm asking for them. All I ask of you is that you take the goods home with you before you unwrap them. Not because we want you to buy a pig in a poke but because the contents vary so much. If the person standing next to you sees you've got a state-of-the-art food processor for a tenner and he's only got a toasted-sandwich maker, a set of heated rollers and a clock radio, it can often cause jealousy, and the last thing we want is fights breaking out because some of our bargains are such outrageously good value for money. Now, I'm going to start with ten-pound parcels. Who's spent money with me here tonight and would like to take advantage of my insane generosity?'

I couldn't help myself. My mouth fell open. A

couple of dozen people were waving their bottles of perfume in the air. Most of them looked like Giro day was the biggest financial event in their lives. Yet they were shelling out hard-hoarded cash on a black bin liner that could have contained a bag of sugar and a half-brick. I wouldn't have believed it if someone had told me about it. Then, as the salesman moved on to fifty-pound lucky bags, I noticed a change in the pattern. It was hardly noticeable, but it was enough. For the first time that evening, I began to believe I was in the right place at the right time.

13

I drove back to Manchester, replaying what I'd just seen, wondering what it meant. If I hadn't been totally focused, I could so easily have missed the tiny alteration to the pattern. It had happened just after the fifty-pound lots had started. Terence had emerged from behind the platform with a black bin liner, just like all the others. Then he'd snaked through the crowd to a short guy in his early twenties with a red baseball cap and a black leather jacket. Even though the guy didn't have his hand stuck in the air, Terence had passed over the bag in exchange for a fat brown envelope. It looked to me like it contained a lot more than fifty pounds, unless the guy in the red hat was paying in roubles.

They said nothing to each other, and the whole exchange took the same few seconds every other transaction had taken. Terence was back serving punters within the minute. But unlike the other mugs, the guy in the red hat wasn't sticking around. As soon as he'd collected his bag of goodies, he was off, shouldering his way through the crowd towards the door, pulling off the red hat and stuffing it inside his jacket. I contemplated following him, but I had no wheels, and besides, I wanted to carry on watching Terence to see what else he'd get up to.

The answer was, nothing. For the short time that remained, he did exactly the same as the other floor men, dishing out black bin liners in exchange for crumpled notes, fending off punters who thought they'd not had the treat they'd been promised at the start of the evening.

Then, with bewildering suddenness, it was over. While the salesman was still speaking, most of his assistants switched their attention from the audience to the platform. With astonishing speed, the boxes that remained on the dais disappeared into the back of the van. By the time his closing speech was over, the platform was bare as my fridge the day before I hit the supermarket.

I worked my way back to the door, joining the punters who were slowly coming back down to planet earth to the depressing realization that they'd been comprehensively ripped off in a completely legal way with no comeback. By the time I made it outside the hall, the satisfied murmurs had turned into discontented mutterings, growing in volume as people began to examine the contents of their blind buying spree. My taxi was waiting, and I didn't hang around to watch them turn into a lynch mob. Neither did the sales crew. As my taxi pulled away from the kerb, I saw the van and the two cars move across the car park. By the time the crowd got angry enough to do anything about it, the lads'd be halfway back across the Pennines.

I pondered all the way to Manchester. It was still almost too slender even to be called circumstantial, but all my instincts told me I was following the right track. I was pretty sure I'd just witnessed the handover of a parcel of illegal substances. I just hoped that it wasn't wishful thinking that was shunting my instincts down the trail of Terence Fitzgerald.

It was nearly twenty to nine when I abandoned the Peugeot on a double yellow line a couple of streets away from the sprawling court complex round Crown Square. I was cutting it fine, since visiting ended at nine. I'd covered my back by phoning ahead *en route* from Sheffield, telling the duty inspector I'd been delayed by a puncture but that I would definitely be there within visiting hours. Looking on the bright side, I'd only have been allowed fifteen minutes anyway. I kicked off the tart's shoes and pulled on the pair of Reeboks I always keep in the car, yanked off the hair band and shook my wavy auburn hair free. I grabbed the plastic bag I'd packed in Richard's bungalow, then I jogged round to the back of the Magistrates' Court building.

I slowed down as I entered the covered walkway

that cuts into the ground floor of the building, and into the range of the video cameras. I didn't want to look like I was storming the building. I pressed the door intercom buzzer. 'Can I help you?' asked a voice with more static than a taxi radio.

'I'm here to visit a prisoner. Richard Barclay. I'm his girlfriend,' I said.

'Go through the double doors to the lift and press the button for the seventh floor,' the voice told me as the door buzzed and the lock was released.

The lift door opened on a different world from the spiffy smartness of the courts. No wood panelling or cool marble floors here. The paintwork was chipped and dirty, the floors pocked with cigarette burns, the walls adorned only with anti-crime posters to intimidate the visitors. I was signed in by a cheerful police officer who ushered me into a tiny cubicle, with two low stools bolted to the floor. The cubicle was divided in half by a metal-topped counter beneath a thick perspex screen. On each side of the counter, there was a telephone handset. I stared through the screen. The other side was identical, except that there was no handle on the inside of the door. I could get up and go any time I wanted, but the prisoner didn't even have that amount of control. I glanced at my watch. It was just after quarter to.

The door opened and Richard walked in, giving a depressing little wave. He sat down, and I found myself noticing all the things I had come to take for granted. The smooth, fluidity of his movements. The way his smile starts on the left side of his mouth before becoming symmetrically cute. I blinked hard and nailed a smile on. His mouth moved, but I couldn't hear a thing. I picked up the phone, waving at him to do the same thing. 'I was beginning to think you weren't coming,' I heard through the earpiece. It wasn't an accusation. His voice sounded strange, disembodied but immediate, not like a normal phone conversation.

'Sorry, but it was your fault I'm so late. I was out there on the mean streets working for you,' I said with a ghost of our usual sparring.

'How's Davy?' he asked.

I swallowed. 'He's fine,' I lied, hoping it didn't show. 'He's in bed asleep.' That bit was true at least.

His eyebrows rose in perfect arcs, just like Paul McCartney's. 'Before nine o'clock? On a Saturday night?'

'Alexis runs a tight ship,' I said confidently. 'She's having so much fun childminding that she's worn him out. Movies, computer games, swimming, enough thick shakes to eliminate the EC milk mountain. Or should that be lake?'

'Depends if it's gone sour yet,' he said. 'Is he missing me?'

'When he has the time to notice you're not there,' I said drily. 'I'm the one that's missing you.'

This time, the smile only made it halfway. 'I

157

feel like Tom Jones in "The Green, Green Grass of Home",' he said. He rubbed a hand over his face. He looked exhausted.

'You don't look like him, thank God,' I told him. 'They treating you OK?'

He shrugged. 'I guess. I've got a cell to myself, which is an improvement on last night. And the food's just about edible. It's the boredom. It's doing my head in. I'd kill for a decent book and a clean shirt.'

I waved the plastic bag. 'Clean shirt, boxers, socks and a couple of books. Alexis chose them.' He looked bemused. I wasn't surprised. 'She says it doesn't mean anything's changed between you,' I added.

He relaxed. 'Thank God for that. I can stand most things, but I don't know if I could bear to go through the rest of my life being grateful to Alexis. Thanks, Brannigan. I appreciate it.'

'You better had,' I growled. 'I don't do this for my clients, you know. You're going to be working flat out till Christmas as it is just to pay me.' I brought him up to speed, stressing how tentative it all was. That didn't stop him looking like a kid who was expecting Santa to turn up with a ten-speed mountain bike *and* a Sega Megadrive.

'OK, I hear you. Gimme the bottom line. Are you going to get me out of here in time to spend some time with Davy?' he asked. The trust I could read in his eyes pushed my stress levels into the stratosphere.

'I sincerely hope so.' I had a horrible feeling that if I didn't, my failure would mean more than one disappointed kid.

Leaving Richard wasn't something I'd relished. But the fresh air outside the court building was. I breathed deep, staring up at the sky, not caring that there was a blur of light rain in the air. I can't remember the last time I felt so low. I checked in with the baby-sitters and Chris told me Davy was still spark out. I drove round by Terence Fitzgerald's house, but the place was in darkness and there was no car outside. I contemplated a bit of burglary, but I knew it was madness. The second rule of successful burglary is: Always make sure you know enough about their lives to know when they're likely to come back. I didn't know nearly enough about Terence's nasty habits. And I didn't relish the thought of being trapped on the top floor with no visible means of escape.

I didn't feel like going home yet. I gunned the car engine into life and cruised back into town. Almost without thinking, I headed for Strangeways. In the long shadow of the Victorian prison commerce thrives. The narrow streets are packed with wholesalers' warehouses, lock-ups and shop fronts, selling casual clothes, electrical goods, jewellery, beauty supplies and furniture. They're mostly family businesses, and the ages of the businesses are like the strata in a geological map. The Jews were here first, then the Cypriots, then the Asians, then a handful of boat people. We're expecting the Bosnians any day now.

A lot of the business that goes on in Strangeways is entirely legitimate. And then, a lot of it isn't. A diligent Trading Standards Officer spending a Sunday poking around the market could find enough infringements to keep a court busy for a week. They regularly do. Only nobody ever answers the summonses.

On a Saturday night, Strangeways looks as empty, dark and moody as a Hollywood film set. Except for the Jewish café, that is. Formally the Warehouse Diner, it's an unpretentious dive frequented by the traders, petty criminals and occasional visitors like me. It's the only decent eating place outside Chinatown that stays open till four in the morning, which makes it handy for all sorts of reasons. Besides, they do the best salt beef sandwiches in town, and the best fry-ups. Some dickhead nominated it for one of those 'cheap and cheerful' good food guides, which means that every now and again a bunch of tourists arrives to gawp at the regulars. I've always enjoyed the atmosphere, though if you want certain items, you have to pick your time carefully. The rabbi's a regular visitor, and the mornings he's due there's no bacon butties and only beef sausages.

I'd hit a lull; the early trade had eaten and gone and the nighthawks weren't in yet. As I'd expected, there were a few familiar faces in the diner. The one I was most pleased to see was

Dennis. He waved to me to join him and his two buddies, but what I wanted to talk about wasn't for public consumption. I shook my head and sat at a table on my own. As my tea and sandwich arrived, so did Dennis. 'What do you know, Kate?' he greeted me, pulling out the chair opposite me.

'Not a lot. Life's a bitch and then you die,' I said wearily.

'Nah,' he said. 'Life's a bitch and then you marry one.'

'That's no way to talk about the love of your life.'

He grinned. 'Me and the wife, we're modern. Into all the latest fashions. That's what keeps a marriage alive. These days we have an S&M relationship.'

I knew I was walking into it, but I walked anyway. 'S&M?'

'Sex and meals.' Dennis roared with laughter. It wasn't that funny, but it was great camouflage. Now everyone would think I was just another victim of Dennis's funny stories.

'Nice one. You know a bloke called Terence Fitzgerald? Lives on the Quays. Drives a black Toyota.'

'Terry Fitz? We were in Durham together.' He didn't mean on holiday. Durham jail is one of the meanest, bleakest places a man can do time. They don't send you there for nonpayment of fines.

'What was he in for?'

'A blag with a shooter. He was the wheels man.

Like Handbrake, only nasty. They never got him for it but he run over an old dear when they was having it away on their toes after a job in Skelmersdale, and he never stopped. Slag,' Dennis added contemptuously.

'He been out long?'

Dennis shrugged. 'A year or so. I don't know what he's doing these days.'

'I do,' I said. 'He's working as a floor man for an outfit doing hall sales.' I handed Dennis the crumpled flyer. 'This outfit.'

Dennis nodded sagely. 'This is his brother-in-law's team. Tank Molloy. He married Fitz's sister Leanne. Good operation he's got there. Makes a lot of money. And he does it all dead legal. He shafts them, but he shafts them within the letter of the law. The BBC had a team following him round for weeks, trying to turn him over, but they couldn't get nothing on him except for being immoral so they had to back off. Burly bloke, hair like a poodle, terrible taste in ties, that's Tank. He's usually the top man.'

I raised one eyebrow. 'The top man?'

'The one that does the patter.'

I nodded. 'Sounds like him. Any drug connection?'

Dennis looked shocked. 'What? Tank Molloy? No way. He's an old-fashioned villain, Tank. He's like me. Wouldn't touch drugs with a bargepole. I mean, where's the challenge in that?'

'What about Terry Fitz?'

Dennis took his time lighting a cigarette. 'Fitz has got no scruples. And he don't give a shit who he works with. If he's got in with the drug boys, you don't want to tangle. He's sharp, Fitz. The only thing he's stupid about is shooters. He thinks they're a tool of the trade. He wouldn't think twice about blowing you away if there was just you standing between him and a good living.'

14

It's a piece of cake, being a lawyer or a doctor or a computer systems analyst or an accountant. Libraries are full of books telling you how to do it. The only textbooks for private eyes are on the fiction shelves, and I don't remember ever reading one that told me how to interrogate an eight-year-old without feeling like I was auditioning for the Gestapo. It didn't help that Alexis was standing in the doorway like a Scouse Boadicea, arms folded, a frown on her face, ready to step in as soon as I stepped out of line.

Davy sat in bed, looking a bit pale, but otherwise normal. I figured if he was well enough to wolf scrambled eggs and cheese cabanos, he was well enough to answer a few simple questions. Somehow, it didn't work out that straightforwardly. I sat on the bed and eventually we established that he was feeling OK, that I wasn't going to tell his mum and we'd negotiate about his dad at a later stage. Already, I felt exhausted.

'Where did you get the transfers from?'

'A boy,' he said.

'Did you know the boy?' I asked.

Davy shook his head. He risked a quick glance at me from under his fringe. I could see he was going to grow up with the same lethal cuteness as his father. However, since I've yet to discover any maternal instincts and I'm not into little boys till they're old enough to have their own credit card, the charm didn't work on me. I stayed firm and relentless. 'You don't usually take presents from strangers, do you, Davy?'

Again, the shake of the head. This time, he mumbled, 'He wasn't a proper stranger.'

'How do you mean?' I pounced.

'Daniel and Wayne knew him,' he said defiantly. 'I wasn't going to, but they said it was all right.'

'Were you playing with Daniel and Wayne?'

This time he nodded. His head came up and he looked me in the eye. He was on surer ground now. Daniel and Wayne were two of the kids from the council estate. He knew I knew who he was talking about. I stood up. 'OK. In future, don't take things from people unless *you* know them. Is that a deal?'

Looking stubborn rather than chastened, he nodded. 'OK,' he dragged out.

'I'm really not cut out for this game,' I muttered to Alexis as I left.

'It shows,' she growled. Walking down the hall, I heard her say, 'You going to lie in your pit all day, soft lad? Only there's a pair of skates at Ice World with your name on, and if you're not ready in half an hour I'm going to have to go on my own.'

'Can't we go later, Alexis?' I heard Davy plead.

'You're not going to lie there half the day, are you?'

'No. But I want to go and watch my dad's team playing football this morning. We always go and watch them when I'm here.'

Silence. I bet standing on a freezing touchline watching the local pub team kick a ball badly round a muddy pitch was as much Alexis's idea of hell as it was mine. I smiled as I headed through the conservatory and back into my own territory. It was nice to know that even Alexis got stiffed now and again. I pulled on last night's jeans. I opened the wardrobe and realized I wasn't going to be able to take a rain check on my date with the iron for much longer. I'd hire someone to do it, but on past experience it only causes me more grief because they never, but never, get the creases in the right places.

Irritated, I grabbed a Black Watch tartan shirt, a leftover from my brief excursion into grunge fashion, hastily abandoned when Della told me I looked like a refugee from an Irish folk group. At least it gave me an excuse to wear the battered old cowboy boots that are more comfortable than every pair of trainers I possess. I put a white T-shirt on under the tartan and headed out the door in search of Daniel and Wayne's mum.

I crossed the common to the rows of four-storey council flats where Cherie Roberts lived. After all this time, I'm still capable of being surprised by the contrast with the neat little enclave where I live. At the risk of sounding like Methuselah at twenty-eight, I can remember council estates where the Rottweilers didn't go around in pairs for security. Oxford isn't famous for its pleasant public housing, but I had school friends who lived out on Blackbird Leys when it was the biggest council housing estate in Western Europe, and it was OK. I don't remember obscene graffiti everywhere, lifts awash with piss and shit, and enough rubbish blowing in the wind between the canyons of flats to mistake the place for the municipal dump. Thank you, Mrs Thatcher.

I walked on to the corner and looked down the narrow cul-de-sac, trying to remember which block Cherie's flat was in. I knew it was on the top floor and on the left-hand side. I'd know it when I saw it, but if I could avoid climbing six sets of stairs, I'd be happier. There was nobody around to ask either. Half past nine on a Sunday morning isn't a busy time on the streets where I live. I set off, chewing over what I knew of Daniel and Wayne's mum.

Cherie was a pale thirty-year-old who looked forty except when she smiled and her bright blue eyes sparked. She didn't smile that often. She was a single parent. She hadn't ever been anything else in practice, even though she'd been married to Eddy Roberts for eight years. Eddy was a Para who'd fallen in love with violence long before Cherie ever got a look-in. They'd married in a moment of madness when he was waiting to be shipped to the Falklands to help win Mrs Thatcher's second term. He'd come back with his head full of Goose Green and gone just crazy enough for them to invalid him out. He stuck around for the few days it took to impregnate Cherie, but before Daniel was much more than a tadpole, her soldier of fortune was off fighting somebody else's war in Southern Africa. He dropped in a year later for long enough to give her a couple of black eyes and another baby before he vanished into Central America.

Davy is the reason I know all this. He'd been coming up to visit regularly for a few months when Cherie turned up on my doorstep one night. Davy had obviously been boasting about my brilliance as a private eye, for Cherie had a task for me. She explained, right up front, that she couldn't afford to pay me in money but she was offering a skill swap. Her cleaning and ironing for my detecting. I was tempted, till she told me about the job. She wanted me to find Eddy. Not because she wanted him back, but because she wanted a divorce.

I'd explained gently that Mortensen and Brannigan don't handle missing persons, which happens to be no less than the truth. I could tell she didn't believe me, even though I spent an hour outlining a few suggestions on how and where she might track down her errant husband. Relations between us weren't helped when the agency was all over the papers a couple of months later because of a very high-profile missing person case that I'd cracked . . . Since then, whenever we'd met in the Post Office or in the dentist's waiting room she'd been frigidly polite, and I guess I'd stood on my dignity. Not the most promising history for a successful interview.

I struck lucky on the third attempt. I recognized Cherie's door as soon as I hit the landing. Daniel's Ninja Turtle stickers were unmistakable, and obviously difficult to remove. Nothing so embarrassing to a kid as the evidence of last year's cult. Taking a deep breath, I knocked. No reply. I banged the letter box, and was rewarded with a scurrying behind the door. The handle turned and the door swung open a couple of inches on a chain and the sound of the TV blasted me, but I couldn't see anybody. Then a small voice said, 'Hiya,' and I adjusted my eye level.

'Hiya, Daniel,' I said to the pyjama-clad figure. I had a fifty per cent chance of being right.

'I'm Wayne,' he said. I hoped that wasn't a sign from the gods.

'Sorry. Hiya, Wayne. Is your mum in?'

He shrugged. 'She's in bed.'

Before he could say more, I saw a pale blue shape in the background and heard Cherie's voice say sharply, 'Wayne. Come away from there. Who is it?'

I cocked my head round the crack in the door

and said, 'Hi, Cherie. It's me, Kate Brannigan. Sorry to wake you, but I wondered if I could have a word.'

Cherie appeared at the door in a faded towelling dressing gown and shoved Wayne out of the way. 'I wasn't asleep.'

I was glad about that. She'd have had to be seriously hearing impaired to have slept through the volume her kids seemed to need from the TV. 'Yeah, right,' I said diplomatically.

'What is it?' she asked.

'I just wanted a word. Em . . . Can I come in?'

Cherie looked defensive. 'If you want,' she said, grudging every word.

'I don't want the whole neighbourhood to hear me,' I said, trying desperately not to sound like I was about to give her a bad time.

'I've nothing to be ashamed of,' she said defensively. She let the chain off and opened the door wide enough to let me in. After I'd entered, she stuck her head out and gave the landing the quick one-two to check who had spotted me.

I pressed against the wall to let her pass and lead me into the living room. 'Out,' she said curtly. Daniel reluctantly uncurled himself from the sofa and walked out of the room. Cherie switched off the TV and stared aggressively at me. 'D'you want a brew, then?' It was a challenge.

I accepted. While she was in the kitchen, I looked around. The room was scrupulously clean and as tidy as my place on a good day. Given she had two kids, it was impressive. It was a shame she didn't have enough cash to upgrade from shabby. The leatherette upholstery of the sofa was mended with parcel tape in places, and in others it had completely worn away. The walls were covered in blown vinyl in a selection of patterns, clearly a job lot of odd rolls. But the paint was still white, if not quite brilliant, and she'd pitched some video shop manager into letting her have some film posters to brighten the place up.

'Seen enough?' Cherie demanded, returning from the kitchen on bare and silent feet. There was nothing I could say about her home that wouldn't sound patronizing, so I said nothing, meekly accepting the mug of tea she held out to me. 'There's no sugar,' she said. 'I don't keep it in.'

'That's OK, I don't use it.'

The door opened a couple of inches and Daniel's head and one shoulder appeared. 'We're going round to Jason's to watch a video,' he said.

'OK. Behave yourselves, you hear me?'

Daniel grinned. 'You wish, Mum,' he giggled. 'See ya.'

Cherie turned her attention back to me. She'd found a moment to drag a brush through her shoulder-length mouse-coloured hair, but it hadn't improved the image a whole lot. She still looked more like a woman at the end of her day rather than the beginning. 'So what's this word you wanted to have with me?'

I swallowed a mouthful of strong tea and dived in at the deep end. 'I'm really worried about something that happened yesterday, and I think you probably will be too. Davy's up for the week. He was out playing yesterday morning for a couple of hours, and when he came in, he was in a hell of a state. He was really hyper, he was sick, and his temperature was all over the place. I got a friend of mine who's a doctor to come around and have a look at him. The bottom line is, he was out of his head on drugs.'

The words were barely out of my mouth before Cherie jumped in. 'And it has to be something to do with my kids, doesn't it? It couldn't be any of those nice middle-class kids from your street, could it? How do you think kids around here get the money for drugs?'

That wasn't one I was prepared to answer. Reminding her of the muggings, burglaries and dole frauds that are the everyday currency of life at the bottom of the heap wasn't going to earn me the answers I was looking for. 'I'm not blaming your lads, Cherie. From what I can gather, they're as likely to be victims as Davy was.'

That wasn't the right response either. 'Don't you accuse my lads of taking drugs,' she said dangerously, her eyes glinting like black ice. 'We might not have much compared to you, but I take care of my kids. You've no shame, have you?'

That was when I lost it. 'Will you for Christ's sake listen to me, Cherie?' I snarled. 'I've not come here to have a go at you or your kids. Something scary, something dangerous, happened to Davy and I don't want it happening to any other kids. Not yours, not anybody's. You and me smacking each other over the heads with our prejudices isn't going to sort things out.'

In the silence that followed, Cherie gave me the hard stare. Gradually, the sullen look left her face. But the suspicion was still there in her eyes. 'OK. You got somebody else's kicking. I had them bastards from the Social round the other day, doing a number about how Eddy's not paying any maintenance and I must know where he is.'

I pulled a face. 'Pick a war, any war.'

'That's more or less what I told them. So, what's all this business with Davy got to do with me?' The adrenaline rush had subsided and her eyes had dulled again, emphasizing the dark blue shadows beneath them. She sat on the arm of the sofa, keeping her eyes firmly fixed on mine.

'These drugs were absorbed through the skin. From those tattoo transfers that the kids stick all over themselves. According to my doctor friend, the tattoos are impregnated with drugs. I don't know why. Maybe it's to give kids the taste for it. You know, a few freebies to get them into the habit, then it's sorry, you've got to cough up some readies.'

Cherie pulled a pack of cheap cigarettes out of her dressing-gown pocket and lit up. 'I've seen my two with a few transfers,' she admitted. 'I know

173

they must have got them from one of the other kids because I don't buy them the stickers, and they've had them some times when they've not had spends. But I've never seen them out of their heads, or anything like it. Mind you, the way they wind each other up, you probably couldn't tell,' she added, in a grim joke.

I mirrored her thin smile. 'The problem seems to have arisen because Davy OD'd on the transfers. He loves them, you see. Given half a chance and a year's pocket money, he'd cover himself from head to foot with them. Especially if they were *Thunderbirds* ones. Now, Davy says he was playing with Wayne and Daniel yesterday. A boy he didn't know gave him the transfers, and he seems to have handed over as many as Davy wanted. He says he thought it was OK to take the transfers from the boy because Wayne and Daniel knew him,' I said.

'I suppose you want to ask my pair who this lad was,' Cherie said with the resignation of a woman who's accustomed to having her autonomy well and truly usurped by the middle-class bastards. Once upon a time I'd have been insulted to be taken for one of them, but even I can't kid myself that I'm still a working-class hero.

I shook my head. 'If you don't mind, I'd rather you asked them. I think you're more likely to get the truth out of them than me. They'd only think I was going to bollock them.'

Cherie snorted. 'They'll *know* I'm going to bollock

them. OK, I'll ask them when I see them. It'll be a few hours, mind you. Once they get stuck into a pile of videos, they lose all track of time.'

'Great. If you get anywhere, can you let me know? I'm going to be in and out a lot, but there'll probably be somebody in next door in Richard's. Or else stick a note through the door. I'd really appreciate it.' I got to my feet.

'You going to hand the slags over to the cops?' Cherie asked. Behind her bravado, I could sense apprehension.

'I don't think people that hand out drugs to kids should be out on the street, do you?'

Cherie shook her head, a despairing look on her face. 'Put them away, another one jumps in to take their place.'

'So we just let them carry on?'

'No way. I just thought you'd know the kind of people that'd put them off drug dealing for life. And put off anybody else that was thinking it would be a good career move.'

People get strange ideas in their heads about the kind of person a private eye hangs out with. The worrying thing for me was that Cherie was absolutely right. I knew just the person to call.

15

Ruth hadn't hung around waiting for me in reception. I spotted her behind the *Independent on Sunday* from the other side of the coffee lounge. There was already a basket of croissants and a selection of cold meats and cheeses on the table. Whipped cream in Alpine peaks was gently subsiding into her hot chocolate, and somehow she'd managed to get a whole jug of freshly squeezed orange juice all to herself. Luckily, she'd chosen a window table which commanded a view of the Quays. On the way to meet her, I'd swung round by Terry Fitz's flat and been relieved to see the Supra sitting on the drive and the curtains still firmly closed. From the hotel, I'd be able to see if he left home.

I sat down and said, 'If I rush off suddenly, it's not because of something you've said.'

She lowered the paper and groaned. 'Oh God, not melodrama over Sunday brunch? Frankly, I can see why you copped out of the law. Not nearly exciting enough to keep you going.'

'I'm not grandstanding,' I bristled. 'I'm trying to get Richard out of jail.'

'You and me both,' Ruth said calmly, dumping her paper, reaching for a croissant and dunking it into her chocolate. I felt faintly sick. 'Any progress?' she asked.

I brought her up to speed. It didn't even fill the gap between me ordering coffee and wholemeal toast and them arriving. Ruth listened attentively in between mouthfuls of soggy croissant. 'How fascinating. It's a novel way of distributing drugs. This sounds very promising for Richard,' she said as I ground to a halt. 'But you're going to need a lot more than that before we can persuade the Drugs Squad that Richard was merely an innocent abroad.'

'What are the next moves, from your point of view?' I asked.

'That depends to some extent on you. If you can come up with enough by Tuesday morning for the Drugs Squad to get going, then I've got a slight chance of getting bail on Wednesday.'

'How slight?' I asked.

Ruth studied the cold meat and speared a slice of smoked ham. 'I'd be lying if I said it looked good. Failing that, what I can go for is a short remand, say an overnight or a couple of days, arguing that investigations are in progress which may produce a significantly different picture within twenty-four hours. If the Drugs Squad then mount a successful operation based on information received from you, the chances are we can then get Richard out on bail. It'll take a little longer to get the charges dropped, but at least he won't be languishing in the CDC while I'm working on it.' She split a croissant and loaded it with ham, followed by a slice of cheese. I envied her appetite. I stared morosely at the toast and poured myself a coffee.

I didn't even have time to add milk. A flash of light as the sun hit the windscreen of Terry Fitz's car alerted me. He was turning out of his drive. I hit the ground running. 'Sorry!' I called back to Ruth. 'Send me the bill.'

'Don't worry about it,' she shouted. 'I'll charge it to the client.'

And I thought I padded my bills. One thing about hanging out with lawyers: they don't half make you feel virtuous.

This time, we headed up the M6. I had no trouble with the tail at first, since half of the North West of England had decided the only place to be on the sunny Sunday of a bank holiday weekend was in a traffic jam on the motorway. Things improved after Blackpool, but there were still a lot of families having the traditional bank holiday argument all the way to the Lakes. The Supra was an impatient outside-lane hogger and flasher of lights, but he had few chances to hammer it till the traffic thinned out after the Windermere turn-off. Then he was off. I prayed he was keeping a look-out for traffic cops up ahead as I watched the speedo creep up past a ton. The last thing I needed was a driving ban.

He slowed as we approached the Carlisle turning, and I hung back till the last minute before I shot off in his wake. His destination was only five minutes off the motorway, a sprawling concrete pillbox of a pub sandwiched between a post-war council estate of two-up two-down flats built to look like semis, and a seventies estate of little 'executive' boxes occupied by sales reps, factory foremen and retail managers struggling with their mortgages. I drifted past the Harvester Moon Inn, watching as he parked the Supra by the truck I recognized from the previous day. I slowed to a halt, twisted my rear-view mirror round and watched Terry Fitz climb out of his car, pick up a black bin liner from the rear seat well and head into the pub.

I parked round the corner from the pub and walked back. The blackboard stood outside the main entrance, announcing today's sales at two p.m. and five p.m. in the pub's upstairs function room. Depressed at the very thought of it, I dragged myself into the pub. It was a huge barn of a place, arbitrarily divided into bar and lounge by a wooden partition at head height. Well, head height for someone with a bit more than my five feet and three inches. The whole place was in dire need of a face-lift, but judging by the desperate tone of the notices on the walls, it wasn't making enough to persuade the brewery to spend the necessary cash. Monday night was 'the best trivia night in town', Tuesday was 'Darts Open Night, cash prizes', Wednesday was 'Ladies Night! With Special House Cocktails', Thursday offered 'Laser Karaoke, genuine opportunities for Talent!', while Friday was 'Disco Dancing! Do the Lambada with Lenny. The Harvester's very own king of the turntables'. And people say Manchester's provincial.

The clientele was marginally up-market of the down-at-heel decor. There were, naturally, more men than women, since somebody has to baste the chicken. I felt out of place, not because of my gender, but because I was the only person who wasn't part of the locals' tribal rituals. The customers sat or stood in tight groups, taking part in what was clearly a regular Sunday lunch-time session with unvarying companions. I carried on walking past the bar, gathering a few inquisitive stares on the way, and through a door at the rear marked 'Harvest Home Lounge'. It led to a small foyer, with stairs climbing upwards, and a set of double doors leading out into the car park. With half an hour to go before the sale, I'd clearly beaten the Carlisle crowds to the draw.

I walked back to the car and headed into the town centre till I found a Chinese chippy next to a corner shop. I drove back crunching worryingly cubic sweet-and-sour chicken, with a bag of apples for afters to make me feel virtuous. I joined the queue for the sale with only a few minutes to go. This time, I hung back as we filed in so I could have a good view of the rest of the punters. The sale followed the same pattern as the previous evening's. The only change was that Molloy, the top man, only offered forty bottles of perfume. I put that down to the slightly smaller crowd that they had drawn. When we got down to the pig-in-a-poke lots, I kept my eyes fixed on Terry Fitz.

The night before hadn't been a fluke. Soon as Molloy announced the fifty-pound lots, Terry appeared with a black bin liner that looked identical to the others. But he took it straight over to a punter I'd already singled out as the man most likely to. Just like the previous night's mark, he was wearing a black leather jacket and a red baseball cap. It was a different guy, there was no question about it. But the clothes were identical.

As soon as I saw the handover, I eased myself away from the audience and ran downstairs. I slipped inside the door leading to the pub and held it open a crack. As I'd expected, Red Cap was only moments behind me. He didn't even pause to look around him, just headed straight out into the car park. I was behind him before he'd gone a hundred yards.

He wasn't hard to tail. He bounced on his expensive hi-tops with a swagger, his red cap jauntily bobbing from side to side. Across the car park, over the road and into the council estate. We walked for half a mile or so through the estate until we came to three blocks of low-rise flats arranged in an H-shape. Red Cap went for the middle block, disappearing into a stairwell. Cautiously, I followed, keeping a clear flight below him as he climbed. I caught a glimpse of his jacket as he turned out of the stairs on the third floor, and I ran the last flight. I cleared the stairs and hit the gallery in time to see a door close behind him. Trying to look as if I belonged, I strolled along the gallery. His was the third door. The glass had been painted over and heavy curtains obscured the windows. I turned and walked back, my eyes flicking from side to side, desperately seeking a vantage point.

One of the legs of the H looked as if it was in the process of being refurbished or demolished. The windows were mostly boarded up and there was no sign of life. I hurried back down the stairs and across to the deserted block. Sure enough, the stairwell was boarded up. It had been padlocked, but the housing had been crowbarred off, some time ago, by the looks of it. I pulled the door open far enough to squeeze round it and cautiously made my way up the gloomy stairs. From what little I could see, it looked like HIV alley, condoms slithering and syringes crunching underfoot. Once I passed the first floor it became lighter and cleaner. I went all the way up to the fourth floor and emerged on the gallery at an oblique angle to Red Cap's front door. Then I settled down to wait.

Half an hour later, there had been four visits to the flat: two separate youths, one couple in their teens and a pair of lads with a girl in tow. Red Cap had opened the door to all of them, and they'd slipped inside, only to emerge less than five minutes later looking a lot happier. I've seen chemists' shops with fewer customers. After the fourth visit, I thought it was time to risk collecting some firm evidence, so I left my sentry post and jogged back to the car. I drove into the private housing estate and headed in the general direction of the flats. I didn't want to leave the car in an exposed place like a pub car park once I'd revealed that it held more than yesterday's newspapers. I parked in a quiet side-street and opened my photographic bag. I put on the khaki gilet Richard brought me back from a business trip to LA. It's got more pockets than a snooker club. I put the Nikon body with the motor drive in one, and slipped my telephoto lens and doubler into inside pockets.

Within ten minutes, I was back on the fourth floor, the long lens resting on the edge of the balcony, focused on Red Cap's front door, motor drive switched on. I didn't have long to wait. In less than an hour, I had six separate groups on film. If I didn't win the Drugs Squad's Woman of the Year award, it wouldn't be for want of trying.

16

I called it a day on the surveillance at half past four and walked back to the car. I swapped cameras, choosing a miniature Japanese one that slots into a pocket in the gilet. The pocket has a hole in it that corresponds to the lens of the camera. I loaded the camera with superfast film so it would capture an image without the need for flash, plugged in the remote shutter release cable and threaded it through the lining so the button sat snugly in the pocket I'd have my hand stuffed into. Before I set off for the five o'clock sale, I called home. There was no reply, either at my house or Richard's, so I assumed everybody was having a good time.

The five o'clock sale ran to the same formula. If I had to do this many more times, I'd be able to take over the top man's job. This time, I'd got near the front of the queue and waited till the red cap and the black leather jacket appeared. This time, it wasn't a man. Nice to see that equal opps is finally making its way into criminal circles. She was about my age, taller, bottle blonde and pale as Normandy butter. I manoeuvred my way through the crowd till I was standing at an angle to her, perfectly positioned for my camera to do the business. The handover came right on cue, the bulky envelope exchanged for a black bin liner. This time, Terry Fitz winked. I'm not sure if it was because she was a woman, or because he knew her, but it was the first time I'd seen him display any kind of recognition towards the happy recipients of his little parcels.

I thought about following the woman, but decided I'd rather stay with Terry Fitz. I knew where the drugs were going now; what I didn't know was where they were coming from. With his record, I couldn't see Terry Fitz standing on for having them stashed in his house. I waited till the woman in the red baseball cap was well clear, then I nipped out ahead of the masses and got my car in position between the pub and the motorway.

Just before eight, Terry Fitz shot past me at a disgraceful speed. On the way back, the bank holiday traffic trapped us again, but in spite of that we were still back in Salford by half past nine. As we turned into the Quays, I hung back. I was a good half-mile away when he pulled up on the street outside his house. He jumped out of the car, trotted up the path and opened the garage, re-emerging seconds later behind the wheel of the Escort Cosworth, still with its trade plates.

I waited till it zoomed past me sounding like

Concorde with a frog in its throat before I spun the Peugeot round and sped off in its wake. Back down the motorway, on to the M63, this time heading south towards Stockport. As we drove over Barton Bridge, the elevated section above the Manchester Shit Canal (so called because of the sewage works that huddle along its banks), I stayed right over in the fast lane. I came rather too close to checking out whether or not there's an afterlife one night on Barton Bridge, and it left me more than a little wary of trusting in the crash barriers.

As we descended the long curve of the bridge, I let my breath out again. I stayed with his tail-lights past Trafford Park and Sale, but I nearly missed him as he cut across three lanes of traffic to shoot off on the slip road for the M56 and the airport. We didn't stay on the motorway for long. He came off at the junction for the sprawling council estate of Wythenshawe, bypassed the shopping centre and made for the far side of the airport, over towards the cargo holding areas. The job suddenly got awkward.

The Cosworth turned right down a narrow lane that wound alongside the perimeter fence of the airport. Following it down there was a risky venture. Sighing, I doused my lights and turned right. My car was black, which meant I had less chance of being spotted. The downside was that anything coming in the opposite direction wouldn't see me either. The things we do for love.

The lane was fairly straight, so I managed easily

to keep the lights of the Cosworth in sight for a mile or so, then, abruptly, they disappeared sharply on the right. Time for a gamble. Since that was the airport side of the road, I didn't think Terry Fitz had turned off on to another minor road. I decided he'd arrived at a rendezvous. I spotted a field gateway a couple of hundred yards ahead on the left, and pulled into it, killing the engine fast. I got out of the car and pushed the door gently to. The click of the lock made me jump, but I told myself it wouldn't carry far, not so close to the airport.

I took a good look round before I crossed the road and moved cautiously towards the spot where the Cosworth had vanished. There was a narrow gap in the hedgerow, and I edged my head round. A rutted, stony track led a few yards off the road, angling round sharply to the double doors of a wooden building. Small barn, large garage, take your pick. The Cosworth was outside, parked next to a Mercedes 300SL with the personalized plate TON 1K. I could see a thin line of yellow light along the top of the door, but nothing more. The side of the lock-up was only feet away from the airport fence.

I felt seriously exposed where I was, so I slipped across the track and inched up to the corner, checking the hedge as I went. Just on the corner, there was a bit of give and I wriggled into the bushes, trying not to think of all the nocturnal creatures that lurk in the English countryside. If you ask me, extinct is quite the best state for mice and rats and most other small furry animals with sharp teeth. Not to mention all the creepy insects that would take one look at my hair and decide it was a better habitat than the filthy maze of the hedgerow.

I gave an involuntary shudder that rippled through the hedge with a noise like *Wuthering Heights* meets *The Wind in the Willows*. 'Get a grip, Brannigan,' I muttered under my breath. I took a deep breath and my nose filled with dust. Predictably, just like the worst kind of wimpy heroine, I felt a sneeze welling up inside. I pinched the bridge of my nose so tight my eyes watered, but not so much that I missed the garage door opening. Terry Fitz appeared in the doorway, called back, 'No problem, speak to you in the week,' and walked briskly to the Cosworth.

He was carrying three Sainsbury's carrier bags, but I didn't think he'd come all the way out to the airport to pick up some groceries. He opened the boot, and in the glow of the courtesy light, I saw him lift the carpet and stow the carrier bags underneath. From the look of it, they were packed into the well where the spare wheel should be. Fitzgerald slammed the boot shut, then got into the Cosworth. He bounced the car round in a tight three-point turn, then he was off, leaving a cloud of dust hanging in the moonlight. I didn't even think about trying to follow him.

Instead, I waited to see who else was lurking inside the garage. I didn't think that anyone who owned a motor like that was likely to be spending the night there. Besides, with Richard behind bars, I had nothing better to do with my Sunday evening.

It was a long half-hour before there was any sign of life. With no warning, the door swung open. Before I had the chance to see who emerged, the inside light snapped off. A tall, burly man in an overcoat came out and turned his back to me as he fastened a couple of big padlocks that closed the heavy steel bars protecting the doors. Then, still with his back to me, he headed towards the Mercedes. I backed out of the hedge, coming out on the track out of his sight, and raced back towards the road as his engine started. I reckoned I had a couple of minutes while he turned the big car around. With a bit of luck, he'd be heading the way my car was facing and I might be able to pick him up. If I lost him, at least I had the car registration number to go at.

I dived behind the wheel of the Peugeot just as his headlights swept the hedge opposite the gap. The gods were smiling. He drove away from me, so I started the engine, left the lights off and followed. I was beginning to feel like I'd got the sucker role in a very bad road movie.

We were only a mile from the main road. I let him glide off before I switched my lights on and rejoined the respectable. I hoped this wasn't going to be a long chase, because my fuel gauge told me I'd soon be running on fumes. At least Mercedes

189

Man didn't drive like a speed freak. I suppose when you're driving round in that much money you don't need to prove anything to anybody.

We cruised through Wilmslow, the town where car dealers aren't allowed to sell anything that costs less than five figures. They're all here – Rolls Royce, Porsche, BMW, Mercedes, Jaguar, even Ferrari. Just before the town centre, the Merc turned right and, a couple of hundred yards down the road, he pulled on to the forecourt of a small car pitch. EMJ Car Sales. Even the second-hand motors were all less than three years old.

The driver got out of the car and let himself into the car showroom. A light came on inside. Now at least I knew where Terry Fitz had come by his trade plates. And why he seemed to go for seriously expensive motors. Five minutes later, the interior light snapped off and the driver got back into his Merc. I still hadn't had a good enough look at him to attempt identification. We drove back into the town centre. It was quiet; not even the designer clothes shops had attracted late-night browsers. We passed the station and headed out of town. By now, I had a shrewd suspicion where we might be headed.

Prestbury has more millionaires per head of population than any other village in England, according to the media-hype types. The only way you'd guess from hanging round in the main street is from the motors parked outside the deli and the *chocolatier*. They don't have sweetie shops run by Asians in places like Prestbury. They don't have anything that isn't one hundred per cent backed up by centuries of English Conservative tradition. But then, in Prestbury, you don't get the kind of *nouveau* millionaire celebs that give the paparazzi palpitations. We're talking captains of industry, backroom boys and girls, the high rollers whose names mean nothing to anyone outside a very select circle. You can tell it's posh, though. They haven't got pavements or streetlights. After all, who needs them when you go everywhere by car or horse?

About a mile from the centre of the village, the Merc signalled a left turn. I signalled right, then killed my lights and pulled on to the verge. Someone was going to have a major tanturm when they saw my tyre marks in the morning. I jumped out of the car and sprinted towards the gateway he'd entered. I crouched behind the gatepost. The deeply incised letters told me I was outside Hickory Dell, the land that taste forgot. The house was built on the side of a slope, a split-level monstrosity that could have housed half Manchester's homeless and still have had room for a wedding reception. A four-car garage bigger than any house on my estate stood off to one side. One garage door was open, the drive outside it spotlit with high-wattage security lights. I heard the soft slam of a car door, then the heavy-set man emerged. As he swung round to check the door was closing behind him, I got a good look at his face.

I'd seen him before, no question about it. The problem was, I didn't have a clue where or when.

17

I stopped running and took a couple of seconds to work out exactly where I was. I could feel the prickle of sweat under my helmet as I swivelled my head from side to side. I turned sharp right and started running again. As I rounded the next corner, my heart sank. I'd hesitated too long. The tank was heading straight for me, blocking the entire width of the street. Desperately, I turned back, in time to see the helicopter closing off my retreat by dropping a block of what looked remarkably like granite into the street.

Resigned to defeat, I pulled off my helmet and glove. In the next playing area, Davy was still inside his helmet, one hand on the joystick that controlled the tank, the other punching the air triumphantly. I hate kids. They're *always* better at the computer games where hand–eye co-ordination is vital.

I tapped the top of his helmet and undid the straps. Reluctantly, he let go the joystick and

193

climbed out of the seat. 'Time up, cybernaut,' I said. I glanced at my watch. 'They'll be closing soon.' The brand new VIRUS Centre (Virtual Reality UniverSe, I kid you not) had proved to be the best possible way of amusing Davy without doing my head in. It had only opened a month before, and secretly I'd been dying to try out the twenty game scenarios promised in their lavish brochure. I'd been wary about coming on a bank holiday Monday, but it had been surprisingly quiet. I blame the parents. Not that I'm complaining – their absence gave me and Davy a lot more scope for enjoying ourselves.

I suppose I should have felt guilty, indulging myself with swords and sorcery while Richard was still languishing, but he seemed to think that his son's enjoyment was just as important as my attempts to get him released. Besides, Alexis had had to go into the office anyway to do some last-minute work on the child porn exposé that would launch the *Chronicle*'s latest campaign. At least I'd pitched her into trying to find out who lived at Hickory Dell.

We headed back to the car via the souvenir shop. 'Enjoy yourself?' I asked. Pretty redundant question, really.

'It was boss. Top wicked.' I took that to mean approval. 'It was a lot better than Ice World,' he said judiciously. 'Skating gets boring after a while. Your ankles get sore. And the other stuff was pretty boring. You know, all that discovering

194

the South Pole stuff. The models are really naff, and they don't *do* anything. 'S not surprising there was hardly anybody there,' he added, dismissing Alexis's attempts to entertain him.

'Wasn't there?' I asked, more for something to say than out of interest.

'There was *no* queues,' he said indignantly. 'Anything worth doing always has queues.' He looked around the souvenir shop, where we were the only customers. 'Except this place,' he qualified.

How bizarre to be part of a generation where queues are a sign of approval. Me, I'd pay money to avoid standing in line. I'm the driver everyone hates, the one who jumps the queue of standing traffic on the motorway and sneaks in just as the three lanes narrow to two. I nearly said something, but Davy was already delving through a box of transfers.

I left him to his browsing and ambled over to the ego board by the door. It displayed five-inch by three-inch colour photographs of the creators and senior staff of the VIRUS Centre, captioned with their names and executive titles. They all looked interchangeable with the mugshots on the board down the local supermarket. I turned back to check on Davy, and suddenly my subconscious swung into action. No queues at Ice World, coupled with the ego board, had finally woken my memory. The answer had been there all the time, only I'd been too dozy to spot it.

*　　*　　*

When we got back, Alexis was sitting in my conservatory, trying to look like she was engrossed in the evening paper. I knew she was only pretending; Chris gave the game away. 'You were right,' she said to Alexis in a surprised voice. 'It *was* Kate's car. Hello, you two. Have a good day?'

That was all the encouragement Davy needed. He launched into a blow-by-blow account of the VIRUS Centre. Like an angel, Chris steered him off towards the kitchen, seducing him with promises of fish fingers and baked beans. I collapsed on the sofa and groaned. 'Thank God for contraception,' I muttered.

'I don't know what you're going on about,' Alexis said. 'He's good as gold. You want to spend a day looking after my nephew. He's hyperactive and his mother's the kind of divvy who fills him up with E numbers. Any more complaints from you and I won't tell you what I've found out today.'

I closed my eyes and leaned back. 'The occupant of Hickory Dell is Eliot James,' I intoned. 'Boss man at Tonik Leisure Services. Owners of, among other things, Ice World. Which, if what Davy says is right, must be struggling. If you're half-empty on a cold bank holiday Sunday morning, you're not going to weather the recession indefinitely.' I sneaked an eyelid half-open. Alexis's expression moved from fury to disappointment to amusement. Luckily for me, it stopped there.

'Nobody loves a smartass,' she growled. 'OK, clever clogs. So what else have you dug up about

196

Jammy James while you've supposedly been off entertaining me laddo? I mean, I don't know why I bother putting myself out when you just bugger off and do it yourself anyway!'

I sat up and tried to look apologetic. 'I haven't been doing any digging, I promise you. Like I said this morning, I knew I'd seen him before, I just couldn't get a handle on it. Then Davy told me Ice World was as lively as Antarctica on a Saturday night, which set me wondering how these theme parks cover their overheads when the punters haven't got enough money to take the family out on a bank holiday. We were in the souvenir shop, and they've got one of those boards with the flattering photos of the top brass that are meant to make you think this is a really user-friendly operation. I was staring at that, and then I remembered that I'd seen the guy I trailed on one of those ego boards. Add that to the personalized number plate on the car . . .'

'What personalized plate?' Alexis protested. 'You never said anything to me about a personalized plate!'

I gave a guilty smile. 'I . . . ah . . . I forgot to mention that. TON 1K. Sorry. I've got a lot on my mind.'

Alexis shook her head. 'I don't know. It's worse working for you than for my brain-dead newsdesk. So what else have you remembered?'

'That's it,' I promised. 'Have you got anything?'

Alexis pulled a face. 'Bits and pieces. Nothing

really. But I've arranged to meet one of my contacts in half an hour, and he's promised me the full SP on Jammy. Oh, and by the way – Ruth's coming round at nine o'clock for a powwow. And so's Della.'

'What?' I howled.

Alexis shrugged. 'Della rang up after Ruth had arranged to come round. I thought they might as well come together to save us having to go over everything twice.'

'Oh God,' I groaned. 'I don't suppose it occurred to you that I might not want them to know the same things?'

Alexis looked amused. 'Which one were you planning on lying to – the lawyer or the copper?'

I left Davy to Alexis and Chris, and headed for the office to develop the films I'd shot in Carlisle. In the cool silence of the darkroom, I concentrated on the job in hand, forcing myself to switch off from the ins and outs of the case. That way, I hoped, my subconscious would get on with processing the information in peace, and come up with some useful inspirations.

I shoved the finished prints into a folder, and headed downstairs to the Mexican restaurant to fortify myself for another soul-destroying visit to the cells. The place was empty, except for one guy sitting alone at a table towards the rear of the restaurant. He gave me a brief glance as I entered, then returned to the magazine he had propped up beside his bowl of chilli. With a jolt of surprise, I recognized the menacing bouncer from the Lousy Hand. If he was a regular here – and I couldn't see any other reason for frequenting the place on a bank holiday Monday, since the food isn't that great – it explained why he'd seemed familiar at the club. Relieved to have cleared that one up, I settled into a window table with my back to his cold eyes and ordered some guacamole and a plate of frijoles. As I ate, I thought about the evening ahead.

Now I'd calmed down, I was pleased Alexis had fixed up the brainstorming session, because I suspected that the dynamic between the four of us might just spark off some fresh ideas. I was desperate for any insight that might take us a step nearer getting Richard out of jail. The hardest thing about being grown up is realizing there are no magic formulas to release the ones we love from pain. Maybe that's why I enjoy computer games so much; you get to be God.

The girls were ready and waiting when I got back from the nick. Alexis had taken charge in my absence. I found it hard to recognize my living room. A flip chart on an easel had materialized from somewhere, and she'd arranged the chairs so we could all see it. She'd also found my cache of Australian Chardonnay and distributed glasses to the other two. I mumbled that I'd stick with the vodka and disappeared into the kitchen to fix myself a lemon Absolut with freshly squeezed pink grapefruit juice. By the time I got back, Alexis was copying some complicated tree structure from her notebook on to the flip chart. Ruth and Della looked as bemused as I felt.

'Alexis, I don't want to be difficult, but . . .'

'Chris is putting Davy to bed, so you don't have to worry about him butting in, if that's what's bugging you,' she said, not even pausing.

'It wasn't, actually. I just wondered what you were doing.'

'I need the diagram to explain about Jammy's empire,' Alexis said in the condescending tones I use to small children and she uses to news editors.

'Maybe Kate could bring us up to date,' Ruth said. 'Then perhaps we'd all have a clue what you're up to, Alexis.' Ever the diplomat.

It took a disturbingly short time to fill everyone in on my weekend activities. 'I waited till James went into the house, then I came home,' I finished up. 'Oh, and I've developed and printed up the films I shot in Carlisle.'

There was a slight pause. I could see Alexis gathering herself together to leap into the breach when Ruth said, 'I'm impressed, Kate. When you told me how little we had to go on, I thought we had as much chance of establishing the identity of the real criminals as I have of becoming Lord Chief Justice.'

'You're right, Kate's done an impressive job, but the Drugs Squad are going to have mixed feelings about it,' Della said ruefully. 'They've been chasing this crack epidemic for some time now, and while there are senior officers who are going to be bloody glad to get a solid handle on it, a lot of people are going to be very pissed off at being shown up by a private eye. And a woman private eye at that.'

'Tell me about it,' I sighed.

'And then there's the question of the accused,' Della went on. 'I've only been in Manchester a matter of months, but that's long enough to know that Eliot James is a name that means money, power and influence.'

Alexis finally managed to get a word in. She jumped to her feet. 'And that's where I come in,' she announced. 'I've been doing some digging into Mr Eliot James.' She picked up her marker pen and attacked the flip chart. For a full fifteen minutes she blinded us with science, taking us on a whirl-wind tour of Jammy James's leisure and property empire, his constant efforts to muscle in on the Olympic bid consortium, the parlous state of his marriage and the debts, loans and mortgages that, added together, put him in what building societies euphemistically call a negative equity situation.

'It's like Maxwell,' she concluded with a flourish. 'On the surface, it looks like everything's hunky-dory. But underneath, there's this huge iceberg of debt ready to smash into Jammy's hull and turn Tonik into the Titanic.'

'She's got a way with words, that girl,' I said. 'Ever thought of becoming a writer, Alexis?'

Della was shaking her head in amazement. 'I think I'll just go and shoot myself now,' she said. 'This has been a bad evening for the police. First, Kate does the Drugs Squad's job. And now you do my job. From what you've said, it looks very like our Mr James is trading while insolvent, so we're looking at one criminal offence at least. I think when the boys from the DS have finished with him, I'll be wanting a word.'

Ruth, who had been unusually quiet, said, 'It certainly explains why he needs the kind of cash injection that the drugs trade can bring. It does, however, give me a slight problem.'

'You're not his brief, are you?' I asked, the cold hand of panic squeezing my chest.

'Thankfully, no,' Ruth said. 'But he does play golf with Peter. My husband,' she added for Della's benefit. Peter hadn't been at Mortensen and Branningan's Christmas party, where the two women had first met. 'And he's supposed to be coming to dinner on Saturday.'

'Who with?' Alexis demanded cheekily. 'The wife or the mistress? Both, incidentally, called Sue. I suppose that way he doesn't run the risk of using the wrong name in bed.'

'Ignore her; it's gone to her head, getting something right for once,' I said.

'Yo, wait till I break this little gem in tomorrow's paper!' Alexis exclaimed.

'No way!' Ruth shouted.

'Don't you *dare*!' Della thundered in unison. 'We

want Jammy James nailed down watertight, not leaping up and down about trial by media.'

'Never mind that,' I butted in. 'Personally, I don't give a toss about nailing Jammy James. This is about getting Richard out of jail. And you printing daft stories in the *Chronicle* is not the way to do that, so forget it, Alexis, OK? What comes next, Ruth?'

Ruth spoke slowly, measuring what she said as she spoke. 'Kate's right, Alexis. I know this must be burning a hole in your notebook, but I think it would be disastrous for Richard if you wrote a story about this.'

Alexis pulled a face. 'All right,' she sighed. 'But when I *can* write about it, I want all of you to talk to me on the record.'

We all nodded wearily. 'Ruth?' I asked.

'Kate, you're going to have to talk to the police. You're also going to have to persuade them to move quickly; the sooner the better from Richard's point of view.'

Della interrupted. 'On that point, they'll already be anxious about how current your information is. These days, most drug dealers alter their distribution patterns every few weeks. Eliot James's team might not be doing that, but as far as the Drugs Squad is concerned, stress that this is up-to-the-minute info and the situation could change any day. There is one significant gap in your evidence, however, which might make them cautious.'

'What's that? Something I've got time to fix?' I

asked anxiously. I'd been right to decide I needed other people's eyes on this case.

Della pulled a face. 'It's not exactly a matter of time. It's a matter of legality. We don't know what's inside this shed out at the airport. If it's just an empty shell, it's not going to be easy to establish a direct connection between James and Fitzgerald. A good brief would argue that James had gone there for reasons entirely unconnected with the drug trade; he could even postulate a hypothetical third party that they were both there to meet.'

I nodded, grateful for the advice. 'Supposing I had that information, how quickly is quickly, in Drugs Squad terms?'

Della shrugged. 'I don't know this lot well, but given your info they should be able to plug straight into the surveillance. If this team is as busy as your material suggests, they could have the bare bones of their evidence within twenty-four to forty-eight hours.'

'Which means what, in terms of Richard's imprisonment?' I asked Ruth.

She bought time by lighting a cigarette. 'Best case, you talk to the Drugs Squad first thing and they stand up in court and support my bail application. Chances of that: almost nil. Worse case, they use your information, make a bundle of arrests and refuse to accept Richard was an innocent bystander. Chances of that: probably low. Most likely scenario, if you get to the Drugs Squad tomorrow, when I argue for bail on Wednesday, it will be refused but the magistrates will agree to a short remand, say till Thursday or Friday; to give the police the chance to evaluate the fresh evidence.'

My disappointment must have been obvious, for Alexis hugged me and Ruth shrugged apologetically. 'Well, we'd better get you fixed up with an appointment to see the Drugs Squad, hadn't we?' Della said briskly. 'Where's the phone?'

I pointed it out, and she wandered into the conservatory to make her call. I watched her through the patio doors. Her face was animated, her free hand expressive. Whatever she was saying, she wasn't pleading. As she ended the call, I remembered something else I wanted to talk to the Drugs Squad about. I turned to Alexis. 'Do you know if Cherie Roberts has been around today? Or if she's left me a note?'

Alexis shook her head. 'Not that I know of. Chris didn't say anything.'

Typical, I thought. Just as well I wasn't relying on Cherie to help get Richard out of jail.

18

It was midnight before I got the house to myself. Much as I enjoy their company, I couldn't wait for the three of them to go home. Ironically, they probably thought they were doing me a favour, keeping me from brooding over Richard's absence. And of course, I couldn't explain why I wanted rid of them, not with two of them being officers of the court. My impatience wasn't helped by the fact that I'd stopped drinking after my first vodka; if discovering what the shed contained was the key to releasing Richard, then I was going to have to get inside there. Preferably before my nine o'clock appointment with DCI Geoff Turnbull of the Drugs Squad.

I went through to my bedroom and changed into the black leggings and black sweat shirt I save for the sort of occasion when nobody I want to impress is likely to see me; illicit night forays, decorating, that sort of thing. I didn't have any black trainers, but I did have a pair of black canvas hockey boots which I'd bought in a moment of madness years before when they'd briefly looked set to be the next essential fashion item. I'd been a first-year student at the time, which is as good an excuse as any. I stuffed my hair inside a black ski cap, and I was all set. I know the Famous Five burned corks and rubbed their faces with the ash, but I couldn't bring myself to do anything that ridiculous. Besides, I had to drive right across town to get to the airport, and I didn't rate my chances of convincing any passing traffic cop that I was on my way to a Hallowe'en party.

On my way out the door, I stopped in my study and picked up one of those compartmentalized mini-aprons that tradesmen stuff with obscure tools. Mine contains a set of lock picks, a glass cutter, a kid's arrow with a sucker on the end, a couple of pairs of latex gloves, a Swiss Army knife, a small camera with a spare film, pliers, a high-powered pencil torch, a set of jeweller's screwdrivers, a couple of ordinary screwdrivers, a cold chisel, secateurs and a toffee hammer. Don't ask. Before I set off, I filled up a mini jug kettle that runs off the car cigarette lighter. Like I said, don't ask.

Less than half an hour later, I was cruising down the country lane I'd been in the night before. I pulled up in the same gateway and plugged in the kettle. As the water boiled, I lifted the lid and let the car fill up with steam. I got out and looked at the windows, satisfied. Anyone passing would be more likely to be jealous than suspicious.

I set off, hugging the infested hedgerows, just in case. I eased round the corner of the track, and saw with relief that there were no cars parked outside the shed. I crept slowly round the edge of the clearing till I was parallel to the big front doors. A quick look around, then I slipped across into the shadow of the shed. I took out my torch and shone it on the lower of the two padlocks. My heart sank. Some locks you can pick after ten minutes' training. Some locks give experts migraine. This wasn't one of the easy ones. I wished I'd brought Dennis with me. I gave it twenty minutes, by which time my hands were sweating so much inside the latex gloves that I couldn't manipulate the picks properly. In frustration, I kicked the door. It didn't swing open. I just got a very sore foot.

I shone the torch on the other padlock, but it was another of the same. The steel bars didn't look too promising either. Muttering the kind of words my mother warned me against, I skirted the corner of the shed and worked my way down the far side. Although it didn't look much, it was actually a deceptively solid building. I'd have expected to find the odd loose board, perhaps even a broken window. But this shed looked like it had been given a good going over by the local crime prevention officer. There was one window on the airport side, but it was barred, and behind it was opaque, wire-reinforced glass. I reached the far corner, but I couldn't get down the back of the shed at all because of the insidious creeping of the undergrowth. Frankly, I doubt if Mickey Mouse could have squeezed through that lot. With a sigh, I turned back. No chance. That was when the spotlight pinned me to the wall.

At least, that's what I thought at first. I froze like a dancer in a strobe, not even daring to blink. Then, as the light swept over me and my brain clocked on, I realized it was only the cyclops headlight of a tow truck from the cargo area. I threw myself to the ground and wriggled back to the front of the shed. Not a moment too soon. As I reached the doors, a battery of floodlights snapped on, bathing an area fifty yards away with harsh bleaching light. A truck was towing a train of boxes from one cargo holding area to another. This wasn't the time or place for burglary, I decided.

I inched backwards on my stomach towards the short drive leading to the road. And that's when I spotted the skylight. Gleaming in the blackness of the roof, it reflected the lights like a mirror. Even though it was a good twelve feet above the ground, the really exciting thing about it was the two-inch gap at the bottom. I gauged the distances involved, and saw there was a way inside the shed.

Getting out again was going to be the problem, I realized as I hung from the edge of the skylight, torch between my teeth. I tried to direct the beam downwards, to see what I was going to land on when I let go. I saw what looked like a chemistry lab constructed by a bag lady. If I dropped from here, I was going to end up either impaled on a bunsen burner or shredded by the shards of a thousand test tubes. That probably explained why the skylight on the blind side of the roof was open.. Even with fume hoods, cooking up designer drugs is a disgustingly smelly occupation. The chemists doubtless decided the need for fresh air was greater than the security benefit of being hermetically sealed. At least having a factory out in the middle of nowhere meant there weren't any neighbours to complain about the pong.

With a groan, I flexed my complaining shoulder muscles and hauled myself back up and out again. I sat on the edge of the skylight and stared into the night. I'd only let myself over the edge in the first place because my torch hadn't been powerful enough to reveal the contents of the shed. And if the torch wasn't, the flash probably wouldn't be either. I had to come up with another idea, and quickly. I'd already had to wait an hour for the cargo area to go dark again, and I didn't know how long it would be before they took it into their heads to shuffle the packing crates again.

I could come up with only one possibility. Sighing, I eased myself off the skylight until my feet were in the guttering. Spread-eagled against the roof, I edged along until I came to the end of the roof. Slowly, cautiously, I slid down the corrugated asbestos until I was crouching, most of my weight on the guttering. I gripped the edge and half rolled off the roof, stretching my legs downwards as far as they would go. Then, thanking God for all the Thai boxing training I'd done, I gradually let myself down. I couldn't feel the roof of the Peugeot under my toes. I'd just have to pray I was in the right place. I released my handholds.

The drop was only a few inches, but it seemed to last minutes. Gasping for the breath I'd been holding, I slithered down the hatch back on to blessedly solid ground and opened the boot. I lifted the carpet, and there, tucked into the spare wheel, was the answer to my prayers. I grabbed the tow rope, coiled it round me like a mountaineer, gently closed the hatch and clambered back up the car and on to the roof.

I fixed the rope to a downpipe that was conveniently near the skylight and dropped it through the hole. I bit on the torch again and slowly started the precarious descent. Needless to say, the tow rope wasn't long enough to take me all the way to the floor, but it left an easy drop of a couple of feet, and I'd be able to reach it again if I moved a lab stool under it.

Getting in was the hard part. Doing the business with the camera was easy. I just started by the doors and worked my way through the shed, photographing the battered equipment, the jars of chemicals, the lists of instructions taped to the walls above the benches, and the plastic bags of white crystalline powder that made my gums numb. I don't know a lot about the drug world, but it looked to me as if there was much, much more than a bit of crack coming out of Jammy James's kitchen.

What there wasn't was paperwork. No filing cabinets, no safe, nothing. Wherever Jammy James kept his records, it wasn't here. I decided I paid enough in taxes. I'd done most of the work; it was time the Drugs Squad did their bit.

Wearily, I shifted a lab stool under the rope and climbed on top of it. My shoulder muscles were threatening to phone the cruelty man as I dragged myself up the rope and over the sill. I carefully lowered the skylight, restoring it to its previous position, give or take a millimetre or two. Then I untied the rope, did my crab imitation along the roof again. This time, the transfer of weight from feet to arms didn't go quite so smoothly; my shoulders were too tired for a gradual lowering, and my arms jerked uncomfortably in their sockets, making me let go sooner than I should have. I wondered how I was going to explain the depression in the roof to the car-leasing company.

My body wanted to get into bed as soon as possible, but my head was singing a different song. I had two films from the shed that needed developing. It would help my case if I could show the prints to Turnbull. The devil on my shoulder told me to go home and crash out for a few hours, then go into the office early to develop my films. But I knew myself well enough to know what my reaction would be when the alarm shattered my sleep at seven. And it wouldn't be to leap out of bed bright-eyed and bushy-tailed, ready to rush to the office and fill my lungs with the noxious fumes of photographic chemicals. With a groan, I shoved *The Best of Blondie* into the cassette player and opened the window all the way. If cold air and Debby Harry's frantic vocals couldn't keep me awake, nothing would.

I managed nearly four hours' sleep. Never mind what Richard owed me in fees; he owed me more sleep than I'd ever catch up on. For once, it wasn't Davy who woke me. It was Chris. She stuck her head round the bedroom door, followed by a hand waving a mug of coffee like a white flag. 'Come in,' I grumbled. 'Time is it?' I would have rolled over to look at the clock, but I couldn't find the energy.

'It's quarter past eight,' she said apologetically, sliding round the door and holding out the mug at arm's length. Alexis had obviously warned her I'm not at my sparkling best first thing.

'Shit!' I growled, as I leaped upright. Or rather, tried to. As soon as I moved, my shoulders went into spasm, and I let out a muffled screech of pain. I managed to shuffle up the bed enough to drink without a straw and seized the mug gratefully. 'Sorry I yelled. I'm in pain, and I've got to be at Bootle Street nick first thing with my brain firing on all four cylinders. So far, it's not looking good.'

Chris tried a smile that turned into a *Spitting Image* grimace. 'I just thought I'd better tell you that I'm off to work now,' she said. Belatedly, I noticed she was suited up, her hair dried and sprayed into the kind of neatly sculpted shape that Frank Lloyd Wright would have turned into an art gallery. 'Davy's had a shower and breakfast, and he's dressed and sitting in front of breakfast telly, which should keep him quiet for approximately twelve minutes, which is when the next news bulletin is due.'

'Has Alexis left?' Pointless question. Alexis is invariably at work by seven.

''Fraid so,' Chris apologized. 'She said she expected to be finished by three, and that you should ring her at the office if you wanted her to pick up Davy later. I'm really sorry we can't help out today.'

'Don't be,' I said. The power of speech seemed to have returned with the second mouthful of coffee. 'You two have done more than enough. Richard owes you.'

Chris smiled, a genuine one this time. 'I know you'll find it hard to believe, but we've enjoyed ourselves. I live with Alexis, don't forget, so I'm used to dealing with the demands of small children, and she loves having someone to play with.'

'You're not getting broody, are you?' I asked suspiciously. It's bad enough that all my straight friends seem to be hellbent on repopulating the world without the lesbians joining in.

'Building a house is more than enough to be going on with,' Chris replied as she headed out the door. In the hall she turned back and gave me a mischievous smile. 'Ask me again in a couple of years.'

If my neck hadn't seized up, I'd have turned my face to the wall. As it was, I gulped the rest of the brew and slowly, excruciatingly, dragged my body out of bed and into an upright position. I walked to the bathroom stiff as a guardsman. Unfortunately, I'd slept too late to have a bath so had to settle for a shower. I tried to relax as the hot water did the business, but I'd only been under for a couple of minutes when I heard Davy's voice outside the door.

'Kate?' he shouted. 'Can I play with your computer?'

'Not here, Davy. I've got to go to work in a minute, so I thought maybe you'd like to play on my machine in the office.' I spluttered.

Silence. That was more unnerving than anything he could have said. I switched off the shower, wrapped myself in a bath sheet and opened the door. He leaned against the wall, looking dejected. My breath stuck in my chest. The line of his body, the angle of his head, the slight frown was so like his father it hurt. He looked up through his long lashes at the sound of the door opening. 'When's my dad coming home?' he asked plaintively.

I managed to get my lungs working again. 'Not for a couple of days, I don't think. I spoke to him on the phone last night, after you'd gone to sleep. He said he misses you too and he'll get back as soon as he can get a plane. I'm sorry, I know I'm not a lot of fun.' I hugged him. Surprisingly, he didn't pull a face and draw away. He hugged back.

'It's not that,' he said. 'I'm having great fun. I just wish he was here too.'

You and me both, pal, I thought but didn't say.

I broke my personal land speed record getting out the door that morning. Dressed in under five minutes, second cup of coffee down the neck in less than a minute, breakfast one of the Pop Tarts I'd bought for Davy. It tasted like sugar-coated polystyrene, but at least it raised the blood sugar level. By the time I parked on the single yellow line round the corner from the office, I was almost functioning.

I hustled Davy up the stairs and into my office, checking the clock as I walked through the door. Seventeen minutes till deadline. Shelley was already at her desk, earphones in, fingers flying over the keyboard. I strode past her with a little wave, shooing Davy into my office. I switched on my PC, showed him the games directory and made him promise not to interfere with any of the other files on the machine. He dumped his backpack by the desk and was absorbed in Lemmings 2 before I'd had time to walk back out. I closed my office door behind me and perched on Shelley's desk, nailing what I hoped was a pathetic and appealing smile on my face.

'No, Kate.' She hadn't even looked up from her

screen. 'I am *not* a child-minder and this is an office, not a crèche.'

'I know it's not a crèche. A crèche is what happens when two BMWs collide in Sloane Street.'

'Not funny,' she retorted, not pausing long enough to let her sense of humour kick in.

'Please, Shelley. He'll be no trouble. Just for this morning. Just till I can get back from court. I promise I'll sort something else out for tomorrow.'

'There's no such thing as an eight-year-old boy who's no trouble. I'm a mother, don't forget. I've told the same lies you're telling now.'

'Shelley, please? I have a meeting with the Drugs Squad in ten minutes. Richard's freedom depends on it. I don't think they're going to be mega-impressed if I turn up with Davy in tow.' I was practically begging. I'd done so much of it lately it was beginning to become second nature. Another bad habit to lay at Richard's door. What's worse is that it doesn't work.

I got up from the desk and went into Bill's office, where I helped myself to his portable TV, a gift from a grateful client who had Mortensen and Brannigan to thank for the ending of his little software piracy problem. I marched through the outer office, wrestled with the door handle and staggered into my office, where I put it down on one of my cupboards. 'There's the TV, in case you get fed up with the computer,' I said to Davy. I can't swear to it, but I don't think he even looked up.

I stalked back into the office and gestured over

my shoulder with my thumb. 'Look at that. You're telling me that's more than you can cope with? God, Shelley, am I disappointed in you.'

When all else fails, go for the ego. The only trouble is, sometimes the ego bites back. Shelley smiled like Jaws and said sweetly, 'Just this once, Kate. And by the way, Andrew Broderick's been on again. He says if he doesn't get his car back soon he's going to have to come to some arrangement about reducing our fee.'

There's nothing like keeping the customer satisfied. I checked the fax machine on the way out, but nothing had arrived from Julia. I hoped that didn't mean it was going to be one of those days. Not when the next item on the agenda was a close encounter with the Drugs Squad.

19

Q: What's the difference between a schneid watch and a policeman? A: Schneid watches keep good time. By the time DCI Geoff Turnbull deigned to fit me into his busy schedule, I'd worn a furrow in the floor tiles of the front office. I was getting more wound up than an eight-day clock.

When he finally appeared, it took all my self-control not to bite his head off. Instead, I smiled sweetly and meekly followed him through the pass door into the real world of the city centre nick. We stopped outside a door that said DRUGS SQUAD – PRIVATE. I thought at first that was a joke, till I saw Turnbull pull out a key to unlock the door. He noticed me noticing and said, 'You can't be too careful, the stuff we have in here. These days, we've got more civilian support staff than we have coppers, and some of them have got more loyalty to their bank balances than they have to The Job.'

How to win friends and influence people, I

thought as I smiled what I hoped would pass for agreement and approval. I followed him into an overcrowded office, crammed with desks, VDUs, bulging files, and not an officer in sight. The walls were lavishly adorned with colour photographs of villains. By the look of the pics, most of them were snatched, like mine. If anything, mine were sharper. Maybe Turnbull would be so impressed with my work that he'd offer me a job as a police photographer.

Turnbull's personal office was partitioned off in one corner. He'd managed to bag the only window, not much of a deal since it looked out on a brick wall all of five feet away. He squeezed his rugby player's frame behind the loaded desk and gave me the hard stare with small sharp blue eyes. He couldn't have looked less like my idea of a Drugs Squad officer. I'd expected an emaciated hippy lookalike with a distressed leather jacket and a pair of jeans. Either that or a flash bastard dripping with personal jewellery who could pass for a major dealer. But Turnbull looked like the only drug you'd suspect him of using was anabolic steroids. He lived up to his name: short curly hair with a forelock like a Charolais, the no-neck and shoulders to match, with the gut of a man whose stomach muscles have given up the unequal struggle with Boddingtons Bitter. I put him in his late thirties, well along the road to the coronary unit.

He rubbed a beefy hand over his jaw, massaging plump flesh. 'So, you're Miss Kate Brannigan,' he said consideringly. He managed to make the 'Miss' sound like an obscenity. 'Not much of you, is there?'

I shrugged. 'Enough to do the job. I don't get many complaints.'

He leered automatically. 'I bet you don't.'

I raised my eyebrows and gave him the bored look. 'DCI Prentice told me you were the person to talk to. I've got some information for you on one of your cases. Richard Barclay?'

'Oh aye,' he said, his Yorkshire accent deliberately exaggerated. 'The boyfriend.' He picked up his phone and dialled an internal number. 'Tommo? Any time you like.' He replaced the receiver and shook his head. 'I suppose you expect me to believe your fella's been fitted up? Well, you're in for a disappointment. It wasn't Drugs Squad officers that picked him up, it was Traffic, and even if they wanted to plant drugs on him, they wouldn't have access to anything like those amounts. So you're barking up the wrong tree there.'

'I don't think he's been fitted up,' I said patiently. 'But the drugs in the car were nothing to do with Richard, and the sooner you realize that, the lower the compo's going to be for the wrongful arrest.'

Turnbull guffawed. 'Was that a threat creeping out of the woodwork? By heck, Miss Brannigan, you like living dangerously.'

Before I could reply, a doorbell sounded. Turnbull leaned back and pressed a button on the wall behind him. I heard the door of the main room open behind me. I resisted the temptation to turn around and see who owned the heavy feet crossing the floor towards me.

Somehow, I wasn't too surprised when the custody sergeant from Longsight walked into Turnbull's office. 'That her?' Turnbull asked.

The sergeant nodded. 'No question about it, sir. That's the woman who purported to be Miss Hunter's assistant the other night. She claimed her name was Kate Robinson.'

'Thank you, Sergeant. I'll talk to you later.'

'Sir,' the sergeant said.

We both held our peace as the feet retreated back across the Drugs Squad office. Turnbull stared at me, a triumphant little smile on his cupid's-bow lips. I kept my eyes on his, determined not to show any weakness. As the door closed behind the custody sergeant, Turnbull said scathingly, 'It's not just you amateurs that can make deductions. I've been wanting to talk to you, Miss Brannigan. DCI Prentice's phone call just made it a bit easier for me to get you in here without a brief hanging on our every word. Especially since your brief's left herself wide open to charges of unprofessional conduct. I'm sure the Law Society would be fascinated to hear about her interpretation of professional ethics. And now we both know there's at least one offence I can hang on to you for, mebbe we can cut the crap and get down to the business.'

I said nothing. When his bluster ran out, he was

going to have to charge me or let me go. Either way he was going to have to listen to what I had to tell him. And I felt sure that his threats against Ruth were emptier than a dosser's bottle. The last thing coppers like him want to do is to antagonize the tightly knit club of criminal solicitors. Turnbull carried on staring at me and started drumming his fingers on the desk. Then he opened his desk drawer and took out a packet of cigars. When I rule the world, the European Court of Human Rights is going to outlaw the obtaining of confessions under cigar- and pipe-smoke torture.

He lit his panatella, the only slim thing about him, and said, 'Soon as I heard the story behind this car, soon as I heard that technically it was your responsibility, I wanted to talk to you. I mean, what better cover for a drug dealer's wheels than supposedly investigating some daft car-finance scam? Count yourself lucky you didn't spend the weekend in the CDC like your boyfriend.'

I shook my head. Clearly, I wasn't going to get anywhere being sweetness and light. Time for no more Ms Nice Guy. 'I don't believe I'm hearing this,' I snarled. 'I come along here with enough information to close down a major drug ring and hand you a bloody great score sheet of arrests, and you treat me like *I'm* the criminal? Jesus, it's no wonder you lot are always whingeing you don't get support from the public. If you threaten to arrest everybody that tries to give you a tip-off, it's a bloody miracle anybody tells you what day it is.'

He leaned forward and sneered. I bet he wouldn't have if he could have seen how badly his teeth needed a scale and polish. I was surprised his breath didn't strip them down to the bare enamel on a daily basis. 'You were supposed to be the bloody lawyer the other night. I shouldn't have to tell you that it's an offence to withhold information about a criminal offence. So cough, Miss Brannigan, or I'll have you banged up so fast your head'll spin.'

I stood up and leaned on Turnbull's desk. I was getting good and tired of being jerked around by the legal system. 'Listen, Turnbull,' I said coldly. 'You threaten me once more and I walk out that door and you don't get another word out of me till you've formally arrested me, cautioned me and allowed me to talk to my solicitor. I might not be a qualified lawyer, but I'd be willing to bet I'd score more points than you on a PACE quiz. Now, are we going to talk like grown-ups, or are we going to carry on playing silly boys' games?'

'Let's be clear about one thing,' he said, still not willing to let the macho bravado slip. 'I'm not doing any deals with you. None of this "I show you mine and you let my boyfriend go" routine. As far as I'm concerned, Mr Richard Barclay's in this up to his fancy tortoiseshell specs.'

I raised my eyes to the ceiling and sighed. 'I just love a man with an open mind. Mr Turnbull, by the time you've heard me out, you'll be dying to release Richard, because if you don't, you're going to look like dickhead of the year after the papers have finished with you. And that's *not* a threat, it's my considered opinion.'

'Sit down,' he growled. 'Let's hear what you've got to say.'

Ignoring his order, I leaned against the wall. I took my miniature tape recorder out of my bag and pressed the 'record' button. 'Since you don't seem inclined to tape our little chat, I'll do it for you,' I said. 'It'll save me having to come back later and make a statement. I know all your instincts tell you not to believe a word that anybody in custody says, but in this instance, you really should have listened. That's all I did. The only clue in Richard's story, as far as I could see, was the business with the trade plates. So I did what any good copper should do: I followed my instincts.' Turnbull looked like he wanted to throttle me, but the part of him that had taken him to the rank of DCI was obviously dying to know what I'd dug up, and right now his curiosity was stronger than his belligerence.

I took him through it from start to finish, omitting only the details of how I came by the photographs of the inside of Jammy James's kitchen. 'Careless of them, leaving the door unlocked, but then, you just can't get the help these days,' I finished up, taking the pics out of my bag and spreading them in a fan across Turnbull's desk.

He poked at the pics with the end of a Biro, as if they'd soil his fingers. Then he shook his head. 'You expect me to believe this taradiddle?' he asked scornfully. 'Eliot James? As in, Eliot James who plays golf with the Chief Constable? Eliot James who runs charity schemes for under-privileged kids at his leisure centres? *That* Eliot James?'

'The same,' I said. 'Having friends in high places doesn't stop you being a crook. Look at the Guinness trials. And if doing charity work was a guarantee of staying out of jail, the Krays would still be running London. Look, James is hanging on to his business empire by his fingernails. Check it out. Go down Ice World, The Dinosaur Adventure, Laser Land, or any of his leisure complexes. They're all empty. His cash flow doesn't. The only reason DCI Prentice isn't running a full-scale fraud inquiry into the sleazeball is that she thinks the drugs angle deserves the first bite of the cherry. But if you're not interested, I know she'll be after James like a greyhound out of a trap.'

Turnbull leaned back in his chair. The legs sounded like an avant-garde string quartet. 'It's funny, isn't it, how you've managed to find all this out so easily when we've been trying to get something on this mob for ages?' he specu-lated. 'If I was a suspicious man, I might think it was because you and your boyfriend were in it up to your eyeballs, and you decided to shop the rest of the team to try and get him off the hook. You wouldn't be the first private dick caught out by the recession who decided to turn their limited knowledge of crime on its head.'

The only thing that stopped me being arrested for assaulting a police officer was the realization that I'd be as much use to Richard as a chocolate fireguard if I ended up behind bars too. So I smiled sweetly at the insult. 'If I was going to turn to crime, Mr Turnbull, I wouldn't have to leave the house. Computer crime. That's where the real, no-risk money is these days. And I've forgotten more about computers than you'll ever know. Look, I'm not asking you for a major favour. I haven't once said, I'll tell you what I know in return for you letting Richard walk away from all of this. I'm handing you all this on a plate, and all I'm asking is that you don't oppose Ruth Hunter's request for a short remand so you can start to test the value of what I've given you.'

'And that's all, is it?' he asked, utter disbelief riddling his voice like a virus in a computer.

'Pretty much, yeah. You see, Mr Turnbull, in spite of your performance this morning, I happen to think you're an honest copper. I don't think you want innocent men put away just to make your clean-up rate look better. And I know the strength of what I've given you. I think after forty-eight hours you'll have the same gut feeling I've got about Richard's innocence, and I don't think you'll be opposing bail then. But I'm not asking for any promises.'

'Just as bloody well,' he grumbled, 'for you'd not

be getting any.' He stared down at the photographs on his desk, slowly sifting through them, assessing what he was seeing with the eyes of an expert. Turnbull eventually looked up. 'So, what has Ruth Hunter told you to ask for?'

'I want you to call the Crown Prosecution solicitor and ask that they don't oppose Ruth's request for a short remand.'

'That it?'

'That's it. Now, are you going to give me something back, or am I going to develop profound amnesia about the events of the last three days?'

He grinned. 'You know, for a girl, you're not short on bottle. OK, I'll do it. I can't say fairer than that, now can I?'

'That's fine,' I said. 'You won't mind if I hang on while you make the call?'

This time he laughed delightedly, his hand making a half-hearted gesture that, if I'd been a bloke, would have turned into a clout on the back that would have brought my breakfast back. 'You're not a Yorkshire lass by any chance, are you? No? Pity.'

I waited while he did as I'd demanded. He was no more charming to the Crown Prosecution Service's solicitor than he'd been to me, but he seemed to achieve the right result. On my way out of the door, I said, 'By the way – Mr Broderick wants to know when you're going to release his very expensive motor from your compound.'

Turnbull snorted. I almost expected him to paw the ground. 'He's been on to you as well, has he? You tell your Mr Broderick that he can have his poncey set of wheels back when I'm good and satisfied that it's going to yield up no more clues to me. And that could be after your boyfriend's trial. Now, bugger off and let me get on. Oh, and leave me that tape, will you? Like you said, it'll save me having to keep you here all day making a statement.'

I handed the tape over with a grim little smile. 'One other thing,' I said. 'Nothing to do with Richard. You know those transfers that kids use – temporary tattoos, that sort of thing?'

Turnbull nodded. 'I've got a seven-year-old that gets in the bath looking like a merchant seaman. What about them?'

'Ever heard of them being impregnated with drugs and used to get kids high?'

Turnbull pulled a face. 'I've heard rumours, but I've never actually come across a case. It's one of them urban legends, isn't it? It always happens to a friend of a friend's cousin's dog. Crap, as far as I'm concerned. If I was wanting to get kids stoned, I'd just stick something in sweets or fizzy drinks. Helluva lot easier. Why d'you ask?'

'Like you said, urban legend. A friend of a friend's cousin's dog asked a doctor I know about it. She said the same as you.' I got to my feet. 'Sorry to have troubled you. Thanks. For phoning.' And

I was gone, quitting while I was still ahead. Let's face it. Telling Geoff Turnbull about Davy's brush with the hallucinogens wasn't the way to get his daddy out of jail.

20

I walked back through the office door on the stroke of twelve. The door to my office was closed. I raised my eyebrows in a question at Shelley. She pursed her lips and said, 'I had to shut the door in case any clients walked in.'

Curious, I opened my door a couple of feet and stuck my head round. I saw instantly what she meant. Davy was still intent on the computer, but now Bill was sitting next to him, clutching his own joystick. Neither of them looked up at the sound of the door. I cleared my throat. Bill glanced up. As soon as he realized it wasn't Shelley with some troublesome business query, I could see his attention leave the game and focus sharply on me. He got up, saying, 'I've got to go and talk to Kate, Davy. Thanks for the game.'

Davy didn't even look up as he said, 'But Bill, you've got one more life!'

'Well, since you've still got four, I guess I'll have to concede. You win,' Bill said, pretending to be petulant about it.

In the glow of the screen, Davy grinned, his body shifting strangely in the chair as he controlled whatever it was that was currently conquering the universe. Bill steered me out of the room and through into his office. 'He's a nice kid,' Bill said. 'No bother.' I was beginning to wonder if there was something wrong with me. Was I the only person on the planet who liked to live in a child-free zone?

Bill sat down and stretched his long legs in front of him. 'So, how did it go?'

I filled him in on the weekend's events. Maybe I should just ring Richard Branson and ask him to release it on CD. It would save me a lot of time. Then I ran through my interview with Geoff Turnbull.

'You think he really will keep an open mind about Richard?' Bill asked.

'I doubt it. I think the only chance he's got is for Turnbull to make a lot of arrests. When he realizes none of them even know Richard's name, he's going to have to unclamp his jaws from off Barclay's leg.'

'But he did go along with the short remand request?'

'Sure, but that's no skin off his nose, is it?' My early jubilation at getting Turnbull to look properly at my evidence had evaporated. I wondered fleetingly how the families of the Guildford Four and the Birmingham Six had put up with this dislocating ordeal for the years it had taken them to have their loved ones released. I took a deep breath. 'And now,' I said, 'I want to ask you a favour.'

'Ask away,' he said. 'Hacking? Bugging? Your wish is my command.'

'None of the above. It's just that I've had enough aggro for one day. Will you phone Andrew Broderick and tell him what Turnbull said about the car? It's hard enough keeping my head together without having to deal with someone else's disappointments.'

Bill jumped up and engulfed me in a bear hug, his thick blond beard tickling my ear. 'Poor old Katy,' he said softly. 'It's not always easy, being as tough as old boots, is it?'

I let myself be held, wallowing in the illusion of security. There's something very solid about Bill. I felt like I was being given a tranquillity transfusion. After a few minutes, I drew back, standing on tiptoe to kiss his beard. 'Thanks,' I said. 'Now, I'm going to take Davy for a swim and a pizza, and then the pair of us are going to get a pile of videos and completely indulge ourselves.'

'You deserve it,' Bill said. 'You've done a helluva job, considering you started with virtually nothing to go at. Richard's a lucky guy.'

'What do you mean, lucky? When he sees our bill, he'll be wishing he was back inside,' I said. 'See you in the morning, Bill. Unless you want to come round and play computer games with Davy tonight?'

'I'll pass,' he said. 'I've got some rather different games in mind for tonight. Abstinence makes the heart grow fonder, you know.' Somehow, I found it hard to believe the heart was the organ in question. I wondered who the lucky woman was this week. One day, he's going to meet one with fancier footwork than him, and that'll be a battle worth seeing. Till then, he's working his way through the intelligent female population of the north of England. He once told me he's never been to bed with a woman yet who didn't teach him something. I don't *think* he was talking about sex.

There were only a couple of dozen people in the fun pool at Gorton, so Davy and I made the most of the slides and the waves, treating the place as our personal pleasure dome. Although my shoulders screamed in complaint at first, the water therapy seemed to help. Afterwards, both ravenous, we scoffed huge pizzas and enough salad to keep Watership Down's bunnies going for a week. Then we hit the video shop and chose more movies than we'd have time to watch. I didn't care. Part of me felt a holiday sense of release. I'd done everything I could to get Richard freed. Now all I could do was wait, and I owed it to Davy to do that as cheerfully as possible.

As we drove across Upper Brook Street and into

Brunswick Street, the traffic slowed to a crawl. I couldn't see what the problem was, only that there was no traffic heading past us in the opposite direction. Eventually, craning my neck, I could see that the road ahead was cordoned off, and that traffic was being diverted down Kincardine Road by a uniformed policeman. Curious, I swung the car out of the queue, and indicated to the policeman that I wanted to turn right, heading back home. He gave me the nod, and I pulled round the corner and parked. I couldn't help myself. There's no way I could ignore something looking that interesting on my own doorstep. At the very least, it looked like someone had raided the local post office. I sometimes wonder whether I chose the career or it chose me. I turned to Davy and said, 'Wait here a minute. I just want to see what's going on.' He flicked a glance heavenwards, sighed and pulled a comic out of his backpack.

I got out of the car and locked it up, then cut through the council estate so that I'd emerge at the mouth of a narrow alley off Brunswick Street, but further down than the road block. I was almost opposite the pelican crossing, and I could see that there was a second road block a little further down in the other direction. On the pedestrianized little shopping precinct on the other side of the street, two police cars and an ambulance were standing, doors open, just outside the post office. Around them milled a bewildered looking knot of people, police officers trying to keep them away from the person the ambulance crew were crouched over. The wailing cries of a child rose and fell like a siren. While I watched, another pair of police cars arrived.

One of the ambulance crew stood up and shook his head while his colleague continued to crouch on the ground. There was a commotion at the heart of the crowd, then a stretcher was loaded into the ambulance. The spectators parted, and the ambulance reversed on to the road and sped off. The crowd stayed back long enough for me to see a policewoman ushering two young boys into the back of a police car, which shot off in the wake of the ambulance, blue light flashing. It was hard to be certain from that distance, but they looked disturbingly like Wayne and Daniel.

By this time, I was a question mark on legs. I'd also spotted a familiar mane of black hair bobbing around on the fringes of the crowd, tapping people on the shoulders and thrusting a tape recorder in their faces. I checked that none of the cops were looking my way, then I nonchalantly nipped out of the alley, crossed the street and headed for Alexis. If anyone had tried to stop me, I'd have insisted I was on my way to a dental appointment in the precinct. If the police were suspicious enough to check it out, Howard's receptionist knew me well enough to back me up.

As I drifted closer, I could see the police officers were working their way through the crowd, taking names and addresses rather than attempting statements. I could hear odd snatches of shocked conversation: 'all over in seconds . . .'; '. . . balaclava over his head . . .'; 'thought it was a car backfiring . . .'; 'police should *do* something about them druggies . . .' Alexis was over on the far side, tape recorder shoved under the nose of a uniformed inspector. I took my notebook and tape recorder out of my handbag and rushed round the fringe of the crowd to Alexis's side. I arrived in time to hear him say in harassed tones, 'Look, I can't tell you any more now, you'll have to wait till we have a clearer idea ourselves.' Then, seeing me and falling for my instant disguise, he added, 'And I haven't got time to go through it all again. Get the details from her,' he said, gesturing towards Alexis with his thumb. She turned and clocked me. Her face, already paler than usual, seemed to go even whiter.

'For Chrissake, what are you doing here?' she hissed.

'I could say the same to you. What's happened? Somebody taken a pot at the post office? And where's the rest of the pack?'

'Still on their way, if they even know about it. I just happened to be driving back to your house when it all came on top. Kate, you've got to get out of here! Now! Move it!' Alexis started hustling me away, back towards the side street where I'd left my car.

'Why?' I protested. 'What's it got to do with me?'

'Where's Davy?' she demanded, still shooing me away from the crowd and back across the street.

'He's in the car.' We'd reached the opening of the alley and I stepped in, then stopped in my tracks. I wasn't going another pace further until she enlightened me. 'What is going on, Alexis? What happened back there?'

She ran a hand through her unruly hair and pulled a crushed packet of cigarettes out of her bag. She lit up and took a deep drag before she spoke. 'I'm sorry, but there is not a gentle way of saying this. Cherie Roberts just got killed,' she said.

I felt like I'd been punched in the chest. The air emptied out of me like a burst balloon. 'A robbery? She got in the way?' I asked.

My face must have betrayed my hope that this had been no more than a horrific accident, a tragic and malignant twist of fate, for Alexis turned her face away and shook her head, smoke streaming down her nostrils in twin plumes. 'No. It was a hit.'

I squeezed the bridge of my nose between my fingers. I didn't want to believe what Alexis was saying. 'That can't be right,' I said half-heartedly. 'For fuck's sake, she was no big deal. She was just another single mum, trying to get through the days and keep her kids out of trouble.'

'I've covered too many stories like this over the last couple of years in the Moss and Cheetham Hill,' Alexis said bleakly, referring to the violent drug wars that have practically doubled Manchester's homicide figures. 'According to the eyewitnesses, Cherie was coming out of the post office after cashing her child benefit. There was a car parked on the other side of the road. When she came out, the car revved up, shot across the road, mounted the pavement and drove towards her. When they were a few feet away from her, she got blasted from the rear window with both barrels of the shotgun. It was, variously, a metallic blue Sierra, a silver Toyota, a grey Cavalier, and nobody's admitting to getting the registration number.'

I closed my eyes and leaned against the wall. I could feel the brick rough against my fingertips. 'Dear God,' I breathed. I'd asked her to find out who had given her kids drug-laced transfers. And two days later, Cherie Roberts was on her way to the mortuary, stamped with the familiar hall-marks of a drug-related murder. Suddenly, my eyes snapped open. 'Davy!' I gasped. I turned on my heel and ran down the alley, panic pumping the blood till my ears pounded with the drum of my heartbeat.

I rounded the corner, imagination painting scenes of bloodshed and violence that even Sam Peckinpah would draw the line at, making all sorts of ridiculous bargains with a god I don't believe in. I skidded to a halt by the car, feeling deeply foolish as Davy waved at me and mouthed. 'Hi,' through the glass. Alexis rushed up behind me, slightly breathless. 'We need to talk,' she said. 'What did you ask Cherie on Sunday?'

'The wrong question, obviously,' I said bitterly. 'I asked her to ask the kids who they got the transfers from. That's all. She must have taken it further than that. Shit, Alexis, I need a drink. Are you finished here, or do you need to talk to some more people?'

'I'm too late for the final edition anyway. I've got the eyewitness stuff for tomorrow's paper. It'll be a while now before the police issue a full statement. Let's go back to your place, eh?' She squeezed my arm sympathetically. 'It's not your fault, KB. It wasn't you that pulled the trigger.'

So why did I feel so guilty?

It took less than a minute to drive round to my house. I parked in the bay outside Richard's house and walked towards mine. Davy hung behind, bouncing up and down at the end of the path, waiting for Alexis to get out of the car so he could show her the videos we'd chosen. You can't see my porch from the parking bays. There's a six foot, gold and green conifer in the way. I'd never thought much about it before. But that afternoon, I was more glad than I can say that the tree was there.

I passed the tree and glanced towards my house. What I saw made me stumble and nearly fall. I regained my balance and took a couple of steps closer to make sure my eyes weren't playing tricks on me. Then I felt sick. The white UPVC of the lower half of the door was pocked with hundreds of little black puncture holes. The glass in the upper half was crazed and starred, no match for the close-range blast it had sustained. Whoever had terminated Cherie Roberts had left me their calling card.

21

I wheeled round as fast as I could and nailed a smile on my face as I headed back towards Alexis and Davy, in a huddle looking at videos. 'We might as well go in through Richard's,' I said, trying to sound breezy. 'I've got some paperwork to do later, and that way you won't have to worry about disturbing me.'

It didn't entirely work. Alexis looked up sharply at the cracked note in my voice. 'All right,' she said casually. 'His video's just as good as yours, and we're nearer the ice-cream there.'

I steered them up the path, carefully using my body to shield Davy from the sight of my front door. I needn't have bothered; he was so engrossed in his chatter with Alexis that he didn't even glance in that direction. She did, though, and I could see from the momentary tightening of her lips that she'd spotted the damage. I unlocked the door and Davy ran into the house ahead of us. 'What the hell's going on, KB?' Alexis demanded.

'Your guess is as good as mine,' I hissed. 'You think this happens all the time?'

Alexis put her arm round my shoulders and squeezed. 'OK, sorry. But we need to get him out of here,' Alexis murmured. 'It's not safe.'

'You think I don't know that? What can we do? Where can we take him?' I asked.

'I'll pitch him into coming to the pictures, then I'll take him back to our house. Fill him up with burgers and popcorn and let him crash out with us while you get this sorted out,' she said softly.

'Gee thanks,' I said, my frustration bubbling up to the surface. 'And how exactly do you suggest I go about that?'

'Calm down, girl,' Alexis protested. 'I was talking about getting the door fixed, not solving the mysteries of the universe.'

I sighed. 'Sorry. I'm kind of edgy, you know?'

Alexis put the other arm round my shoulders and gave me a quick hug. 'I'll go and get Davy before he gets stuck into one of those videos.' She headed down the hall. I leaned against the wall and took some deep breaths, doing the mental relaxation exercises my Thai boxing coach taught me. I heard her say, 'Hey, soft lad, you can't watch a film without popcorn. Tell you what, why don't we go to the proper pictures? Then we can go to the McDonald's drive-in near my house and take the burgers back and watch your videos there.'

'What are we going to go and see?' Davy demanded.

'Hang on a minute,' Alexis said. She emerged from the living room and said, 'Did I see the local freesheet scrunched up in the porch? They've got the multi-screen listings in, haven't they?'

'I think so,' I said, exhaling the last of the twenty breaths.

Alexis moved past me and picked up the crumpled newspaper that had been stuffed gratuitously through Richard's letter box some time over the weekend. 'You know, I really object to trees being cut down so that rubbish can be dumped in my porch without my permission or invitation,' I grumbled.

'I hate freesheets too,' Alexis said, flicking through the pages. 'Because they get distributed to so many homes, advertising managers just lie about how many people read the bloody things, so local businesses spend their limited budgets advertising in wastepaper rather than taking an ad in the *Chronicle*. So the number of pages we print decreases, so we don't hire as many journalists. And the freesheets don't take up the slack on account of they're crap editorially,' she added for good measure.

'Not that you're biased or anything,' I muttered. 'Found the listing yet?' As I spoke, a rumpled sheet of blue writing paper slid out from between the newspaper's pages and fluttered to the floor.

'Mmm,' Alexis said, frowning in concentration as she moved back down the hall.

Absently, I bent down and picked up the paper.

It was a sheet from a writing pad, folded in half. On the outside, in unfamiliar writing, I read: 'Kate Brannigan'. Before I opened it, I knew what it was. I closed my eyes until the wave of nausea passed, then, slowly, apprehensively I unfolded it.

The hand was uncertain but perfectly legible. 'Kate – I came round Monday afternoon but there was nobody in. I asked the boys where they got the transfers from, and they told me who's handing them out. I spoke to the lad and found out where he's getting them from, and there's more to it than the drugs. You're right, it shouldn't be going on, and I'm going round tonight to tell him so. If you want to come with me, come to my flat about seven o'clock. Yours sincerely, Cherie.'

I slid down the wall till I was crouching in a tight bundle. I'd let Cherie down. I'd been so busy running around being a hero for Richard that I hadn't made the time to check back with her. And now she was dead, all because I hadn't managed to prevent her from sticking her head into a hornet's nest.

I'd probably have stayed like that forever if I hadn't heard wagons roll from the living room. Davy was shrieking with delight over some movie or other, Alexis's rumble of enthusiasm a lower counterpoint. 'Come on then, I'll race you to the car,' I heard her say. I forced myself into an upright position and I'd managed to find something approximating a smile by the time Davy was close enough to notice.

'See you later, super troopers,' I said as they passed at a run.

'We'll be at our house,' Alexis said. 'Phone Chris and tell her, would you? Only, don't tell her why, she'll only get fear of loss. I'll tell her when she gets home.'

I watched them drive off in the car. I don't think I've ever been so sorry to see Alexis leave. I pulled myself together with the assistance of a strong vodka and grapefruit juice and cut through the conservatory to my house. I didn't think I was up to approaching from the front. What amazed me was that the place wasn't crawling with police. But then, my bungalow's on the end of the row. No one overlooks the front of it, and even though it's got a postcode that whacks my insurance up into the stratosphere, it's still the kind of area where people assume a loud bang is a backfire from one of the MOT failures that sit on bricks all over the council estate, and not the shoot-out at the OK Corral.

From the inside, the front door looked just about as lethal. Time to call in a favour. I rang the office, and told Shelley I was on my way in. 'Oh, and Shelley? I'd like to make a contribution to your household budget.'

'You what?'

'I need a new front door. Pronto monto. I mean tonight. Can you get Ted to see to it?' Ted Barlow is the man Shelley strenuously insists she's not actually, technically, living with. They fell in love

246

when he turned up in our office looking forlorn, with the bank about to foreclose on his conservatory business. While I was busy sorting out the mess, the pair of them gazed into each other's eyes and whispered sweet nothings. Now Shelley's got a conservatory that takes up a good half of her back garden, and Ted tends to answer her phone first thing in the morning.

'What's happened? Have you had a burglary?'

'I wish,' I said with feeling. 'Unfortunately, it's a little bit more personal than that. I'll tell you all about it when I come in.'

'What about a key? Shall I get him to come by the office and pick one up?'

I pictured the door. 'I think a key's a bit academic,' I said. 'If I can get the key in, I'll leave the outside door unlocked, OK? So if it's still locked, he'll know just to kick it in.' I couldn't believe the words that were coming out of my mouth. I was instructing someone to kick my door in? Sooner or later, somebody was going to pay for all this. For scaring me, for killing Cherie, for giving drugs to little kids.

I felt safer in the office. Illogical, I know, but fear and logic are hardly ever on speaking terms, never mind pals. I perched on the edge of the leather sofa in Bill's office and told him all about the latest crisis. 'I'm sorry to lay it all on you,' I apologized, 'but I need to talk it through.'

His blue eyes smiled. 'We're partners, aren't we?

In my book, that makes this as much my business as yours.'

'I know, but, I feel like it's always me that's in the shit up to the neck. I seem to be accident-prone these days. I remember when this agency never did anything more dramatic than prowling through somebody else's database. Now I seem to spend half my life in a state of panic.'

Bill chewed his beard and shrugged. 'So walk away from it.' He saw my look of instant outrage and grinned. 'You see?' he teased. 'You like answers too much, Kate. But this time, I think we really should walk away from it. This is one for the cops.'

I shook my head vehemently, my nervous fingers plaiting the streamers from the waste basket of his shredder. 'No can do, Bill. Sorry.'

Bill prowled the room like a huge blond bear who's forgotten where he left the honey jar. 'It's too much of a risk,' he insisted. 'These people are serious, Kate. They've given you a warning. If they think you're ignoring that, then they won't hesitate to give you the same treatment they dished out to that poor woman. And frankly, I haven't got the time to find another partner right now.'

'I *can't* go to the police, Bill. I'm not just being bloody-minded!'

'It wouldn't be the first time,' he said, a wry smile counteracting the bitter edge to his voice.

I stood up, his restlessness infecting me. I walked across to his desk and perched on the edge of it and explained. 'Bill, the Drugs Squad are supposedly checking out the info I handed over to them, and if it stands up, Richard will be released on bail on Thursday morning. If I go to the bizzies now and say, "Excuse me, some drug dealer's hit man's just taken a shotgun to my front door, but it's got absolutely nothing to do with the fact that you've got my partner locked up on drugs charges," they're going to fall about. There's no way they're not going to connect it to what's happened to Richard, and that'll be the end of any chance he's got of being turned loose.'

Bill stopped pacing and threw himself down on the sofa. He breathed out deeply through his nose. 'Kate, I don't want you to take this the wrong way, but hadn't you considered the possibility that it just might be connected to Richard's case rather than Cherie's death?'

'It's hard for me to get my head round the idea that there were two lunatics with shotguns wandering round Ardwick at the same time. The only credible explanation is that when Cherie fronted up whoever is pushing these drugs to kids, she mentioned my name. She might even have used me as an insurance policy. You know – "if anything happens to me, Kate Brannigan knows where to come looking". If that's what happened, then hiring some psycho with a sawn-off to kill Cherie gets even more cost-effective. It not only gets rid of someone who knows more than the dealer wants her to, it also serves as a warning to me to keep my nose out and to stay away from the cops investigating the shooting. And it lets everybody else who's involved with the racket know just what's coming to them if they step out of line. A real bargain, when you think about it,' I added angrily.

Bill said, 'But I don't necessarily think that there *were* two psychos driving round Ardwick with a shooter. Manchester isn't LA. Having a gun in your glove box or under your car seat so the girls all know you're a big man and the yobs all know to give you a wide berth is a different kettle of fish from being a hired gun. It could be that while there was only one gunman, there were two paymasters. That would explain why Cherie was killed and you were only warned.'

Suddenly, I saw the flaw in Bill's theory. 'It was *my* front door,' I said.

'Yes?' Bill said.

'Not Richard's. It was *my* front door. Don't you see?' I was excited now, banging the desk with my fist. 'If they'd wanted to warn me off the case, they'd have blasted Richard's front door. *He's* the one that's vulnerable, *he's* the one that's banged up with a load of villains, *he's* the one with the eight-year-old pressure point. Besides, the only people who know there's any connection between me and Richard are the Drugs Squad.'

Bill slumped in his office chair and chewed a pencil. 'And we trust the Drugs Squad not to have a leak? We think they don't have any bent officers who might just be in Eliot James's golf club?'

I sighed. 'I don't exactly *trust* Geoff Turnbull. Not even on Della's say-so. But he's an ambitious man, and self-interest's one of the most powerful engines there is. I bet the thought of nailing a smooth operator like Eliot James is a bigger aphrodisiac than oysters to a man like Turnbull. And he'll want all the credit for himself; I doubt very much if he's told a living soul he got his information from a private eye.'

'I can't argue with that,' Bill said, resignation all over his face. 'So, what now?'

I told him. And since his only alternative was to betray me by going behind my back to the police, Bill reluctantly agreed to help where he could.

The main problem for me now was that I'd argued myself out of any chance of feeling secure. At least if I'd believed the shooting had anything to do with Jammy James and his merry men, I'd have known that the Drugs Squad were about to rob the gunman of any future playdays from that direction. Now, I had to live with the uncomfortable fact that some complete stranger out there wanted me to give up an inquiry so badly that they'd blown a hole in my front door. If I was going to stop them doing the same thing to me, I'd better find out who they were. And fast.

22

The rush-hour traffic had already started to build by the time I left the office. I sat smouldering in the jam at the top of Plymouth Grove, listening to GMR cheerily telling me where the traffic black spots were. I could have crossed town faster on foot than I was managing by car. I watched the seconds tick past on my watch, muttering darkly about what the transport policy would be when I ruled the world. It was twenty to five by the time I'd inched up Stockport Road and turned off into the car park behind the Longsight District Centre. I parked illegally as near as I could get to the Social Services office. I wanted to make sure I didn't miss my target.

Like the rest of the city's social workers, the family placement officer theoretically knocks off work at half past four. But like most of her colleagues, Frankie Summerbee knows that the only way to come close to dealing with her workload is to stay at the office long after the town hall bureaucrats have gone home. So, like most of her colleagues, Frankie's chronically over-tired, over-stressed and prone to making decisions that don't always look too wonderful in the cool light of day under cross-examination. That's what I was relying on this afternoon.

I've known Frankie almost as long as I've known Richard. Before he moved in next door to me, he lived in Chorlton-cum-Hardy, that Manchester suburb whose trendiness quotient rises and falls in tandem with the Green Party's electoral share. He lived in the downstairs flat of an Edwardian terraced cottage. Frankie had the flat upstairs. Luckily for her, that included the attic. I don't know if that had always been her bedroom, but after Richard moved in downstairs I suspect that sleeping at least two floors away from his stereo became an imperative.

Of course, as a trained social worker, she couldn't avoid helping him out; cooking the odd meal, picking up his washing from the launderette, grabbing a stack of pizzas every now and again as she whizzed past the chill cabinet in the supermarket on her weekly shop. I don't expect she got any thanks, but he did take her out to dinner a few times, and so she became another victim of the Cute Smile.

The bonking bit didn't last too long. I suspect they both realized after the first time that it was a big mistake, but they're both much too kind to have hurt the other's feelings by saying so. Luckily, Frankie also has the good social worker's ruthless streak, otherwise they'd probably both still be hanging on till the last minute every Saturday night because nice people come second. Under normal circumstances, I was glad she'd forced a return to uncomplicated friendship so he was unencumbered when he met me. After the events of the past few days, I wasn't so sure.

I could have short-circuited the waiting period by picking up my mobile phone and dialling Frankie's direct line, but I was glad of a breathing space to try to organize my thoughts into something approaching order. I didn't get one.

I'd been sitting there less than ten minutes when Frankie's spiky black hair appeared like a fright wig on top of a stack of files. The files teetered forward above a pair of black leggings and emerald green suede hi-tops. I jumped out of the car and rushed forwards to help her. 'Hi, Frankie,' I said, putting my arms out to steady the files as I stopped her in her tracks.

The hair tilted sideways and two interested brown eyes peered round the stack of files. Her granny glasses were slowly sliding down her nose, but not so far that she didn't recognize me. 'Hi, Brannigan,' she said. She didn't sound surprised, but then she's been a social worker for the best part of ten years. Nothing surprises Frankie any more.

'Let me help,' I said.

'The car's over there,' she said, sounding slightly baffled as I grabbed the top half of her pile. 'The red Astra.'

I carried the files over to the car and we did small talk while she fiddled with her keys and unlocked the hatchback. It wasn't easy, avoiding the subject of Richard's incarceration, but I managed it by dragging Davy's visit into the conversation two sentences in. We loaded the boot, and Frankie slammed it shut, then leaned against it, catching me eye to eye. Not many people manage that, but Frankie and I are so alike physically that if I ever get signed up to star in a movie with nude scenes I could get her to be my body double. 'This is not serendipity, is it?'

I shook my head sheepishly. 'Sorry.'

She sighed. 'You should know better.'

'It's not business, Frankie,' I said in mitigation. 'It's personal, and it's not for me.'

She raised her eyebrows and looked sceptical. I can't say I blamed her. 'I'm in a hurry,' she said. 'I've got a meeting this evening. I was on my way to grab a quick curry since I skipped lunch. If you think there's any point in telling me what you're after, follow me to the Tandoori Kitchen. You're buying. Deal?'

'Deal,' I said. I've always liked the Tandoori Kitchen. The food's consistently good, but the best thing of all is the chocolate-flavoured lollipops they give you when they bring you the bill. I wasn't particularly hungry, but I ordered some onion bhajis and pakora to keep me occupied while Frankie worked her way through the biggest mushroom biryani I've ever seen.

'So what's this favour you're after, Brannigan?'

'Who said anything about a favour?' I said innocently.

'A person doesn't need to have A Level Deduction to know you're after something more than a share in my poppadums when you turn up on the office doorstep. What are you after?' Frankie persisted.

So much for gently working round to it. I plunged in. 'You took a couple of kids into care this afternoon. Daniel and Wayne Roberts. Their mum was shot in Brunswick Street?'

Frankie nodded cautiously. 'Mmm?'

'I knew Cherie quite well, because Davy always plays with Daniel and Wayne when he's staying with Richard. Also, I helped her out when she was trying to get a divorce from Eddy, her ex.' I paused, but Frankie didn't lift her eyes from her curry.

Nothing for it but to soldier on. 'I was driving home with Davy this afternoon just after Cherie had been shot. The place was jumping with police and ambulance crews, and we saw the boys being taken away in a police car. Then when we got home, all the neighbours were talking about Cherie being shot. The bottom line is that Davy's in a hell of a state. He's terrified because Cherie's been shot, but he's even more frightened because Daniel and Wayne have been carted off in a police car.'

'Not particularly surprising,' Frankie said sympathetically. 'Poor Davy. So what do you want me to do?'

'I just wondered if there was any chance you could fix up for me to take Davy to see Daniel and Wayne this evening. I know it's bending the rules and all that, but I don't see how I'm going to get him to sleep otherwise. He's climbing the walls. He thinks Daniel and Wayne have gone to prison, you see.' I sighed and shrugged. 'I've tried to explain, but he won't believe me.'

'I wonder why not,' Frankie said drily. She gave me a shrewd look. 'Are you sure you're asking for Davy and not for yourself?'

'Give me a break, Frankie,' I complained. 'You know I don't do murders. Strictly white collar, that's Mortensen and Brannigan.'

She snorted, not a wise move when you're dealing with curry spices. After she'd finished spluttering and sneezing, she said, 'And Patrick Swayze's strictly ballroom. OK. I believe you. God knows why. But if I find out you've been lying to me, Brannigan, I'll be really disappointed in you.'

Just as well I'm not a Catholic or I'd never get out of bed in the morning with the weight of guilt on my shoulders. I smiled meekly and said, 'You won't regret this, Frankie.'

'Where is Davy now?' she asked. 'Is he with Richard?'

'My friend Alexis is looking after him. She was going to take him to the pictures to see if she could take his mind off what's happened.' I glanced at my watch. 'They should be back within the next half-hour or so.'

Frankie ran a hand through her spiky hair. 'I hope for your sake I don't live to regret this, Brannigan. I'll tell you what would make me feel happier, though.'

'What's that?' I asked, willing to go along with anything half-reasonable so long as I still had the chance to hit the boys with a few questions.

'I'd be a lot happier if Richard brought Davy along rather than you. Then I could be sure there wasn't a hidden agenda.' Frankie said calmly.

I hoped the dismay I felt didn't reach the surface. I pulled a face and said, 'You and me both. But the boy wonder is out of town tonight. He's gone to Birmingham to see some international super-star I've never heard of at the NEC. He went off this afternoon early. He doesn't even know about Cherie.'

Frankie sighed. 'I'll just have to live with it, then. OK. We've placed Wayne and Daniel with emergency foster parents in Levenshulme. Normally, it would take a few days to organize a visit while we checked out the credentials of the person claiming to be friends or family, but in this case, I don't see why we shouldn't speed the wheels of bureaucracy since I know both you and Davy. Besides, it might just help the boys to settle, feel less abandoned. After we've eaten, I'll find a phone box and call the foster parents, see what time will fit in with their arrangements.'

I put my mobile phone on the table. 'Have this one on me,' I said, nudging it towards her.

Frankie shook her head, smiling wryly. 'Since I've known you, I've come to realize what the essential quality of a private investigator is,' she said, reaching across and picking up the phone.

'What's that?'

'You simply don't recognize the point where the rest of the world backs off,' she said. 'Now, how do I work this thing?'

It was just after seven when Davy and I pulled up outside a trim between-the-wars semi off Slade Lane. The street was quiet; one of the few in the area that motorists driven demented by traffic don't think is a short cut to anywhere. I'd had a difficult half-hour with Davy, explaining what had happened to Cherie and the boys. I thought I should keep it low-key so I wouldn't frighten him, but I'd forgotten how small boys like things to be gory. He hadn't seen it happen right in front of his eyes, so it was no more real, no more frightening than a cartoon or a video. I was glad Frankie had gone off to her meeting; anything less like a terrified nervous wreck than Davy it would be hard to imagine.

You couldn't say the same for Daniel and Wayne. They sat huddled together on a settee in the front room. The television was on and their eyes were pointing at it, but they weren't watching. They didn't look up when the foster mother showed Davy and me into the room, but when she spoke, they both turned their heads towards us, a look of bafflement on their faces. They had the bewildered, desperate air we've all grown used to seeing in endlessly recurring TV film of refugees from disaster areas.

'Hi, lads,' I said. 'Davy and I were wondering if you fancied going to the ice-cream parlour.'

Wayne got to his feet and, after a moment, Daniel joined him. I felt like a monster, dragging these two shattered kids out of the nearest thing they were going to have to a home, just to satisfy my curiosity. Then I looked at Davy and remembered my front door. That reminded me there was a lot more at stake than my nosiness. 'Or we could go somewhere else, if you'd rather,' I said.

'It's good there,' Davy said anxiously, disturbed by his friends' silence.

'I want to go home,' Wayne said. 'That's where I want to go.'

The foster mother, a bulky, comfortable-looking woman in her late thirties, stepped past me and gave Wayne a hug. 'You've got to stay with us for a while, Wayne,' she said in a soothing voice. 'I know it's not the same as home, but tomorrow we'll go back to your house and get your clothes and the rest of your stuff and you can be at home here, OK?'

'We'll go to the ice-cream place, then,' he said grudgingly to me. Wayne shrugged off the woman's arm and pushed past her into the hall, where he stood expectantly by the door. Daniel followed him, and, after a quick glance at me for permission, so did Davy.

'I'll have them back in an hour,' I promised.

'Don't worry about it,' she said. 'Quite honestly, love, the more worn out they are tonight the better.'

For the first twenty minutes, I said nothing about Cherie or the shooting. We pumped money into the Wurlitzer, we argued the relative merits of everything on the menu. Then I sat back and watched while the boys wolfed huge ice-cream sundaes, gradually returning to something approaching normal behaviour, even if it was tinged with a kind of hysteria. I even joined in some of their fun, dredging my memory for old and sick jokes. When I reached the point where the only one I could remember was the one about the Rottweiler and the social worker, I reckoned it was time to change tack.

'Davy got a lot of new transfers yesterday, didn't you?' I said brightly.

'Where did you go?' Daniel asked.

'VIRUS,' said Davy and proceeded to enthuse about the virtual reality centre.

'Maybe we could all go together the next time Davy's up,' I suggested. 'Show them your tattoos, Davy.'

He took off his New York blouson to reveal tattoos that spread up from his wrists and finally disappeared into the sleeves of his T-shirt. Wayne and

Daniel studied the intergalactic warriors and dinosaurs, desperately trying not to look impressed.

'Huh,' Wayne finally said. 'I've had ones just as good as that.'

'Where from?' Davy challenged.

'From Woody on the estate. You know, him that gave you a load last week.'

There is a god. 'I don't think I know Woody,' I said. 'Where does he live?'

'Up the top. Near the Apollo. Where the chip van parks,' Daniel said positively.

'Wasn't your mum going to go and see him last night?' I asked, feeling like I was walking on eggshells. It was the first time Cherie had been mentioned, and I didn't know how they would react.

Wayne stared into his sundae dish, scraping his spoon round the sides. But Daniel didn't seem bothered. 'Nah,' he said scornfully. 'It wasn't Woody she went to see. She'd already seen Woody and gave him a right gobful about giving things to us. And Woody said he was just doing what he was told to do, and she said he was a waste of space and who told him, and he said, the guy in the house on the corner. And that's where she went.'

'What guy is that, do you know?'

Daniel shook his head. 'Don't know his name. We don't go there.'

'What house is it?'

'You know I said where Woody lives? Well, if you was standing at the chip van and you looked across the street that way,' he said, gesturing with his right arm, 'it's the house on the corner. That's where my mum went last night,' he added.

I was impressed. 'Were you with your mum when she saw Woody?' I asked. Daniel's information seemed almost too good to be true.

''Course *we* weren't,' Wayne said contemptuously. 'She didn't even know we were out. We followed her. We always follow her. She says we're the men of the house and she needs us to take care of her, so we follow her, but she don't know. We watch and listen so we'll know if anyone did bad things to her and we could get them back later. She never saw us,' he added proudly.

'I wish I was that good at following people,' I said. 'It would come in really handy in my job. You'll have to give me lessons one of these days. Where did you learn your tricks? From the TV?'

Wayne shook his head, swinging it elaborately from side to side. 'Our dad showed us. He trained us to be silent and deadly, just like the Paras.'

I felt a chill in my heart. According to Cherie, Crazy Eddy hadn't been near the kids in years. 'When was this?' I asked casually.

'For ages. He just turns up at the common where we go with our bikes and takes us up Levenshulme and trains us. But he made us promise we wouldn't tell anybody because he didn't want Mum to know. But now Mum's not here, it doesn't matter about telling, does it?' Wayne's face crumpled and he rubbed his eyes savagely with his fists.

'No, it doesn't matter. Your dad must be really proud of you. When did you see him last?'

'We saw him yesterday,' Daniel said. 'But he's been around for ages. He came back at Easter.'

23

I knew that if I betrayed my surprise I wouldn't get another word out of Daniel or Wayne. Somehow, I had to keep superficially calm at the news that Crazy Eddy was back in town. I breathed softly and thought about something restful; a room freshly painted barley white, actually. 'I thought your dad worked away,' I said.

Daniel stuck his chest out like a sergeant major. 'He does. He's a warrior, my dad. He teaches whole armies how to fight like him. But when they've learned how to do it, he comes home and sees us.'

'Does he come home often?' I asked.

'Once or twice a year,' Wayne muttered. 'The first time was just after I was five. We were playing in the playground at school at break time and this soldier came up to us, and he crouched down beside us and said, "You know who I am, don't you?" And we did, because Mum had his picture on her dressing table.' At the mention of the photograph, something clicked inside my head. Wayne looked up and met my eyes. 'Do you think we can go and live with him now? Be soldiers with him?'

'You'll have to ask your foster mother about that,' I said, distracted by the piece of the jigsaw that had just fallen into place. 'Where does your dad stay when he's here?' I tried to sound casual.

'In the Moss. With a man that used to be one of his squaddies,' Daniel said. 'He's never taken us there. He's too busy training us.'

'Of course he is. It's a tough job, being a good soldier.' Out of the corner of my eye, I could see Davy getting restive. I pretended to be stern. 'And you soldiers are letting the side down now.' All three looked puzzled. 'Do you know what's wrong with this picture?' I asked, gesturing at the table. They all held their breath and shook their heads. 'Empty plates!' I mock-roared. 'Time for seconds! Who wants more?'

I didn't have to ask twice. After the waiter had brought the second round of ice-creams, I said, 'So what training were you doing with your dad yesterday?'

'Tracking and observation,' Daniel reported. 'We met Dad round the common, and then we went and hid across the main road, on the waste ground. We had binoculars, and we watched the outside of the flats and we waited for Mum to come out, then we trailed her and spied on her talking to Woody. Dad said she should keep her nose out of other people's business when we told him she was on about the transfers.'

'Did he know about the transfers, then?' I asked through a mouthful of chocolate hazelnut. I'd succumbed the second time around.

''Course he does,' Wayne said, scornful again. 'He told us to get the transfers off Woody and get the other kids to use them. He said they'd all want them and that way they'd do what we told them to. But we don't use the ones we take off Woody. Dad said that would be a sign of weakness, so we don't.'

Eddy wasn't wrong about the transfers being a sign of weakness. I couldn't help wondering just how much he knew about what was going on in the house on the corner. It was time I paid it a visit. But first, I had to keep my side of the bargain I'd made with myself. I'd had my needs met; now, Daniel and Wayne were entitled to the same thing. I dug my hand in my pocket and dumped a handful of change on the table. 'Who wants to play?' I demanded, gesturing with one thumb towards the array of video-game machines at the far end of the ice-cream parlour.

I kept half an eye on them as I struggled with the significance of what Wayne had told me without realizing. Now I knew why the big bouncer at the Lousy Hand seemed so familiar. It wasn't because he was a regular in the Mexican restaurant downstairs from the office.

I'd once seen that photograph that Cherie kept

in her bedroom. She'd shown me it when she'd asked me to hunt her husband down. He'd been in uniform, the maroon beret of the Paras cocked jauntily on his head. He'd been nearly ten years younger too. But that scar clinched it. The man who was fingering cars for Terry Fitz was none other than Crazy Eddy Roberts. At the very least, it was a strange coincidence.

It takes more than bereavement to divert small boys from arcade games. By the time they'd fought in the streets, driven several grand prix, played a round or two of golf and done enough terminating to get us jobs with Rentokil, the effects of the afternoon's trauma had receded noticeably. When we all piled back into my car, the haunted look had left their eyes. I didn't doubt that it was only a temporary respite, but even that was enough to ease my guilt at having taken advantage.

I dropped them off, promising that we'd keep in touch, then I drove Davy back to Alexis's. Of course, he was fired with curiosity as to why they'd moved back to their house and why he was staying with them there instead of with me in Coverley Close. Luckily, he was tired enough to be fobbed off with the excuse that Alexis and Chris needed to be at home now they were back at work because all their clothes and stuff were there. Alexis greeted him like a long-lost friend and hustled him off to the spare room, where she'd moved the video and the portable TV from their bedroom. I made the coffee while she made sure he was sufficiently engrossed in *The Karate Kid* for the dozenth time.

'You all right, girl?' Alexis asked when she returned. 'You look about as lively as a slug in a salt cellar.'

'Gee thanks. Remind me to call you next time my self-confidence creeps above the parapet. I'm just tired, that's all. I've not had a decent night's kip since last Wednesday.'

'Why don't you crash out here now? You can have the sofa bed in the study.'

'Thanks, but no thanks. I've got to go and sit outside a house in the dark.'

'Hey, the sofa bed's not that bad,' Alexis protested, joking. 'I've slept there myself.'

'Sorry to hear that, Alexis,' I said, pretending deep concern. 'I hadn't realized your relationship was in such a bad way.'

'Hey, carry on getting it that wrong and you could get a job on the *Chronicle*'s diary column.'

'Tut-tut' I scolded. 'And you the one that's always telling me how unfairly you journos are maligned for your inaccuracies. Anyway, enough of this gay repartee. I've got work to do, and you've got a child to mind. I'll call you later.' I headed for the door. 'And Alexis? I know you probably think I'm over-reacting, but don't open the door to anyone unless you know them.' I was through the door before she could argue.

I got in the car, revved up noisily, and drove round the corner. I gave it a couple of minutes, then turned back on to Alexis's street, stopping as soon as I had a clear view of the path leading to the house. I picked up my mobile and dialled a familiar number. It rang out, then I heard, 'Hello?'

'Dennis? It's Kate. Are you busy tonight?'

'I don't have to be,' he said, his voice too crackly for me to hear whether he sounded pissed off or not.

'I need a major favour.'

'No problem. Whereabout?'

I gave him brief directions and settled back to wait. OK, so I was being paranoid. But like they say, that doesn't mean they're not out to get you. There was no way I was leaving this street until I was sure that Davy, not to mention Alexis and Chris, had someone to watch over them. And there was no minder I'd trust more than Dennis. He had an added advantage. Years of earning his living as a burglar had developed in him an astonishing ability to stay awake and alert long after the rest of us are crashed out snoring with our heads on the steering wheel. If he was sitting outside the house in his car, I'd feel a lot less worried about the possibility of Jammy James wanting to use me or Davy as a lever against Richard. Not that I believed for one minute that the demolition of my front door was a message from James. I just thought it was better to be safe than sorry. Or something.

While I was waiting, I wondered how Richard was coping. I felt bad about missing the evening's visit, but I figured he could live without seeing me for a day. Whereas, if I didn't do all I could to finger the people who were responsible for the holes in my door, he might have to get used to the idea of not seeing me again. Ever. It wasn't a comforting thought.

The house on the corner of Oliver Tambo Close wasn't the ideal place for a stake-out. The chip van's presence meant a constant flow of people up and down the street, as well as the gang of local yobs who hung round the van every evening just for the hell of it. Add to that the general miasma of poverty and seediness up this end of the estate, and I knew without pausing to think that the Peugeot would stick out like a sore thumb as soon as that evening's rock audience from the Apollo had gone home. I swung round by the office lock-up and helped myself to the Little Rascal van we've adapted for surveillance work.

I stopped behind the chip van, bought fish, chips and cholesterol and ostentatiously drove the Little Rascal back round the corner on to the street running at right angles to Oliver Tambo Close. From the tinted rear windows of the van, I had a perfect view of the house, front door and all. I pulled down one of the padded jump seats and opened my fragrant parcel. I felt like I'd done nothing but eat all day, yet as soon as I smelled the fish and chips, I was ravenous. I sometimes think we're imprinted with that particular aroma while we're still in the womb.

While I tucked in, I checked out the house. I'd once been inside one of the other houses on the estate demanding action against the toerag who'd been anti-social enough to smash my car window and walk off with my radio cassette. Sparky, who runs the car crime round here, wasn't too pleased about a bit of private enterprise on his patch, especially from someone who was too stupid to work out which cars belonged to locals and which were fair game. Incidentally, he's not called Sparky because he's bright; it's because he uses a spark plug whirling on the end of a piece of string to shatter car windows. Anyway, I thought it was fair to assume this house would have the same layout as Sparky's. It looked the same from the outside, and Manchester City Council's Housing Department has never been renowned for its imagination.

The door would open into a narrow hall, the kitchen off to the right and the living-room to the left. Behind the kitchen was the staircase, a storage cupboard underneath. I'd gone upstairs to use the bathroom and noted two other doors, presumably leading to bedrooms. That checked out with what I could see of the house on the corner. My job wasn't made any easier by the vandals who had busted the streetlamp in front of it. I could see heavy curtains were drawn at every window, even the kitchen. That was unusual in itself. If you've *got* curtains for all your windows in Oliver Tambo Close, the Social Security snoopers come round and ask where you're getting your extra income from.

I could see a crack of light from a couple of the windows, but apart from that there was no sign of life until nearly half past ten. The front door opened a couple of feet and spilled a long tongue of pale light on to the path. At first, there was no one to be seen in the doorway, then, sudden as sprites in an arcade game, two kids barrelled down the hall and out on to the path. They were both boys, both good-looking in the way that most lads have grown out of by adolescence. Unfortunately for the teenage girls. I'd have put them around nine or ten, but I'm not the best judge of children's ages. One had dark curls, the other had mousey brown hair cut in one of those trendy styles, all straight lines and heavy fringes that remind me of BBC TV versions of Dickens.

The two boys seemed in boisterous, cheerful moods, pushing each other, staggering about, giggling and generally horsing around. They stopped on the corner and pulled chocolate bars out of the pockets of their jeans. They stood there for a few minutes, munching chocolate, then they ran off down the street towards the blocks of flats where Cherie Roberts had tried to bring her kids up as straight as she knew how. A slow anger had started to burn inside me when those kids appeared on the path, all alone at a time of night that's a long way from safe in this part of town. Apart from anything else, it's an area that's always full of strangers in the evening, since the city's major rock venue is just round the corner. If a child was lifted from these streets, the police would have more strange cars to check out than if they clocked every motor that cruises the red-light zone.

I bit down on my anger and carried on watching. About twenty minutes later, the door opened again, more widely this time, and a young man appeared. He couldn't have been more than five-six, slim build, blond, late twenties, cheekbones like chapel hat pegs. He had his jacket collar turned up and sleeves rolled up. Clearly no one had told him *Miami Vice* is yesterday's news. He walked with a swagger to a Toyota MR2 parked at the kerb. I toyed with the idea of following him, but rejected it. I didn't know that he was anything to do with the drugs being foisted on kids, and besides, chasing a sports car in a delivery van is about as much fun as that nightmare where you're sitting an exam and you don't understand any of the questions, and then you realize you're stark naked as well.

So I stayed put. The MR2 revved enough to attract the envy of the chip-van gang, then shot off leaving a couple of hundred miles' worth of rubber on the road. Ten minutes later, the door opened again. This time, the hall light snapped off. Two men emerged. In the dimness, it was hard to see much, except that they both looked paunchy and middle-aged. They walked towards my van, near enough for me to see that they both wore

Sellafield suits – those expensive Italian jobs that virtually glow in the dark. Surprisingly, they got into an elderly Ford Sierra that looked perfectly in keeping with the locale, and drove off.

I carried on with my vigil. There were no lights on that I could see, but I figured there might still be someone in the bathroom, or the bedroom at the rear of the house. The chip van packed up at midnight, and the gang wandered off to annoy someone else. By half past midnight, it had started to drizzle and the street was as quiet as it was ever going to get. There was still no sign of life at the house. I unlocked the strongbox in the floor of the van, and helped myself to some of the essential tools of the trade. Then I pulled on a pair of latex surgical gloves.

I got out of the van and walked towards the narrow alley that runs up the back of Oliver Tambo Close so the bin men have more scope to strew the neighbourhood with the contents of burst black rubbish sacks. As nonchalantly as possible, I made sure I wasn't being watched before I nipped smartly down the alley. The house on the corner had a solid fence about seven feet high, with a heavy gate about halfway along. Luckily, one of the neighbours was trusting. A couple of doors down was a dustbin. I retrieved the bin and climbed on top of it.

The rear of the house was in darkness, so I scrambled over the fence and dropped into a tangle of Russian vine. Come the holocaust, that's all there will be left. Cockroaches and Russian vine. I freed myself and stood on the edge of a patchy lawn staring up at the house. There was a burglar alarm bell box on the gable end of the house, but I suspected it was a dummy. Most of them round here are. Even if it was for real, I wasn't too worried. It would take five minutes before anyone called the cops, and by the time they got here, I'd be home, tucked up in bed.

The back door had two locks, a Yale and a mortise. The patio doors looked more promising. You can often remove a patio door from its runners in a matter of minutes. All it takes is a crowbar in the right place. Only problem was, I was fresh out of crowbars. With a sigh, I started in with the lock picks. The mortise took me nearly twenty minutes, but at least the rain meant nobody with any sense was out walking curious dogs with highly developed senses of smell and powerful vocal cords. When the lock clicked back, I stretched my arms and flexed my tired fingers. The Yale was a piece of cake, even though I couldn't slide it open with an old credit card and had to use a pick. Cautiously, I turned the handle and inched the door open.

Silence. Blackness. I slipped into the carpeted hall and left the door on the latch. Slowly, painstakingly, I inched forward down the hall, my right hand brushing the wall to warn me when I reached the living-room doorway. As my eyes grew accustomed to the dark, I made out a patch of lesser blackness on the left. The stairs. As I drew level,

I paused and held my breath. I couldn't hear a thing. Feeling slightly more relaxed, I carried on.

The living-room door was open. I moved through the doorway tentatively, scared of tripping over furniture, and closed the door softly behind me. I switched on the big rubber torch I'd taken from the van's glove box and slowly played it over the room.

It was like two separate rooms glued together in the middle. In the far end of the room, the walls were painted cream. There was a cream leather armchair, a pair of school desks with child-sized chairs, and a pair of bunk beds complete with satin sheets. Where there should have been a light fitting hanging from the ceiling there was a microphone. At the midpoint of the room, a camcorder was fixed on a tripod, flanked by a couple of photographer's floodlights.

The other half of the room, where I was standing, was like the distribution area of a video production company. There was one of those big video-copying machines that do a dozen copies at a time, a desk set up for home video editing, boxes of Jiffy bags and shelf upon shelf of videos, one title to a shelf. Titles like, *Detention!, Bedtime Stories* and *You Show Me Yours* . . . There were also sealed packets of photographs. Now I began to understand why kids were being handed free drugs that would smash their inhibitions to smithereens and make them see the funny side of being exploited to hell. I could only come up with one explanation of what was going on here, and the very thought of it was so sickening that part of me didn't want to hang around checking the evidence. The only thing that forced me to do it was the thought of some smartass from the Vice Squad doing the 'so if you didn't look at these videos, how do you know they weren't Bugs Bunny cartoons?' routine on me.

I picked a title at random and slotted it into the player on the editing desk. I turned on the TV monitor. While I waited for the credits to come up, I slit open a packet of photographs. Twelve colour five-by-sevens slid out into my hand. I nearly lost my fish and chips. I recognized the blond man who'd left earlier in the Toyota, but the children in the shots were, thank God, strangers. I'd have been fairly revolted to see adults in some of those poses, but with children, my reaction went beyond disgust. At once, I understood those parents who take the law into their own hands when the drunk drivers who killed their kids walk free from court.

If the photographs were bad, the video was indescribably worse, all the more so because of the relentlessly suburban locations where these appalling acts were taking place. I could barely take five minutes of it. My instincts were to empty a can of petrol on the carpet and raze the place to the ground. Then common sense prevailed and reminded me it would be infinitely preferable if those bastards ended up behind bars rather than me. I switched off the video and ejected the tape. I picked up the photographs and stuffed them inside my jacket. I grabbed another couple of videos off the shelf. The night relief at Longsight police station were in for an interesting shift.

I stood up. I heard a sickening crunch. My eyes filled with red, shot through with yellow meteors. A starburst of pain spread from the back of my head. And everything went black.

24

Mosquito. Unmistakable. High-pitched whine circling my head, in one ear and then in the other. Bluebottle. Low, stuttering buzz mixing in with the mozzy. You wouldn't think two little insects could make enough noise to give you a splitting headache, I thought vaguely as I surfaced.

Then the pain hit. You know when you catch your finger in a door? Imagine doing that to your head, and you'll start to get the picture. The sharp edge of the agony snapped my brain back into gear. In the tiny gaps between waves of pain and nausea, I started to remember where I'd been and what I was doing when something seriously brutal put my memory on pause.

As that memory returned, so my senses started to catch up. I still couldn't force my eyes open, but my hearing had recovered from its dislocation. I wasn't hearing a mozzy and a bluebottle. I was hearing a voice. The words drifted in and out, like listening to a pirate radio station on the edge of its transmission area. 'I don't fucking *know* how she got in,' I heard. 'I was fucking sleeping, wasn't I? Look, it's your job to sort out problems . . .' The voice tailed off. The silence was blissful.

Moments later, the voice started yapping again. This time, I registered that it was a man. 'I don't give a shit what you're doing. Look, you're paid to do this sort of thing. I'm just paid to copy videos and *be* here, not whack people over the head with tripods. You'd better get your arse over here now and deal with this cow.' Silence again. Then the voice, higher pitched, angry. 'You've already been paid once to warn her off, and it didn't work, did it? So you'd better come round here and finish the job or else I'll have to ring Colin and tell him you're not prepared to turn out, and he won't be pleased about that, not being disturbed this time of night.'

It finally dawned on me that this was me he was talking about. If I'd had the energy to be afraid, I'd have been gibbering. As it was, the immediate prospect of being executed helped focus my mind even more. My eyes still refused to open, but I became aware of a shooting pain in my shoulders and managed to work out my position. I was suspended by my wrists, which were manacled by something warm and solid that was biting into the flesh. My hands were jammed up against what felt like hot and cold water pipes. My body was dangling, my legs were crumpled under me, not actually taking any of my weight.

Before I could test whether it was possible to shift my weight to my feet without making a noise, the voice started yammering again. 'Look, it's your responsibility. She's got to be dealt with, and now. She's seen the videos, for God's sake. You might want to spend the next ten years being buggered by some Neanderthal in the nick, but I don't.' He paused. 'Fine. You better be here, that's all, or I'll be right on the phone to Colin. And if you want another wage packet like today's, you won't want me doing that.' I heard the sound of a phone being slammed down. The jangling crash cut through my head like a blunt axe, snapping my eyes open.

I closed them to a slit at once, eager to look like I was still out for the count. If I had any chance of getting clear of this place before the hit man arrived, it was by playing dead and hoping my captor would leave me alone. Through my lashes, I could see I was in the kitchen, the fluorescent light a stab behind the eyes. At the far end of the room, the man who'd been using the wall-mounted phone turned towards me. He was tall and slim, his gingerish hair tousled from sleep. He had a neat, full moustache that jutted out like a ledge above thin lips and a sharp chin. The bleary eyes he focused on me narrowed vindictively. 'Bitch,' he said, savagely tightening the belt of his towelling dressing gown.

I knew him. Not his name, or anything like that, but I knew him. I'd seen him around, in the local shops, and in Manto's café bar on one of the handful of occasions I'd been in there waiting for Richard. We were on nodding terms, talking about the weather in the corner-shop terms. It was hard to get my head round the idea of being trussed up by someone I knew. I've never had the slightest desire to explore S&M, and I sure as hell didn't want to start now.

He turned away from me and picked up the kettle. He filled it up and switched it on. While he was waiting for it to boil he came over to me. I let my eyelids sink shut and tried to ignore the cramps that were sending spasms of agony from my lower back muscles through my shoulders and down into my triceps. I let my body hang limp. I was just fine till he kicked me in the ribs.

I think I passed out again for a moment, for the next time I cracked my eyes open he was pouring boiling water into a teapot. I had a funny feeling that he wasn't going to offer me a cup. I took the opportunity of his back being turned to check out my position.

I was handcuffed to water pipes, each about an inch in diameter. What was holding me up was the brackets that were screwed into the wall to keep the pipes in place. What worried me most of all was that I wasn't wearing my jacket or my cotton sweater. I was stripped down to my sports bra, and the entire length of my arms was covered in temporary tattoos. No wonder I was feeling out of it. The gratuitous kick had given me a vague feeling that I ought to be really, really angry, but

I couldn't seem to get worked up. However, I was a long way from being totally stoned. Maybe the lack of circulation in my arms and hands had slowed down the process of absorption. Just how long had the tattoos been in place, and how long did I have before I became a silly giggling maniac?

While I worried about this, Moustache was brewing his tea. He poured himself a mug, gave me a last glance and walked out of the room. Judging by the shuffle of his slippers, he'd only gone as far as the living room.

I knew I didn't have a lot of time. The hit man was on his way, and I needed to be free and clear by then. Taking a deep breath, I shifted round so the soles of my feet were on the floor. Gradually, I allowed my legs to take the weight off my shoulders. For a moment, the pain in my shoulders vanished like magic. Then the pins and needles set in. From my hands to my shoulders, I twitched with a million stabs of irritation. I bit my lip to gag the whimpers that I couldn't stop escaping.

Slowly, inch by cautious inch, I straightened my legs, relieving all the strain on my arms and shoulders. It seemed to take forever, especially since I had to do it all in silence and the pounding in my head seemed to be growing rather than subsiding. When I was upright, I took stock again. The pipes looked pretty strong, but there were a couple of bends in them which might indicate weak points. The downside was that my arms were weak, my muscles twitching with pain. On the other hand, I had nothing to lose since the hit man was already on his way.

I took a deep breath and raised one leg, placing the sole of my foot against the wall, on a level with my hips. Then, gritting my teeth, I leaned back, taking my weight on my arms again, and swung my other leg up, bracing it against the wall on the other side of the pipe. With all my strength, I straightened my legs, pulling back against the handcuffs as hard as I could, my weight lending maximum force to my efforts.

At first, nothing happened. The cuffs dug into my hands, thankfully in a different place to the weals from my earlier suspension, but nothing moved. Then, suddenly, one of the brackets popped out of the walls like the pearl stud on a tight cowboy shirt. Another bracket followed it almost at once, and the pipe came away from the wall, bowing dramatically towards me. I bent my legs slightly, then prepared for a final, all-out effort. With a grunt that Monica Seles would have been proud of, I straightened my legs and hauled with everything I had. Just when I thought I would dislocate my shoulders, the pipe snapped about five feet from the ground and I crashed to the floor.

The roar of gushing water mingled with the roar of anger from behind me. I dragged myself upright and hauled my hands over the broken ends of the pipes, fast as I could. Even so, Moustache was on me as I swivelled round to face him. He'd grabbed the first thing to hand, which was the kettle, swinging it at my battered head. I did a staggering sidestep, as much to get away from the scalding blast of the hot pipe as to avoid the kettle. Moustache got the hot water straight in the face as the momentum of his running blow carried him past me and into the wall.

His scream would have been music to my ears if my head hadn't been splitting. Instead, all I wanted to do was shut him up. I aimed a Thai boxing kick at the crook of his knee. It was a pretty feeble kick, but he was off balance anyway. He dropped to his knees like a sack of spuds and I brought my clenched hands, complete with nasty sticking-out bits of handcuffs, down hard on the back of his neck. With a groan like an abandoned harmonium, he slumped against the wall and slithered down into the growing pool of water like something out of a Tom and Jerry cartoon.

I leaned against the sink, trying to catch my breath. I looked at the inert body crumpled at my feet and realized that all I had to do was walk away to get my own back for that gratuitous boot in the ribs. Given the rate the water was pouring into the kitchen, it wouldn't be long before Moustache said good night, Vienna.

Call me a wimp, but I couldn't do it. I crouched down, grabbed his hair and hauled his poleaxed head out of the water. I yanked him on to his back and propped him in a sitting position between the wall and the sink unit. I'm too nice for my own good.

Keeping one eye on him, I backed across the kitchen to the phone. Using both hands, I picked up the receiver and tucked it into my left shoulder. I punched in a familiar number and listened to it ring out. I was starting to panic when it reached the thirteenth ring: it's not easy being patient when you know someone's on their way to send you to the crematorium.

Just as I was about to abandon the phone and leg it, the ringing stopped and a blurred voice muttered, ''Lo?'

'Della? It's Kate. This is an emergency. Are you awake?'

There was a grunt, then Della said, 'Getting there. What is it?'

'Della, there's a guy on his way to kill me. It'll take too long to explain it all now, but he's the hit man who killed Cherie Roberts, the single mum who got blown away this afternoon? He's coming after me!' I could hear the hysteria rising in my voice, and I was overwhelmed by the urge to giggle.

'Kate? Are you pissed?' Della asked incredulously.

'No, but I think I've been drugged,' I said. 'I swear this isn't a wind-up, Della. I know it's not your beat, but you've got to get a posse out here right away, double urgent. This guy's a paid killer.

And he's after me!' Even to me, my voice sounded like Minnie Mouse.

'OK, calm down. Where exactly are you?'

'I'm in a house on the corner of Oliver Tambo Close, near the Apollo. The house is full of kiddy porn. They've been drugging the kids to get them to perform,' I gabbled.

'Later, Kate, later,' Della interrupted. 'I'm going to hang up now and get the local lads to send the area car round there pronto. And I'll be there myself as soon as I can. But I want you to get out of there right now. Don't hang about. Just get out. Go back to your house and I'll meet you there.'

I snorted with insane laughter. I was beginning to feel really silly. 'I can't go there,' I giggled. 'He knows where I live. He's already blown my door away.' Before she could make another suggestion, the line went dead. Not the way it goes when someone hangs up on you. This was dead, hollow, a void. Suddenly, I didn't feel like giggling any more. Somewhere outside the house was the man who had been sent to kill me. And his automatic first action was to cut the lines of communication.

I checked my pockets for the van keys, but they weren't there. Wildly, I looked around the kitchen. I spotted them on one of the worktops, along with my wallet. I paddled through the water and picked them up, stuffing my wallet in my trouser pocket. In the kitchen doorway, I hesitated, water flowing like a spring stream round my ankles, trying to decide whether the assassin would approach from the front or the rear.

I didn't wonder for long. With a crash that reverberated round my skull, the back door slammed against the wall. I didn't even wait to look. I whirled round to the front door. The gods were on my side, for the key was in the lock. I turned the key, pulled it out of the lock and yanked the door open. I was through it and had it closed in the time it took the hit man to travel the length of the hall. I shoved the key in the lock and turned it. Then I stumbled and weaved down the path, my breath coming in ragged sobs.

I'd reached the pavement when the night exploded in a pair of catastrophic bangs. I turned to look back at the house. The door was hanging drunkenly on one of its hinges, and the silhouette of a man was pushing it aside. In his right hand, he carried a sawn-off shotgun. I drew in my breath in a horrified moan and ran for my life.

Now I was swerving madly by design as I approached the van. I pressed the burglar alarm remote-control button, which unlocks the doors as well as deactivating the alarm. I was barely at the back of the van, and I could hear him gaining on me. Then, suddenly, the sound of his footsteps stopped. I knew he was taking aim. Desperately, I threw myself into a rolling somersault round the rear of the van to the passenger side, putting the van between him and me.

Weeping with fear, sweating in spite of the cold

night air on my freshly grazed skin, I scrambled to my feet and staggered along the side of the van to the passenger door. I grabbed the door handle like a lifeline and pulled myself into the cab. I had the presence of mind to lock the doors behind me. I fumbled the key into the ignition at the second attempt.

I was still cuffed, so driving wasn't going to be easy. I swivelled round to shift the gear stick into first, then released the handbrake. Movement at the edge of my peripheral vision made me swing round to look out of the driver's window. The shock of what I saw nearly had me stalling the engine. As it was, I let the clutch out way too fast and the van bucked forward in a series of jumps like a kangaroo on acid.

In my wing mirror, I saw him step back involuntarily to avoid having his feet run over by the van's rear wheels. Crazy Eddy Roberts, locked somewhere on the slopes of Mount Tumbledown, clutching his gun like mothers clutch frightened children. A man who'd lost touch with human feelings to the point where there was nothing difficult about taking a damn sight more than thirty pieces of silver to kill the mother of his children.

For a fraction of a second, our eyes locked. The engine was screaming a protest at still being in first, so I took my hands off the steering wheel to change up into second. When I looked in my mirror again, the twin barrels of the gun gleamed dully in the distant streetlights as Eddy swung it up towards me. I put my foot down and grabbed the steering wheel. I could feel the van fishtailing as I tried to wrench the wheel round to clear the oncoming corner.

I heard the boom of the gun as the window shattered. I'd lost control of the van almost simultaneously. I hit the kerb at speed and clipped a lamppost. As the van toppled over on its side, the last thing I saw was a pair of flashing blue lights.

25

I couldn't believe how blue the sea was. It glittered under Mediterranean sunlight like one of those crystal beds that New Age fanatics have lying around their living-rooms. I propped myself up on one elbow and watched the lumbering half-tracked harvesters further down the beach, gathering and refining the spice that had caused the planet wars that had ravaged Dune for a generation. Suddenly, the sand shifted, only feet away from my leg, and the head of a huge, carnivorous sandworm reared up. The ferocious jaws opened, to reveal Moustache's face.

I swam up the levels to consciousness, passing from dreaming to awareness via that state where you know that you've just been dreaming, but you're not quite awake. My head felt like an oversized block of stone, though there didn't seem to be as much pain as I remembered enduring before the accident. The accident!

My eyes snapped open. I was in a small room,

dimly illumined by lights glowing through frosted glass from the corridor outside. I tried to lift my head, but it was too much of an effort. Instead, I shifted my feet to check I was still functioning below the neck. You put your left leg in, you put your left leg out . . . Yeah, the lower limbs all did the hokey cokey. I breathed deeply. There was a bit of pain from my ribs and chest, but nothing felt broken, which was pretty miraculous given that I hadn't been wearing my seat belt when I crashed the van. I raised my right arm, which seemed fine, apart from the puffy bruises that ran round hand and wrist like designer bangles by the Marquis de Sade. My left arm had no watch on it, only grazes from shoulder to wrist, and a drip running into the back of my hand, which was more than a little disconcerting.

I moved my head to one side, trying to see if there was a clock anywhere. To my surprise, Della was fast asleep on a plastic bucket chair next to my bed. I felt mildly outraged. Someone had tried to kill me tonight, and she should have been down the police station, going through the hoops of the Police and Criminal Evidence Act to make sure Crazy Eddy spent the foreseeable future living at the taxpayers' expense in a room with a bucket to piss in and bars on the windows. Then a horrible thought struck me. What if Eddy Roberts had managed to give the plod a body swerve? What if Della was Greater Manchester Police's idea of a bodyguard? What if Crazy Eddy was still out there with his pump-action double-barrelled shotgun packed with cartridges with my name on?

I opened my mouth. My brain said, 'Della?' but my mouth was too dry to play along. All I managed was a sort of strangulated croak.

She must only have been catnapping, for her eyes opened at once. Momentarily, she had the startled look of someone who has lost track of where she is. Then her conscious mind checked in and she sat bolt upright, staring at me with undisguised relief. 'Kate?' she said softly. 'Can you hear me?'

I tried to nod, but it wasn't in my repertoire yet. I waved my arm in the direction of the locker, where there was a jug of water and a bottle of orange juice. 'Drink?' I mouthed.

Della jumped up and poured a glass of water. She leaned over me and tipped the glass to my lips. Most of the water went down my cheeks and on to the pillow, but I didn't care. All I was concerned about was getting some in my parched mouth. The water was warm and stale and blissful. I didn't want to swallow, just hold it there in my mouth. Della gave me a concerned, anxious look as I waved her away.

Finally, I let the water trickle down my throat. 'Thanks,' I said in something approaching my normal voice. 'What are you doing here? Shouldn't you be down the cells beating a confession out of that mad bastard with the shotgun?' She gave me an odd look. 'You did *catch* him, didn't you,'

I demanded, panic gripping my chest and turning my stomach over.

'We caught him,' Della said grimly. 'The officers from Longsight got slightly over-enthusiastic with their truncheons when they realized he had a gun. Your assailant has a broken collar bone and a shattered wrist, you'll be sorry to hear.'

'Is that why you're here and not down the nick taking a statement?' I asked.

Della looked awkward. 'Actually, no,' she said, shifting in her seat. 'Kate, this isn't the same day,' she said in a rush.

I frowned. 'Not the same day? What do you mean?'

'You called me in the early hours of Wednesday morning.' She glanced at her watch. 'It's now four forty-seven a.m. on Thursday. You've been out cold for over a day.'

'Over a day?' I echoed foolishly. I couldn't take it in. I had no sense of having lost a day of my life. I felt like I'd woken up from a strange dream after a brief spell of unconsciousness. Did people feel like this when they came out of comas that lasted weeks or years? No wonder they felt dislocated. I'd only lost a day and I felt like I'd stumbled into an episode of the *Twilight Zone*. I managed a twisted grin. 'You know it's a bad case when the only way you can catch up on your sleep is to get unconscious.'

'I'm glad you can joke about it. We were starting to get really worried. The doctors gave you a brain scan and said there seemed to be no damage, but they couldn't say how long you'd be out.'

'Does Richard know?' I asked.

'I discussed it with Bill and Ruth, and we decided not to tell him before this morning's hearing. It seemed the best solution.'

'Yeah,' I sighed. 'He couldn't have done anything, and they wouldn't have let him out unless I was really at death's door. It would only have had him climbing the walls. The last thing he needs right now is to be charged with assaulting a police officer.' The only good thing I could see about having lost an entire day was that I wouldn't have to wait so long to see Richard again. With luck, he'd be out on bail by lunch time.

'How are you feeling?' Della asked.

'Took your time asking, didn't you?' I teased.

Della looked hurt for a few seconds, before it sank in that I was at the wind-up. 'Listen, Brannigan,' she said, pretending to be stern, 'I don't have to be here. I'm not on duty. I'm here out of the goodness of my heart, you know.'

'Thanks,' I said, meaning it. 'I'm impressed. I've never known you go this long without a cigarette voluntarily. Actually, I don't feel too bad. A bit woozy, that's all. And my head's throbbing. And now I'm awake, they'll probably give me something for that. At least I know I'll be out of here in a few days. How's Crazy Eddy handling it, being locked up in a cell?'

Della stiffened to attention again. Her face shifted

from concerned friend to alert copper. 'You *know* who this guy is?'

'Why? Don't you?'

She looked faintly embarrassed. 'As it happens, we don't. He won't say a word. He had nothing on him that would identify him, and his prints don't seem to be on record. Who is he?'

'His name's Eddy Roberts. He's an ex-Para. He got invalided out a couple of years after the Falklands war because he was out to lunch and not coming back. He's supposedly been working all over the globe as a mercenary. He's been back in Manchester since Easter. Apparently working as a hired gun. Among other things.' I stopped, suddenly exhausted.

'Kate, I know you've been through it, and I'm sorry to have to keep on at you. This isn't the time to take a formal statement, but this is really important information. How do you know all this? Have you been chasing him?' She had the good grace to look ashamed of herself.

I gave one of those laughs that turns into a cough halfway through. 'No, Della. He was chasing me, remember. The reason I know so much about Crazy Eddy is because his wife and kids told me. Eddy Roberts used to be married to Cherie Roberts. The woman he blew away outside the post office on Tuesday.'

That was revelation enough to shatter Della's official cool. 'You mean, that wasn't a professional hit job? It was a domestic?'

'It was a hit job all right. Cherie had found out about the child porn racket. And I expect she threatened that she'd spill the beans to me. The fact that Eddy used to be married to her was, I suspect, totally irrelevant. If anything, it probably made it more exciting.'

'And that's how you got involved? Through Cherie?'

I was growing wearier by the second, but I forced a smile. 'I thought you weren't taking a statement?' Della started to apologize but I waved it aside. 'Only joking, honest. No, I got involved because Davy came home stoned out of his mind.' I gave Della the thirty-second version of events around Oliver Tambo Close. I'd just got to the bit about interviewing Wayne and Daniel when we were interrupted.

She was only in her mid-twenties, but the night sister was fierce. 'Is the patient awake?' she demanded. 'Chief Inspector, I gave you strict instructions to ring for a nurse if the patient showed signs of coming round. You've got no right to interrogate her on my ward without my permission.'

'It's my fault,' I butted in. 'I wanted to know what had happened.'

The sister busied herself with my pulse. 'You're in no fit state to discuss it,' she said firmly. 'Chief Inspector, I'm going to have to ask you to leave. You can come back after Mr Rocco has seen the patient and if he decides she's fit to be interviewed.'

Della got to her feet meekly and winked. 'See you soon, Kate,' she said.

'I hope so,' I sighed. 'Oh, Della – before you go . . . Sister, can I ask the officer one question?'

The sister smiled, unexpectedly. 'If you must. But keep it short,' she added, frowning pointedly at Della.

'The van. What sort of state is it in?'

'Amazingly enough, it's just superficial damage. You'll be relieved to hear it's not a write-off, according to Bill last night.' She edged towards the door. 'Thanks for your help, Kate.'

I watched her retreating back while the sister bustled about doing sisterly things to my reflexes. She asked me who the Prime Minister was, and I told her about the pain, so she gave me some pills once she'd finished her neurological observations. The last thing I remembered as I drifted into sleep was being grateful that I hadn't written off the Little Rascal. It was only seven months since another homicidal nutter had sent my last company car to the great scrap yard in the sky. Any more of that, and the insurance premiums were going to be higher than the price of a new set of wheels.

The next time my eyes flickered open, I thought I was hallucinating. There, sitting on the uncomfortable chair, brown hair flopping across his forehead, eyes intent behind his glasses, was Richard. Seeing me waken, a slow, joyful smile spread across his face. I'd never seen a more welcome sight. 'Hiya,

Brannigan,' he said. 'You're not fit to be let out on your own, are you?' He stretched out an arm and gripped my right hand tightly. The bruises sent out a protest bulletin on all frequencies, but I didn't care.

'You're a fine one to talk,' I said. 'This is all your fault anyway.'

'I had a funny feeling it was going to be,' he said, grinning. 'I see the blow to your head hasn't improved your grasp of logic. They tell me you've not got brain damage, but I told the consultant different. He said there was nothing they could do about the state you were in before the accident. So I'm just going to have to live with it.'

'Did you get bail, or was it Group 4 that escorted you to court this morning?'

'The police withdrew their objections to bail, and they let me go without conditions. Ruth says they'll drop charges once they've nailed the real guys in the black hats and cleared me. I came straight here, you know. I didn't even go home for fresh clothes and a joint. You did a great job, Brannigan.' He released my hand and dropped to his knees, hands clenched in supplication. 'How can I ever repay you?'

'I'll think of something,' I said. 'You can start by giving me a kiss.'

He jumped to his feet. 'I'll have to close my eyes,' he said, mock-seriously.

'I look that bad?' I demanded, suddenly discovering a new anxiety. I put my hand up to my head, discovering a thick turban of bandage that extended halfway down my forehead.

'Two lovely black eyes, two lovely black eyes,' he sang. 'And a whopping great bruise on your jaw. Linda Evangelista won't be worrying about you taking her place on the catwalk for a while.' Before I could say anything more, he stooped over me and kissed me gently on the lips.

'Call that a kiss?' I snarled.

It got better after that.

When he finally came up for air, he said softly, 'I love you, Brannigan.'

'Don't go getting soft on me,' I murmured. 'You're only saying that because I got you out of jail.'

'And you took care of my kid. I've heard all about what went on. Bill came to court this morning and told me how you'd ended up in here.'

'Speaking of which,' I interrupted before he got hopelessly sentimental in the way that only cynical journos can. 'Where is Davy?'

'Alexis took the day off to look after him. They've gone off to some fun palace this morning. She told Bill she'd meet me here . . .' he glanced at his watch. 'In about ten minutes, actually.'

'God, you'd better not let him in here if I'm as much of a sight as you seem to think I am. He'll have nightmares for weeks.'

'Brannigan, you're talking about a kid who thought *Dracula* was a fun movie. I don't think a couple of bruises and a heavy-duty headscarf are going to freak him out. He knows you were in a car crash. The only thing I'm worried about is what he's going to tell his mother.'

Epilogue

On the first day of Davy's summer holidays, the
three of us giggled our way along Blackpool prom
on the open top deck of a tram. I was wearing
a baseball cap that said 'Kiss me slow'. Tacky, I
know, but it covered the uneven hair growth. At
least it wasn't stubble any more. I'd been less than
thrilled to discover I had a bald patch where they'd
had to shave me when they stitched up the hole
that Moustache's tripod had made in the back of
my head. The hair seems to be coming back just
fine over the scar, but it's knackered my attempts
at growing my hair. I'm back to short and spiky.
Passé, sure, but I hadn't had a lot of choice. And
I didn't look too much like a punk now the deep
bruising had finally faded.

Davy had insisted on coming back north for
part of the summer because he'd had such a good
time at half-term. I can only presume he gave his
mother a highly edited version of events, since
she made no objection. We'd spent most of the

day at the Pleasure Beach, only giving up on the white-knuckle rides when Richard dumped his lunch down the drain after a spectacular trip round the Grand National.

Now we were heading for the tower. Richard had decided that physically being on top of the world was the best way to symbolize the fact that as of tomorrow he'd officially be a free man. 'I can't wait,' he said as we queued for the lift.

'I didn't think you were into views,' I said.

'No, for tomorrow, stupid. I can't wait to hear the prosecuting solicitor saying they're dropping all the charges against me.'

I squeezed his hand. 'Me too.' It had been an interesting few weeks. In spite of his misgivings about my information, Geoff Turnbull had put full surveillance on Terry Fitz, Jammy James and the chemical kitchen. They'd swooped in the early hours of Friday morning. They'd actually caught Terry Fitz red-handed in a stolen Mazda MX5 halfway down the M40 with trade plates and five kilos of crack in the boot. A dozen bodies had been remanded in custody at Saturday morning's Magistrates' Court. According to Ruth, nothing had come up in the interviews that even remotely implicated Richard or me. The police had even managed to establish that James and his team of dealers still had no idea who had driven off in a 'stolen' car with a boot full of crack. Best of all, the police seemed to think they wouldn't need me to testify in court, which I reckoned significantly increased my chances of celebrating my thirtieth birthday. After all, Crazy Eddy wasn't the only hit man in Greater Manchester.

Speaking of Crazy Eddy, he'd been charged with murdering Cherie and attempting to murder me. According to Della, it looked like he was also going to be charged with a couple of other street shootings in Moss Side just after Easter. He was still doing the Trappist monk routine with all of the coppers who'd done their brains in trying to interview him. He hadn't even asked for a solicitor. Interestingly, it turned out that Terry Fitz had been in the Paras with Crazy Eddy, which was how Eddy had got involved as spotter for the car stealing racket. The police also suspected that Jammy James's outfit was responsible for recommending him to the child-porn merchants as a hit man.

There was another connection between the two teams. It turned out that James's mob were supplying the designer drugs for the kids to the child-porn gang in exchange for videos they could sell on through their own network. Or, in the case of one of Terry Fitz's cronies, hang on to for their own sick purposes. Which explained the mysterious Polaroid that had slipped down the side of the seat in the Gemini coupé.

The house in Oliver Tambo Close had been a proper little gold mine for the Vice Squad. Not only had they put a stop to the racket, they'd found the porn makers' mailing list, investigation of which was currently causing marital difficulties from Land's End to John O'Groats; or rather, from an executive housing estate in Penzance to a croft on the Shetland Isles. Served them right too. The only bleak piece of news was that the two middle-aged bastards who'd made most of the profits from the sleazy trade had legged it at the first sign of trouble. The word is they're somewhere on the Algarve, playing golf.

And the police had finally released Andrew Broderick's Leo Gemini turbo super coupé. In his shoes, I'd have been less than thrilled at being deprived of one of my company's flagship motors for so long, but Andrew was a happy man. More than two months had passed since Richard and I had started doing the groundwork to expose the fiddle that the car dealerships were up to. And not a single one of the cars we'd purchased had been reported sold to his finance company. Which meant Andrew had been absolutely right about the scam, and with every day that passed without the cars being notified, he had more ammo to fight the war for his new distribution system.

Not only that, but the vague hunch I'd had had paid off in spades. With all the aggro there had been the day after the bank holiday, I'd completely forgotten Julia was supposed to be sending me a fax. When I finally got out of hospital, it was sitting in my in-tray, buried in a pile of correspondence that Shelley had been carefully nurturing for me.

What I'd asked Julia for was a company check

on both Richmond Credit Finance and the chain of car dealerships that had been the main target of our investigation. It wasn't difficult to come by the information. The only reason we don't have it on-line ourselves is that it's more cost-effective for us to get the info from Josh than to subscribe to the appropriate database. Anyway, when I'd been able to get my eyes to focus properly, I'd compared the two sets of directors. Surprise, surprise. The managing director and principal shareholder of Richmond Credit Finance was the wife of the managing director and principal shareholder of the garages, an interesting coincidence that is currently occupying some of the working hours of Detective Chief Inspector Della Prentice.

So, instead of trying to bully us into cutting our bill, Andrew was keen to make sure we felt Mortensen and Brannigan were properly rewarded for our efforts. I wasn't about to argue with him.

After the tower, there was nothing for it but fish and chips. I suggested beating the traffic by going back to Harry Ramsden's in Manchester, and the idea was supported by two votes to one. To take Davy's mind off his disappointment, we challenged him to a race back to the car. We let him win, of course. He looked much more appealing than the Rolls Royce silver lady sitting on the bonnet of my slightly shop soiled, midnight blue Leo Gemini turbo super coupé GLXi. Some days you eat the bear.

Star Struck

ACKNOWLEDGEMENTS

I was a journalist for many years on a newspaper that became increasingly obsessed with the world of soaps. As a result, I have forgotten more than any respectable person would want to know about the private lives of many household names. Nevertheless, the fictional soap *Northerners* and its cast are entirely creatures of my imagination. Any resemblances to the real or fictional characters of any actual regular drama series are entirely coincidental and purely accidental. Besides, I'm not worth suing.

The legal advice came from Brigid Baillie, Jai Penna and Paula Tyler; any errors are either deliberate mistakes for dramatic effect, or just plain stupidity. Jennifer Paul also provided crucial information, in exchange for which I promise never to tell the story about the golden retriever.

Thanks too to my agents Jane Gregory and Lisanne Radice and my editors Julia Wisdom and Karen Godfrey who, because of the wonders of e-mail, were able to shower me with queries the length and breadth of three continents.

Prologue

Extract from the computer database of
Dorothea Dawson, Seer to the Stars

Written in the Stars for Kate Brannigan,
private investigator.

Born Oxford, UK, 4th September 1966.

* Sun in Virgo in the Fifth House
* Moon in Taurus in the Twelfth House
* Mercury in Virgo in the Fifth House
* Venus in Leo in the Fourth House
* Mars in Leo in the Fourth House
* Jupiter in Cancer in the Third House
* Saturn retrograde in Pisces in the Eleventh House
* Uranus in Virgo in the Fifth House
* Neptune in Scorpio in the Sixth House
* Pluto in Virgo in the Fifth House
* Chiron in Pisces in the Eleventh House
* Ascendant Sign: Gemini

1

SUN IN VIRGO IN THE 5TH HOUSE

On the positive side, can be ingenious, verbally skilled, diplomatic, tidy, methodical, discerning and dutiful. The negatives are fussiness, a critical manner, an obsessive attention to detail and a lack of self-confidence that can disguise itself as arrogance. In the 5th House, it indicates a player of games.

From *Written in the Stars*, by Dorothea Dawson

My client was about to get a resounding smack in the mouth. I watched helplessly from the other side of the street. My adrenaline was pumping, but there was no way I could have made it to her side in time. That's the trouble with bodyguarding jobs. Even if you surround the client with a phalanx of Rutger Hauer clones and Jean Van Damme wannabes in bulletproof vests, the moment always comes when they're vulnerable. And guess who always gets the blame? That's why, when people come looking for a minder, the house rule at

Brannigan & Co: Investigations & Security states, 'We don't do that.'

But Christmas was coming and the goose was anorexic. Business had been as slow as a Post Office queue and even staff as unorthodox as mine expect to be paid on time. Besides, I deserved a festive bonus myself. Eating, for example. So I'd sent my better judgement on an early Yuletide break and agreed to take on a client who'd turned out to be more accident prone than Coco the Clown.

For once, it wasn't my fault that the client was in the front line. I'd had no say in what was happening out there on the street. If I'd wanted to stop it, I couldn't have. So, absolved from action for once, I stood with my hands in my pockets and watched Carla Hardcastle's arm swing round in a fearsome arc to deliver a cracking wallop that wiped the complacent smirk off Brenda Barrowclough's self-satisfied face. I sucked my breath in sharply.

'And cut,' the director said. 'Very nice, girls, but I'd like it one more time. Gloria, loved that smug little smile, but can you lose it at the point where you realize she's actually going to thump you? And let us see some outrage?'

My client gave a forbearing smile that was about as sincere as a beggar asking for tea money. 'Whatever you say, Helen, chuck,' she rasped in the voice that thrilled the nation three times a week as we shovelled down our microwave dinners in front of Manchester's principal contribution to the world of soap. Then she turned to me with an exaggerated wink and called, 'You're all right, chuck, it's only make believe.'

Everyone turned to stare at me. I managed to grin while clenching my teeth. It's a talent that comes in very handy in the private-eye business. It's having to deal with unscrupulous idiots that does it. And that's just the clients.

'That's my bodyguard,' Gloria Kendal – alias Brenda Barrowclough – announced to the entire cast and crew of *Northerners*.

'We'd all worked out it wasn't your body double,' the actress playing Carla said, apparently as sour in life as the character she played in the human drama that had wowed British audiences for the best part of twenty years.

'Let's hope you only get attacked by midgets,' Teddy Edwards added. He'd once been a stand-up comedian on the working men's club circuit, but he'd clearly been playing Gloria's screen husband for so long that he'd lost any comic talent he'd ever possessed. I might only be five feet three in my socks, but I wouldn't have needed to use too many of my Thai-boxing skills to bring a lump of lard like him to his knees. I gave him the hard stare and I'm petty enough to admit I enjoyed it when he cleared his throat and looked away.

'All right, settle down,' the director called. 'Places, please, and let's take it again from the top of the scene.'

'Can we have a bit of hush back there?' someone else added. I wondered what his job title was and how long I'd have to hang around the TV studios before I worked out who did what in a hierarchy that included best boys, gaffers and too many gofers to count. I figured I'd probably have long enough, the way things were going. There was a lot of time for idle reflection in this job. When Gloria was filming, silence was the rule. I couldn't ask questions, eavesdrop or burgle in pursuit of the information I needed to close the case. All there was for me to do was lean against the wall and watch. There was nothing remotely glamorous about witnessing the seventh take of a scene that was a long way from Shakespeare to start with. As jobs went, minding the queen of the nation's soaps was about as exotic as watching rain slide down a window.

It hadn't started out that way. When Gloria had swanned into our office, I'd known straight off it wasn't going to be a routine case. At Brannigan & Co, the private investigation firm that I run, we cover a wide spectrum of work. Previously, when I'd been in partnership with Bill Mortensen, we'd mostly investigated white-collar fraud, computer security, industrial espionage and sabotage, with a bit of miscellaneous meddling that friends occasionally dropped in our laps. Now Bill had moved to Australia, I'd had to cast my net wider to survive. I'd clawed back some process-serving from a handful of law firms, added 'surveillance' to the letterheading and canvassed insurance companies for work exposing fraudulent claims. Even so,

Gloria Kendal's arrival in our front office signalled something well out of the ordinary.

Not that I'd recognized her straight away. Neither had Shelley, the office administrator, and she's got the X-ray vision of every mother of teenagers. My first thought when Gloria had swept through the door on a wave of Estée Lauder's White Linen was that she was a domestic violence victim. I couldn't think of another reason for the wide-brimmed hat and the wraparound sunglasses on a wet December afternoon in Manchester.

I'd been looking over Shelley's shoulder at some information she'd downloaded from Companies House when the woman had pushed open the door and paused, dramatically framed against the hallway. She waited long enough for us to look up and register the expensive swagger of her mac and the quality of the kelly-green silk suit underneath, then she took three measured steps into the room on low-heeled pumps that precisely matched the suit. I don't know about Shelley, but I suspect my astonishment showed.

There was an air of expectancy in the woman's pose. Shelley's, 'Can I help you?' did nothing to diminish it.

The woman smiled, parting perfectly painted lips the colour of tinned black cherries. 'I hope you can, chuck,' she said, and her secret was out.

'Gloria Kendal,' I said.

'Brenda Barrowclough,' Shelley said simultaneously.

Gloria chuckled. 'You're both right, girls. But we'll just let that be our little secret, eh?' I nodded blankly. The only way her identity was ever going to stay secret was if she kept her mouth shut. It was clear from three short sentences that the voice that had made Brenda Barrowclough the darling of impressionists the length and breadth of the comedy circuit wasn't something Gloria took on and cast off as readily as her character's trademark bottle-blonde beehive wig. Gloria really did talk in broad North Manchester with the gravelly growl of a bulldozer in low gear.

'How can I help you, Ms Kendal?' I asked, remembering my manners and stepping out from behind the reception desk. She might not be a CEO in a grey suit, but she clearly had enough in the bank to make sure we all had a very happy Christmas.

'Call me Gloria, chuck. In fact, call me any-thing except Brenda.' After twenty years of TV viewing, the raucous laugh was as familiar as my best friend's. 'I'm looking for Brannigan,' she said.

'You found her,' I said, holding out my hand.

Gloria dropped a limp bunch of fingers into mine and withdrew before I could squeeze them – the professional sign of someone who had to shake too many hands in a year. 'I thought you'd be a bloke,' she said. For once, it wasn't a complaint, merely an observation. 'Well, that makes things a lot easier. I were wondering what we'd do if Brannigan and

6

Co didn't have women detectives. Is there some place we can go and talk?'

'My office?' I gestured towards the open door.

'Grand,' Gloria said, sweeping past me and fluttering her fingers in farewell to Shelley.

We exchanged a look. 'Rather you than me,' Shelley muttered.

By the time I closed the door behind me, Gloria was settled into one corner of the sofa I use for informal client meetings. She'd taken off her hat and tossed it casually on the low table in front of her. Her own hair was a subtle ash-blonde cut in a gamine Audrey Hepburn style. Somehow it managed not to look ridiculous on a woman who had to be nudging sixty. She had the clear skin of a much younger woman, but none of the Barbie-doll tightness that goes with the overenthusiastic face-lift. As I sat down opposite her, she took off the sunglasses and familiar grey eyes crinkled in a smile. 'I know it's ridiculous, but even though people stare at the bins, they don't recognize Brenda behind them. They just think it's some daft rich bitch with delusions of grandeur.'

'Living a normal life must be tough,' I said.

'You're not kidding, chuck. They see you three times a week in their living room, and they think you're a member of the family. You let on who you are and next thing you know they're telling you all about their hernia operation and the state of their veins. It's a nightmare.' She shrugged out of her coat, opened her handbag and took out a packet of those long skinny brown cigarettes that look like cinnamon sticks, and a gold Dunhill lighter. She looked around, eyebrows raised.

Stifling a sigh, I got up and removed the saucer from under the Christmas cactus. I'd only bought it two days before but already the buds that had promised pretty cascades of flowers were predictably starting to litter the windowsill. Me and plants go together like North and South Korea. I tipped the water from the saucer into the bin and placed it on the table in front of Gloria. 'Sorry,' I said. 'It's the best I can do.'

She smiled. 'I used to work in a cat food factory. I've put my fags out in a lot worse, believe me.'

I preferred not to think about it. 'Well, Gloria, how can I help you?'

'I need a bodyguard.'

My eyebrows rose. 'We don't normally . . .'

'These aren't normal circumstances,' she said sharply. 'I don't want some thick as pigshit bodybuilder trailing round after me. I want somebody with a brain, somebody that can figure out what the heck's going on. Somebody that won't attract attention. Half my life I spend with the bloody press snapping round my ankles and the last thing I need is stories that I've splashed out on a hired gun. That's why I wanted a woman.'

'You said, "somebody that can figure out what the heck's going on",' I said, focusing on the need I probably could do something useful about. 'What seems to be the problem?'

'I've been getting threatening letters,' she said. 'Now, that's nothing new. Brenda Barrowclough is not a woman who minces her words, and there are a lot of folk out there as can't tell the difference between *Northerners* and the real world. You'd be too young to remember, but when I was first widowed in the series, back about fifteen years ago, I was snowed under with letters of condolence. People actually sent wreaths for the funeral, addressed to fifteen, Sebastopol Grove. The Post Office is used to it now, they just deliver direct to the studios, but back then the poor florists didn't know what to do. We had letters from cancer charities saying donations had been made to their funds in memory of Harry – that was my screen husband's name. Whenever characters move out, we get letters from punters wondering what the asking price is for the house. So whenever Brenda does owt controversial, I get hate mail.'

I dredged my memory for recent tabloid headlines. 'Hasn't there been some storyline about abortion? Sorry, I don't get the chance to watch much TV.'

'You're all right, chuck. Me neither. You know Brenda's granddaughter, Debbie?'

'The one who's lived with Brenda since she was about ten? After her mum got shot in the Post Office raid?'

'You used to be a fan, then?'

'I still watch when I can. Which was a lot more back when Debbie was ten than it is now.'

'Well, what's happened is that Brenda's found out that Debbie's had an abortion. Now, Brenda had a real down on Debbie's boyfriend because he was black, so the audience would have expected her to support Debbie rather than have a mixed-race grandson. But Brenda's only gone mental about the right to life and thrown Debbie out on her ear, hasn't she? So me and Sarah Anne Kelly who plays Debbie were expecting a right slagging off.'

'And that's what's happened?'

Gloria shook her head, leaving a ribbon of smoke drifting level with her mouth. 'Sort of,' she said, confusing me. 'What happens is the studio goes through our post, weeding out the really nasty letters so we don't get upset. Only, of course, you ask, don't you? I mean, you want to know if there's any real nutters out there looking for you.'

'And the studio told you there was?'

'No, chuck. It weren't the studio. The letters I'm worried about are the ones coming to the house.'

Now I was really confused. 'You mean, your real house? Where you actually live?'

'Exactly. Now, I mean, it's not a state secret, where I live. But unless you're actually a neighbour or one of the reptiles of the press, you'd have to go to a bit of trouble to find out. The phone's ex-directory, of course. And all the official stuff like electricity bills and the voters' roll don't come

10

under Gloria Kendal. They come under my real name.'

'Which is?'

'Doreen Satterthwaite.' She narrowed her eyes. I didn't think it was because the smoke was getting into them. I struggled to keep my face straight. Then Gloria grinned. 'Bloody awful, isn't it? Do you wonder I chose Gloria Kendal?'

'In your shoes, I'd have done exactly the same thing,' I told her. I wasn't lying. 'So these threatening letters are coming directly to the house?'

'Not just to my house. My daughter's had one too. And they're different to the usual.' She opened her handbag again. I wondered at a life where it mattered to have suit, shoes and handbag in identical shades. I couldn't help my mind slithering into speculation about her underwear. Did her coordination extend that far?

Gloria produced a sheet of paper. She started to pass it to me, then paused. I could have taken it from her, but it was an awkward reach, so I waited. 'Usually, letters like this, they're semi-literate. They're ignorant. I mean, I might have left school when I were fifteen, but I know the difference between a dot and a comma. Most of the nutters that write me letters wouldn't know a paragraph if they woke up next to one. They can't spell, and they've got a tendency to write in green ink or felt-tip pens. Some of them, I don't think they're allowed sharp objects where they live,' she added. I've noticed how actors and audiences often

11

hold each other in mutual contempt. It looked like Gloria didn't have a whole lot of respect for the people who paid for the roof over her head.

Now she passed the letter across. It was plain A4 bond, the text printed unidentifiably on a laser printer. *'Doreen Satterthwaite, it's time you paid for what you've done. You deserve to endure the same suffering you've been responsible for. I know where you live. I know where your daughter Sandra and her husband Keith live. I know your granddaughter Joanna goes to Gorse Mill School. I know they worship at St Andrew's Church and have a caravan on Anglesey. I know you drive a scarlet Saab convertible. I know you, you bitch. And soon you're going to be dead. But there'll be no quick getaway for you. First, you're going to suffer.'* She was right. The letter sounded disturbingly in control.

'Any idea what the letter writer is referring to?' I asked, not really expecting an honest answer.

Gloria shrugged. 'Who the heck knows? I'm no plaster saint, but I can't think of anybody I've done a really bad turn to. Apart from my ex, and I doubt he could manage a letter to me that didn't include the words, "you effing bitch". He certainly can't manage a conversation without it. And besides, he wouldn't threaten our Sandra or Joanna. No way.' I took her response for genuine perplexity, then reminded myself how she made her living.

'Have there been many of them?'

'This is the third. Plus the one that went to

12

Sandra. That were about the sins of the mother. To be honest, the first couple I just binned. I thought they were somebody at the wind-up.' Suddenly, Gloria looked away. She fumbled another cigarette from the packet and this time, the hand that lit it shook.

'Something happened to change your mind?'

'My car tyres were slashed. All four of them. Inside the NPTV compound. And there was a note stuck under the windscreen wipers. "Next time your wardrobe? Or you?" And before you ask, I haven't got the note. It'd been raining. It just fell to bits in my hand.'

'That's serious business,' I said. 'Are you sure you shouldn't be talking to the police?' I hated to lose a potential client, but it would have verged on criminal negligence not to point out that this might be one for Officer Dibble.

Gloria fiddled with her cigarette. 'I told the management about it. And John Turpin, he's the Administration and Production Coordinator, he persuaded me not to go to the cops.'

'Why not? I'd have thought the management would have been desperate to make sure nothing happened to their stars.'

Gloria's lip curled in a cynical sneer. 'It were nowt to do with my safety and everything to do with bad publicity. Plus, who'd want to come and work at NPTV if they found out the security was so crap that somebody could walk into the company compound and get away with that?

Anyway, Turpin promised me an internal inquiry, so I decided to go along with him.'

'But now you're here.' It's observational skills like this that got me where I am today.

She flashed a quick up-and-under glance at me, an appraisal that contained more than a hint of fear held under tight control. 'You're going to think I'm daft.'

I shook my head. 'I don't see you as the daft type, Gloria.' Well, it was only a white lie. Daft enough to spend the equivalent of a week's payroll for Brannigan & Co on a matching outfit, but probably not daft when it came to a realistic assessment of personal danger. Mind you, neither was Ronald Reagan and look what happened to him.

'You know Dorothea Dawson?' Gloria asked, eyeing me out of the corner of her eye.

'"The Seer to the Stars"?' I asked incredulously. 'The one who does the horoscopes in *TV Viewer*? The one who's always on the telly? "A horse born under the sign of Aries will win the Derby"?' I intoned in a cheap impersonation of Dorothea Dawson's sepulchral groan.

'Don't mock,' she cautioned me, wagging a finger. 'She's a brilliant clairvoyant, you know. Dorothea comes into the studios once a week. She's the personal astrologer to half the cast. She really has a gift.'

I bet she had. Gifts from all the stars of *Northerners*. 'And Dorothea said something about these letters?'

14

'I took this letter in with me to my last consultation with her. I asked her what she could sense from it. She does that as well as the straight clairvoyance. She's done it for me before now, and she's never been wrong.' In spite of her acting skills, anxiety was surfacing in Gloria's voice.

'And what did she say?'

Gloria drew so hard on her cigarette that I could hear the burning tobacco crackle. As she exhaled she said, 'She held the envelope and shivered. She said the letter meant death. Dorothea said death was in the room with us.'

2

SUN TRINE MOON

Creative thinking resolves difficult circumstances; she will tackle difficulties with bold resolution. The subject feels at home wherever she is, but can be blind to the real extent of problems. She will not always notice if her marriage is falling apart; she doesn't always nip problems in the bud.

From *Written in the Stars*, by Dorothea Dawson

Anybody gullible enough to fall for the doom and gloom dished out by professional con merchants like astrologers certainly wasn't going to have a problem with my expense sheets. Money for old rope, I reckoned. By Gloria's own admission, hate mail was as much part of the routine in her line of work as travelling everywhere with stacks of postcard-sized photographs to autograph for the punters. OK, the tyre slashing was definitely more serious, but that might be unconnected to the letters, an isolated act of vindictiveness. It was only

16

because the Seer to the Stars had thrown a wobbler that this poison pen outbreak had been blown up to life-threatening proportions. 'Does she often sense impending death when she does predictions for people?' I asked, trying not to snigger.

Gloria shook her head vigorously. 'I've never heard of anybody else getting a prediction like that.'

'And have you told other people in the cast about it?'

'Nobody,' she said. 'It's not the sort of thing you go on about.'

Not unless you liked being laughed at, I reckoned. On the other hand, it might mean that the death prediction was one of Dorothea Dawson's regular routines for putting the frighteners on her clients and making them more dependent on her. Especially the older ones. Let's face it, there can't be that many public figures Gloria's age who go through more than a couple of months without knowing somebody who's died or dying. Gloria might have been catapulted into panic by her astrologer, but I couldn't imagine it being anything more than a stunt by Dorothea Dawson. Minding Gloria sounded like a major earner with no risk attached. Just what the bank manager ordered. I said a small prayer of thanks to Dorothea Dawson and told Gloria that for her, I'd be happy to make an exception to company policy. In fact, I would take personal responsibility for her safety.

The news seemed to cheer her up. 'Right then,

we'd better be off,' she said, stubbing out her cigarette and gathering her mac around her shoulders.

'We'd better be off?' I echoed.

She glanced at her watch, a chunky gold item with chips of diamond that glittered like a broken windscreen in a streetlight. 'Depends where you live, I suppose. Only, if I'm opening a theme pub in Blackburn at eight and we've both got to get changed and grab a bite to eat, we'll be cutting it a bit fine if we don't get a move on.'

'A theme pub in Blackburn,' I said faintly.

'That's right, chuck. I'm under contract to the brewery. It's straightforward enough. I turn up, tell a few jokes, sing a couple of songs to backing tapes, sign a couple of hundred autographs and off.' As she spoke, she was setting her hat at a rakish angle and replacing her sunglasses. As she made for the door, I dived behind the desk and swept my palmtop computer and my moby into my shoulder bag. I only caught up with her because she'd stopped to sign a glossy colour photograph of herself disguised as Brenda Barrowclough for Shelley.

Something terrible had happened to the toughest office manager in Manchester. Imagine Cruella De Vil transformed into one of those cuddly Dalmatian puppies, only more so. It was like watching Ben Nevis grovel. 'And could you sign one, "for Ted"?' she begged. I wished I had closed-circuit TV cameras covering the office. A video of this would keep Shelley off my back for months.

'No problem, there you go,' Gloria said, signing the card with a flourish. 'You right, Kate?'

I grabbed my coat and shrugged into it as I followed Gloria into the hall. She glanced both ways and down the stairwell before she set off. 'The last thing I need is somebody clocking me coming out of your office,' she said, trotting down the stairs at a fair pace. At the front door I turned right automatically, heading for my car. Gloria followed me into the private car park.

'This sign says, "Employees of DVS Systems only. Unauthorized users will be clamped,"' she pointed out.

'It's all right,' I said in a tone that I hoped would end the conversation. I didn't want to explain to Gloria that I'd got so fed up with the desperate state of car parking in my part of town that I'd checked out which office car parks were seldom full. I'd used the macro lens on the camera to take a photograph of a DVS Systems parking pass through somebody else's windscreen and made myself a passable forgery. I'd been parking on their lot for six months with no trouble, but it wasn't something I was exactly proud of. Besides, it never does to let the clients know about the little sins. It only makes them nervous.

Gloria stopped expectantly next to a very large black saloon with tinted windows. I shook my head and she pulled a rueful smile. I pointed the remote at my dark-blue Rover and it cheeped its usual greeting at me. 'Sorry it's not a limo,' I said to Gloria as we piled in. 'I need to be invisible most of the time.' I didn't feel the need to mention that the engine under the bonnet was very different from the unit the manufacturer had installed. I had enough horsepower under my bonnet to stage my own rodeo. If anybody was stalking Gloria, I could blow them off inside the first five miles.

I drove home, which took less than five minutes even in early rush-hour traffic. I love living so close to the city centre, but the area's become more dodgy in the last year. I'd have moved if I hadn't had to commit every spare penny to the business. I'd been the junior partner in Mortensen & Brannigan, and when Bill Mortensen had decided to sell up and move to Australia, I'd thought my career prospects were in the toilet. I couldn't afford to buy him out but I was damned if some stranger was going to end up with the lion's share of a business I'd worked so hard to build. It had taken a lot of creative thinking and a shedload of debt to get Brannigan & Co off the ground. Now I had a sleeping partner in the Cayman Islands and a deal to buy out his share of the business piecemeal as and when I could afford it, so it would be a long time before I could consider heading for the southern suburbs where all my sensible friends had moved.

Besides, the domestic arrangements were perfect. My lover Richard, a freelance rock journalist, owned the bungalow next door to mine, linked by a long conservatory that ran along the back of

20

both properties. We had all the advantages of living together and none of the disadvantages. I didn't have to put up with his mess or his music-business cronies; he didn't have to deal with my girls' nights in or my addiction to very long baths.

Richard's car, a hot-pink Volkswagen Beetle convertible, was in its slot, which, at this time of day, probably meant he was home. There might be other showbiz journos with him, so I played safe and asked Gloria to wait in the car. I was back inside ten minutes, wearing a bottle-green crushed-velvet cocktail dress under a dark-navy dupion-silk matador jacket. OTT for Blackburn, I know, but there hadn't been a lot of choice. If I didn't get to the dry cleaner soon, I'd be going to work in my dressing gown.

Gloria lived in Saddleworth, the expensively rural cluster of villages that hugs the edges of the Yorkshire moors on the eastern fringe of Greater Manchester. The hills are still green and rolling there, but on the skyline the dark humps of the moors lower unpleasantly, even on the sunniest of days. This is the wilderness that ate up the bodies of the child victims of Myra Hindley and Ian Brady. I can never drive through this brooding landscape without remembering the Moors Murders. Living on the doorstep would give me nightmares. It didn't seem to bother Gloria. But why would it? It didn't impinge either on her or on Brenda Barrowclough, and the half-hour drive out to Saddleworth was long enough for me to realize these were the only criteria that mattered to her. I'd heard it said that actors are like children in their unconscious self-absorption. Now I was seeing the proof.

In the December dark, Saddleworth looked like a Christmas card, early fairy lights twinkling against a light dusting of snow. I wished I'd listened to the weather forecast; the roads out here can be closed by drifts when there hasn't been so much as a flake on my roof. Yet another argument against country living. Gloria directed me down the valley in a gentle spiral to Greenfield. We turned off the main street into a narrow passage between two high walls. I hoped I wouldn't meet something coming the other way in a hurry. About a hundred yards in, the passage ended in two tall wrought-iron gates. Gloria fumbled with something in her handbag and the gates swung open.

I edged forward slowly, completely gobsmacked. I appeared to have driven into the set of a BBC period drama. I was in a large cobbled court-yard, surrounded on three sides by handsome two-storey buildings in weatherworn gritstone. Even my untrained eye can spot early Indus-trial Revolution, and this was a prime example. 'Wow,' I said.

'It were built as offices for the mill,' Gloria said, pointing me towards a pair of double doors in the long left-hand side of the square. 'Leave the car in front of my garage for now. Then the mill became a cat food factory. Sound familiar?'

'The factory where you used to work?'

'Got it in one.' She opened the car door and I followed her across the courtyard. The door she stopped at was solid oak, the lock a sensible mortise. As we went in, a burglar alarm klaxoned its warning. While Gloria turned it off, I walked across the wide room that ran the whole depth of the building. Through the tall window, I could see light glinting off water. The house backed on to the canal. Suddenly life looked better. This house was about as impregnable as they come. Unless Gloria's letter writer had the Venetian skill of climbing a ladder from a boat, I was going to be able to sleep in my own bed at night rather than across the threshold of Gloria's bedroom.

'It's beautiful,' I said.

'Especially when your living room used to be the cashier's office where you picked up your wages every week smelling of offal,' Gloria said ironically.

I turned back to look round the room. Wall uplighters gave a soft glow to burnished beams and the exposed stone of the three outer walls. The furnishings looked like a job lot from John Lewis, all pastel-figured damask and mahogany. The pictures on the wall were big watercolour landscapes of the Yorkshire moorland and the expanse of stripped floorboards was broken up by thick pile Chinese rugs. There was nothing to quarrel with, but nothing that spoke of individual taste, unlike Gloria's clothes. 'You live here alone?' I asked.

'Thank God,' she said with feeling, opening a walk-in cupboard and hanging up her coat.

'Anyone else have keys?'

'Only my daughter.' Gloria emerged and pointed to a door in the far wall. 'The kitchen's through there. There's a freezer full of ready meals. Do you want to grab a couple and stick them in the microwave while I'm getting changed?' Without waiting for an answer, she started up the open-plan staircase that climbed to the upper floor.

The kitchen was almost as big as the living room. One end was laid out as a dining area, with a long refectory table and a collection of unmatched antique farm kitchen chairs complete with patchwork cushions. The other end was an efficiently arranged working kitchen, dominated by an enormous freestanding fridge-freezer. The freezer was stacked from top to bottom with meals from Marks and Spencer. Maybe country living could be tolerable after all, I thought. All you needed to get through the winter was a big enough freezer and an endless supply of computer games. I chose a couple of pasta dishes and followed the instructions on the pack. By the time they were thawed and reheated, Gloria was back, dressed for action in a shocking-pink swirl of sequins. All it needed was the Brenda Barrowclough beehive to define camp kitsch better than any drag queen could have.

'Amazing,' I said faintly, scooping chicken and pasta into bowls.

'Bloody awful, you mean,' Gloria said, sitting down in a flounce of candyfloss. 'But the punters are paying for Brenda, not me.' She attacked her pasta like an extra from *Oliver Twist*. She finished while I was barely halfway through. 'Right,' she said, wiping her mouth with the back of her hand. 'I'll be five minutes putting on me slap and the wig. The dishwasher's under the sink.'

With anyone else, I'd have started to resent being ordered around. But I was beginning to get the hang of Gloria. She wasn't bossy as such. She was just supremely organized and blissfully convinced that her way was the best way. Life would inevitably be smoother for those around her who recognized this and went along with it unquestioningly. For now, I was prepared to settle for the quiet life. Later, it might be different, but I'd deal with that when later rolled round. Meanwhile, I loaded the dishwasher then went outside and started the car.

The drive to Blackburn was the last sane part of the evening. Gloria handed me a faxed set of directions then demanded that I didn't mither her with problems so she could get her head straight. I loaded an appropriate CD into the car stereo and drove to the ambient chill of Dreamfish while she reclined her seat and closed her eyes. I pulled up outside the pub three-quarters of an hour later, ten minutes before she was due to sparkle. She opened her eyes, groaned softly and said, 'It's a bit repetitive, that music. Have you got no Frank

Sinatra?' I tried to disguise my sense of impending doom. I failed. Gloria roared with raucous laughter and said, 'I were only winding you up. I can't bloody stand Sinatra. Typical man, I did it my own bloody-minded way. This modern stuff's much better.'

I left Gloria in the car while I did a brief reconnaissance of the venue. I had this vague notion of trying to spot any suspicious characters. I had more chance of hitting the Sahara on a wet Wednesday. Inside the pub, it was mayhem on a leash. Lads with bad haircuts and football shirts jostled giggling groups of girls dressed in what the high-street chain stores had persuaded them was fashion. Mostly they looked like they'd had a collision with their mothers' cast-offs from the seventies. I couldn't think of another reason for wearing Crimplene. The Lightning Seeds were revealing that football was coming home at a volume that made my fillings hurt. Provincial didn't begin to describe it. It was so different from the city-centre scene I began to wonder if we could have slipped through a black hole and ended up in the Andromeda galaxy. What a waste of a good frock.

The special opening night offer of two drinks for the price of one had already scored a clutch of casualties and the rest of the partygoers looked like they were hellbent on the same fate. I ducked back out and collected Gloria. 'I'll try to stay as close to you as I can,' I told her. 'It's a madhouse in there.'

She paused on the threshold, took a swift look round the room and said, 'You've obviously led a very sheltered life.' As she spoke, someone spotted her. The cry rippled across the room and within seconds the youth of Blackburn were cheering and bellowing a ragged chorus of the theme song from *Northerners*. And then we were plunged into the throbbing embrace of the crowd.

I gave up trying to keep Gloria from the assassin's knife after about twenty seconds when I realized that if I came between her and her public, I was the more likely candidate for a stiletto in the ribs. I wriggled backwards through the crowd and found a vantage point on the raised dais where the DJ was looking as cool as any man can who works for the local building society during the day. I was scanning the crowd automatically, looking for behaviour that didn't fit in. Easier said than done, given the level of drunken revelry around me. But from what I could see of the people crammed into the Frog and Scrannage, the natives were definitely friendly, at least as far as Gloria/Brenda was concerned.

I watched my client, impressed with her energy and her professionalism. She crossed the room slower than a stoned three-toed sloth, with a word and an autograph for everyone who managed to squeeze alongside. She didn't even seem to be sweating, the only cool person in the biggest sauna in the North West. When she finally made it to the dais, there was no shortage of hands to help her up. She turned momentarily and swiftly handed the DJ a cassette tape. 'Any time you like, chuck. Just let it run.'

The lad slotted it into his music deck and the opening bars of the *Northerners* theme crashed out over the PA, the audience swaying along. The music faded down and Gloria went straight into what was clearly a well-polished routine. Half a dozen jokes with a local spin, a clutch of anecdotes about her fellow cast members then, right on cue, the music swelled up under her and she belted out a segued medley of 'I Will Survive', 'No More Tears', 'Roll With It' and 'No Regrets'.

You had to be there.

The crowd was baying for more. They got it. 'The Power of Love' blasted our eardrums into the middle of next week. Then we were out of there. The car park was so cold and quiet I'd have been tempted to linger if I hadn't had the client to consider. Instead I ran to the car and brought it round to the doorway, where she was signing the last few autographs. 'Keep watching the show,' she urged them as she climbed into the car.

As soon as we were out of the car park, she pulled off the wig with a noisy sigh. 'What did you think?'

'Anybody who seriously wanted to damage you could easily get close enough. Getting away might be harder,' I said, half my attention on negotiating a brutal one-way system that could commit us to Chorley or Preston or some other fate worse than death if I didn't keep my wits about me.

'No, not that,' Gloria said impatiently. 'Never mind that. How was I? Did they love it?'

It was gone midnight by the time I'd deposited Gloria behind bolted doors and locked gates and driven back through the empty impoverished streets of the city's eastern fringes. Nothing much was moving except the litter in the wind. I felt a faint nagging throb in my sinuses, thanks to the assault of cigarette smoke, loud music and flashing lights I'd endured in the pub. I'd recently turned thirty; maybe some fundamental alteration had happened in my brain which meant my body could no longer tolerate all the things that spelled 'a good night out' to the denizens of Blackburn's latest fun pub. Perhaps there were hidden benefits in aging after all.

I yawned as I turned out of the council estate into the enclave of private housing where I occasionally manage a full night's sleep. Tonight wouldn't be one; Gloria had to be at the studios by nine thirty, so she wanted me at her place by eight thirty. I'd gritted my teeth, thought about the hourly rate and smiled.

I staggered up the path, slithering slightly on the frosted cobbles, already imagining the sensuous bliss of slipping under a winter-weight feather-and-down duvet. As soon as I opened the door, the dream shattered. Even from the hallway I could see the glow of light from the conservatory. I could hear moody saxophone music and the mutter of voices. That they were in the conservatory rather than Richard's living room meant that whoever he was talking to was there for me.

My bag slid to the floor as my shoulders drooped. I walked through to the living room and took in the scene through the patio doors. Beer bottles, a plume of smoke from a joint, two male bodies sprawled across the wicker.

Just what I'd always wanted at the end of a working day. A pair of criminals in the conservatory.

3

VENUS SQUARES NEPTUNE
This is a tense aspect that produces strain in affairs of the heart because she has a higher expectation of love and comradeship than her world provides. She has a strong determination to beat the odds stacked against her.

From *Written in the Stars*, by Dorothea Dawson

It's not every night you feel like you need a Visiting Order to enter your own conservatory. That night I definitely wanted reinforcements before I could face the music or the men. A quick trip to the kitchen and I was equipped with a sweating tumbler of ice-cold pepper-flavoured Absolut topped up with pink grapefruit juice. I took a deep draught and headed for whatever Dennis and Richard had to throw at me.

When I say the conservatory was full of criminals, I was only slightly exaggerating. Although

Richard's insistence on the need for marijuana before creativity can be achieved means he cheerfully breaks the law every day, he's got no criminal convictions. Being a journalist, he doesn't have any other kind either.

Dennis is a different animal. He's a career criminal but, paradoxically, I trust him more than almost anyone. I always know where I am with Dennis; his morality might not be constructed along traditional lines, but it's more rigid than the law of gravity, and a hell of a lot more forgiving. He used to be a professional burglar; not the sort who breaks into people's houses to steal the video and rummage through the lingerie, but the sort who relieves the very rich of some of their ill-gotten and well-insured gains. Some of his victims had so many expensive status symbols lying around that they didn't even realize they'd been burgled. These days, he's more or less given up robbing anyone except other villains who've got too much pride to complain to the law. That's because, after his last enforced spell of taking care of business from behind high walls with no office equipment except a phone card, his wife told him she'd divorce him if he ever did anything else that carried a custodial sentence.

I've known Dennis even longer than I've known Richard. He's my Thai-boxing coach, and he taught me the basic principle of self-defence for someone as little as I am – one crippling kick to the kneecap or the balls, then run like hell. It's saved my life more than once, which is another good reason why Dennis will always be welcome in my house. Well, almost always.

I leaned against the doorjamb and scowled. 'I thought you didn't do drugs,' I said mildly to Dennis.

'You know I don't,' he said. 'Who's been telling porkies about me?'

'Nobody. I was referring to the atmosphere in here,' I said, wafting my hand in front of my face as I crossed the room to give Dennis a kiss on a cheek so smooth he must have shaved before he came out for the evening. 'Breathe and you're stoned. Not to mention cutting your life expectancy by half.'

'Nice to see you too, Brannigan,' my beloved said as I pushed the evening paper to one side and dropped on to the sofa next to him.

'So what are you two boys plotting?'

Dennis grinned like Wile E. Coyote. My heart sank. I was well past a convincing impersonation of the Road Runner. 'Wanted to pick your brains,' he said.

'And it couldn't wait till morning?' I groaned.

'I was passing.'

Richard gave the sort of soft giggle that comes after the fifth bottle and the fourth joint. I know my man. 'He was passing and he heard a bottle of Pete's Wicked Bohemian Pilsner calling his name,' he spluttered.

'Looking at the number of bottles, it looks more

like a crate shouting its head off,' I muttered. The boys looked like they were set to make a night of it. There was only one way I was going to come out of this alive and that was to sort out Dennis's problem. Then they might not notice if I answered the siren call of my duvet. 'How can I help, Dennis?' I asked sweetly.

He gave me the wary look of a person who's drunk enough to notice their other half isn't giving them the hard time they deserve. 'I could come back tomorrow,' he said.

'I don't think that'll be necessary,' I said repressively. 'Like the song says, tonight will be fine.'

Dennis gave me a quick sideways look and reached for his cigarettes. 'You never finished your law degree, did you?'

I shook my head. It was a sore point with my mum and dad, who fancied being the parents of the first graduate in the family, but all it brought me was relief that business could never be so bad that I'd be tempted to set up shop as a lawyer. Two years of study had been enough to demonstrate there wasn't a single area of legal practice that wouldn't drive me barking within six months.

'So you couldn't charge me for legal advice,' Dennis concluded triumphantly.

I raised my eyes to the heavens, where a few determined stars penetrated the sodium glow of the city sky. 'No, Dennis, I couldn't.' Then I gave him the hard stare. 'But why would I want to?

34

We've never sent each other bills before, have we? What exactly are you up to?'

'You know I'd never ask you to help me out with anything criminal, don't you?'

''Course you wouldn't. You're far too tight to waste your breath,' I said. Richard giggled again. I revised my estimate. Sixth bottle, fifth joint.

Dennis leaned across to pick up his jacket from the nearby chair, revealing splendid muscles in his forearm and a Ralph Lauren label. It didn't quite go with the jogging pants and the Manchester United away shirt. He pulled some papers out of the inside pocket then gave me a slightly apprehensive glance. Then he shrugged and said, 'It's not illegal. Not as such.'

'Not even a little bit?' I asked. I didn't bother trying to hide my incredulity. Dennis only takes offence when it's intended.

'This bit isn't illegal,' he said firmly. 'It's a lease.'

'A lease?'

'For a shop.'

'You're taking out a lease on a shop?' It was a bit like hearing Dracula had gone veggie.

He had the grace to look embarrassed. 'Only technically.'

I knew better than to ask more. Sometimes ignorance is not only bliss but also healthy. 'And you want me to cast an eye over it to see that you're not being ripped off,' I said, holding a hand out for the papers.

Curiously reluctant now, Dennis clutched the

papers to his chest. 'You do know about leases? I mean, it's not one of the bits you missed out, is it?'

It was, as it happened, but I wasn't about to tell him that. Besides, since I'd quit law school, I'd learned much more practical stuff about contracts and leases than I could ever have done if I'd stuck it out. 'Gimme,' I said.

'You don't want to argue with that tone of voice,' Richard chipped in like the Dormouse at the Mad Hatter's tea party. Dennis screwed his face up like a man eating a piccalilli sandwich, but he handed over the papers.

It looked like a bog standard lease to me. It was for a shop in the Arndale Centre, the soulless shopping mall in the city centre that the IRA tried to remove from the map back in '96. As usual, they got it wrong. The Arndale, probably the ugliest building in central Manchester, remained more or less intact. Unfortunately, almost every other building within a quarter-mile radius took a hell of a hammering, especially the ones that were actually worth looking at. As a result, the whole city centre ended up spending a couple of years looking like it had been wrapped by Christo in some bizarre pre-millennium celebration. Now it looked as if part of the mall that had been closed for structural repairs and renovation was opening up again and Dennis had got himself a piece of the action.

There was nothing controversial in the document, as far as I could see. If anything, it was skewed in favour of the lessee, one John Thompson, since it gave him the first three months at half rent as a supposed inducement. I wasn't surprised that it wasn't Dennis's name on the lease. He's a man who can barely bring himself to fill in his real name on the voters' roll. Besides, no self-respecting landlord would ever grant a lease to a man who, according to the credit-rating agencies, didn't even exist.

What I couldn't understand was what he was up to. Somehow, I couldn't get my head round the idea of Dennis as the natural heir of Marks and Spencer. Karl Marx, maybe, except that they'd have had radically different views of what constituted an appropriate redistribution of wealth. I folded the lease along its creases and said, 'Looks fine to me.'

Dennis virtually snatched it out of my hand and shoved it back in his pocket, looking far too shifty for a villain as experienced as him. 'Thanks, love. I just wanted to be sure everything's there that should be. That it looks right.'

I recognized the key word right away. Us detectives, we never sleep. 'Looks right?' I demanded. 'Why? Who else is going to be giving it the once-over?'

Dennis tried to look innocent. I've seen hunter-killer submarines give it a better shot. 'Just the usual, you know? The leccy board, the water board. They need to see the lease before they'll connect you to the utilities.'

'What's going on, Dennis? What's really going on?'

Richard pushed himself more or less upright and draped an arm over my shoulders. 'You might as well tell her, Den. You know what they say – it's better having her inside the tent pissing out than outside pissing in.'

I let him get away with the anatomical impossibility and settled for a savage grin. 'He's not wrong,' I said.

Dennis sighed and lit a cigarette. 'All right. But I meant it when I said it's not criminal.'

I cast my eyes upwards and shook my head. 'Dennis O'Brien, you know and I know that "not criminal" doesn't necessarily mean "legal".'

'Too deep for me,' Richard complained, reaching for another bottle of beer.

'Let's hear it,' I said firmly.

'You know how I hate waste,' Dennis began. I nodded cautiously. 'There's nothing more offensive to a man like me than premises standing empty because the landlords' agents are crap at their job. So I had this idea about making use of a resource that was just standing idle.'

'Shop-squatting,' I said flatly.

'What?' Richard asked vaguely. 'You going to live in a shop, Den? What happened to the house? Debbie thrown you out, has she?'

'He's not going to be living in the shop, dope-head,' I said sarcastically.

'You keep smoking that draw, you're going to

38

have a mental age of three soon,' Dennis added sententiously. 'Of course I'm not going to be living in the shop. I'm going to be selling things in the shop.'

'Take me through it,' I said. Dennis's latest idea was only new to him; he was far from the first in Manchester to give it a try. I remembered reading something in the *Evening Chronicle* about shop-squatting, but as usual with newspaper articles, it had told me none of the things I really wanted to know.

'You want to know how it works?'

Silly question to ask a woman whose first watch lasted only as long as it took me to work out how to get the back off. 'Was Georgie Best?'

'First off, you identify your premises. Find some empty shops and give the agents a ring. What you're looking for is one where the agent says they're not taking any offers because it's already let as from a couple of months ahead.'

'What?' Richard mumbled.

Dennis and I shared the conspiratorial grin of those who are several drinks behind the mentally defective. 'That way, you know it's going to stay empty for long enough for you to get in and out and do the business in between,' he explained patiently.

'Next thing you do is you get somebody to draw you up a moody contract. One that looks like you've bought a short-term lease in good faith, cash on the nail. All you gotta do then is get into the shop and Bob's your uncle. Get the leccy and the water turned on, fill the place with crap, everything under a pound, which you can afford to do because you've got no overheads. And the Dibble can't touch you for it, on account of you've broken no laws.'

'What about criminal damage?' I asked. 'You have to bust the locks to get in.'

Dennis winked. 'If you pick the locks, you've not done any damage. And if you fit some new locks to give extra security, where's the damage in that?'

'Doesn't the landlord try to close you down?' Richard asked. It was an amazingly sensible question given his condition.

Dennis shrugged. 'Some of them can't be bothered. They know we'll be out of there before their new tenant needs the premises, so they've got nothing to lose. Some of them have a go. I keep somebody on the premises all the time, just in case they try to get clever and repo the place in the night. You can get a homeless kid to play night watchman for a tenner a time. Give them a mobile phone and a butty and lock them in. Then if the landlord tries anything, I get the call and I get down there sharpish. He lays a finger on me or my lad, he's the criminal.' Dennis smiled with all the warmth of a shark. 'I'm told you get a very reasonable response when you explain the precise legal position.'

'I can imagine,' I said drily. 'Do the explanations come complete with baseball bat?'

'Can people help it if they get the summons

when they're on their way home from sports training?' He raised his eyebrows, trying for innocent and failing dismally.

'Profitable, is it?' I asked.

'It's got to be a very nice little earner, what with Christmas coming up.'

'You know, Dennis, if you put half the effort into a straight business that you put into being bent, you'd be a multimillionaire by now,' I sighed.

He shook his head, rueful. 'Maybe so, but where would the fun be in that?'

He had a point. And who was I to talk? I'd turned my back on the straight version of my life a long time ago. If Dennis broke the law for profit, so did I. I'd committed burglary, fraud, assault, theft, deception and breaches of the Wireless and Telegraph Act too numerous to mention, and that was just in the past six months. I dressed it up with the excuse of doing it for the clients and my own version of justice. It had led me into some strange places, forced me into decisions that I didn't like to examine too closely in the harsh light of day. Once upon a time, I'd have had no doubt whether it was me or Dennis who could lay claim to the better view from the moral high ground.

These days, I wasn't quite so sure.

4

MOON SQUARES MARS

An accident-prone aspect, suggesting she can harm herself through lack of forethought. She is far too eager to make her presence felt and doesn't always practice self-control. Her feelings of insecurity can manifest themselves in an unfeminine belligerence. She has authoritarian tendencies.

From *Written in the Stars*, by Dorothea Dawson

Anyone can be a soap star. All you need is a script-writer who knows you well enough to write your character into their series, and you're laughing all the way to the BAFTA. I'd always thought you had to be an actor. But two hours on the set of *Northerners* made me realize that soap is different. About ten per cent of the cast could play Shakespeare or Stoppard. The rest just roll up to the studios every week and play themselves. The lovable rogues are just as roguish, the dizzy blondes are just as empty-headed, the salts of the earth make you thirst just as much for a long cold alcoholic drink and the ones the nation loves to hate are every bit as repulsive in the flesh. Actually, they're more repulsive, since anyone hanging round the green room is exposed to rather more of their flesh than a reasonable person could desire. There was more chance of me being struck by lightning than being star struck by that lot of has-beens and wannabes.

They didn't even have to learn their words. TV takes are so short that a gnat with Alzheimer's could retain the average speech with no trouble at all. Especially by the sixth or seventh take most of the *Northerners* cast seemed to need to capture the simplest sentiment on screen.

The main problem I had was how to do my job. Gloria had told everyone I was her bodyguard. Not because I couldn't come up with a decent cover story, but because I'd weighed up both sides of the argument and decided that if there was somebody in cast or crew who was out to get her it was time for them to understand they should back off and forget about it. Gloria had been all for the cloak and dagger approach, hoping I could catch the author of her threatening letters in the act of extracting vengeance, but I pointed out that if I was going to stay close enough to protect her, I'd be an obvious obstacle to nefarious doings anyway.

Besides, members of the public weren't allowed on the closed set of *Northerners*. The storylines were supposed to be top secret. NPTV, the company who made the soap, were so paranoid they made New Labour look relaxed. Everyone who worked on the programme had to sign an agreement that disclosure of any information relating to the cast characters or storylines was gross misconduct, a sacking offence and a strict liability tort. Even I had had to sign up to the tort clause before I was allowed into the compound that housed the interior and exterior sets, as well as the production suite and admin offices. Apart from location shooting to give the show that authentic Manchester ambience, the entire process from script conference to edited master tapes took place behind the high walls that surrounded NPTV's flagship complex.

A fat lot of good it did them. *Northerners* generated more column inches than any other TV programme in the country. The fuel for the flames had to come from somewhere, and tabloid papers have always had deep pockets. There's not a tabloid journalist I've ever met who couldn't explain in words of one syllable to a nervously dithering source that the NPTV legal threat of suing for civil damages was about as solid as the plyboard walls of Brenda Barrowclough's living room.

But NPTV insisted on their power trip, and I'd persuaded Gloria it would be simpler all round if we were upfront. The downside of being out in the open was that everyone was on their guard. Nobody was going to let anything slip accidentally. If my target was a member of the *Northerners* team, they'd be very careful around me.

In order to be effective protection for my client, I had to be visible, which meant that I couldn't even find a quiet corner and catch up with my e-mail and my invoices. If Gloria was in make-up, I was in make-up. If Gloria was on set, I was hovering round the edges of the set, getting in everybody's way. If Gloria was having a pee, I was leaning against the tampon dispenser. I could have made one of those video diary programmes that would have had any prospective private eye applying for a job as a hospital auxiliary.

I was trying to balance that month's books in my head when a hand on my shoulder lifted my feet off the floor. Spot the alert bodyguard. I spun round and found my nose level with the top button of a suit jacket. I took a step back and looked up. The man must have been six-three, wide shouldered and heavy featured. The suit, whose tailoring owed more to Savile Row than to Armani, was cut to disguise the effects of too many business lunches and dinners, but this guy was still a long way off fat. On the other hand, he looked as if he was still only in his early forties and in the kind of trim that betrays a commitment to regular exercise. In a few years, when his joints started complaining and his stamina wasn't what it had been, he'd swiftly slip into florid flabbiness. I'd seen the type. Greed was always a killer.

The smile on his broad face softened the stern good looks that come with a square jaw, a broad brow and deep-set eyes under overhanging brows.

'You must be Kate Brannigan,' he said, extending a hand. 'I didn't mean to startle you. I'm John Turpin.'

For a man who'd gone out of his way to try to persuade Gloria to keep her problems in the family, he seemed amazingly cordial. 'Pleased to meet you,' I said.

'How are your investigations proceeding?' he asked, smiling down on me benevolently.

'I could ask you the same question.' If the guy was trying to win me over with his affable helpfulness, the least I could do was take advantage and trawl for some information.

His smile curved up at one corner, suddenly turning his expression from magnanimous to predatory. 'I'm afraid I'm more of a guardian of company confidentiality than Ms Kendal,' he said, with a note of acid in his voice.

'But you expect me to share with you?' I asked innocently.

He chuckled. 'Not really, but it never hurts to try. As you yourself so ably demonstrated. I had hoped we could keep Ms Kendal's little problem in-house, but if she insists on wasting her money on services we can provide more effectively and for free, I can't stop her.'

'Can I tell her when to expect the results of your internal inquiry?' I wasn't playing the sweetness and light game any more. It hadn't got me anywhere so I figured I might as well turn into Ms Businesslike.

Turpin thrust one hand into his jacket pocket, thumb sticking out like Prince Charles always has. 'Impossible to say. I have so many calls on my time, most of them rather more serious than the antics of some poison-pen writer.'

'She had her car tyres slashed. All four of them. On NPTV premises,' I reminded him.

'It's a bitchy business, soap,' he said calmly. 'I'm far from convinced there's any connection between the letters and the car tyres. I can't believe you find it hard to credit that Ms Kendal could annoy a colleague enough for them to lose their temper and behave so childishly.'

'You're really not taking this seriously, are you?' I said, struggling to keep the incredulity out of my voice.

'That's what you're being paid for, Ms Brannigan. Me, I've got a television production company to run.' He inclined his head and gave me the full charm offensive again. 'It's been a pleasure.'

I said nothing, just watched his retreating back with its double-vent tailoring that perfectly camouflaged the effects of too many hours sitting behind a desk. If our conversation was par for the course around here, the only surprise was that it had taken Gloria so long to get round to hiring me.

In spite of Turpin's intervention, by lunchtime I was more bored than I'd been in the weeks before I finally managed to jettison A level Latin. If anyone had asked, I'd have admitted to being up for any distraction. I'd have been lying, as I discovered when my moby rang, right in the middle of the fifth run-through of a tense scene between my client and the putative father of her granddaughter's aborted foetus.

Mortified, I twisted my face into an apologetic grimace as the actor playing opposite Gloria glared at me and muttered, 'For fuck's sake. What is this? Fucking amateur city?' The six months he'd once spent on remand awaiting trial for rape (according to the front page of the *Sun* a couple of months back) hadn't improved his word power, then.

I ducked behind a props skip and tucked my head down into my chest as I grunted, 'Hello?'

'Kate? I've been arrested.' The voice was familiar, the scenario definitely wasn't. Donovan Carmichael was a second-year engineering student at UMIST. He'd just started eking out his pathetic student grant by working part time for me as a process-server, doing the bread and butter work that pays his mother's wages. Did I mention Shelley the office tyrant was his mother? And that she hated the thought that her highly educated baby boy might be tempted to throw it all away to become a maverick of the mean streets like her boss? That probably explained why said boy was using his one phone call on me rather than on his doting mother.

'What for?'

'Being black, I think,' he said angrily.

'What happened?'

'I was in Hale Barns.' That explained a lot. They don't have a lot of six-feet-three-inch black lads in Hale Barns, especially not ones with shoulders wider than the flashy sports cars in their four-car garages. It would lower the property values too much.

'Doing what?'

'Working,' he said. 'You know? Trying to make that delivery that came in yesterday afternoon?' His way of telling me there were other ears on our conversation. I knew he was referring to a domestic violence injunction we'd been hired to serve. The husband had broken his wife's cheek-bone the last time he'd had a bad day. If Donovan succeeded in serving the paper, there might not be a next time. But there were very good reasons why Donovan was reluctant to reveal his target or our client's name to the cops. Once you get outside the high-profile city-centre divisions that are constantly under scrutiny, you find that most policemen don't have a lot of sympathy for the victims of domestic violence. Especially when the guy who's been doing the battering is one of the city's biggest football stars. He'd given a whole new meaning to the word 'striker', but that wouldn't stop him being a hero in the eyes of the boys in blue.

'Are they charging you with anything?'

'They've not interviewed me yet.'

'Which nick are you in?'

'Altrincham.'

I looked at my watch. I stuck my head round the side of the skip. They were about to go for a take. 'I'll get someone there as soon as I can. Till then, say nothing. OK?' I said in a low voice.

I didn't wait for a reply, just ended the call and tiptoed back to the set. Gloria and the idiot boy she was acting opposite went through their interaction for the eighth time and the director announced she was satisfied. Gloria heaved a seismic sigh and walked off the set, dragging Brenda's beehive from her head as she approached me. 'That's me for today, chuck,' she said. 'Drop me at home and you can have the rest of the day off.'

'Are you staying in?' I asked, falling into step beside her as we walked to the dressing room she shared with Rita Hardwick, the actress who played Thelma Torrance, the good-time girl who'd never grown up.

'I am that. I've got to pick up next month's scripts from the office on the way out. I'll be lying in the Jacuzzi learning my lines till bedtime. It's not a pretty sight, and I don't need a spectator. Especially one that charges me for the privilege,' she added with an earthy chuckle.

I tried not to look as pleased as I felt. I could have sent a lawyer out to rescue Donovan, but it didn't sound as if things had reached the point where I couldn't sort it out myself, and lawyers cost either money I couldn't afford or favours I didn't want to owe.

*   *   *

Two hours later, I was walking Donovan back to my car. The police don't like private eyes, but faced with me threatening a lawsuit for false imprisonment and racial harassment, they were only too happy to release Donovan from the interview room where he'd been pacing the floor for every one of the minutes it had taken me to get there.

'I didn't do anything, you know,' Donovan complained. His anger seethed just below the surface. I couldn't blame him, but for all our sakes, I hoped the cycle ride back into town would get it out of his system.

'According to the copper I spoke to, one of the neighbours saw you sneaking round the back of the house and figured you for a burglar,' I said drily.

'Yeah, right. All I was doing was checking if he was in the snooker room round the back, like his wife said he usually is if he's not training in the morning. I reckoned if he was there, and I walked right up to the French windows, he'd be bound to come over and open up, at least to give me a bollocking. When I saw the place was empty, I came back down the drive and went and sat on a wall down the road, where I could see him come home. It's not like I was hiding,' he continued. 'They only arrested me because I'm black. Anybody black on the street in Hale Barns has got to be a burglar, right?'

'Or a drug dealer. The rich have got to get their coke and heroin from somewhere,' I pointed out reasonably. 'Where's your bike?'

'Hale Barns. Chained to a lamppost, I hope.'

'Let's go back out there and do it,' I sighed.

The leafy lanes of Hale Barns were dripping a soft rain down our necks as we walked along the grass verge that led to our target's house. Wrought-iron gates stood open, revealing a long drive done in herringbone brick. There was enough of it there to build a semi. At the top of the drive, a matching pair of Mercedes sports cars were parallel parked. My heart sank. 'I don't believe it,' I muttered.

We walked up the drive towards a vast white hacienda-style ranch that would have been grandiose in California. In Cheshire, it just looked silly. I leaned on the doorbell. There was a long pause, then the door swung silently open without warning. I recognized his face from the back pages of the *Chronicle*. For once, I didn't have to check ID before I served the papers. 'Yeah?' he said, frowning. 'Who are you?'

I leaned forward and stuffed the papers down the front of the towelling robe that was all he was wearing. 'I'm Kate Brannigan, and you are well and truly served,' I said.

As I spoke, over his shoulder, I saw a woman in a matching robe emerge from an archway. Like him, she looked as if she'd been in bed, and not for an afternoon nap. I recognized her from the *Chronicle* too. From the diary pages. Former model

Bo Robinson. Better known these days as the wife of the man I'd just served with the injunction her solicitor had sweated blood to get out of a district judge.

Now I remembered what I'd hated most about my own days as a process-server.

The last thing Donovan had said before he'd pedalled off to the university library was, 'Don't tell my mum I got arrested, OK? Not even as a joke. Not unless you want her to put the blocks on me working for you again.'

I'd agreed. Jokes are supposed to be funny, after all. Unfortunately, the cops at Altrincham weren't in on the deal. What I didn't know was that while I'd been savouring the ambience of their lovely foyer (decor by the visually challenged, furnishings by a masochist, posters from a template unchanged since 1959) the desk sergeant had been calling the offices of Brannigan & Co to check that the auburn-haired midget and the giant in the sweat suit really were operatives of the agency and not a pair of smart-mouthed burglars on the make.

I'd barely put a foot inside the door when Shelley's voice hit me like a blast furnace. 'Nineteen years old and never been inside a police station,' came the opening salvo. 'Five minutes working with you, and he might as well be some smackhead from Moss Side. That's it now, his name's on their computer. Another black bastard who's got away with it, that's how they'll have him down.'

I raised my palms towards her, trying to fend off her fury. 'It's all right, Shelley. He wasn't formally arrested. They won't be putting anything into the computer.'

Shelley snorted. 'You're so street smart when it comes to your business. How come you can be so naive about our lives? You don't have the faintest idea what it means for a boy like Donovan to get picked up by the police! They don't see a hard-working boy who's been brought up to respect his elders and stay away from drugs. They just see another black face where it doesn't belong. And you put him there.'

I edged across reception, trying to make the safe haven of my own office without being permanently disabled by the crossfire. 'Shelley, he's a grown man. He has to make his own decisions. I told him when I took him on that serving process wasn't as easy as it sounded. But he was adamant that he could handle it.'

'Of course he can handle it,' she yelled. 'He's not the problem. It's the other assholes out there, that's the problem. I don't want him doing this any more.'

I'd almost reached the safety of my door. 'You'll have to take that up with Don,' I told her, sounding more firm than I felt.

'I will, don't you worry about that,' she vowed.

'OK. But don't forget the reason he's doing this.'

Her eyes narrowed. 'What are you getting at?'

'It's about independence. He's trying to earn his own money so he's not dipping his hand in your pocket all the time. He's trying to tell you he's a man now.' I took a deep breath, trying not to feel intimidated by the scowl that was drawing Shelley's perfectly shaped eyebrows into a gnarled scribble. My hand on the doorknob, I delivered what was supposed to be the knockout punch. 'You've got to let him make his own mistakes. You've got to let him go.'

I opened the door and dived for safety. No such luck. Instead of silent sanctuary, I fell into nerd heaven. A pair of pink-rimmed eyes looked up accusingly at me. Under the pressure of Shelley's rage, I'd forgotten that my office wasn't mine any more. Now I was the sole active partner in Brannigan & Co, I occupied the larger of the two rooms that opened off reception. When I'd been junior partner in Mortensen & Brannigan it had doubled as Bill Mortensen's office and the main client interview room. Now, it was my sanctum.

These days, my former bolthole was the computer room, occupied as and when the occasion demanded by Gizmo, our information technology consultant. In our business, that's the polite word for hacker. And when it comes to prowling other people's systems with cat-like tread, Gizmo is king of the dark hill. The trade off for his computer acumen is that on a scale of one to ten, his social skills come in somewhere around absolute zero. I'm convinced that was the principal reason he was made redundant from his job as systems wizard with Telecom. Now they've become a multinational leading-edge company, everybody who works there has to pass for human. Silicon-based life forms like Gizmo just had to be downsized out the door.

Their loss was my gain. There had had to be changes, of course. Plain brown envelopes stuffed with banknotes had been replaced with a system more appealing to the taxman, if not to the company accountant. Then there was the personal grooming. Gizmo had always favoured an appearance that would have served as perfect camouflage if he'd been living on a refuse tip.

The clothes weren't so hard. I managed to make him stop twitching long enough to get the key measurements, then hit a couple of designer factory outlets during the sales. I was planning to dock the cost from his first consultancy fees, but I didn't want it to terrify him too much. Now he had two decent suits, four shirts that didn't look disastrous unironed, a couple of inoffensive ties and a mac that any flasher would have been proud of. I could wheel him out as our computer security expert without frightening the clients, and he had a couple of outfits that wouldn't entirely destroy his street cred if another of the undead happened to be on the street in daylight hours to see him.

The haircut had been harder. I don't think he'd

spent money on a haircut since 1987. I'd always thought he simply took a pair of scissors to any stray locks whose reflection in the monitor distracted him from what he was working on. Gizmo tried to make me believe he liked it that way. It cost me five beers to get him to the point where I could drag him across the threshold of the city centre salon where I'd already had to cancel three times. The stylist had winced in pain, but had overcome his aesthetic suffering for long enough to do the business. Giz ended up with a seriously sharp haircut and I ended up gobsmacked that lurking underneath the shambolic dress sense and terrible haircut was a rather attractive man. Scary.

Three months down the line, he was still looking the business, his hollow cheeks and bloodshot eyes fitting the current image of heroin addict as male glamour. I'd even overheard one of Shelley's adolescent daughter's mates saying she thought Gizmo was 'shaggable'. That *Trainspotting* has a lot to answer for. 'All right,' he mumbled, already looking back at his screen. 'You two want to keep the noise down?'

'Sorry, Giz. I didn't actually mean to come in here.'

'Know what you mean,' he said.

Before I could leave, the door burst open. 'And another thing,' Shelley said. 'You've not done a new client file for Gloria Kendal.'

Gizmo's head came up like it was on a string.

'Gloria Kendal? *The* Gloria Kendal? Brenda Barrow-clough off *Northerners*?'

I nodded.

'She's a client?'

'I can't believe you watch *Northerners*,' I said.

'She was in here yesterday,' Shelley said smugly. 'She signed a photograph for me personally.'

'Wow! Gloria Kendal. Cool! Anything I can do to help?' The last time I'd seen him this excited was over an advance release of Netscape Navigator 3.0.

'I'll let you know,' I promised. 'Now, if you'll both excuse me, I have some work to do.' I smiled sweetly and sidled past Shelley. As I crossed the threshold, the outside door opened and a massive basket of flowers walked in. Lilies, roses, carnations, and a dozen other things I didn't know the names of. For a wild moment, I thought Richard might be apologizing for the night before. He had cause, given what had gone on after Dennis had left. The thought shrivelled and died as hope was overtaken by experience.

'They'll be from Gloria Kendal,' Shelley predicted.

I contradicted her. 'It'll be Donovan mortgaging his first month's wages to apologize to you.'

'Wrong address,' Gizmo said gloomily. Given the way the day had been running, he was probably right.

'Is this Brannigan and Co?' the flowers asked. For such an exotic arrangement, they had a remarkably prosaic Manchester accent.

'That's right,' I said. 'I'm Brannigan.' I stepped forward expectantly.

'They're not for you, love,' the voice said, half a face appearing round the edge of the blooms. 'You got someone here called Gizmo?'

5

JUPITER IN CANCER IN THE 3RD HOUSE
Jupiter is exalted in Cancer. She has a philosophical outlook, enjoying speculative thinking. She is good humoured and generous, with strong protective instincts. Her intuition and imagination are powerful tools that she could develop profitably. She has a good business sense and communicates well in that sphere. She probably writes very thorough reports.

From *Written in the Stars*, by Dorothea Dawson

It was hard to keep my mind on Gloria's monologue on the way in to the studios the next morning. The conundrum of Gizmo's mysterious bouquet was much more interesting than her analysis of the next month's storylines for *Northerners*. When the delivery man had announced who the flowers were for, Shelley and I had rounded on Gizmo. Scarlet and stammering, he'd refused to reveal anything. Shelley, who's always been quick on her feet, helped herself to the card attached to the bouquet and ripped open the envelope.

All it said was, 'www gets real'. I know. I was looking over her shoulder. The delivery man had placed the flowers on Shelley's desk and legged it. He'd clearly seen enough blood shed over bouquets to hang around. 'So who have you been chatting up on the Internet?' I demanded. 'Who's the cyberbabe?'

'Cyberbabe?' Shelley echoed.

I pointed to the card. 'www. The worldwide web. The Internet. It's from someone he's met websurfing. Well, not actually met, as such. Exchanged e-mail with.'

'Safer than body fluids,' Shelley commented drily. 'So who's the cyberbabe, Gizmo?'

Gizmo shook his head. 'It's a joke,' he said with the tentative air of a man who doesn't expect to be believed. 'Just the guys trying to embarrass me at work.'

I shook my head. 'I don't think so. I've never met a techie yet who'd spend money on flowers while there was still software on the planet.'

'Honest, Kate, it's a wind-up,' he said desperately.

'Some expensive wind-up,' Shelley commented. 'Did one of your mates win the lottery, then?'

'There is no babe, OK? Leave it, eh?' he said, this time sounding genuinely upset.

So we'd left it, sensitive girls that we are. Gizmo retreated back to his hi-tech hermitage and Shelley shrugged. 'No use looking at me, Kate. He's not going to fall for the, "You can talk to me, I'm a woman, I understand these things," routine. It's down to you.'

'Men never cry on my shoulder,' I protested.

'No, but you're the only one around here who knows enough about computers to find who he's been talking to.'

I shook my head. 'No chance. If Gizmo's got a cybersecret, it'll be locked away somewhere I won't be able to find it. We'll just have to do this the hard way. First thing tomorrow, you better get on to the florist.'

Call me a sad bastard, but as I was driving Gloria to the studios, I was busy working out how we could discover Gizmo's secret admirer if she'd been clever enough to cover her tracks on the flower delivery. So I almost missed it when Gloria asked me a question that needed more than a grunt in response. 'So you don't mind coming along tonight?'

'No, that's fine,' I said, not quite certain what I'd agreed to.

'I'm really buggering up your social life, chuck,' she continued. 'If you've got a fella you want to bring along, you're welcome, you know.'

I must have shown how unlikely a prospect that was, since Gloria chuckled. 'He's a rock journalist,' I said.

She roared with laughter. 'Better not bring him anywhere I'm singing, then,' she spluttered. 'I'm too old to be insulted.'

By the time we reached the studios, the sky had clouded over and large raindrops were plopping on the windscreen. 'Oh bugger,' Gloria said.

'Problems?'

'We're supposed to be filming outside this morning. When it's raining like this, they'll hang on to see if it clears up and fill the time with the indoor scenes scheduled for this afternoon. I'm not in any of them, so not only do I lose an afternoon off but I get a morning hanging around waiting for the weather to change.' She rummaged in the bulging satchel that contained her scripts and pulled out a crumpled schedule. 'Let's see . . . Could be worse. Teddy and Clive are in the same boat. D'you play bridge, Kate?'

'Badly. I haven't played against humans since I was a student, and these days the computer usually gives me a coating.'

'You can't be worse than Rita Hardwick,' she said firmly. 'That's settled then.'

'Two spades,' I said tentatively. My partner, Clive Doran (Billy Knowles, the crooked bookmaker with an eye for his female employees) nodded approval.

'Pass,' said Gloria.

'Three hearts.'

'Doubled,' announced Teddy Edwards, Gloria's screen husband, the feckless Arthur Barrowclough, cowboy builder and failed gambler. I hoped he had as much luck with cards in real life as he did on screen. What Gloria had omitted to mention in the car was that we were playing for 10p a point. I suppose she figured she was paying me so much she needed to win some of it back.

I looked at my hand. 'Redoubled,' I said boldly. Clive raised one eyebrow. My bid passed round the table, and we started playing. I soon realized that the other three were so used to each other's game that they only needed a small proportion of their brains to choose the next card. The bridge game was just an excuse to gossip in the relative privacy of Gloria's dressing room.

'Seen the *Sun* this morning?' Clive asked, casually tossing a card down.

'It'd be hard to miss it,' Gloria pointed out. 'I don't know about where you live, but every newsagent we passed on the way in had a board outside. Gay soap star exposed: Exclusive. I sometimes wonder if this is the end of the nineteenth century, not the twentieth. I mean, who gives a stuff if Gary Bond's a poof? None of us does, and we're the ones as have to work with the lad.'

'They're bloody idle, them hacks,' Teddy grumbled, sweeping a trick from the table that I'd thought my ace of diamonds was bound to win.

Clive sucked his breath in over his teeth. 'How d'you mean?'

'It couldn't have taken much digging out. It's not like it's a state secret, Gary being a homo. He's always going on about lads he's pulled on a night

64

out in the gay village.' Teddy sighed. 'I remember when it were just the red light district round Canal Street. Back in them days, if you fancied a bit, at least you could be sure it was a woman under the frock.'

'And it's not as if he's messing about with kids,' Gloria continued, taking the next trick. 'Nice lead, Teddy. I mean, Gary always goes for fellas his own age.'

'There's been a lot of heavy stories about *Northerners* lately,' I said. I might be playing dummy in this hand, but that didn't mean I had to take the job literally.

'You're not kidding,' Clive said with feeling, sweeping his thin hair back from his narrow forehead in a familiar gesture. 'You get used to living in a goldfish bowl, but lately it's been ridiculous. We're all behaving like Sunday-school teachers.'

'Aye, but you can be as good as gold for all the benefit you'll get if the skeletons are already in the cupboard,' said Gloria. 'Seventeen years since Tony Peverell got nicked for waving his willy at a couple of lasses. He must have thought that were dead and buried long since. Then up it pops on the front of the *News of the World*. And his wife a churchwarden.' She shook her head. I remembered the story.

'He quit the programme, didn't he?' I asked, making a note of our winning score and gathering the cards to me so I could shuffle while Gloria dealt the next hand with the other pack.

'Did he fall or was he pushed?' Clive intoned. It would have sounded sinister from someone who didn't have a snub nose and a dimple in his chin and a manner only marginally less camp than Kenneth Williams. It was hard to believe he was happily married with three kids, but according to Gloria, the limp-wristed routine was nothing more than a backstage affectation. 'And I should know,' she'd winked. I didn't ask.

'What do you mean?' I asked now.

'John Turpin's what he means,' Gloria said. 'I told you about Turpin, didn't I? The management's hatchet man. Administration and Production Coordinator, they call him. Scumbag, we call him. Just a typical bloody TV executive who's never made a programme all his born days but thinks he knows better than everybody else what makes good telly.'

'Turpin's in charge of cast contracts,' Clive explained, sorting his cards. 'So he's the one who's technically responsible when there's a leak to the press. He's been running around like all Four Horsemen of the Apocalypse rolled into one for the last six months. He threatens, he rants, he rages, but still the stories keep leaking out. One diamond.'

'Pass. It drives him demented,' Teddy said with a smug little smile that revealed rodent teeth.

'One heart?' I tried, wondering what message that was sending to my partner. When he'd asked what system of bidding I preferred, I'd had to smile weakly and say, 'Psychic?' He hadn't looked impressed.

'It's not the scandals that really push his blood pressure through the ceiling. It's the storyline leaks.' Gloria lit a cigarette, eyeing Teddy speculatively. 'Two clubs. Remember when the *Sunday Mirror* got hold of that tale about Colette's charity?'

'Colette Darvall?' I asked.

'That's right.'

'I must have missed that one,' I said.

'Two diamonds,' Clive said firmly. 'Off the planet that month, were you? When her daughter was diagnosed with MS, Colette met up with all these other people who had kids in the same boat. So she let them use her as a sort of figurehead for a charity. She worked her socks off for them. She was always doing PAs for free, giving them stuff to raffle, donating interview fees and all sorts. Then it turns out one of the organizers has been ripping the charity off. He legged it to the West Indies with all the cash. Which would have been nothing more than a rather embarrassing tragedy for everyone concerned if it hadn't been for the unfortunate detail that he'd been shagging Colette's brains out for the previous three months.'

'Oops,' I said.

'By heck, you private eyes know how to swear, don't you?' Teddy said acidly. 'I don't think "oops" was quite what Colette was saying. But Turpin was all right about that. He stuck one of the press officers on her doorstep night and day for a week and told her not to worry about her job.'

'That's because having a fling with somebody else's husband is sexy in PR terms, whereas flashing at schoolgirls is just sleazy,' Clive said. 'Have you taken a vow of silence, Teddy? Or are you going to bid?'

'Oh God,' Teddy groaned. 'Who dealt this dross? I'm going to have to pass. Sorry, Glo.'

'Pass,' I echoed.

'And I make it three in a row. It's all yours, Clive.' Gloria leaned back in her chair and blew a plume of smoke towards the ceiling. 'God, I love it when Rita's not here to whinge about me smoking.'

'Better not let Turpin catch you,' Clive said.

'He sounds a real prize, this Turpin,' I said. 'I met him yesterday and he was nice as ninepence to me. Told me nothing, mind you, but did it charmingly.'

'Smooth-talking bastard. He did the square root of bugger-all about sorting out my security. Bloody chocolate teapot,' Gloria said dismissively. 'At least this latest furore about the future of the show has stopped him going on about finding out who's leaking the storylines to the press.'

'The future of the show? They're surely not going to axe *Northerners*?' It was a more radical suggestion than abolishing the monarchy, and one that would have had a lot more people rioting in the streets. For some reason, the public forgave the sins of the cast of their favourite soap far more readily than those of the House of Windsor, even though they paid both lots of wages, one via their taxes, the other via the hidden tax of advertising.

'Don't be daft,' Gloria said. 'Of course they're not going to axe *Northerners*. That'd be like chocolate voting for Easter. No, what they're on about is moving us to a satellite or cable channel.'

I stared blankly at her, the cards forgotten. 'But that would mean losing all your viewers. There's only two people and a dog watch cable.'

'And the dog's a guide dog,' Teddy chipped in gloomily.

'The theory is that if *Northerners* defects to one of the pay-to-view channels, the viewers will follow,' Clive said. 'The men in suits think our following is so addicted that they'd rather shell out for a satellite dish than lose their three times weekly fix of an everyday story of northern folk.'

'Hardly everyday,' I muttered. 'You show me anywhere in Manchester where nobody stays out of work for more than a fortnight and where the corner shop, the fast-food outlet and the local newsagent are still run by white Anglo-Saxons.'

'We're not a bloody documentary,' Teddy said. He'd clearly heard similar complaints before. His irritation didn't upset me unduly, since it resulted in him throwing away the rest of the hand with one hasty lead.

'No, we're a fantasy,' Clive said cheerfully, sweeping up the next trick and laying down his cards. 'I think the rest are ours. What we're providing, Kate, is contemporary nostalgia. We're harking back to a past that never existed, but we're translating it into contemporary terms. People feel alienated and lonely in the city and we create the illusion that they're part of a community. A community where all the girls are pretty, all the lads have lovely shoulders and any woman over thirty-five is veneered with a kind of folk wisdom.'

I was beginning to understand why Clive hid behind the camp manner. Underneath it all there lay a sharper mind than most of his fellow cast members ever exhibited. He was just as self-absorbed as they were, but at least he'd given some thought to how he earned his considerable living. I bet that made him really popular in a green room populated by egos who were each convinced they were the sole reason for the show's success. 'So you reckon the tug of fantasy is so strong that the millions who tune in three times a week will take out their satellite subscriptions like a bunch of little lambs?' I said, my scepticism obvious.

'*We* don't, chuck,' Gloria said, lighting a fresh cigarette while Clive dealt the cards. 'But the management do.'

'That's hardly surprising,' Teddy said. 'They're the ones who are going to make a bomb whatever happens.'

'How come?' I asked.

'The contract NPTV has with the ITV network is due for renegotiation. The network knows NPTV have been talking to satellite and cable companies with a view to them buying first rights in *Northerners* for the next three years. So the network knows that the price is going to have to go up. There's going to be a bidding war. And the only winners are going to be the management at NPTV, with their pocketfuls of share options. If they're wrong and the viewers don't follow the programme in droves, it doesn't matter to them, because they'll already have their hot sticky hands on the cash,' Clive explained.

'So Turpin needs to plug the storyline leak,' Gloria said, examining her cards.

'I'm not sure I follow you. Surely any publicity is good publicity?'

'Not when it involves letting the public know in advance what's going to happen,' Teddy said, raising his eyes to the heavens as if I was stupid. I didn't react. After all, I wasn't the one who was currently fourteen quid out of pocket.

Clive took pity on my puzzlement. 'If people know the big storylines in advance, a lot of them think it won't be the end of the world if they miss a few eps, because they know what they'll be missing. Once they get out of the habit of watching every ep religiously, their viewing habits drift.'

'They find other programmes on at the same time that they get to like. They don't bother setting the video to watch us because they think they already know what's going to happen. Or they just go down the pub. Before you know it, they've lost touch with the programme,' Gloria continued. 'One heart.'

'Especially now we're three times a week. You dip out for two, three weeks and when you come back, you don't know some of the faces. I'm going to pass this time.'

Teddy tugged at his shirt collar, a mannerism either he'd borrowed from Arthur Barrowclough or the character had borrowed from him. 'Two hearts. And every time the viewing figures drop, John Turpin sees his share of the profits going down.'

'And we get to watch his blood pressure going up,' Gloria said. 'Three hearts,' she added, noting my shake of the head.

'I'd have thought he'd be on to a loser, trying to find out who's behind it. It's too good an earner for the mole to give it up, and no journalist on the receiving end of a series of exclusives like that is going to expose a source,' I said.

'It won't be for want of trying,' Gloria said. 'He's even got every script coded so that any photocopied pages can be traced back. I hope whoever it is really is making a killing, because they're not going to earn another shilling off NPTV if they're caught.'

'You'll never work in this town again,' Teddy drawled in a surprisingly convincing American accent. I was so accustomed to him behaving in character I'd almost forgotten he was an actor.

'And speaking of making a killing, Gloria, any more news from your stalker?'

Gloria scowled. 'By heck, Clive, you know how to put a girl off her game. No, I've heard nowt since I took Kate on. I'm hoping we've frightened him off.'

'How do you know it's a he?' Clive said.

'Believe me, Clive, I know.'

We played out the hand in silence for a moment. In bridge as in life, I've always been better at defence than attack. Clive also seemed to relish the taste of blood and we left Gloria and Teddy three tricks short of their contract. My client raised her eyebrows and lit another cigarette. 'She lied so beautifully, Teddy. I really believed her when she said she was crap at this.'

'Don't tell Turpin,' Teddy said sharply. 'He'll hire her out from under you.'

'My dears, for all we know, he's done that already,' Clive said archly.

I should be so lucky, I thought as they all stared at me. I'm not proud about whose money I take. Maybe I should engineer another encounter with Turpin the hatchet man and kill two birds with one stone. Gloria's eyes narrowed, either from the smoke or because she could see the wheels going round in my head. 'Don't even think about it,' she warned me. 'Chances are it's one of our brain-dead mates who's ratting to the vampires, and I don't want that on my conscience.'

I nodded. 'Fair enough. Whose deal is it?'

6

VENUS IN LEO IN THE 4TH HOUSE
*She can show great extravagance, both practical
and emotional, to those she cares for. She is loyal
but likes to dominate situations of the heart. She
has creative ability, which can sometimes lead to
self-dramatization. Her domestic surroundings must
be easy on the eye.*

From *Written in the Stars*, by Dorothea Dawson

My second evening bodyguarding Gloria Kendal
taught me that I really should pay more attention to the client. The evening engagement I'd
so blithely agreed to turned out to be another
of the nights from hell that seemed to be how
Gloria spent her free time. That night, she was
guest of honour at the annual dinner dance of
the ladies' division of the North West branch of
the Association of Beverage and Victuals Providers.
I've never been in the same room as that much
hairspray. If taste were IQ, there would only have

75

been a handful of them escaping Special Needs education. I'd thought the Blackburn outfit would have blended in nicely at a women-only dinner, but I was as flash as a peahen at a peacock convention. I should have realized Gloria wasn't wearing those sequins and diamanté for a bet.

About ten minutes after we arrived in Ormskirk, I sussed this wasn't one of those dinners you go to for the food. I know '70s food is coming back into fashion, but the Boar and Truffle's menu of prawn cocktail, boeuf bourguignon and, to crown it all, Black Forest gateau, owed nothing to the Style Police or the foodies. You could tell that every cooking fashion in the intervening twenty years had passed them by. This was a dinner my Granny Brannigan would have recognized and approved of. It wasn't entirely surprising; nobody who had any choice in the matter would spend a minute longer than they had to in a town characterized by a one-way system that's twice the size of the town centre itself. It's the only place I know where they're so proud of their back streets they have to show them to every unwary motorist who gets trapped there on the way to Southport.

The landladies, most of whom almost certainly served better pub grub back home, didn't care. The only function of the food they were interested in was its capacity to line the stomach and absorb alcohol. It wasn't a night to be the designated driver, never mind bodyguard.

Gloria was on fine form, though. She'd heeded

what I'd said about keeping her back to the wall and trying to make sure there was a table between her and her admirers. It wasn't easy, given how many of the female publicans of the North West desperately needed to have their photographs taken in a clinch with my client. But she smiled and smiled, and drank her gin and made a blisteringly funny and scathing speech that would have had a rugby club audience blushing.

'I'm sorry you've been landed with all this ferrying me around,' she said as I drove across the flat fields of the Fylde towards the motorway and civilization.

'Who normally does it?' I asked.

'A pal of mine. He got the sack last year for being over fifty. He's not going to get another job at his age. He enjoys the driving and it gives him a few quid in his back pocket.' She yawned and reached for her cigarettes. It was her car, so I didn't feel I could complain. Instead, I opened the window. Gloria shivered at the blast of cold air and snorted with laughter. 'Point taken,' she said, shoving the cigarettes back in her bag. 'How much longer do you think we're going to have to be joined at the hip?'

'Depends on you,' I said. 'I don't think you've got a stalker. I've seen no signs of anybody following us, and I've had a good look around where you live. There's no obvious vantage point for anybody to stake out your home –'

'One of the reasons I bought it,' Gloria interrupted.

'Those bloody snappers with their long lenses make our lives a misery, you know. All those editors, they all made their holier-than-thou promises after they hounded Princess Di to her death, but nothing's changed, you know. They're still chasing us every chance they get. But they can't catch me there. Not that I'm likely to be doing anything more exciting than planting out my window boxes, but I'm buggered if the *Sun*'s readers have any right to know whether I'm having Busy Lizzies or lobelia this year.'

'So that probably confirms that whoever has been sending the letters is connected to the show; they can keep tabs on you because they see you at work every day. And they can pick up background details quite easily, it seems to me. The cast members talk quite freely among themselves and you don't have to set out to eavesdrop to pick up all sorts of personal information. I've only been on the set for a couple of days and already I know Paul Naylor's seeing an acupuncturist in Chinatown for his eczema, Rita Hardwick's husband breeds pugs and Tiffany Joseph's bulimic. Another week and I'd have enough background information to write threatening letters to half the cast.' What I didn't say was that another week among the terminally self-obsessed, and threatening letters would be the least of what I'd be up for.

'It's not a pretty thought, that. Somebody that knows me hates me enough to want me to be frightened. I don't like that idea one little bit.'

'If the letters and the tyre slashing are connected, then it almost certainly has to be somebody at NPTV, you know. Of course, it is possible that the tyre slasher isn't the letter writer, just some sicko who took advantage of your concern over the letters to wind you up. I've asked you this before, but you've had time to think about it now: are you sure there isn't anybody you've pissed off that might just be one scene short of a script?'

Gloria shook her head. 'Come on, chuck. You've spent time with me now. You've seen the way I am with the folk I work with. I'm a long way off perfect, but I don't wind them up like certain other people I could mention.'

'I'd noticed,' I said drily. 'The thing is, now everybody at NPTV knows you're taking what Dorothea said seriously. The person who wrote you those letters is basking in a sense of power, which means that he or she probably won't feel the need to carry the threats through any further. Besides, they won't know whether I'm off the case altogether or I've taken the surveillance undercover. Much as I'd love to be on this hourly rate indefinitely, I'd be inclined to give it another couple of days and then I'll pull out.'

'You're sure I'll be safe? I'm not a silly woman, in spite of how I come across, but what Dorothea said really scared me, coming on top of the business with the tyres. She's not given to coming the spooky witch, you know.'

'When is she in next?'

'Day after tomorrow. Do you want to see her?'

'I want to interview her, not have a consultation,' I said hastily.

'Oh, go on,' Gloria urged. 'Have it on me. You don't have to take it seriously.' She opened her bag and took out a pen and one of the postcard-sized portraits of herself she carried everywhere for the fans who otherwise would have had her signing everything from their library books to any available part of their anatomies. 'Give us your time, date and place of birth.' She snapped on the interior light, making me blink hard against the darkness. 'Come on, sooner you tell me, the sooner you get the light off again.'

'Oxford,' I said. 'Fourth of September, 1966.'

'Now why am I not surprised you're a Virgo?' Gloria said sarcastically as she turned off the light. 'Caligula, Jimmy Young, Agatha Christie, Cecil Parkinson, Raine Spencer and you.'

'Which proves it's a load of old socks,' I said decisively. A couple of miles down the road, it hit me. 'How come you can rattle off a list of famous Virgoans?'

'I married one. Well, not a famous one. And divorced him. I wish I'd known Dorothea then. Virgo and Leo? She'd never have let it happen. A recipe for disaster.'

'Aren't you taking a bit of a chance, working with me?'

Gloria laughed, that great swooping chuckle that

gets the nation grinning when things are going right for Brenda Barrowclough. 'Working's fine. Nobody grafts harder than a Virgo. You see the detail while I only get the big picture. And you never give up. No, you'll do fine for me.'

It's funny how often clients forget they've said that when a case doesn't work out the way they wanted it to. I only hoped Gloria wouldn't live to regret her words. I grunted noncommittally and concentrated on the road.

It was almost one when I walked through my own front door. Both my house and Richard's were illuminated only by the dirty orange of the sodium streetlights. I'd hoped he'd be home; I was suffering from what my best friend Alexis calls NSA – Non-Specific Anxiety – and my experience of self-medicating has told me the best cure is a cuddle. But it looked like he was doing whatever it is that rock journos do in live music venues in the middle of the night. It probably involved drugs, but Richard never touches anything stronger than joints and these days all the cops do with cannabis is confiscate it for their own use, so I wasn't worried on that score.

I turned on the kitchen light, figuring a mug of hot chocolate might prevent the vague feeling of unease from keeping me awake. I couldn't miss the sheet of paper stuck under a fridge magnet. 'Babysitting for Alexis + Chris. Staying over. See you tomorrow. Big kisses.' I didn't need to be a handwriting expert to know it was from my besotted lover. The only problem was, it wasn't me he was besotted with.

I'd know how to fight back if it was a beautiful blonde waving her perfectly rounded calves at him. But how exactly can a woman keep her dignity and compete with a nine-month-old baby girl?

The following day, we were let out to play. Because *Northerners* traded so heavily on its connection to Manchester, the city of cool, they had to reinforce the link with regular exterior and interior shots of identifiable landmarks. It had led to a profitable spin-off for NPTV, who now ran *Northerners* tours at weekends. The punters would stay in the very hotel where Pauline Pratt and Gordon Johnstone had consummated their adulterous affair, then they'd be whisked off on a walking tour that took in sites from key episodes. They'd see the tram line where Diane Grimshaw committed suicide, the alley where Brenda Barrowclough was mugged, the jewellery shop that was robbed while Maureen and Phil Pomeroy were choosing an engagement ring. They'd have lunch in the restaurant where Kamal Sayeed had worked as a waiter before his tragic death from streptococcal meningitis. In the afternoon, they visited the sets where the show was filmed, and a couple of cast members joined them for dinner, persuaded by veiled threats and large fees.

To keep that particular gravy train running, the show had to film on the streets of the city at least once a month. That day, they were filming a series of exterior shots at various points along the refurbished Rochdale Canal. According to Gloria, a new producer was determined to stamp his authority on the soap with a series of themed episodes. The linking theme of this particular week was the idea of the waterway providing a range of backdrops, from the sinister to the seriously hip. Gloria had drawn the short straw of an argument with Teddy outside Barca, Mick Hucknall's chic Catalan bistro. On a summer afternoon, it might have been a pleasant diversion. On a bleak December morning, it was about as much fun as sunbathing in Siberia. It took forever to film because trains and trams would keep rattling across the high brick viaducts above our heads when the cameras were rolling.

I couldn't even take refuge in the cast or crew buses, since I needed to keep a close eye on Gloria. In spite of what I'd said the night before, I hadn't entirely ruled out the possibility of an obsessive fan who was stalking her. The fact that she spent so much of her time inaccessible might actually fuel his derangement. He could be planning to take action against her only when she was in a public place and in character.

I huddled under the awning of the catering truck where a red-haired giant with a soft Highland accent supervised the pair of young women who were responsible for making sure there was a constant flow of bacon, sausage and/or egg butties for anyone who wanted them. They served me with a steaming carton of scalding coffee, which I held under my chin. Not for long, though. If my nose thawed out too quickly, there was always the possibility of it shearing off from the rest of my face.

I half listened to the conversation in the van behind me. It was a lot more interesting than the script Teddy and Gloria were working their way through. The caterers were discussing that day's lunch menu and the cast members in roughly equal proportions. I can't think why, but they seemed not to have a lot of respect for their customers. I was stifling a giggle at one particularly scurrilous comment about the randiness of one of the show's young studs being in inverse proportion to the size of his equipment when I was aware that I had company under the awning. The Rob Roy lookalike had abandoned his assistants and slipped out for a fag. The environmental health department would have been impressed.

He grinned. Close up, he was even more attractive than he was with a steaming array of food between us. His thick red-gold hair was swept back from a high, broad forehead. Eyes the blue of the Windows 95 intro screen sparkled above high cheekbones. He had one of those mouths romantic novelists always describe as cruel, which lets you know the heroine's probably going to end up in the guy's arms if not his bed. 'Hiya,' he said. 'I'm Ross Grant. I own the location catering company.'

The coffee had defrosted my lips enough for me to return his smile. 'Kate Brannigan. I'm –'

'I know who you are,' he interrupted, sounding amused. 'You're Gloria's bodyguard. Dorothea Dawson, the Seer to the Stars, told her she was going to be murdered, and she hired you to protect her.'

'You've been watching too much television,' I said lightly. 'People don't lash out the kind of money I cost without having good reason.'

'I'm sorry,' he said. 'I didn't mean to insult your professionalism. Or to take the piss out of Dorothea. She's been really good to us.'

'Predicting a sudden rush on bacon butties, you mean?'

He gave a sheepish grin. 'Very funny. No, I mean it. You know how she's always on the telly? Well, she's recommended us to quite a few of the programmes she's been on. We've got a lot of work off the back of it. She's great, Dorothea. She really understands what it's like trying to make a living out of a business where you're constantly dependent on goodwill. So she goes out of her way for folk like us, know what I mean? Not like most of them round here, it's self, self, self. Working with people that are so full of themselves, we find it hard to take anything about them seriously.'

This time it was my turn to smile. 'They do lack a certain sense of proportion.'

'But you're more than just a bodyguard, aren't

you? Somebody said you're a proper private investigator.'

'That's right. In fact, I almost never do this kind of work. But Gloria can be very persuasive.'

'Don't I know it. This is the woman that had me up all night making petits fours for her granddaughter's birthday party. Is she really in danger, then?'

I shrugged. 'Better safe than sorry.'

'I'm sorry to hear that. She's the best of the bunch. I don't like to think of her in fear of her life. I wasn't asking out of nosiness,' he added quickly. 'I just wondered how long you were going to be tied up working for Gloria.'

'Why? Are you missing me already?'

He went that strange damson-purple that redheads go when they blush. 'Actually, I wanted to hire you.'

'Hire me?' Suddenly this was a lot more interesting than a mild flirtation to keep the cold out. 'What for?'

'I don't know if you know, but *Northerners* has got a mole. Somebody's been leaking stuff to the press. Not just the usual sordid stuff about people's love lives and creepy things they did twenty years ago, but storylines as well.' All the humour had left him now.

'I'd heard. John Turpin's supposed to be finding out where the leak is.'

'Yeah, well, Turpin's trying to pin it on me or my staff,' Ross said bluntly.

'Why would he do that?'

He inhaled sharply. 'Because we're convenient scapegoats. Our contract's up for renewal at the end of January, and Turpin seems to be determined to ditch me. Knowing that slimy bastard, he's probably in bed with one of the other firms tendering for the contract and he figures if he can blame me for the leaks he can feather his own nest easier.'

'But why would anybody believe him?' I asked.

Ross flicked his cigarette end on to a frozen puddle where it bounced once then sank through the hole it made. 'We're the outsiders, aren't we? We're not part of the team like the ones who work inside the compound are.'

'So how are you supposed to come by the advance storylines?' I objected.

'We're involved in location filming for the show nearly every week. With them filming four weeks ahead of transmission, it's not hard to pick up the direction the stories are heading. The cast are always standing round the food wagon shooting their mouths off about storylines they don't like, or taking the piss out of each other about what their characters are up to. If me or my lassies had a mind to, we could be moles. It would be dead simple. But we're not.'

'How can you be sure?'

'Well, I know it's not me. And I know it's not my wife.' He gestured towards the open side of the van with his thumb. 'She's the one with the red

87

sweatshirt on. And I'd put money on it not being Mary, the other lassie, because she owns twenty per cent of the business and she's never been a woman who went for the short-term benefit.'

I sighed. 'I sympathize. But it's always impossible to prove a negative.'

'I know that,' he said. 'That's not what I want to hire you for. I want you to find out who the real mole is and get me off the hook.'

I shook my head. It nearly killed me, turning business down. 'I'm already fully occupied taking care of Gloria. You'd be better off going to another firm.' I gritted my teeth. 'I could probably recommend somebody.'

He shook his handsome head. 'There would be no point. Turpin would never let them on to the location shoots, never mind inside the compound. I'm amazed Gloria's got away with having you on set. That's why you're the only one who can help me. I'll pay the going rate, I don't expect anything less.'

I finished my coffee and tossed the cup in the nearby bin. 'No can do,' I said. 'I can't take money under false pretences. I'd be lying if I said I could investigate the leaks at the same time as taking care of Gloria.'

He looked as if he was going to burst into tears. His big shoulders slumped and his mouth turned down at the corners. I glanced back to the serving hatch in the side of the van and caught a murderous look from his wife. 'Look,' I sighed. 'I tell you what I'll do. I'll keep my eyes and ears open, maybe make a couple of phone calls. If I come up with anything, you can pay me on results. How does that grab you?'

Laughing boy was back. He grinned and clapped a beefy arm round my shoulders. I thought my lungs had collapsed. 'That's terrific. Fabulous. Thanks, I really appreciate it.' He leaned over and smacked a sloppy kiss on my cheek.

'Ross?' his wife called sharply. 'I need a hand in here.'

'No problem,' the big man said. 'I'll be hearing from you then, Kate.'

Somehow I doubted it. Before I could say anything more, I noticed Gloria rushing off the set and into the make-up caravan. Grateful for the chance to get out of the northerly wind that was exfoliating the few square centimetres of skin I had allowed to be exposed, I ran across and climbed aboard.

Gloria was sitting in front of a mirror, blowing on her hands as a make-up artist hovered around her. 'Here she is,' Gloria announced. 'Me and my shadow,' she sang in her throaty contralto. 'Are you as cold as I am?'

'How many fingers have you got left?'

Gloria made a show of counting. 'Looks like they're all still here.'

'In that case, I'm colder,' I said, waving a hand with one finger bent over.

'Freddie, meet Kate Brannigan, my bodyguard.

Kate, this is Freddie Littlewood. It's his job to stop me looking like the raddled old bag I really am.'

'Hi, Freddie.'

He ducked his head in acknowledgement and gave me a quick once-over in the mirror. He had a narrow head and small, tight features framed by spiky black hair. With his black polo neck and black jeans like a second skin, he looked as if he'd escaped from one of those existential French films where you don't understand a bloody word even with subtitles. 'Honestly, Gloria,' he said. 'I don't know why you listen to that Dorothea Dawson.' His voice was surprising. There wasn't a trace of the high camp of his physical appearance. He could have read the radio news without a complaint.

'It's surprising how often she gets things right,' Gloria said mildly as he expertly applied powder to her cheeks.

'And how often she causes trouble,' he added drily. 'All those sly little hints that people take a certain way and before you know it, old friends are at each other's throats. You watch, now she's got you all wound up and scared witless, I bet this week she'll tell you something that starts you looking out the corner of your eye at one of your best friends.'

'I don't know why you've got it in for Dorothea,' Gloria said. 'She's harmless and we're all grown-ups.'

'I just don't like to see you upset, Gloria,' he said solicitously.

'Well, between me and you and the wall, Freddie, it wasn't what Dorothea said that upset me. I was already in a state. I'd been getting threatening letters. I'd had my tyres slashed to ribbons. All Dorothea did was make me realize I should be taking them seriously.'

I could have clobbered her. I'd told her to carry on keeping quiet about the threatening letters and the vandalism, to let everyone think it was Dorothea's eerie warning that was behind my presence. And here she was, telling all to the man perfectly placed to be the distribution centre of the rumour factory. 'Nice one, Gloria,' I muttered.

It's not the people you go up against that make this job a bitch; it's the clients, every time.

7

SUN CONJUNCTION WITH MERCURY
She has a lively mind. Her opinions are important to her and she enjoys expressing them. Objectivity sometimes suffers from the strength of her views. Exchanging and acquiring information which she can subsequently analyse matters a lot.

From *Written in the Stars*, by Dorothea Dawson

When she finally finished filming her outdoor scene with Teddy, Gloria announced we were going shopping. I must have looked as dubious as I felt. 'Don't worry, chuck,' she laughed as I drove her into the NPTV compound. 'We won't get mobbed. How do you think I manage when I've not got you running around after me?'

I was gobsmacked by the result. I'd seen her in plain clothes already, not least when she'd first come to the office. But this was something else again. I thought I was the mistress of disguise until

92

I met Gloria. When she emerged from her dressing room after a mere ten minutes to slough off Brenda Barrowclough, I nearly let her walk past me. She'd cheated; this wasn't the outfit she'd worn when I'd driven her to work that morning. Wearing jeans and cowboy boots under a soft nubuck jacket that fell to mid-thigh, the image was entirely different. On her head perched a designer version of a cowboy hat, tilted to a jaunty angle. Instead of sunglasses, she'd gone for a pair of slightly tinted granny glasses that subtly changed the shape of her face. She looked twenty years younger. I wasn't going to be the only person who wouldn't instantly recognize Gloria now she'd ditched the wig and adopted a wardrobe that didn't include polyester.

Thankfully, she didn't have a major expedition in mind. Her granddaughter had been invited to a fancy dress party and she wanted to go as Esmeralda from *The Hunchback of Notre Dame*. 'They've got outfits at the Disney store, but they cost a fortune and I could make better myself,' Gloria explained as I squeezed the car into a slot in the Arndale Centre car park. She never ceased to amaze me. This was a woman who could afford a hundred Esmeralda outfits without noticing the dent in her bank balance. But her pretence of meanness didn't fool me. Making the costume wasn't about saving money; it was about giving her granddaughter something of herself. It was also a way, I suspected, of reminding herself of the life she had come from.

We descended a claustrophobic concrete stairwell that reeked so strongly of piss it was a relief to step out into the traffic fumes of High Street. Gloria led me unerringly through the warren of Victorian warehouses that house the city's rag trade till we fetched up at a wholesaler who specialized in saris. Judging by the warmth of the welcome, she was no stranger. Merely because I was with her, I was offered tea too. While Gloria sipped from a thick pottery mug and browsed the dazzling fabrics, I hung around near the door, peering into the street with the avidity of the truly paranoid. The only people in sight were hurrying through the dank cold of the dying December day, coat collars turned up against the knife edge of the wind that howled through the narrow streets of the Northern Quarter. It wasn't a day for appreciating the renaissance of yet another part of the inner city. Nobody was going to be browsing the shop windows today. The craft workers must have been blessing their good fortune at having an enclosed market.

We emerged on the street just as darkness was falling, me staggering two steps behind Gloria toting a bale of fabric that felt heavy enough to clothe half of Lancashire. As we approached the Arndale from a slightly different angle, I realized we must be close to Dennis's latest venture. I couldn't help smiling at the thought of the double act Dennis and Gloria would be. It had been a long week, and I felt like some light relief, so I said, 'A

mate of mine has just opened a shop this end of
the Arndale. Do you mind if we just drop in to say
hello?'

'What kind of shop?'

'You remember what they used to say about
how cheap it was to shop at the Co-op? On account
of you could never find anything you wanted
to buy?'

Gloria chuckled. 'That good, eh? Oh well, why
not? We've got nowt else on till tomorrow morning.'

'I don't think it'll take that long.'

It wasn't hard to spot Dennis's establishment.
Sandwiched between a cut-price butcher and a
heel bar in the subterranean section of the mall,
it was notable for the dump bins of bargains virtually blocking the underpass and the muscle-bound
minder keeping an eye on potential shoplifters. All
he was wearing was a pair of jogging pants and
a vest designed to show off his awesome upper
body development. 'High-class joint, then,' Gloria
remarked as we followed the chicane created by
the dump bins, artfully placed to funnel us past
whitewashed windows proclaiming, 'Everything
Under a Pound!' and into the shop.

By the door were three tills, all staffed by slack-
jawed teenagers. The girls were the ones with the
mascara. I think. Dennis was up near the back of
the shop, stacking shelves with giant bottles of
lurid green bath foam. We squeezed up a narrow
aisle packed with weary shoppers who had the

look and smell of poverty. My awkward parcel of material earned me a few hard words and a lot of harder looks.

Of course, I didn't get anywhere near Dennis before he noticed us. I swear that man has eyes in the back of his head. 'Kate,' he said, his face creasing up in a delighted grin. 'Fabulous!' He cleared a way through for us, telling his customers to kindly move their arses or take the consequences. 'So, what do you think?' he asked almost before I was within bear-hug reach.

I gave the shelves the quick once-over. Exactly what I'd expected. Cheap and nasty, from the toys to the toiletries. 'I think you're going to make a mint,' I said sadly, depressed at the reminder of how many skint punters there are out there who needed to fill Christmas stockings on a weekly budget of the same amount that most MPs spend on lunch.

'Are you not going to introduce us, chuck?' Gloria said. I half turned to find her giving Dennis the appraising look of a farmer at a fatstock show. That was all I needed. Dennis has a habit of forgetting he's married, which is fine by me as long as I'm not personally involved with aiding and abetting it. I'm very fond of his wife Debbie, even if she doesn't have the brains God gave a lemming.

'I don't think so,' I said. 'This is just a flying visit.'

I was too late. Dennis was already sliding round me and extending a hand to Gloria. 'Dennis O'Brien at your service, darling,' he said. Gloria slid her hand into his and he raised it to his lips, all the time fixing her with the irresistible sparkle of his intense blue eyes. I groaned.

'I'm Gloria Kendal.'

His smile reminded me of crocodiles at feeding time. 'I know,' he said.

'It's the voice,' I muttered. 'Total giveaway.'

'It's got nothing to do with the voice,' he said. 'It's because this lovely lady's with you. I can read, you know, Kate.'

'What do you mean, it's because she's with me?'

Dennis cast his eyes heavenwards. 'Tonight's *Chronicle*. You mean you've not seen it?'

'No. What about it?'

He jerked his head towards a door at the rear of the shop. 'Through the back. It's in my ski-jacket pocket.'

I looked at him. I looked at the door. I looked at Gloria. 'On you go, chuck,' she said. 'I think I'm in safe hands here.'

'That's all you know,' I mumbled. But I dumped the fabric parcel on Dennis and left them to it while I went to chase whatever he'd seen in the evening paper. I didn't have to look hard. There wasn't much room in the bare concrete back shop to hide anything as big as Dennis's ski jacket, which was draped over one of two folding chairs by a cardboard computer carton doing a bad impersonation of a table. The paper was sticking out of a pocket and the story I was clearly supposed to be looking for was splashed across the front page. '*NORTHERNERS' STAR IN DEATH THREAT DRAMA,*' I read.

> '*Gloria Kendal, busybody Brenda Barrowclough in top soap* Northerners, *is at the heart of a real-life drama tonight. The award-winning actress has been warned that threatening letters sent to her home could mean death.*
>
> '*The desperate warning was spelled out by her personal astrologer Dorothea Dawson, the TV Seer to the Stars. But following a savage act of vandalism on her Saab sports car, Ms Kendal has taken the danger to heart and has hired top local private investigator Kate Brannigan to act as bodyguard.*
>
> '*The star of the Manchester-based soap has vowed not to be driven underground by the vicious poison-pen writer . . .*'

I skimmed to the end of the article, but there didn't seem to be any more meat on the bones. There were a couple of paragraphs mentioning previous cases where my name had unfortunately made it into the press, but nothing too damaging. What I couldn't figure out, apart from where the story had come from, was why nobody had called me all afternoon about it. Shelley should have been straight on to me the minute the paper landed, I thought. I was almost glad of the rare opportunity to put her in the wrong.

Then I took my moby out of my bag and realized

I'd forgotten to switch it back on after I'd had it muted for the filming.

There were fourteen messages. I wasn't strong enough to deal with them yet. Besides, if the situation was out in the open, I needed to get my client away from the public eye as fast as possible. The last thing I needed was for some care-in-the-community case to hit on the idea of making a name for himself by metamorphosing into the secret stalker.

I hurried back to the shop, clutching the paper. I was too late. When I opened the door, it looked as if a small riot had enveloped the shop. At the eye of the storm was Dennis, standing on a counter with Gloria perched next to him. The massive bouncer had moved inside the store and was brandishing one of the red plastic under-a-pound fun cameras like King Kong with a fire engine. 'Did you get that, Keith? Did you get that?' Dennis kept asking.

The shoppers had lost all interest in Dennis's wares, but for once he didn't care. 'Melody, get on the blower to the *Sun* and tell them we've got exclusive pictures to sell of Gloria Kendal defying death threats and shopping in Manchester's best value-for-money store.'

'Ah, shit,' I muttered, lowering my head and thrusting through the crowd. Getting through to Gloria was a lot harder than Moses parting the Red Sea. Eventually I managed it, but only by elbowing a couple of elderly ladies in the ribs and stepping hard on the instep of a teenage girl who was still yelping in complaint minutes later. 'Come on, Gloria, time to go home,' I said grimly.

'I was just starting to enjoy myself,' she complained good-naturedly, pushing herself to her feet.

'You're not whisking this wonderful woman off before we've had the chance to get to know each other?' Dennis demanded, sounding aggrieved.

'That's as good a reason as any,' I grunted, trying to force a way through the clamouring crowd to the door.

Gloria turned to wiggle her fingers at him. 'See you around, Dennis. I hope.'

'Keith,' I shouted. 'Stop poncing around pretending to be David Bailey and give us a hand here. I need to get Gloria home.'

The big bouncer looked to Dennis for guidance. He gave a rueful smile and nodded. 'Sort it,' he said.

Keith picked up the parcel of fabric and carved a path to the door in seconds flat. One look at biceps the size of cannonballs, and the obstructive punters just melted into the shelves. Gloria signed postcards as she walked, automatically passing them into the grasping hands of the fans. Out in the underpass, Keith thrust the bundle into my arms and I hustled Gloria towards a nearby bank of lifts that would take us back to the car park. 'I like your friend,' she said as we crammed in beside a pushchair and a harassed-looking woman who was too busy pacifying her toddler to care who was in the lift with her.

'He obviously likes you too. But then, his wife's a big fan of *Northerners*,' I said drily.

'That's a pity,' she said.

'I thought you needed all the viewers you could get just now.'

Gloria raised her eyebrows, not entirely amused by my deliberate misunderstanding. 'I meant, the existence of a wife. I was going to ask you for his number, but if he's a married man, I'm not interested.'

'Worried about the press?'

She shook her head. 'It's not fear of the *Sun* that stops me having affairs with married men. There are enough people out there ready to make women's lives a misery without me joining in.'

The lift doors opened and Gloria stepped out, turning to give the young mother a hand with her pushchair. 'You never cease to amaze me, Gloria,' I said as we crossed the car park. 'You must have *some* bad habits.'

In response, she took out her cigarette packet and waved it at me. 'One for the road,' she said, climbing into the passenger seat of her Saab. 'And I like a drink,' she added as I started the engine. 'And I have been known to play the odd game of bingo.'

'You're too good for this world,' I said wryly.

She plucked the *Chronicle* from the pocket where

I'd stowed it and stared grim-faced at the front page. 'I flaming hope not,' she said.

After I dropped Gloria at home where she planned a quiet night in with her sewing machine and a stack of Fred Astaire and Ginger Rogers movies, there was only one logical place to go. Even if it did involve one of those cross-country routes that looks sensible on the map but suddenly develops a mind of its own as soon as all human habitation falls out of sight.

My best friend Alexis and her partner Chris live in the wilds of the Derbyshire Peak District. Alexis claims she can be in her office in central Manchester twenty-three minutes after leaving home, but that's only because she's the crime correspondent of the *Chronicle* and so she starts work around half past six in the morning. I always feel like I need a Sherpa and a St Bernard with a barrel of brandy to make it to the dream home they built themselves. Chris is an architect, and she designed the small development in exchange for the skills of her neighbours who did a lot of the heavy work as well as the plumbing and electrics. They ended up spending about eighty grand on a property that would sell for three times that on the open market.

Then they found the perfect way to spend all the money they'd saved. They had a baby. Chris actually did the bit that makes most people wince and cross their legs, but Alexis has just as much of a stake in Jay Appleton Lee. I'm about as fond of woodlice as I am of children, but even I have to admit – if only to myself – that I can see why Richard finds this particular baby as delightful as her parents do.

But that night I wasn't interested in admiring Jay's shock of black spiky hair or her latest tooth. It was Alexis I needed to see. I'd timed my arrival perfectly. Jay was en route from bath to bed, so all I had to do was make a few admiring noises before Chris whisked her away. Five minutes later, the three of us were installed in the comfortable living room, Chris and Alexis with dark smudges under their eyes that just about matched the glasses of Murphy's stout they were drinking.

'You having a night off, then, girl?' Alexis asked, her Scouse accent as rich as the creamy head on her glass. 'Rather you than me, minding a soap star for a living.'

'Just let me lie down for five minutes then I'll throw some pizza at the oven,' Chris said, stifling a yawn and stretching out on the sofa, dumping her feet in Alexis's lap. 'So what's she like, Gloria Kendal?'

'Brenda Barrowclough with a bit more insight, humour and style,' I said. 'At first, all I saw was that total self-absorption you get with actors. But the more I've got to know her, the more I've come to realize there's more to her than that. She's forthright, funny, generous. I'm amazed, but I actually like her.' I told them about our adventures with Dennis. They both knew him well enough to fill in the gaps for themselves.

'I wish I'd been there. It sounds like one to cut out and keep,' Alexis said, reaching for her cigarette packet. She took out a fag and began to go through the motions of smoking without actually lighting up. Another consequence of motherhood. She'd gone from fifty Silk Cut a day to smoking about a dozen and using a few others as the adult equivalent of a dummy. The only person who didn't see this as an improvement was Alexis herself.

'Thanks to the *Chronicle*.' I scowled.

'The newsdesk were on to me about it,' Alexis said. 'I told them there wasn't any point in me ringing you for a quote. Or in them ringing you for a quote. I gave them this whole spiel about how you've got this Philip Marlowe code of conduct and you'd never grass up a client.'

'Very noble of you,' Chris said drily. 'Respecting Kate's professional code. You really love pissing off the newsdesk, don't you?'

'Well,' Alexis drawled. 'They ask for it, don't they? So, is she really getting death threats?'

'I'll swap you,' I said. 'I'll give you some nonattributable background if you tell me where the story came from in the first place.'

Alexis pulled a face and flicked the nonexistent ash from her cigarette. 'You got me there, KB. You know I have as little to do with the brain-dead dickheads on the newsdesk as possible. And this didn't actually come as a tip directly to news. The story came through features, from Mack Morrissey who does the showbiz beat. It'll have come from a contact.'

'Any chance you could find out who?'

Alexis shrugged. 'I don't know. Mack's a bit precious, you know. He wouldn't let any of us hairy-arsed hacks anywhere near his valuable artistic contacts.'

'You could ask him,' Chris chipped in.

'I could,' Alexis admitted. 'But there's a better way of finding out. I can't believe he got a tale like this for free. He'll have had to put a payment through the credits book.'

'He won't have stumped up readies?' I asked.

Alexis shook her head. 'Not this amount. It'll have been a few hundred. I'm surprised his contact gave the story to us, to be honest. It would have been worth a lot more to the nationals.'

Another interesting piece of information to tuck away in the file marked, 'Makes no sense'. When the oddments of data reached critical mass, seemingly unrelated facts collided and rearranged themselves into logical sequences. It's a process normally called 'woman's intuition'.

'I'll check out the credits book in the morning,' Alexis promised. 'So what's the score with Gloria? Has she really had death threats? And does she really think you're going to throw yourself between her and the assassin's bullet?'

'How else will I catch it with my teeth?' I asked

innocently. 'People in Gloria's position are always getting hate mail. Recently, she's had a few letters that have seemed a bit more sinister than the usual run-of-the-mill stuff, and Dorothea Dawson threw some petrol on the flames. Bloody irresponsible, but what can you expect from a con merchant? None of these psychics and clairvoyants would earn a shilling if they had to stop preying on people's irrational fears. Take it from me, Alexis, nothing is going to happen to Gloria Kendal. All I'm there for is to put the frighteners on anybody who might be thinking about taking advantage of the situation.'

Alexis's eyebrows rose and she ran a hand through thick dark hair recently shorn from a wiry thicket to a shrubby bush less accessible to tiny grasping fists. Another consequence of mother-hood. 'You've not met Dorothea yet, then?'

I frowned. 'No, but what difference does that make?'

'I didn't think you'd be calling her a con artist if you'd met her.'

I stared open-mouthed at Alexis. 'You're not telling me you believe in that crap, are you?'

'Of course not, soft girl. But Dorothea Dawson's not a charlatan. She's sincere about what she does. I interviewed her a few years back, when I was still working for features. Before I actually met her, I was saying exactly the same as you're saying now. And I had to eat my words. It wasn't that she told me anything world shattering, like I was going to

106

meet a tall dark handsome stranger and do a lot of foreign travel. She didn't make a big production number out of it, just said very calmly that I had already met the love of my life, that my career was going to make a sideways move that would make me a lot more satisfied and it probably wouldn't be the fags that killed me but they wouldn't help.'

I shook my head. 'And this revelation turned you into a believer?' I said sarcastically.

'Yeah. Because she didn't grandstand. She was dead matter-of-fact, even apologized for not having anything more exciting to tell me. She came across as a really nice woman, you know? And she's not just in it for the money. Sure, she charges rich bastards like the *Northerners* cast an arm and a leg, but she does a lot of freebies for charity.'

'That's right,' Chris added. 'She donated a full personal horoscope to the Women's Aid charity auction last month. And you remember that mental health job I designed a couple of years ago?'

I nodded. It had been a major renovation project for Chris, turning an old mill in Rochdale into housing units for single homeless people with mental health problems. 'I remember,' I said.

'Well, I happen to know that Dorothea Dawson was the biggest single donor for that scheme. She gave them fifty grand.'

'You never told me that,' Alexis complained. 'That would have made a good diary piece.'

'That's precisely why I didn't tell you,' Chris

said drily. 'It was supposed to be confidential. She didn't want a big song and dance about it.'

'It's a lot of money,' I said diplomatically.

'So she can't be a con artist, can she?' Alexis demanded. 'They rip people off. They don't donate that sort of cash to charity. It's not like she'd need a tax loss, is it? I mean, a load of her earnings must be cash, so she could stash a bundle undeclared anyway.'

I held my hands up in submission. 'OK, I give in. Dorothea Dawson is a sweet little old lady, grossly misunderstood by cynical unbelievers like me. It must be written in my stars.'

'Anyway, KB, you sure taking care of Gloria isn't just a front?' Alexis demanded, changing tack in an obvious bid to wrong-foot me.

'For what?' I asked, baffled.

'Working for the management at NPTV. They've got a major mole in there, which is the last thing you need when you're trying to finesse a major deal with the networks. I heard they've got a mole hunt going on. You sure they've not hired you to find out who's stirring the shit for them?'

I shook my head. 'Sorry. You'll have to get your follow-up somewhere else.'

'I thought they'd be happy about all the press stories about the show,' Chris said. 'I'd have thought it would increase the ratings. I had to go to London the other day on the train, and the two women opposite me talked about *Northerners* nonstop.'

'I think the scandalous stories about the stars

108

whet people's appetites,' I said. 'According to my sources, what the management don't like are the storyline leaks. They reckon that makes people turn off.'

Before anyone could say more, my moby began to bleat insistently. 'Goodbye, pizza,' I said mournfully, grabbing my bag and reaching for the phone. 'Brannigan,' I grunted.

'It's me.'

My heart sank. 'Donovan, you've not been arrested again?'

8

MOON IN TAURUS IN THE 12TH HOUSE

The emotional swings of the moon are minimized in this placing, leading to balance between impulsiveness and determination. She is sociable, but needs to recharge her batteries in solitude which she seeks actively. Imaginative and intuitive, she has an instinctive rapport with creative artists though not herself artistic.

From *Written in the Stars*, by Dorothea Dawson

This time it was Alderley Edge, the village that buys more champagne per head of population than anywhere else in the UK. Donovan had been there to serve a subpoena on a company director who seemed to think the shareholders should fund the entire cost of his affair with a member of the chorus of Northern Opera. The detached house was in a quietly expensive street, behind tall hedges like most of its neighbours. Donovan had borrowed his mother's car and sat patiently parked a few doors down from the house for about an hour waiting for his target to return.

When the man came home, Donovan had caught him getting out of his car. He'd accepted service with ill grace and stormed into the house. Donovan had driven home via his girlfriend's student residence bedsit to pick up some tutorial handouts for the essay he was writing. He'd arrived home to find the police waiting. They hadn't been interested in an explanation. They'd just hauled him off in a police car to the local nick where they'd informed him he was being arrested on suspicion of burglary.

By the time I arrived, tempers were fraying round the edges. It turned out that at some point during the day, a neighbour of the company director had been burgled. And another nosy neighbour had happened to jot down Shelley's car number because, well, you just don't get black people sitting around in parked cars in the leafy streets of Alderley Edge. The neighbour had arrived home a few minutes after Donovan had driven off, discovered the burglary and called the police. When the nosy neighbour saw the police arrive (within five minutes, because Alderley Edge is middle-class territory, not a council estate where you wait half an hour for a response to a treble-niner reporting a murder in progress) he nipped across to tell them about the suspicious black man.

The police computer spat out Shelley's address in response to the car registration number, and the bizzies were round there in no time flat. Things were complicated by the fact that the bloke Donovan had served the subpoena on decided to get his own back and denied all knowledge of a young black process-server with a legitimate reason for being in the street.

It took me the best part of an hour to persuade the police that Donovan was telling the truth and that I wasn't some gangster's moll trying to spring my toy boy. Thighs like his, I should be so lucky.

The one good thing about the whole pathetic business was that Shelley had been out when the police had turned up. With luck, she'd still be out. As I drove him home, I said, 'Maybe this isn't such a good idea, you doing the process-serving.'

'I'm serving the papers properly, what's the problem?' he said defensively.

'It's not good for your image or your mother's blood pressure if you keep getting arrested.'

'I'm not letting those racists drive me out of a job,' he protested. 'You're saying I should just lie down and let them do it to me? The only places I have a problem are the ones where rich white people think that money can buy them a ghetto. People don't call the cops when *you* go to serve paper in Alderley Edge, or when I turn up on a doorstep in Hulme.'

'You're right. I'm sorry. I wasn't thinking it through,' I said, ashamed of myself for only seeing the easy way out. 'The job's yours for as long as you want it. And first thing tomorrow, I'll get your

112

mother to have some proper business cards and ID printed up for you.'

'Fine by me. Besides, Kate, I need the money. I can't be scrounging off my mother so I can have a beer with my mates, or go to see a film with Miranda. The process-serving's something I can fit around studying and having fun. You can't do that with most part-time jobs.'

I grinned. 'You could always get an anorak and work with Gizmo on the computer security side of things.'

Donovan snorted. 'I don't think Gizmo'd let me. Have you noticed he's got well weird lately?'

'How can you tell?' I signalled the right turn that would bring me into the narrow street of terraced brick houses where the Carmichael family lived.

'Yeah, right. He's always been well weird. But this last few weeks, he's been totally paranoid android about his files.'

'He's always been secretive about his work,' I reminded him. 'And not unreasonably. A lot of what we do for clients on computer security is commercially sensitive.'

'There's secretive and there's mentally ill. Did you know you even need a password to get out of his screen savers?'

'Now you are exaggerating,' I said.

'You think so? You try it the next time he goes to the loo. Touch a key when one of the screen savers is running and you'll be asked for a password. You didn't know?' Donovan's eyebrows rose in surprise. He opened the car door and unfolded his long body into the street. Then he bent down and said anxiously, 'Check it out. I'm not making it up. Whatever he's up to, he doesn't want anybody else to know. And it is your hardware he's doing it on.'

'It'll be OK,' I said, trying to reassure myself as much as Donovan. 'Gizmo wouldn't take risks with my business.' Which was true enough, I thought as I drove home. Except that what Gizmo thought was fair game didn't necessarily coincide with the law's view. And if he didn't think it was wrong, why would he imagine it might be risky?

The response to the *Chronicle*'s story sharply polarized the *Northerners* cast in a way I hadn't seen before. Up to that point, I'd been beginning to wonder whether I could possibly be right about this being an inside job. Ten minutes in the NPTV compound that morning showed me the truth. People who had been all smiles and friendship the day before now had pursed lips and suddenly found they had somewhere else to look when Gloria passed. I actually heard one minor cast member say to another, supposedly apropos of something else, 'Too grand for the likes of us, of course.'

'What happened to that lot?' I asked as soon as Gloria closed the dressing room door behind us.

Rita Hardwick, who shared the room and played

rough and ready tart with a heart Thelma Torrance, paused in stitching the tapestry she passed the slack time with. 'Got the cold shoulder, did she?' she said with grim good humour.

'Yeah,' I said, not caring about showing my puzzlement. 'Yesterday, everybody's everybody's pal and today, it's like we've got a communicable disease.'

'It happens when you get a big show in the papers,' Gloria said, putting her coat on a hanger and subsiding into a chair. 'It's basically jealousy. The people below you in the pecking order resent the fact that you're important enough to make the front page of the *Chronicle* and have the story followed up by all the tabloids the next day.'

I'd already seen the evidence of Gloria's importance to the tabloids. When I'd arrived to collect her that morning, we'd had to run the gauntlet of reporters and photographers clustered round the high gates that kept Gloria safe from their invasive tendencies.

'Aye,' said Rita. 'And the ones above you in the pecking order reckon you need cutting down to size before you start snapping too close at their heels. Not that there's many above you these days, Glo.'

'Stuff like this shows you who your real friends are,' Gloria added.

'Aye, and we've all got precious few round here,' Rita said, thrusting her needle ferociously into the material. 'There's plenty would stab you in the back soon as look at you if they thought they could get away with it.'

If a bit of newspaper coverage was all it took to create a poisonous atmosphere like the one we'd just walked through, I hated to think how Gloria's colleagues would react if someone actually did them serious damage. 'Have you had much personal publicity lately?' I asked, wondering if an excess of press attention had provoked one of her fellow cast members into sending her the original threatening letters.

Gloria shook her head. Rita disagreed. 'There's been a lot of stories about the abortion issue, Glo. Brenda and Debbie have been all over the tabloids.'

'But that's Brenda, not me. The punters don't know the difference, but the people who work here do.'

'It doesn't make any odds to some of that lot,' Rita said. 'Eaten up with jealousy, they are.' She glanced at her watch. 'Bloody hell, is that the time? I've got an appointment with Dorothea in five minutes.' She shoved her sewing into a tapestry bag.

'You're all right. I didn't see the van when we parked up.' Gloria gave me a considering look. 'You wanted a word with Dorothea, didn't you, chuck?'

Rita stared. 'By heck, Kate, I'd not have put you down as a lass who wanted her horoscope reading.'

I bristled. 'The only stars I want to ask Dorothea

Dawson about are the ones that work for *Northerners.*'

Rita giggled. 'If that crystal ball could talk . . .'

'Aye, but going to Dorothea's like going to the doctor. You can say owt you like and know it'll go no further,' Gloria said. 'Rita, chuck, do you mind if I just pop in ahead of you for a quick word with Dorothea, to see when she can fit Kate in?'

'Be my guest. I'll walk across with you.'

The three of us left the studio building and crossed the car park. Over at the far end, near the administration block, I noticed a camper van that hadn't been there when we'd arrived shortly before. It was painted midnight-blue, but as we drew closer, I could see there was a Milky Way of golden stars arcing across the cab door and the van's side. The door into the living section of the van had a zodiac painted on it in silver, the glyphs of the signs picked out in gold. Even I could recognize the maiden that symbolized my Virgo star sign. I also identified the familiar three-legged symbol of Mercedes Benz. I didn't need my background information from Chris to realize there was obviously serious money in Dorothea Dawson's profession.

Rita knocked and a familiar husky voice told us to come in. I expected a full blast of the histrionic mystic, complete with joss sticks and Indian cotton, but when it came to her personal environment, Dorothea clearly preferred the opulent to the occult. Leather, velvet, shag-pile carpet and wood panelling lined the luxurious interior. In the galley, I could see a microwave and a fridge. On a pull-out shelf sat a laptop and a portable colour printer, an ensemble that must have cost the thick end of three grand. Instead of a bloody awful tape of rainforest noises backed by Pan pipes and whales singing, the background music sounded like one of those 'not available in the shops' collections of Romantic Classics. The only concession to the mystic world of the zodiac was the dining table, surrounded on three sides by a bench seat. It was covered in a dark-blue chenille cloth and on it sat a massive crystal ball. If it had had a set of finger holes, we could have gone ten-pin bowling.

'Nice to see you all, ladies,' Dorothea Dawson said as we piled through the door. She was smaller than I expected from TV. But then, they all were. Her hair was pure silver, cut in a chin-length bob that hid the fact that her jaw was too heavy for her small features. Her skin was criss-crossed with the fine wrinkles of an apple that's been left lying around too long. Either she was older than she sounded or she'd loved the sun too much when she was younger. 'And you must be Kate Brannigan,' she said, acknowledging me with a nod, assessing me with eyes like amethyst chips.

'Saw me in your crystal ball, did you?' I asked more pleasantly than I wanted to. I've never liked charlatans.

'No, I saw you in the *Manchester Evening Chronicle*,' she said with wry amusement. I found myself liking her in spite of all my prejudices against people who prey on the gullible. 'You want to talk to me about my last session with Gloria?'

'Good guess,' I said.

'And I want you to cast her horoscope,' Gloria butted in, as usual incapable of holding her tongue.

Dorothea cocked her head, a knowing smile on her lips. 'Virgo, with ... an air sign rising, at a guess. Probably Gemini, with such a smart mouth.'

I tried not to look as surprised as I felt. A one-in-twelve chance of getting my sun sign right multiplied up to a one-in-a-gross chance of hitting the sun sign and the ascendant. Not that I believed any of that rubbish; I only knew my rising sign because I'd spent half an hour the night before on the computer with some astrological chart-casting shareware I'd pulled down from the internet. But however she'd reached her conclusion, Dorothea was right. 'I couldn't say,' I lied, determined to show her my scepticism. 'Gloria can give you my details.'

'I have a very full diary today,' Dorothea said, sounding far more like a businesswoman than she had any right to. She looked businesslike too, in a high-necked Edwardian-style white blouse under a soft black wool crepe jacket. A silver and amethyst brooch the size of a credit card was pinned to the jacket, like an abstract representation of her hair and eyes. She flicked open a desk diary on the seat beside her while Gloria produced a piece of paper with a flourish. 'That's Kate's time, date and place of birth.'

Dorothea put it on the seat beside her without a glance. 'I couldn't possibly take you through your chart *and* answer your questions, Kate.'

'It's the answers to my questions I'm interested in.'

Dorothea raised one eyebrow. I used to do that, but I grew out of it. 'Pity. You should always seize opportunity when it presents itself. Who knows when you'll get a second chance to find out what really makes you tick?' She sounded amused.

'I'll manage somehow,' I said.

'I'm sure you will, and that's without reading your chart. Gloria, you're my final appointment today. How would it be if I saw Kate then? Or are you in a hurry to get home?'

'That's fine, Dor,' Gloria said. 'We'll get out your road now and let Rita get her money's worth. See you at half past five.'

She shooed me out ahead of her into the car park. 'We'd better get a move on,' she said. 'I'm due in make-up and I'm not frocked up yet.'

'Gloria, is Dorothea normally fully booked?' I asked, trailing in her wake.

'Oh aye. If you're not one of her regulars, you can wait a month or more for her to fit you in unless you're prepared to go to her consulting room.'

'All half-hour appointments?'

120

'That's right. From nine till half past five,' Gloria confirmed.

'Just as a matter of interest, how much does Dorothea charge?'

'For half an hour, she charges twice what you do for an hour, chuck.'

It was one of those bits of information that stops you dead in your tracks. I'm not cheap. Well, only where Richard's concerned, but even he hasn't worked that out yet. Four times my hourly rate was serious money. Sometimes I wonder if I'm in the right business.

The day passed. Wardrobe, make-up, rehearsal, film. No diverting phone calls, no murderous attacks on the client. No chance either of finding out who had written the poison-pen letters or the identity of the mole that Ross Grant wanted me to drag kicking and screaming into the daylight; thanks to the *Chronicle*, nobody was talking to me. I supposed the cast members had fallen out of love with me because for today I was more famous than them. The crew were just too busy and besides, the novelty of having a real live private eye about the place had worn off.

By the time five rolled around, I was beginning to think that I should start charging boredom money the way that some people charge danger money. I was convinced by now that whoever was writing threatening letters to Gloria was getting satisfaction from knowing they'd frightened her enough to hire me. Given the number of opportunities to cause her serious harm, even with me in tow, it was significant that we'd not even had so much as a near miss in the car. I'd accompany her on her weekend personal appearances, then I intended to call it a day.

Her face restored to street levels of make-up and Brenda's outfit back in wardrobe where it belonged, Gloria was ready for her session with Dorothea. 'Walk me across to the van, chuck,' she said. 'I'll see Dorothea on my own, but if you come over about five to six, you can walk me back to my dressing room then pop back to ask her whatever it is you want to know.'

An unrelenting sleet was falling as we joined the dozens of people scurrying across the car park, desperately seeking shelter. I'd helped myself to one of the umbrellas in an equipment skip by the entrance to the outdoor set, and I wrestled with the gusty wind to keep it over Gloria's head. At the caravan, I knocked. I heard Dorothea tell Gloria to come in. She disappeared inside and I closed the umbrella and sprinted for Gloria's car, parked only a few spaces away. Waiting for her there, I could at least listen to the radio.

I closed my eyes and leaned back in the seat, the day's news washing over me. The traffic reporter warned about drifting snow on trans-Pennine routes. 'Great,' I muttered, wondering how bad the road to Saddleworth would be. If the weather was going to close in, it might be worth suggesting

122

to Gloria that she spend the night in my spare room to save myself the double journey over snowy moorland roads.

Almost before I knew it, the twenty-five minutes were up. I abandoned the condensation-fogged car and legged it for Dorothea's camper. I knocked on the door of the van and Gloria called, 'Just coming, chuck.' The door opened, the warm light from inside spilling on to the Tarmac and revealing the waterlogging that was creeping up the sides of my brown ankle boots. 'I'll send her right back,' Gloria said over her shoulder as she emerged, closing the door behind her.

I did my trick with the umbrella and escorted Gloria back to her dressing room. The production area already felt deserted. Nobody on *Northerners* loved their job so much they wanted to hang around after the end of filming on a Friday. I was slightly concerned about leaving Gloria vulnerable in her dressing room. Both Rita and Dorothea knew about my appointment with the astrologer, and either could have mentioned it unthinkingly to a third party. Given the speed rumour moved at in NPTV, the cleaners and secretaries all probably knew Gloria would be alone in a virtually empty building from six o'clock.

'I want you to lock the door behind me, OK?' I told her. 'And don't let anybody in except me. It doesn't matter how much you think you can trust them. If anyone turns up, tell them they'll have to wait until I get back. Promise?'

Gloria grinned. 'All right, boss. Whatever you say.'

I waited outside the door until I heard the Yale lock snap into place behind me. Then I hurried out of the building and ran back across the car park to Dorothea's van. There was no answer to my knock, but I knew she was expecting me to return. Besides, it wasn't the kind of night where you hang around in freezing sleet waiting for someone else to stop playing power games. I opened the door and stepped into the dimly lit interior.

Dorothea Dawson lay sprawled across her chenille tablecloth, one side of her head strangely misshapen and dark with spilled blood. A few feet away, her crystal ball glowed in the lamplight at the end of a flecked trail of scarlet clotting the deep pile of the champagne-coloured carpet.

I backed away momentarily, dragging my eyes from the compelling horror before me. I stared wildly around, checking there was no one else in the confined space. Then the thought hit me with the force of a kick to the stomach that Dorothea might still be alive. For a long moment I didn't know if I could bring myself to touch her.

But I knew that if she died because I'd been squeamish that the guilt would far outweigh the revulsion I felt now. I tried to swallow whatever it was that was preventing me from breathing and inched forward, carefully avoiding the track the crystal ball had left. I stretched my hand towards Dorothea's outflung arm and grasped her wrist.

Her skin was the same temperature as mine, which made it all the more horrible that I couldn't find a pulse.

I backed away, appalled. I'd been right to warn Gloria to take care. There was a killer out there.

I'd been catastrophically wrong about the target, though.

9

MARS OPPOSES THE MIDHEAVEN

She has a high opinion of herself and is not always diplomatic enough to hide it. She can be too bold and belligerent in pursuit of what she knows to be right. But this opposition provides great energy, allowing her to be enterprising and independent. Her speed and competitiveness often take the wind out of the sails of authority figures.

From *Written in the Stars*, by Dorothea Dawson

I didn't know what to do. I didn't think I could bear to stay in that confined space with Dorothea's corpse, but I couldn't just walk away leaving the camper van unsecured. Besides, I couldn't stand guard outside because I'd be soaked to the skin in minutes. It seemed important to me that I shouldn't face the police looking like a drowned rat.

The compromise I found was to move down to the cab. The passenger seat was designed so that it could either face out through the windscreen or swing round to act as an extra chair in the living section of the van. Luckily for my peace of mind, it was currently configured to face forwards.

I scrambled through the gap between the seats, surprised to find myself gasping for air as if I'd been running. I gripped the armrests and forced myself to breathe evenly. I wanted to make sure I didn't sound like an emergency operator's idea of a murderer. I concentrated on the tracks of the melting sleet slithering down the windscreen that blurred the floodlights around the car park and tried to forget the image branded on my mind's eye. Only when my breathing had returned to normal did I take out my phone and dial 999. Once I was connected to the police control room, I said, 'My name is Kate Brannigan and I am a private investigator. I want to report what appears to be a murder.'

The woman on the end of the phone had obviously assimilated her training well. With no apparent indication that this was any more extraordinary an occurrence than a burglary in progress, she calmly said, 'Where are you calling from?'

'My mobile. I'm in the car park of the *Northerners* compound. It's just off Alan Turing Way, near the velodrome.'

'And can you tell me what appears to have happened?'

'I'm in a camper van. It belongs to Dorothea Dawson. The astrologer? I'd arranged a meeting with her. I walked in and found her lying dead. It looks like someone's caved her head in with her crystal ball. I tried to find a pulse, but there's nothing.' I could hear my voice cracking and swallowed hard.

'Are you still there?'

'Yes. I'm in the camper van. You can't miss it. It's a big dark-blue Mercedes. Down the far end, away from the entrance. Most of the cars have gone now; there's just a few down this end of the car park.' I was gabbling, I knew, but I couldn't stop myself.

'We'll have some officers with you very soon. Please don't touch anything. Can you give me your number, please?'

I rattled off the number automatically. 'We will be with you very shortly,' she concluded reassuringly. I wasn't comforted. This was an opportunist killing. Normally, there would be people in the car park, chatting and gossiping on their way to their cars, pausing and taking notice. But tonight, the weather meant everyone had their heads down, rushing for shelter and paying no attention to anything except the quickest route to their wheels.

Then there was the time element. There had only been a gap of ten minutes at the very outside between Gloria and me leaving the van and me returning. But someone had been bold or desperate enough to seize that tiny window of opportunity to invade Dorothea's camper van. They'd caught her unawares, obviously, and smashed the heavy crystal ball into her skull so swiftly she'd had no time to react.

Then they'd slipped back into the night. No time to search or steal. Time only to kill and to disappear again. Suddenly, I realized the killer might only have been feet away from me as I pounded across the car park through the sleet. Minutes – no, seconds – earlier and I could have come face to face with someone ruthless enough to have killed me too.

The thought hit me like a blow to the heart. My mouth went dry and a violent shiver ran through me from head to foot. My stomach started to heave and I barely got the door open in time. Second-hand lunch splattered on to the puddled car park. I retched and retched long past the point where my stomach was empty, hanging on grimly to the door with one hand.

That's how the police found me. I hadn't even been aware of the approaching sirens. I figured they must have turned them off when they reached the security gates at NPTV. Now, it was only the flashing blue lights that announced their arrival. I looked up blearily, my hair stuck to my head with sleet and sweat, and took in two liveried police cars and an ambulance. The occupants were out and running almost before the cars came to a standstill.

They headed towards me. I straightened up and pointed weakly to the door that led directly into the living section. 'She's in there,' I croaked. Three of them shifted their angle of approach. The fourth moved towards me, blocking any getaway I might have planned. He wasn't to know we were on the same side. Not surprising; it was a role I found pretty unfamiliar myself. After a quick scan of his colleagues' faces to check there was no opposition, the first policeman opened the door and cautiously stuck his head inside the van. I heard the hiss of indrawn breath and a muffled curse.

Now the paramedics were also at the door, trying to get past the knot of police officers. 'Let us in,' I heard one of them say impatiently.

'No way,' the cop who'd seen the body said. 'That's a crime scene.'

'She could be alive,' the paramedic protested, attempting to shove through the barrier of blue uniforms.

'No way,' the policeman repeated. He looked about as good as I felt. 'Take it from me, there's nothing you can do for her.'

'She didn't have a pulse when I found the body,' I said.

'When was that?' the officer keeping an eye on me asked.

'About two minutes before I made the treble-niner.'

My unthinking use of a professional term won me a quizzical look. One of his colleagues was speaking into his radio, collar turned up against the wind-driven sleet. Grumbling, the paramedics headed back to the shelter of their ambulance. I inched back so that I was out of the worst of the weather, making sure I kept my hands in sight. I knew that right now I had to be their prime suspect. One being a prime number.

Another car splashed through the puddles, illuminating a couple of executives making for their cars, too worried about getting wet to care about the presence of police cars and ambulances. The new arrival skidded to a halt only feet away from the front of Dorothea's Mercedes. The doors swung open, switching on the interior light and the impossible happened.

Things got worse.

Twenty minutes later, I was sitting in the *Northerners* green room, instantly commandeered by the police as a temporary incident room until their own purpose-built caravan could be brought over. Opposite me sat Detective Sergeant Linda Shaw, her hands wrapped around a cardboard cup of instant coffee. I didn't mind Linda; she probably had more in common with me than she'd ever have with the hard-nosed bastard she worked for.

I suspected Detective Chief Inspector Cliff Jackson had an auburn-haired doll in his desk drawer. I was convinced he stuck pins into it at regular intervals. It was the only explanation I could think of for that stabbing pain I sometimes got in my left ankle. Jackson had been one of the senior murder detectives in the city for the last seven years or so. You'd think he'd be pleased that I've made a significant contribution to his clear-up rate. You'd be wrong. Now, whenever the planets really want to gang up on me, they send me an encounter with Jackson.

Linda Shaw stood between Jackson and me like a buffer zone between warring Balkan armies. As soon as he'd seen me pale-faced and shivering in the cab of Dorothea's van, the wheels had started going round in his head as he imagined the many ways he could use my presence at the murder scene to make my life hell. He'd sped across the intervening Tarmac without even pausing to put on his raincoat. 'What the fuck are you doing here?' he greeted me.

'Working,' I said. 'How about you?'

He turned scarlet. 'Don't push your luck, Brannigan,' he stormed. 'I'm here less than a minute and already you're looking at spending the night in the cells. You just don't know when to keep your smart mouth shut, do you?'

'If you want me to keep my mouth shut, that's fine by me. I'll make my one call to my solicitor and then you'll get "no comment" from here to eternity,' I snarled back. 'And as soon as I get home, I'll be on the phone to Alexis Lee. The world should hear how a material witness in the murder of the nation's favourite astrologer gets treated by Manchester's finest.'

'Sir.' Linda's voice was quiet but urgent. 'Sir, you're needed inside the van. The scene-of-crime lads are right behind us, and the rest of the team has just got here. Why don't I find a quiet corner and take a statement from Ms Brannigan? Then we'll have an idea where we're up to?'

'I don't want you sticking your nose in this, Brannigan,' Jackson snapped, straightening an electric-blue tie that clashed disturbingly with his lilac shirt. 'You give your statement to DS Shaw and then you bugger off out of it. That's not an invitation, it's an instruction. I'd love to arrest you for obstruction. But then, I shouldn't have to tell you that, should I? She's all yours, Detective Sergeant.'

I had led Linda from the van to the production building, suggesting it would be a good idea to get someone to contact John Turpin to tell NPTV what was going on and find out where we could talk. She'd got it sorted, right down to discovering where the nearest coffee machine was. Finally we had a moment to give each other the once-over. I saw a woman hovering around the crucial cusp of thirty, the skin around her eyes starting to show the attrition of long hours and late nights, the slight downturn to her mouth revealing the emotional price of dealing with people who have been violently bereaved, and the ones responsible for smashing those lives to smithereens.

I didn't want to think about what she saw. I opened the batting. 'Detective Sergeant, eh? Congratulations.'

'Thanks. I hear you've come up in the world too.

Brannigan and Co, not Mortensen and Brannigan any more.'

'Cliff keeps tabs on me, does he? At least I get to be my own boss. But you're still stuck being Jackson's bag carrier.'

'There are worse jobs in the police service,' she said drily.

'Especially if you're a woman.'

She inclined her head in agreement. 'So, help me to keep my job and tell me what happened here tonight?'

'You know I don't have any problem with you, Linda. Ask what you want. As long as you don't expect me to breach my client's confidentiality, I'll tell you all I can.'

She took me through the reason for my presence, then on to the precise circumstances of my discovery. We'd just got to the part where I described trying to find Dorothea's pulse when the door crashed open. Gloria staggered in dramatically, hair plastered to her head, eye make-up spreading like a bad Dusty Springfield impersonation. 'Kate,' she wailed. 'Thank God you're all right! Oh Kate, I can't believe it. Not Dorothea,' she continued, stumbling towards me. Think Vanessa Redgrave playing King Lear. I had no choice but to jump to my feet and support her. She'd have had no problem collapsing in a heap for effect. I had no doubt that she was sincerely upset, but being a thespian she couldn't help going over the top so much she made the Battle of the Somme look like a little skirmish.

I put an arm round her and steered her to the nearest sofa. Linda was staring at her with avid eyes. I didn't think it was Gloria's bedraggled appearance that had gobsmacked her. She was star struck. I've seen it happen. Normal, intelligent people faced with their heroes become open-mouthed, wittering wrecks. Back before she became crime correspondent, Alexis once got to interview Martina Navratilova for the features department. She claims the most intelligent question she managed to come out with was, 'What did you have for breakfast, Martina?'

So now I had a star struck detective, an hysterical soap star and a cop who wanted to arrest me for daring to find a murder victim. This was turning into the worst night for a very long time.

'I can't believe it,' Gloria was saying for the dozenth time. This time, however, she moved the narrative forward. 'I keep thinking, I must have been the last person to see her alive.'

The words brought Linda back to something approximating normality. 'What do you mean, Ms Kendal?' she asked gently, crossing to the sofa and sitting next to Gloria.

'Gloria, this is Detective Sergeant Shaw. She's involved in the inquiry into Dorothea's death.'

Gloria fixed Linda with eyes brimming with sooty tears. When this was all over, I'd have to speak to her about waterproof mascara. 'What happened, chuck? All they'd say out in the car park was that there had been an accident, that

135

Dorothea were dead. I'd gone out looking for you. You were gone so long, I was beginning to worry. I had this feeling . . .' Her voice tailed off into another whooping sob. 'Oh God, I can't believe it,' she wailed. I got up and silently fetched her a glass of water. She emptied it in a few swift gulps then clutched it histrionically to her bosom.

Linda patted her free hand. 'It's hard to grasp, losing a friend,' she said. 'But the best thing you can do for Dorothea now is to help us find the person responsible for this.'

'It wasn't an accident, then?' Gloria demanded. I saw an alertness spring into her eyes that hadn't been there a moment before.

Linda obviously hadn't. 'You'll have to brace yourself for a shock, I'm afraid, Gloria. It looks like Dorothea has been murdered.'

Gloria's face froze. The tears stopped as suddenly as they would when the director yelled, 'Cut'. 'Murdered?' she said, her voice an octave lower. 'I don't understand. Dorothea were fine when I left her. And Kate went right back to her. How could anybody have murdered her?'

'That's what we're here to find out,' Linda said reassuringly. Much more of this and I was going to throw up. A couple of generations ago, it was the professional classes who got this kind of veneration from the police. Before that, you had to have a title. But in Britain in the 1990s, the prerequisite for deference from Officer Dibble was celebrity.

I cleared my throat. 'Apart from the killer, it

seems likely that Gloria was the last person to see Dorothea alive.'

'Do you have any idea what time that might have been?' Linda asked Gloria.

'Just before six,' I said. 'I'd been sitting in Gloria's car in the car park, waiting for her to finish her half past five session with Dorothea. And before you ask, I didn't notice anyone hanging around suspiciously, just a lot of people rushing to their cars and a few others crossing from the production building to the admin block. At five to six, I left the car and went to the camper van. I knocked, and Gloria came out.'

'Did you see Dorothea?' Linda asked me. I couldn't believe she was getting into this with Gloria present. It broke all the unwritten rules about interviewing witnesses separately.

'No, I didn't enter the van.'

'Did you hear her voice?'

I shook my head. 'The wind was blowing, there were cars driving past, she wouldn't have been shouting anyway.'

I could see the implications registering with Linda. I could also see her dismissing the possibility that Gloria could have killed Dorothea for no more substantial reason than that Brenda Barrowclough could never have done such a thing. 'She said cheerio to me and said she'd expect Kate along in a few minutes. But Kate's right. She wasn't shouting. There was no reason why she should, and she wasn't one for raising her voice at the best of times,' Gloria said kindly, as if she was explaining something obvious to a child.

'Was the door on the latch, or did it automatically lock behind you?' Linda asked.

'Just on the latch. We'd all knock and walk in when it were time for our appointments,' Gloria said. 'She were strict about not overrunning, was Dorothea.'

'And how long was it before you got back to the van?' Linda asked me.

I'd already given the timing a lot of thought. 'Ten minutes, tops. Maybe three minutes to walk Gloria back to her dressing room, a few minutes to make sure she was going to lock the door behind me, then a couple of minutes back.'

'It's not long,' Linda observed.

Suddenly, Gloria burst into tears again. 'It's terrible,' she wailed. 'It's a warning. It's a warning to me. All those letters, and Dorothea's premonition. There's a killer out there and he's after me!'

I couldn't quite see the logic, but Gloria's fear seemed real enough. She sobbed and hiccuped and wailed. Linda and I exchanged desperate looks, neither sure how to deal with this. Then as abruptly as her hysterics had begun, they ended and she took control of herself. 'This is aimed at me,' Gloria said, her voice shaky. 'Everybody knew I relied on Dorothea. Everybody knew Dorothea had predicted there was death in the room that last time I saw her. She's been killed to put the fear of death into me.'

'I don't think that's likely,' Linda said soothingly. 'It's a very extreme thing to do if all this letter writer wants to do is frighten you. It's more likely that it's all just a horrible coincidence.'

'Oh aye?' Gloria sat upright, her shoulders straightening. It was a classic Brenda Barrowclough move that signalled to *Northerners* viewers that it was flak-jacket time. 'And is it just a horrible coincidence that I was the last person to see Dorothea alive? If somebody had it in for Dorothea, there must have been plenty of other times they could have killed her without taking the risk that somebody would see them going in or out of the van. Or even walk in on them. The only reason anybody would have for killing her when they did was to make it look like I was the killer. You mark my words, whoever killed my friend has got it in for me an' all.'

There was a moment's stunned silence. 'She has a point,' I said.

'So what are your lot going to do to protect me?' Gloria demanded.

Linda just stared.

'The short answer is, nothing,' I told her. 'Even if they had the bodies, you wouldn't be a priority, on account of your poison-pen letters don't actually threaten to kill you. That's right, isn't it, Linda?'

Linda made a strangled sort of noise. I figured she was agreeing with me.

'Right then,' said Gloria. 'I'll have to keep relying on Kate.' She gathered herself together. I suddenly understood the expression 'girding your loins'. Gloria stood up and said, 'Come on, chuck. I've had enough of this. I'm distraught and I need to go home and have a lie-down.'

She was halfway to the door when she looked behind to check I was following. I gave Linda a hapless shrug. 'We'll need formal statements,' Linda tried plaintively.

'Call my lawyer in the morning,' Gloria said imperiously. 'Kate, who's my lawyer?'

I grinned. Jackson was going to love this. 'Same as mine, of course. Ruth Hunter.'

The last thing I heard as the door swung shut behind us was Linda groaning, 'Ah, shit.' In grim silence we marched out of the building. The sleet had stopped, which was the one good thing that had happened since lunchtime. Gloria swept straight through the mêlée of activity around Dorothea's van, looking neither to right nor left. I scuttled in her wake, trying to look invisible to anyone who might be tempted to alert Jackson. We made it to the car without a challenge.

Once we'd got past the two bobbies working with the NPTV security men on the main gate, all the fight went out of Gloria. Her shoulders slumped and she reached for her cigarettes. 'This is an emergency,' she said. 'Don't you dare open that bloody window.' She inhaled deeply. 'You know I didn't kill Dorothea, don't you?'

I pulled a wry smile. 'You're an actress, Gloria. Would I know if you had?'

She snorted. 'I'm no Susan Sarandon. I play myself with knobs on. Come on, Kate, did I kill Dorothea?'

'I can't believe you did,' I said slowly.

'That'll do me. So you'll try and find out who's done this? Before he decides it's my turn? Or my granddaughter's?'

'Cliff Jackson, the cop that's in charge of this? He's not a bad investigator. But he's been wrong before. I'll give it my best shot.'

'I'll sleep easier knowing that,' she said, toking on her cigarette as if it gave life instead of stealing it.

'Speaking of sleep . . . Do you want to stay over at my place tonight? I'm thinking partly of the weather and partly from the security point of view.'

Gloria frowned. 'It's nice of you to offer, but I could do with being in my own space. I need to feel grounded. And I don't want to be under your feet. You're going to have to get stuck into your inquiries tomorrow, and I don't want to get in the road.'

'I don't want to leave you on your own. Even behind those high walls.' I thought for a moment, then pulled over to the roadside and took out my phone. A couple of phone calls and I had it sorted. It meant an awkward detour via the students' union, but as soon as Gloria saw Donovan in all his hulking glory, she was perfectly happy for me to hoof it the mile across town to my house while she disappeared over the hills and far away

141

with the best-looking bodyguard either side of the Pennines. The only question was whether she'd still respect him in the morning.

I stepped out briskly. The temperature was plummeting now the sleet had stopped, the pavements rapidly icing over. Twice the only thing that saved me from crashing to the pavement was a handy lamppost. All I wanted was to curl up in my dressing gown with a very large amount of Absolut Citron and a smudge of grapefruit juice. With luck, Richard might be home early, preferably armed with a substantial Chinese. He always says Friday night is amateurs' night out as far as live music is concerned. I could almost taste the salt and pepper king prawns.

I should have known better. Nights like that just don't get better. The man I suppose I love was home all right. But not home alone. I found him fast asleep in his bed, his arms around someone else. When I walked into the room, her eyes snapped open. She took one look at me and screamed.

Sensible girl.

10

MERCURY IN VIRGO IN THE 5TH HOUSE
*She can turn her hand to anything. She has a discrim-
inating intellect but tends to be overcritical of herself
and others in times of stress. She analyses problems
with tenacity and is capable of painstaking research.
She is logical, sceptical and can be obsessive.*
From *Written in the Stars*, by Dorothea Dawson

Divorce may have deprived Richard of most of the
last five years of his son Davy's life, but because a
lot of his work is done at night, he did most of
the daytime childcare for the first three. Thankfully
the old skills hadn't deserted him. That meant I
didn't have to take any responsibility for the most
remarkable child on the planet (if you believed
Alexis and Chris). I watched with a mixture of
relief and astonishment as he spooned greyish-pink
mush into the eager mouth of his nine-month-old
girlfriend. He managed it almost without looking,
and without ever breaking off in mid-sentence.

He'd already changed a nappy without flinching, which was a long way away from my idea of getting the day off to a good start.

I remember when northern men would have died rather than admit they knew how Pampers worked. Now, they pin you to the wall in café bars and tell you it's possible for men to produce tiny amounts of breast milk. Certainly, Jay's arrival had already achieved the seemingly impossible task of ending the superficial hostilities between Alexis and Richard. Before Jay, Alexis maintained she was a real journo and Richard a sycophant; Richard that he was a real journo and Alexis a police lackey. Work never entered their conversations any more.

As he did about once a week, Richard had taken Jay for the night to give Chris a chance at a straight eight hours. Oddly, when Jay spent the night with him, she slept through till seven in the morning. When Chris was within earshot, Jay would invariably pierce the night with her cries at two, four and six o'clock. I could see she was going to grow up into the kind of clever manipulator I wouldn't mind having on the staff. Never mind putting her name down for Eton, I was putting her name down for Brannigan & Co.

'So what are your plans for today?' Richard asked as we sat in the conservatory watching wet snow cascading from the sky.

'I've got Donovan minding Gloria, so I probably

don't need to go over there. I've told him she's to stay indoors, but looking at the weather, I don't think there'll be much temptation to leave the fireside. I'm going to do some background research in the *Chronicle* library so I can start asking sensible questions about Dorothea Dawson.'

'Great,' he said enthusiastically. 'You can take Jay in with you. I was supposed to drop her at the *Chronicle* crèche so Alexis can pick her up, but if you're going in anyway, I can stay home and get on with some writing.'

Time for the application of the Kate Brannigan irregular verb theory of life. In this case, 'I am diplomatic, you are economical with the truth, s/he is a lying little gobshite.' 'No problem,' I said. Why should I mind drumming my fingers on the table while Richard finished feeding her, changing her, swaddling her for the outside world, swapping the baby seat from his car to mine then strapping her in? It wasn't as if I had anything important like a murder to solve, after all.

I eventually tracked Alexis down in the office canteen. 'Your daughter is in the crèche,' I told her. 'So's her car seat.'

'That's great,' she said. 'I'll bob along in a minute and say hello. We really appreciate it, you know. It's the only time we get a decent night's sleep. She been OK?'

'As far as I know. She screamed her socks off when I got home last night, but that's just because she can't stand any competition for Richard's attention. So I left them to it. She probably had a better night's sleep than I did.'

Alexis shook her head, smiling. 'I know you love her really.'

She knew more than I did. I smiled vacantly and said, 'Dorothea Dawson.'

'She didn't see that coming, did she?'

I love journalistic black humour. It always comforts me to know there are people more cynical than me around. 'What's this morning's story?'

'What's your interest?' she asked, instantly on the alert. Her cigarettes came out and she lit one for real.

'I found the body.'

Alexis ran her free hand through her hair so it stood up in a punk crest. 'Shit,' she said. 'The bizzies never said anything about that at the press conference. They said the body had been discovered by a member of staff, the lying gets.'

'You're surprised?'

'No. Cliff Jackson would superglue his gob shut before he let the name "Brannigan" pass his lips. Unless the sentence also contained the words, "has been charged with". So give, KB. A first-person colour piece, that's just what I need for the city final.' Her notebook had appeared on the table.

'What are they saying?'

'That she was killed in her camper van in the car park of the NPTV compound by a blow to the head

146

around six last night. And that's about all. What can you give me?'

I sighed. 'It isn't exactly something I want to dwell on. I needed to talk to Dorothea about the warning she'd given Gloria the last time she'd done a reading for her. I'd arranged to see her after her final client of the day. When I got there, I knocked but there was no reply. I knew she was expecting me, so I opened the door and walked in. She was lying face down on the table with her head caved in. It was obvious she was dead. Her crystal ball was lying on the carpet at the end of a track of blood. It looked to me as if that's what the killer used. It's much bigger than the usual crystal ball. It must be nine, ten inches across.'

Alexis nodded as she took notes. 'She was famous for it. Claimed it came from some mystical mountain mine. Me, I reckon it came from Pilkington Glass at St Helens.' She gave me an apologetic grin. 'Sorry about this but . . . How did you feel?'

'Sick. Can we talk about something else?'

'What, like Cliff Jackson's marital problems?'

'He's got marital problems?'

Alexis nodded, a grim little smile on her face. 'In spades. His wife's run off with another bloke.'

'What took her so long?'

'She probably couldn't find the key to the handcuffs. The best bit, though, is who she's run off with.' Alexis paused for effect. I rotated my wrist in the classic 'get on with it' gesture. 'His oldest lad's in his second year at Liverpool University. His wife's only run off with the lad's best mate.'

'You're kidding!'

'Would I lie to you?'

'How long have you been sitting on this?' I demanded.

'I only found out this morning. I was trying to get a comment from Jackson and he was going totally ballistic. I know one of his DCs from way back, so I cornered her and asked why Jackson was being even more of a pain than usual and she told me. So don't expect any favours.'

'I'll bear that in mind.' I grinned. 'Couldn't happen to a nicer bloke, though. By the way, did you get anywhere in tracking down who was the source of your story about me minding Gloria?'

Alexis savoured her last mouthful of smoke and regretfully crushed the stub in the ashtray. 'One of those things. Every Friday, the news credits book goes up to accounts so the payments can be processed. It doesn't come back till Monday morning. I was too late getting to it yesterday. Sorry.'

'I'll just have to possess my soul in patience,' I complained.

'So who was Dorothea's last appointment with? Which member of the *Northerners* cast was the last person to see her alive?'

'You'll have to ask Jackson that one.' I didn't have much hope that I'd be able to keep Gloria's name out of the papers, but the longer I could, the better for her. 'Any chance I can pillage the library? I could use some background on Dorothea.'

'You digging into this, then?'

I shrugged. 'If he's not made an arrest overnight, the chances are Jackson's stuck. Which means he'll be wasting time making my life hell. The best way to get him out of my face is to give him something else to think about. I figured if I took a trawl through the cuttings, something might occur to me that I could slip to Linda Shaw.'

I could see from her eyes that Alexis didn't believe a word of it, but she knew better than to try to push me in a direction I didn't want to travel. 'You'll tell me when you're ready,' she said. 'Come on, I'll sort you out.'

Ten minutes later, I was beginning to wish I hadn't asked. A stack of manila files six inches deep contained the *Chronicle*'s archive on Dorothea Dawson, newly returned from the news reporters who had been writing the background feature for that day's paper. Another two ten-inch stacks contained the last year's cuttings about *Northerners*.

I tore a hole in the lid on the carton of coffee I'd brought up from the canteen, took the cap off my pen and began to explore Dorothea Dawson's past.

I'd got as far as her early TV appearances when Alexis burst in, a fresh cigarette clamped between her teeth. The librarian shouted, 'Crush that ash, shit-for-brains!' Alexis ignored him and grabbed my arm, hustling me out into the corridor.

'Where's the fire? What the hell's going on, Alexis?'

'Your mate Dennis has just been arrested for murder.'

I understood each of the words. But together they made no sense. 'They think Dennis killed Dorothea Dawson?' I asked uncomprehendingly.

'Who said anything about Dorothea?'

'Alexis, just explain in words of one syllable. Please?'

'Some villain called Pit Bull Kelly was found dead early doors in one of the underground units in the Arndale. The place was empty, but apparently it had been squatted. According to my contact, they had a tip-off that it'd been Dennis who'd been using the place, and when they checked his fingerprints with records, they found them all over the place. So they've arrested him.'

I still couldn't get my head round it. Dennis was a hard man, no stranger to violence. But for a long time, he'd not lifted a hand in anger to anyone. The crimes he'd committed had all been against property, not people. The notion of Dennis as a killer struck at the heart of everything I believed about him. Alexis's words were a blow that felled my confidence in my own judgement. 'I need to speak to Ruth,' I said, pushing past her and heading blindly down the corridor towards the lifts. I was halfway there when I had to turn back and collect my jacket and bag from the library.

'Calm down, KB,' Alexis said pointlessly as I passed her.

'I don't want to be calm,' I shouted over my shoulder. 'Sometimes I get fed up with calm.' I half ran down the corridor and, too wound up to wait for the lift, started down the stairs. I could hear Alexis's feet pounding down behind me. 'He's not a killer, Alexis,' I shouted up at her. 'He loves his wife, he loves his daughter too much. He wouldn't do this to them.'

Her footsteps stopped. I could hear her gasping for breath. 'Phone me,' she managed to get out.

I didn't bother to reply. I was too agitated. Alexis would forgive me, I knew that. Specifically, she'd forgive me when she got the inside story. At the bottom of the stairwell, I pushed open the door to the car park and got into my car. My breath was coming in deep gulps and my hands were shaking. I realized it was probably delayed shock from the night before kicking in as soon as my defences were down. I was close to Dennis, but not that close, I told myself.

When my pulse was back within the normal range, I took my phone out and dialled the number of Ruth Hunter's moby. If being hated by the police and the judiciary is a measure of success in criminal defence work, Ruth must be one of the best solicitors in the North West. Behind her back, they call her firm Hunter, Killer & Co. A big woman in every sense of the word, she sails into court in her bespoke tailoring like an outsize catwalk queen and rips the Crown Prosecution case to rags. If she didn't have clients, I suspect she'd do it anyway, just for the hell of it. She drives Officer Dibble wild by turning up to cop shops in the middle of the night in her millionaire husband's Bentley Mulsanne turbo. She can park that car in streets where my Rover would be stripped to the chassis in ten minutes and know it'll be there unscathed when she comes back. If she wasn't one of my closest friends, I'd string garlic round my neck just to walk past her office.

'Ruth Hunter,' the voice said briskly.

'It's Kate. I heard about Dennis.'

'What took you so long?' she asked drily. 'It's at least three hours since they lifted him.'

'Are they charging him?'

'I can't talk now as I'm sure you'll appreciate.'

That meant she was in a police station, probably with a custody sergeant breathing down her neck. 'When can we talk?'

'Your office, three o'clock.'

'I'll be there. Should I go and see his wife?'

'I'd leave it for now. Maybe tomorrow. Things are a little . . . volatile at the moment. I'll see you later.' The line went dead.

I could imagine. Most of the contents of the glass cupboard were probably in bits. Debbie's never had a problem expressing her emotions and Dennis was on his final warning following the twelve-month stretch he'd recently done. She'd told him then, one more serious nicking and she'd file for divorce. She'd probably started shredding his suits by now, unless she was saving that for when they charged him.

The clock said half past eleven. I couldn't face sitting in the *Chronicle* library for another three hours, and I didn't want to kick my heels at home. It's ironic. I spend half my life complaining that I never have time to do my washing or ironing, then when I get a couple of hours to myself, I'm too wound up to do anything constructive. I needed to find something that would make me feel like I was being effective. Then I remembered Cassandra Cliff. Cassie had once been one of the household names among the stars of *Northerners*. Then some creepy hack had left no stone unturned to find the slug who revealed that years before she'd been cast as Maggie Grimshaw, the bitch goddess gossip queen of *Northerners*, Cassie had been Kevin.

In the teeth of the hurricane of publicity, NPTV pointed out that they had an equal opportunities policy that protected transsexuals and that Cassie's job was safe with them. They were using 'safe' with that particular meaning Margaret Thatcher inaugurated when she claimed the National Health Service was safe in her hands. Within months, Maggie Grimshaw had been killed off and Cassie was not only unemployed but unemployable.

She didn't run weeping into the wilderness. She sold the inside story of life on *Northerners* to the highest bidder, and there were no holds barred. Cassie never featured in any of the show's

153

regular anniversary celebrations, but I suspected that didn't keep her awake at night. She'd chosen not to be bitter and instead of frittering away the money she made from her exposé, she set up a shop, magazine and social organization for transvestites and transsexuals.

Cassie had been a key source for Alexis for years, and we'd met following the death of a transvestite lawyer I'd been investigating. I'd met her a couple of times since then, most recently at Alexis and Chris's housewarming party. I knew she still kept in touch with a couple of people from *Northerners*. She might well know things Gloria didn't. More to the point, she might well tell me things Gloria wouldn't.

Energized by the thought of action, I started the car and headed for Oldham. Cassie's shop, Trances, was in one of those weary side streets just off the main town centre where some businesses survive against all the odds and the rest sink without trace, simply failing to raise the metal shutters one morning with no advance warning. There was little traffic and fewer pedestrians that afternoon; the wet snow that was melting away in Manchester was making half-hearted attempts at lying in Oldham, and ripples of slush were spreading across the pavements under the lash of a bitter wind. Anyone with any sense was sitting in front of the fire watching a black and white Bette Davis movie.

The interior of Trances never seemed to change.

There were racks of dresses in large sizes, big hair on wig stands, open shelves of shoes so big I could have got both feet in one without a struggle, racks of garish magazines that no one was ever going to read on the tram. The key giveaway that this was the land of the truly different was the display case of foam and silicone prostheses – breasts, hips, buttocks. The assistant serving behind the counter took one look at me and I could see her contemptuously classifying me as a tourist. 'Hi,' I said. 'Is Cassie about?'

'Have you an appointment?'

I shook my head. 'I was passing.'

'Are you a journalist? Because if you are, you're wasting your time. She's got nothing to say to anybody about *Northerners*,' she said, her Adam's apple bobbing uncontrollably.

'I'm not a journalist,' I said. 'I know Cassie. Can you tell her Kate Brannigan's here?'

She looked doubtful, but picked up the phone anyway. 'Cassandra? There's someone here called Kate Brannigan who wants to see you.' There was a pause, then she said, 'Fine. I'll send her up.' The smile she gave me as she replaced the receiver was apologetic. 'I'm sorry. The phone hasn't stopped ringing all day. It's always the same when there's some big *Northerners* story. If it's not that, it's Channel Four researchers doing documentaries about TSs and TVs.'

I nodded and made for the door at the back of the shop that I knew led to Cassie's office and, beyond that, to her private domain. Cassie was waiting for me at the top of the stairs, immaculate as ever in a superbly tailored cream suit over a hyacinth-blue silk T-shirt. I'd never seen her in anything other than fabulous clothes. Her ash-blonde hair was cut in a spiky urchin style, her make-up subtle. From below, her jawline was so taut I had to suspect the surgeon's knife. If I earned my living from looking as convincing as Cassie, even I'd have submitted to plastic surgery. 'Kate,' she greeted me. 'You've survived, then.'

I followed her down the hallway and into her office, a symphony in limed wood and grey leather. She'd replaced the dusty-pink fabric of the curtains and cushions with midnight-blue and upgraded the computer systems since I'd last been there. She'd obviously tapped a significantly profitable niche in the market. 'Survived?' I echoed.

Cassie sat on one of the low sofas and crossed legs that could still give any of her former colleagues a run for their money. 'I saw the story in the *Chronicle*. My idea of hell would be running interference for Gloria Kendal,' she said.

'Why do you say that?' I sat down opposite her.

'Unless she's changed dramatically, she's got a schedule that makes being Prime Minister look like a part-time job, she's about as docile as a Doberman and she thinks if she's hired you, she's bought you.'

I grinned. 'Sounds about right.'

'At least you're not a bloke, so you're relatively safe,' Cassie added archly.

I hoped Donovan was. 'I expect you can guess why I'm here?'

'It's got to be Dorothea. Except that I can't think why you'd be investigating her murder when it's Gloria you've been working for.'

I pulled a face. 'It's possible that the person who killed Dorothea is the same one who is threatening Gloria. I'm just nosing around to see what I can dig up.'

Cassie smiled, shaking her head slightly. 'You'll never make an actress until you stop pulling your earlobe when you're stretching the truth.'

My mouth fell open. I'd never realized what my giveaway body language was, but now Cassie had pointed that out, I became instantly self-conscious. 'I can't believe you spotted that,' I complained.

She shrugged. 'My business depends on being able to spot deception. I've got good at it. It's all right, Kate, I don't need to know the real reason you're interested in who killed Dorothea. I'm happy to tell you whatever I know. I liked Dorothea. She was a worker, like me.'

'How did the connection with *Northerners* begin?'

Cassie frowned in concentration. 'I've got a feeling it was Edna Mercer who first discovered her. You remember Edna? Ma Pickersgill?'

'She's dead now, isn't she?'

Cassie's smile was sardonic. 'Ma Pickersgill died of a heart attack when her house was burgled five years ago. Edna's still alive, though you'll never see her at an NPTV function.'

'She left under a cloud?'

'Alzheimer's. Towards the end, it was touch and go whether she'd stay lucid long enough for them to get her made up and on set. As for learning lines, forget it. Anyway, I'm pretty sure it was Edna who brought Dorothea to the studios. She'd come across her in some dead-end seaside town and Dorothea had hit a couple of nails on the head. So Edna, who was a woman given to enthusiasms, persuaded enough of us to sign up for sessions with Dorothea to make it worth her while coming over for the day. I was impressed, in spite of myself.'

'You surprise me,' I said. 'I'd have thought your feet were too firmly planted on the ground to care what's written in the stars.'

Cassie smiled wryly. 'Dorothea was very good. Whether you believed in it or not when you went in to see her, by the time you came out you were convinced she'd got something. After that first visit, we were all eating out of her hand. So it became a regular thing. The word spread through the cast, and soon she was coming more or less every week.'

'What kind of stuff did she tell you?'

'She'd cast your horoscope, and she'd kick off every session by explaining some little thing in your chart. That was one of the clever things about the way she operated – you had to keep going to see her if you wanted her insight into every element of your personal horoscope. Then she'd talk about the current relationships between the planets and how they might affect you.

'She did phenomenal research, you know. She knew everything there was to know about everybody she had dealings with. Dorothea made a habit of gathering every snippet, no matter how insignificant it seemed. You know how these things go – Edna would say something in passing about Rita's son, then three months later Dorothea would say something to Rita about her son, knowing full well that Rita knows she's never mentioned the boy to Dorothea. It all contributed to the myth of omniscience.'

'Making a virtue out of being a know-all. That is clever,' I acknowledged. 'So was that it?'

Cassie shook her head. 'She'd finish off by asking if there was anything bothering you that you wanted guidance with. You'd tell her and she'd gaze into her crystal ball and give you advice. She didn't go in for the riddle of the Sphinx stuff – she'd say things like, "You're never going to have emotional support from your husband while you're married to an Aries with Capricorn rising. You either have to get out of the marriage or find what you're lacking in your friendships."'

'More therapy than prediction, then?'

'A mixture of both. And actors are very gullible people.' Her smile reminded me that she'd once been an actor, and not just on the screen.

'So why would anyone have it in for her?' I asked.

'I haven't a clue. I hadn't heard that anybody had fallen out with her. She could be irritating when she was trying to impress you with how mystical and spiritual she was, but that's no reason to kill somebody.'

Changing tack, I said, 'What about Gloria? Has anybody from *Northerners* got it in for her?'

Cassie chuckled, a warm, throaty sound. 'How long have you got? The only surprising thing about Gloria is that she's still alive.'

11

MOON SQUARES MIDHEAVEN

She can feel insecure socially because she tends to find herself in conflict with conventional norms. She will construct a world of her own where she can be herself, but will maintain the pretence of being tough and self-sufficient to the outside world. She does not express emotion readily, but nevertheless will often choose a caring or self-sacrificing role in life.

From *Written in the Stars*, by Dorothea Dawson

It was the first time anybody had even hinted that Gloria wasn't the most popular girl in the school. I leaned forward and said as calmly as I could manage, 'And there was me thinking everybody loved Gloria.'

'They do. That's why she provokes thoughts of murder on a regular basis. Or at least, she always used to. It drives you insane to be around somebody who's always kind, always generous, always doing charity work, always making time for the

161

fans. There are people in the cast of *Northerners* who have a permanent inferiority complex thanks to Gloria.' Cassie's voice was light, but there was an edge of something harder in her eyes.

'But like you just said, that's no reason to kill somebody.'

Cassie raised her perfectly shaped eyebrows. 'No? Well, you have more experience in these matters than I do. I tell you what people would kill for, though, and that's their roles in *Northerners*. Gloria's hot right now. The public adore her, and the management knows it. Granted, nobody's bigger than the show, but when actors are riding the crest of the wave, they do get a certain amount of input into the storylines. If somebody in the cast knew Gloria was suggesting a storyline that would see them written out, that'd be a strong enough motive for some of the idiots in the cast to put her out of the picture. But then, it's not Gloria who's been murdered, is it?'

I sighed. 'No. But one way or another, Dorothea's death has rebounded quite nastily on Gloria's life. She was the one who was in the room when Dorothea talked about the presence of death. She never said anything similar to anyone else, as far as I've been able to find out.'

Cassie suddenly jumped to her feet. 'Stay there a minute,' she said, crossing to a door in the far wall. 'I'll be right back.'

The minute stretched into two, then five. The more I thought about what she'd suggested, the more uneasy I became. I pulled out my phone and rang Gloria's number. 'Hiya, chuck,' she greeted me.

'Everything OK?' I asked.

'Grand as owt. We're watching a Bette Davis video and having a lovely time.'

All right for some. 'Can I speak to Donovan?' I waited while she summoned him. He came on the line almost immediately. 'Don? How's things?'

'Nothing except endless phone calls from the papers. Gloria just tells them she's too devastated to talk and puts the phone down. It's a class act.' He sounded both admiring and cautious.

'I've got something to do in town, but I'll be over in a couple of hours to relieve you. Is that OK?'

'Great.' I wasn't imagining the relief in his voice. Considering they've grown up in the inner city, Shelley's kids have led remarkably sheltered lives. There was no way Donovan had the sophistication to deal with a demanding woman like Gloria indefinitely. If I didn't rescue him before nightfall, his mother almost certainly would, and then we'd have another corpse on our hands. And I'm still too young to die.

Cassie returned just as I finished the call, carrying a paperback. She held it up so I could see the cover, a misty head-and-shoulders shot of Dorothea looking significantly younger than when I'd met her. *If I'd Known Then, by Dorothea Dawson. The Life of a Stargazer*, was emblazoned top and bottom across the cover. 'It was published about four years ago,' Cassie said, handing it to me. 'Bestseller list for four weeks, then the remainder pile, I suspect.'

I opened it. The title page had an inscription. *To my darling Cassie. Fire and water make for a steamy combination! Where you are is better for you than where you were. Go in peace. Love, Dorothea Dawson.* 'She seemed to know you well,' I remarked.

'Not as well as she liked to think,' Cassie said drily. 'Like most people, she thought anyone whose sexuality or gender was expressed differently from the mainstream had to be obsessed with sex. Anyway, you're welcome to borrow it. It's life with all the edges smoothed down, but it does show you a bit of what the woman herself was like.'

I pocketed the book and thanked her. It was clear from the way she was still standing that as far as Cassie was concerned, there was no more to be said. But before I left, I had to ask her one thing. 'You know they've got a mole,' I said. 'Any ideas who it might be?'

An indefinable bitterness crept into Cassie's face. She knew all about the damage that moles could do to the foundations of a life. 'John Turpin must be biting the carpet,' she said. 'There's nothing the management hates more than storyline leaks.'

'This isn't just storyline leaks,' I pointed out. 'It's the kind of stuff that ruined your career.'

She sighed. 'I know. I try not to think about it because it reminds me of what was probably the worst point in my life. When I was splashed all over the tabloids, I think I was actually more depressed than I ever was when I was still trapped inside a male shape. So when I see other people's lives being trashed in the same way, I just try to tune out and remind myself that it turned into the best thing that could have happened to me. But I don't know who's ratting on the *Northerners* cast any more than I know who gave me up.'

'You never found out?'

'I never found out. There were so few people who knew, you see, and I trusted them all with my life. I always thought someone from the Amsterdam clinic where I had my surgery must have been over here on holiday or on business or something and seen me on the TV.'

I got to my feet. 'Was Ross Grant doing the outside catering when you were on the show?'

'Ross? Big cuddly Scotsman? Wife with eyes like a hawk? Yeah, he took over the contract about a year before I was demolished. Wait a minute . . . You're not suggesting Ross is the mole?'

'I'm not, but Turpin seems determined to give it a whirl.'

Cassie laughed scornfully. 'Ross hasn't got the malice to do it or the brains to cover his tracks.'

'What about his wife?'

'Why should she? Why risk the goose that lays the golden eggs?'

'Greed?'

Cassie looked sceptical. 'I can't see her going in for that kind of short-term thinking.'

'Not even if she thought they were going to lose the contract? That way she kills two birds with one stone. She gets her revenge on Turpin for dumping them and she earns a nice little nest egg to cushion the blow while they look for other work.'

'They already have other work,' Cassie objected. 'Or they used to, at any rate. *Northerners* is their most regular source of income, but they do cater for other people's location shoots. So it wouldn't be the end of the world if they did lose the contract. And if she was discovered, it would mean the end of their business altogether. I just don't see it.'

As I walked back to my car, I pondered what Cassie had said. For it to be worth the mole's while, he or she had to be indifferent to the outcome of being found out. That meant it was either someone sufficiently skilled to overcome the stigma of being known in the TV business as the *Northerners* mole, or someone who was prepared to risk their career to vent their venom against the programme or its makers.

However I cut it, it didn't sound like a cast member to me.

I was back in my office by three. I wasn't alone; Gizmo was in the computer room in weekend uniform of jeans, Converse baseball boots with holes in the toes, and three shirts. When I'd stuck my head round the door, he'd lifted his head long enough to tell me he was working on some new computer security sub-routines for a local mail order company that had started direct selling via the Internet. Who was I to doubt him? Even if he had gone pink around the ears?

As soon as I had five minutes that I didn't need for sleeping, I was going to have to do some digging.

Ruth walked through the door with ten seconds to spare. She's the only person I know who's even more punctual than me. One of the mysteries of the universe for both of us is how we ended up hitched to men who think if you get to the cinema in time to see the British Board of Film Censors certificate, you're far too early. If I could change one thing about Richard, that's what it would be.

She pulled me into her arms and gave me the kind of hug that always makes me feel five years old. It was exaggerated today because she was swathed in a vast silver-grey fake fur that felt like the best fluffy toy a child ever held. 'You look like the Snow Queen,' I said, disentangling myself and giving her an admiring look from the perfectly pleated blonde hair to the soft leather boots that clung to her well-shaped calves.

'I was aiming for the scary-monster effect,' she said, shrugging out of her fur and dropping into a chair.

'Did it work?'

She pulled a face. 'Dennis is still in custody, so it rather looks as if I failed.'

'What's the score?' I asked, switching on the

cappuccino machine that was one of the few permanent reminders of my former business partner Bill Mortensen.

Ruth shook her head wearily. 'It's really not looking good for him. Especially with a record that includes burglary, robbery and GBH.'

'GBH? I didn't know about that.'

'He was twenty-two and he'd just come out of the Paras after a tour in Northern Ireland where his best friend was shot by a sniper in front of his eyes. Post-traumatic shock hadn't been invented then, otherwise a good brief would have walked him out of the door on that set of circumstances. He hasn't been convicted of a violent offence since, but it's still sitting there among his previous convictions like a great fat toad. Any battered body found in the vicinity of his fingerprints is always going to point to Dennis.'

I passed her a cup of frothy coffee and perched with my own on the corner of the desk. 'What exactly happened?'

Ruth filled me in succinctly. Patrick 'Pit Bull' Kelly was one of a gang of eight brothers from the unappetizing redbrick terraces of Cheetham Hill in North Manchester. They were all small-time criminals, good only at getting caught. Pit Bull had been running a shop-squat scam like Dennis, but since he lacked Dennis's nerve or imagination, he'd steered clear of the city centre and worked his own familiar turf with its restricted numbers of punters, none of whom had much cash to spare.

When he'd heard about Dennis's operation, he'd decided he wanted a slice so last night he'd told two of his brothers he was going into town to 'take that scumbag O'Brien's shop off him'.

The next anyone had seen of Pit Bull Kelly had been early that morning. The manager of the cut-price butcher's shop next door to Dennis's squat got more than he'd bargained for when he went to open up. He'd opened the door to the service corridor that ran behind the six-unit section. Facing him was a brindle-and-white pit bull terrier, the bulges of muscle making the hair on its shoulders and ribs stand out like a bristly halo. Its teeth were bared in a rictus that would have made Jaws look friendly, but instead of growling, it was whimpering. The poor bloke froze in his tracks, but the dog showed no signs of attacking him. Instead, it had backed up to Dennis's back door and started howling. According to Ruth, the witness claimed it sounded like the hound from hell.

He didn't know what to do, so he shut the door and called the mall security. Grateful for something more interesting than teenage troublemakers, two uniformed guards had arrived within minutes. They had the local beat bobby in tow, less than thrilled at having his illicit tea break with the security men broken up. When they opened the corridor, the same thing happened. The dog showed its teeth, backed off and started howling outside the door to Dennis's shop.

The bobby decided they should take a look

inside. The door obviously wasn't locked, but there was something heavy behind it. A bit of brute force got the door far enough open for the copper to stick his head inside and check out the obstruction. Which happened to be the corpse of Pit Bull Kelly.

How he'd died was far from obvious. There was no blood, no visible wound. But the bobby was sensible enough to realize that somebody who looked as dodgy as Pit Bull Kelly probably hadn't dropped down dead with a heart attack. He'd radioed for back-up. By mid-morning, the finger-print team had matched Dennis's prints with the ones all over the curiously empty shop. And the pathologist had given them the tentative infor-mation that he thought Pit Bull Kelly had died from a sub-arachnoid haemorrhage.

'What's a sub-arachnoid haemorrhage?' I asked, my first interruption. Ordinarily I'm not that restrained, but, unusually in lawyers, Ruth act-ually tells a story with all the pertinent details in place.

Ruth tilted her head sharply to one side and pressed her fingers under the angle of her jaw. 'Just behind the jawbone here, there's a very vulnerable blood vessel. Rupture that and you're brain-dead in seconds. Normally it's protected by the jaw. And by the way we instinctively duck our heads when any threat approaches. It's almost impossible to hit accidentally, but it could be caused by, for exam-ple, a stiff-fingered karate blow to the neck.'

'And Dennis was a Para,' I said hollowly.

'Dennis was indeed a Para. He says he never learned any karate in the service, but we both know what a bugger it is to try proving a negative.'

'So the police are saying that Dennis was there, Dennis had good reason to get into a ruck with Pit Bull Kelly, so Dennis must have murdered him then emptied his stock out of the shop to cover his tracks?'

Ruth nodded. 'That's about the size of it. That, or Dennis caught Pit Bull Kelly in the act of stealing all his stock.'

'What's Dennis's version?'

'Perfectly plausible, as you'd expect. According to him, the landlord turned up yesterday with a couple of heavies who were even bigger than Keith. He gave Dennis twenty-four hours to get out or suffer the consequences. Dennis thought this was a not unreasonable proposition, so he spent yesterday evening with Keith and a couple of the lads, loading the stock into a van. Keith and the others went off with the van around half past nine, and Dennis went home, where he spent the rest of the evening watching a video with Debbie. They then went to bed, together, and woke up, again together, at around eight this morning.'

'That's his alibi? The blonde with no brain?'

'The blonde with no brain who has previously been caught out giving him false alibis,' Ruth said drily.

'Wasn't Christie home?' I asked. Dennis's daughter obviously couldn't testify that he'd been in bed all night, but at least she'd have been a more credible witness to his TV viewing.

'She stayed overnight with a friend.' Ruth carefully placed her empty cup on the side table. 'I won't deny it's looking bad, Kate.'

I nodded. 'I'll do what I can.'

Ruth stood up and enveloped herself in the fake fur. 'I know Dennis will appreciate it. I think they'll probably charge him tomorrow and bring him before the Mags on Monday. Once he's remanded, you'll be able to visit him and see if there's anything he can tell you that he'd prefer me not to know. If you need anything, you know where to find me.'

We hugged, the silken fur stroking my face. 'Just leave the coat,' I said. 'I've got to go to Saddleworth.'

Ruth groaned. 'It's not the coat you'll need, it's a team of huskies and a sled. You're surely not going there for pleasure, are you?'

I laughed. 'They do pleasure in Saddleworth? A place where their idea of a good time is brass bands, Morris dancing and the annual Ducking of the Greenfield Trollop? I don't think so.'

'So, strictly business,' Ruth said, adjusting her pelt so not a breath of chill air could penetrate. 'No fun Saturday night with Richard, then.'

'He's probably babysitting,' I said, more of an edge in my voice than I'd intended.

Ruth's eyebrows rose. 'The boy getting broody, is he?'

'If he is, he's wasting his energy,' I told her firmly.

'I'd keep an eye on that, if I were you,' Ruth said ominously as she swept out.

Where would we be if it wasn't for the love and support of our friends?

12

MERCURY SQUARES THE ASCENDANT

She is inclined to keep her own counsel, but can't resist poking her nose into everybody else's business. She's never quite got to grips with the idea that there are times when it's tactful to keep her advice to herself. She is a quick worker, energetic and inventive. She tends to be a chameleon, appearing all things to all people.

From *Written in the Stars*, by Dorothea Dawson

It's not often I feel sorry for journalists. But I had to admit my heart went out to the handful of hacks still staking out the entrance to Gloria's enclave. The temperature was already below zero, and the interiors of their cars were no match for a winter's night on the edge of Saddleworth Moor. They perked up momentarily when I swung into the narrow lane, a couple of them even getting out and trotting through the freezing slush in my wake.

But I was through the gate and gone long before they caught up. I hadn't had to use the intercom; I'd phoned Donovan just as I was approaching precisely so I wouldn't have to run the gutter-press gauntlet. As I got out of the car, Gloria appeared in her doorway. She was wearing a high-necked, sparkling, midnight-blue evening dress that hung straight down from her bosom in an elegant fall. On her feet were glittering gold strappy sandals. She looked ready for the Oscars on a balmy California evening, not a charity auction in a Manchester hotel on the coldest night of the year. My charcoal wool crepe suit that doubles up for evening wear and impressing the hell out of clients left me feeling seriously underdressed. Gloria clearly agreed.

'You do know this is a black-tie affair?' she asked.

'I'm a minder, not a model,' I snapped, forcing her to step backwards as I hurried inside. Donovan was looming in the living room, a certain tension noticeable around his deep-set eyes. 'Any problems, Don?'

'Everything under control,' he reported, thrusting his big hands into the pockets of his jeans, which made his shoulders look even more like an American footballer's padding. 'Are you going to drop me off in town, or what?'

Gloria swept past me and slipped her arm through one of Donovan's. His eyes widened like a startled Bambi. 'Kate, don't you think it would be better if

175

Donovan escorted me tonight? All I'm thinking is that you've been splashed all over the papers, and I don't want you to have to spend your evening fending off nosy parkers.'

She didn't want anyone stealing her limelight, more like. Besides, women like Gloria like to impress people. What better fashion accessory than a drop-dead-gorgeous toy boy like Donovan? That would take everyone's mind off death threats and on to prurient scandal. 'I thought you just said it was black tie,' I said sourly.

Gloria gazed up at Donovan. 'Have you not got a dinner jacket, chuck?'

'Sorry, no.' Relief relaxed his features into a smile.

'Never mind,' Gloria said. 'Harry Gershon the tailor's on the committee for tonight's do. I'll give him a bell and you can tell him your measurements and he'll bring a suit along.'

'Oh,' Donovan croaked. 'But . . .'

Gloria gave him the hundred-watt smile. I could see sweat on his upper lip and it was nothing to do with the central heating. 'We'll have a great time, Donovan. I promise you.' Her throaty chuckle left almost nothing to the imagination.

'That might not be such a bad idea,' I said slowly, an idea beginning to form.

'But Kate,' Donovan protested, apprehension and betrayal in his voice.

'If I take Gloria's car and shove a Brenda wig over my hair, I can act as a decoy and pull the press off. Then you'll get a clear run into town. I've got some work to do digging into Dorothea's past, so I can get on with that while you two are out enjoying yourselves.'

Donovan looked like I'd just given him life with a recommendation for twenty-five years. 'You mean you want me to carry on bodyguarding Gloria?' he asked desperately.

'At least, chuck,' Gloria purred, delighted to be getting her own way.

'And I'll pick Gloria up later at the hotel and bring her back here,' I said sweetly, enjoying the irritation that flashed in her eyes as she watched her bubble burst.

Donovan grinned with relief. 'That's great. I don't think I can do tomorrow, Kate, because I've got to finish an essay for Monday.'

And I am Marie of Romania, I thought to myself. 'No problem. I'll handle it. OK?' I asked Gloria.

'You're the boss,' she pouted. 'I'll get you my spare Brenda wig.' She disentangled her arm from Donovan, gave him a little pat on his iron-hard gluteus maximus and sashayed out of the room.

Donovan moved to my side and stooped close to my ear. 'I thought you were going to make me spend another night here,' he whispered. I thought only the prospect of his mother's anger had the power to make him that twitchy.

'You survived last night intact, didn't you?' I asked sweetly.

He straightened up and scowled. 'Only just,' he muttered. 'What's the polite way to tell somebody ten years older than your mum to take her hand off your thigh?'

'You obviously found one,' I said drily.

'I went to the toilet a lot,' he said bitterly. 'And the spare bedroom's got a bloody big chest of drawers that fits nicely behind the door. It took me all my time to get it shifted, and it's just as well I did because I swear I woke up to the sound of the door handle turning.'

I stifled a snort of laughter. 'Sorry, Don,' I giggled. 'I know it's not funny. What happened?'

'I did snoring. Loudly. Eventually she went away. She must think I'm a pretty crap bodyguard if I can sleep through that.'

I grinned. 'Somehow I don't think it's the guarding capabilities of your body that she's interested in. Don't worry, I'll come and rescue you in good time tonight.'

We shut up and moved apart as we heard Gloria's approach. She came in twirling a rigid platinum-blonde beehive on the end of her finger. 'There you go, chuck. One Brenda Barrowclough barnet.' She tossed it in my direction. Donovan stretched out a long arm and intercepted it, then handed it ceremoniously to me.

'Let's see what you look like,' he said, a mischievous grin lighting up his eyes.

I pulled the wig over my head. It wasn't a bad fit, and in the poor light of the streetlamps

I reckoned it would be good enough to fool anyone expecting Gloria. Five minutes later and I was proving myself right, always a feeling I enjoy. At the end of the narrow lane leading to Gloria's, I slowed to turn on to the main road. To either side, headlights snapped on and engines coughed into life. 'Gotcha,' I said under my breath as I led the cavalcade down the road towards Oldham. As far as I could see, they were all nailed to my tail. I was just grateful there were no tunnels between Saddleworth and Manchester. And that it was too cold for riding motorbikes.

I drove to the office, not particularly wanting to invite the rat pack back to my own doorstep. I managed to find a parking space that wasn't illegal enough to earn a ticket on a Saturday night, aware of the four press cars hovering nearby, trying to find nonexistent spaces where they could abandon ship and follow 'Gloria'. I got out of the car, pulled the wig off and ran my hand through my hair. I wiggled my fingers at the hacks and walked round the corner to my office. Nobody followed me. Like private eyes, journos always know when they've just been had over by an expert. One humiliation was enough for one evening.

The office was dark and empty, Gizmo having finally remembered he had a home to go to. I brewed myself a cappuccino and stretched out on the clients' sofa to skim the authorized version of Dorothea's life. The two hundred and fifty pages of largish print left a lot of scope for the imagination.

The rosy glow of a happy Lancashire childhood in a poor but honest family, followed by an adolescence troubled only by the upheavals surrounding the discovery of her psychic powers and the difficulties of coming to terms with a 'gift' that set her apart from her contemporaries.

She had married at twenty to a man eight years older than her, referred to only as Harry. The marriage lasted less than a chapter. If Dorothea's cursory dismissal was anything to go by, the real thing hadn't endured much longer. Because she'd needed to support herself, she'd started charging for astrological consultations. By the time Edna Mercer had stumbled across her, she'd graduated from her front room to her own booth on a seaside pier.

Northerners had changed everything. Within months of becoming the personal astrologer to a handful of cast members, she was the most sought-after stargazer in the country. A year after Edna Mercer had plucked her from relative obscurity, she had a monthly slot on daytime TV, syndicated weekly newspaper columns and pre-recorded local radio horoscopes. Now, a few years after her book had appeared, she had been edged from pole position among astrologers by the high-profile appearances of Mystic Meg on the national lottery broadcasts, but Dorothea Dawson was still Seer to the Stars in the public's mind. The amazing thing, the one fact that had kept her going through the tough times, was the certain knowledge that once she reached a particular point in her astrological cycle, she would be a star herself. And the moon is made of green cheese.

Bored by the book's relentless tabloid prose and frustrated by its deliberate superficiality, I gave up on it after an hour or so. I knew that compared to the police, my chances of uncovering Dorothea's killer were slim. They had forensic evidence and teams of trained officers who could question everybody who'd ever crossed the threshold of the NPTV compound. All I had going for me was the chance that my informal networks could produce information that was denied to the police. Cassie had been some help, but I needed a lot more.

There was one source that I suspected wouldn't occur to Cliff Jackson if he thought from now till next Christmas. Even if it did, a private operator like me was always going to get a far better response from the anarchic community of the Internet than a copper ever would. Even the straightest suit turns into a bit of a rebel when he – or she – ventures into cyberspace.

Reluctantly abandoning the comfort of the sofa, I slouched in front of my PC and got on-line. I went straight to one of the search engines that act as the nearest thing the ever-expanding web has to a road map. Within minutes, I had a list of addresses for websites and newsgroups that might be useful sources of information. I posted a message in a dozen places – the technological equivalent of the personal column of the newspaper, with considerably faster and better results. While I was on-line, I posted a couple of other inquiries, to see if something I'd half remembered was the truth or just wishful thinking. Finally, I checked my own e-mail and printed out a couple of requests for information from investigators abroad. They were after routine background checks that would take them days or weeks but which I could polish off in a matter of hours thanks to my local knowledge. It used to be a lot easier for people to disappear abroad. Now it's really true that you can run but you can't hide.

I switched off the computer and checked the time. Way too early to pick up Gloria. There was no chance of Richard being home on a Saturday night, at least not before *Match of the Day*. But I knew someone who would be.

As I parked outside the O'Briens' house, a couple of pairs of curtains in the deeply suburban close twitched open, shards of light sparking on their frosted lawns like glitter on Christmas cards. Even thick middle managers know that nobody as small as me gets into the police, so the pale stripes of curtain gaps soon disappeared. Debbie answered the door with a defiant glower that turned her beauty into a threat. 'Oh, it's you,' she said. 'I thought it was the Old Bill come back for another run through the laundry basket. Bastards. Come on in.'

It was hardly a gracious invitation, but I don't

suppose I'd have been any better behaved in the circumstances. I followed her into the immaculate and characterless kitchen. I'd been right about the glasses. The cabinet was empty. I didn't think that was because Debbie was secretly having a party in the next room. 'Want a drink?' she asked.

When I started working in Manchester, the first time someone had asked me that I'd said, 'No thanks, I'm driving.' He'd given me a very strange look. It took me about six months and a lot of thirsty encounters to realize that when you're offered a drink around here, they mean tea or coffee. 'Coffee,' I said. 'White, no sugar.'

The silence grew thick between us while Debbie brewed up, the hiss as boiling water exploded coffee granules perfectly audible. She's never quite sure what to make of me. Being a woman whose IQ is around the same as her continental shoe size, she can't quite make herself believe that any woman would prefer to go out to work to support herself from choice. She also finds it hard to get her head round the notion that any heterosexual woman could spend serious time with her husband without having designs on his body. Every now and again Dennis or I or their teenage daughter Christie convinces her that our relationship is purely platonic. Then she forgets what platonic means and we have to start all over again. Sometimes I think it would just be easier if I told her I was a lesbian.

On second thoughts, perhaps not.

'Ruth says you're going to help him,' Debbie said flatly as she plonked the mug in front of me.

'I'll do what I can. But I'm not sure what I can usefully do. It's not like I can track down missing alibi witnesses or anything.'

Debbie bristled. 'That's because he was here with me all night.'

'You're sure he didn't pop out for a packet of fags or anything?' I asked.

Debbie glared at me. 'Whose side are you on? You sound like the bloody bizzies. Look, he didn't pop out for a packet of fags because I buy his fags at the supermarket, right?' She swung away from me and yanked open one of the tall kitchen units. The cupboard contained an unbroached carton of Dennis's brand and a half-full wrap of hers. 'Even Dennis can't smoke two hundred fags a night.'

'I'm just checking, Debbie,' I said calmly. 'I'm on Dennis's side. I only asked because if he did bob out for ten minutes, you can bet the dibble are going to find out and use that to make you look like a liar.'

She lit a cigarette, then gripped her right elbow with her left hand in a classic defensive gesture. 'Look, I know I gave him a moody alibi one time. But you've got to when it's your man. And I'm not lying this time. He really was here all night. Him and Keith and the lads had been loading up the stock. He was too knackered even to go out for a pint.'

I held my hands up in a placatory gesture.

'I believe you. The problem I've got is that I'm not up to speed with who hates who among the Cheetham Hill villains. Until I can speak to Dennis, I haven't a clue whose doors I should be kicking in.'

Debbie sighed a long ribbon of smoke. 'No point in asking me. I've always kept my nose out. There is one thing, though,' she added, frowning as she thought. The absence of permanent lines on her forehead demonstrated what a rare event I was witnessing.

'What's that?' I had little hope of a result, but my mother brought me up to be polite.

'The dog. I can't understand how come the dog was in the corridor and Pit Bull Kelly was in the shop.'

'Pit Bull must have been attacked as he walked in the door.'

'So how did whoever killed him get out past the dog? That's a killer dog, that. It wouldn't let Pit Bull's killer walk. It'd rip his throat out.'

She had a point. I sipped my coffee and thought about it. 'A bit of a puzzle, that,' I said.

'Plus,' she added with a triumphant air, 'if Pit Bull went down the shop to front up Dennis, he'd never have moved an inch without the dog. If Dennis had been in the shop, it would have been the dog that went through the door first, not that gutless wonder Pit Bull. Plus, if Dennis had still been using the shop, his night watchman would have been inside.'

185

'Of course,' I breathed.

'So the dog being in the corridor proves Dennis wasn't there.'

Somehow, I thought a jury might need a bit more convincing than the dog that didn't rip a throat out in the night. But at least it gave me somewhere to start.

Traditionally, the serious players in Manchester's drug wars have been the black gangs of Moss Side and the white gangs of Cheetham Hill. The Cheetham Hill lads have been around longer, their criminal roots deep in the cracks between the paving stones of the narrow terraced streets north of the wholesale district of Strangeways, their horizons bisected by the central tower of the Victorian prison and the slender black chimney of Boddingtons Brewery. Most of them are descended from long lines of gangsters and scam artists; it's a mark of status in Cheetham Hill to reveal your great-granddad did time for black marketeering during the war.

The Kellys were one of the oldest families, and most of them stuck to the old ways. Protection rackets and schneid sports gear, long firm frauds and small-time thieving, that was the Kellys' style. The team of brothers had always had contempt for the drug lords, which was about the only good thing you could say for them.

I had to endure three boozers where I drank beer straight from the bottle because I wasn't prepared to risk the glasses before I found a pair of grieving Kelly brothers. The Dog and Brewer was the kind of dump where your feet stick to the carpet and the fag ash forms a paste on the bottom of ashtrays that nobody has bothered to dry after rinsing them under the tap. Most of the punters had the blurred jawlines and bleary eyes of people who have smoked and drunk so much for so long change seems pointless. The women wore clothes that might have flattered them fifteen years before but now insulted them even more than the flabby men in ill-fitting casual clothes who were buying them drinks. Tom Jones was rejoicing loudly that again he'd touch the green, green grass of home.

I brazened out the eyes on me and bought a bottle of Carlsberg. 'Any of the Kelly boys in?' I asked the barman, my fingers resting lightly on the fiver on the bar.

He looked at the money and gave me the once-over. I obviously didn't look like a cop, for he jerked his head towards two shaggy-haired men in padded flannel work shirts at the far end of the bar. Before I could turn back, the fiver was gone. One good thing about lowlife dives is that the information comes cheap.

I picked up my bottle and pushed through the crowd until I was standing next to the two men. Their blue eyes were bloodshot, their stubbled cheeks scarlet with the stout and whisky they were pouring down their throats. 'I'm sorry for your loss, gentlemen,' I said. 'Will you let the *Evening Chronicle* buy you a drink?'

The taller of the two managed a half-hearted leer. 'I'll let you buy me a drink any time, darling.'

I signalled the barman and blew a tenner on drink. 'Hell of a shock,' I said, raising my bottle to clink against their glasses.

'I told him he was a dickhead, going up against Dennis O'Brien. Hard bastard, that one,' the smaller brother slurred.

'I heard the dog was supposed to be good protection,' I said. 'Bit of a handful, I heard. They say he gave the Old Bill a hard time.'

The taller one grinned. 'Thank fuck for that. I'm Paul, by the way, and this is Little Joe.'

I shook the outstretched paw. 'I'm Kate. How come Patrick went to see O'Brien on his own? If the guy's so tough?'

Little Joe snorted. 'Because he was a big girl's blouse. He was always trying to prove he was a hard man, our Patrick, but he was about as hard as Angel Delight. He was complaining that Dennis O'Brien had muscled in on his racket, and we all got so fucked off with listening we told him to go and sort O'Brien out if he was so pissed off.'

'And he'd had enough to drink to think he was man enough to take on that South Manchester scumbag.' Paul shook his head. 'He was an eejit, Patrick.'

'Especially when he had a drink in him.' Little Joe shook his head too.

'And a draw,' Paul concluded.

'So he'd been drinking and smoking dope before he went off to the Arndale to front up O'Brien?' I asked.

'That's right,' Little Joe confirmed. 'I mean, what kind of bastard has to top some drunken tosser just to make a point? O'Brien could just have broken a few bones and chucked Patrick out on his ear. He didn't have to go and kill him. Anybody could see Patrick was an eejit.'

'What about the dog, though?' I persisted.

Paul gave a contemptuous bark of laughter. 'Yeah, well, even a hard nut like O'Brien might have thought twice about taking on that mad bastard dog. I can't figure out how the dog didn't rip his throat out.'

Suddenly, Little Joe's eyes were full of tears. 'He didn't have to kill him, though, did he? The bastard didn't have to kill my baby brother.' His hand snaked out and grabbed my lapel. 'You tell them that in your paper. My baby brother was a big soft lump. Even with a drink and a draw in him, he wouldn't have done to O'Brien what that shit O'Brien done to him. You tell them, d'you hear? You tell them.'

I promised I'd tell them. I promised several times. I listened to the Kelly boys telling me the same things a few more times, then made my excuses and left. I carried my own haze of stale smoke and spilled drink into the car and made for the city centre.

I virtually had to drag Gloria off Donovan in the end. She'd been taking advantage of having a driver to attack the champagne with the brio of an operatic tenor. As she slid from happy to drunk to absolutely arseholed, so her amorousness had grown, according to Donovan, who I found with a slew of red lipstick below one ear and one shirt-tail hanging down the front of his trousers. He was keeping Gloria upright by pure strength, lurking in a corner near the revolving doors.

'Why didn't you sit her down in a quiet corner of the bar?' I hissed as we steered her into the street. It was like manipulating one of those wooden articulated models artists use, only life-sized and heavy as waterlogged mahogany.

'Every time I sat down she climbed on my lap,' he growled as we poured Gloria into the passenger seat of her car.

'Fair enough.' I slammed the door and handed him my car keys. 'Thanks, Don. You did a good job in very trying circumstances.'

He scratched his head. 'I expect it'll be reflected in my pay packet.'

Like mother, like son. 'It would be nice to find my car outside my house sometime tomorrow, keys through the letterbox. I'll talk to you soon.' I patted his arm. It was like making friends with one of the Trafalgar Square lions.

Gloria was snoring gently when I got behind the wheel. The engine turning over woke her up. She rolled towards me, hand blindly groping for my knee. 'I don't think so,' I said firmly, returning it to her own lap.

Her eyes snapped open and she looked at me in astonishment. 'Hiya, chuck,' she said blearily. 'Where did Donovan go?'

'Home to bed.'

She gurgled. I hoped it was a chuckle and not the overture to a technicolour yawn. 'Lucky girl,' she slurred. 'Poor old Glo. Whatchou been up to, then? Bit of nookie with the boyfriend?'

We turned into Albert Square where the giant inflatable red and white figure of Santa Claus clutched the steeple that rises out of the middle of the town hall roof. It looked vaguely obscene in the garish glare of the Christmas lights. I jerked my thumb upwards. 'He's seen more action than I have tonight. I've been trying to find out about Dorothea's past,' I said, more to fill the space than in any hope of a sensible response.

'Bloody tragic, that's what it was. Tragic,' Gloria mumbled.

'Murder always is.'

'No, you daft get, not the murder, her life. It was tragic.' Gloria gave me one of those punches to the shoulder that drunks think are affectionate. The car swerved across two lanes and narrowly missed a bus. Gloria giggled as I wrestled with the wheel.

191

'What was tragic?' I asked, my jaw clenched so tight the muscles hurt.

'She never got over losing him.' She groped in her evening purse for a cigarette and lit up.

'Losing who? Her husband?'

'Flamin' Nora, Kate. When did a woman ever regret losing a no-good waste of space like her old man?' she reproached me. 'Her son, of course. She never got over losing her son.'

'I didn't know she'd had a son.'

'Not a lot of people know that,' Gloria intoned in a very bad impersonation of Michael Caine. 'She had a son and then she had post-natal depression.'

'And the baby died?'

''Course he didn't die,' she said scornfully. 'He got taken off her. When she got put away.'

This was beginning to feel like one of those terrible black and white Northern kitchen sink dramas scripted by men with names like Arnold and Stanley. 'When you say "put away", do you mean sectioned, Gloria?' I asked as sweetly as I could manage.

'Tha's right,' she said. 'Put away in the loony bin. He did that to her. Her old man had her put away because having the baby had sent her a bit off her rocker. Christ, every woman goes a bit off her rocker when she's had a littl'un. If they put us all away just because we went a bit daft, there'd be a hell of a lot of men changing nappies. Right bastard he must have been.'

'So Dorothea's baby was adopted then, is that what you're saying?'

'Aye. Taken off her and given to somebody else. And they gave her electric shocks and cold showers and more drugs than Boots the Chemist and wondered why it took her so bloody long to get better. Bastards.' She spat the last word vehemently, as if it was personal, her eyes on the swirl of pinprick snowflakes tumbling thinly in the cones of sulphur-yellow street-lights.

'Did Dorothea tell you about this?'

'Who else? It were when I asked her to do a horoscope for my granddaughter. We'd gone out for a meal and we ended up back at my place, pissed as farts. And she started on about how she could be a grandmother half a dozen times over and she'd never be any the wiser. When she sobered up, she made me swear not to tell another living soul. And I haven't, not until now. Tragic, that's what it was. Tragic.'

I came at the subject half a dozen different ways before we finally arrived back at the deserted alley leading to her fortification. Each time I got the same version. No details added, no details different. Dorothea might have been lying to Gloria, but Gloria was telling me the truth.

I helped her out of the car and across cobbles covered in feathery white powder to her front door. I wasn't in the mood to go any further. I wanted home and bed and the sleep that would

make sense of the jumbled jigsaw pieces of information that were drifting through my head like
the snow across the windscreen. And not a snow-
plough in sight.

God, I hate the country.

13

SUN CONJUNCTION WITH PLUTO

Compromise is not in her vocabulary. She is not afraid of initiating confrontations and is a great strategist. She enjoys conflict with authority, she will not stand for personal or professional interference, but she is capable of transforming her own life and the world around her. People can be nervous of her, but this is a splendid aspect for a detective.

From *Written in the Stars*, by Dorothea Dawson

I woke up with that muffled feeling. It didn't go away when I stuck my head out from under the duvet. Richard only grunted when I slipped out of bed and pulled on my dressing gown before I died of hypothermia. The central heating had obviously been and gone while I was still sleeping, which made it sometime after nine. I lifted the curtain and looked out at a world gone white. 'Bugger,' I said.

Richard mumbled something. 'Whazza?' it sounded like.

'It's been snowing. Properly.'

He pushed himself up on one elbow and reached for his glasses. 'Lessee,' he slurred. I opened one side of the curtain. 'Fabulous,' he said. 'We can make a snowman.'

'And what about Gloria? I'm supposed to be minding her.'

'Not even a mad axeman would be daft enough to go on a killing spree in Saddleworth in this weather,' he pointed out, not unreasonably. 'It'll be chaos on the roads out there. And if Gloria's got the hangover she deserves, she won't be thinking about going anywhere. Come back to bed, Brannigan. I need a cuddle.'

I didn't need asking twice. 'I obey, o master,' I said ironically, slipping out of my dressing gown and into his arms.

The second time we woke, the phone was to blame. I noted the clock as I grabbed the handset. I couldn't believe it was nearly noon. I'd obviously needed the sleep. Or something. 'Yes?' I said.

'It's me, chuck.' It was the voice of a ghost. It sounded like Gloria had died and somehow missed the pearly gates.

''Morning, Gloria,' I said cheerfully, upping the volume in revenge for her attempt at groping my knee. 'How are you today?'

'Don't,' she said. 'Just don't. For some reason, I seem to have a bit of a migraine this morning. I thought I'd just spend the day in bed with the phone turned off, so you don't have to worry about coming over.'

'Are you sure? I could always send Donovan,' I said sadistically.

I sensed the shudder. 'I'll be fine,' she said. 'I'll see you tomorrow, usual time.' Click. I didn't even get the chance to say goodbye.

Richard emerged, blinking at the snow-light. 'Gloria?' he asked.

'I'm reprieved for the day. She sounds like the walking dead.'

'Told you,' he said triumphantly. 'Shall we make a snowman, then?'

By the time we'd made the snowman, then had a bath to restore our circulation, then done some more vigorous horizontal exercises to raise our core body temperatures, it was late afternoon and neither of us could put off work any longer. He had some copy to write for an Australian magazine fascinated by Britpop. Personally, I'd rather have cleaned the U-bend, but I'm the woman who thinks the best place for Oasis is in the bottom of a flower arrangement. I settled down at my computer and trawled the Net for responses to last night's queries.

I downloaded everything, then started reading my way through. I immediately junked the tranche from people who thought it must be cool to be a private eye, would I give them a work-experience placement? I also quickly dumped the ones that were no more than a rehash of what had been in the papers and on the radio. That left me with half a dozen that revealed Dorothea had had a breakdown back in the 1950s. There were two that seemed to have some real credibility. The first came from someone who lived in the picturesque Lancashire town where Dorothea had grown up.

Dear Kate Brannigan, it read, I am a sixteen-year-old girl and I live in Halton-on-Lune where Dorothea Dawson came from. My grandmother was at school with Dorothea, so when I saw your query in the astrology newsgroup, I asked her what she remembered about her.

She said Dorothea was always a bit of a loner at school, she was an only child, but there was nothing weird or spooky about her when she was growing up, she was just like everybody else. My gran says Dorothea got married to this bloke Harry Thompson who worked in the bank. She says he was a real cold fish which I think means he didn't know how to have a good time, except I don't know what they did then to have a good time because they didn't have clubs or decent music or anything like that.

Anyway, Gran says Dorothea had this baby and then she went mad and had to go into the loony bin (Gran calls it that, but she really means a mental hospital). Anyway, her husband went away and was never seen again, and when Dorothea came out of the hospital after a couple of years, she only came back to pack her bags and get the next bus out.

I don't know what happened to the baby, Gran says it probably got put in a home, which is not a good place to be brought up even if your mum is a bit barking.

I hope this helps.

Yours sincerely

Megan Hall

The other was better written. I didn't much care; literary style wasn't what I was after.

Dear Ms Brannigan

It may come as a surprise that a man of my age knows how to <surf the Internet>, but I am a contemporary of Dorothea Dawson. I was a year younger than her, but my sister was in the same class at school, and was the nearest Dorothea had to a close friend. Dorothea used regularly to come to our house for tea, and the two girls often played together.

That all changed when Dorothea met Harry Thompson. He was a bank clerk, good-looking in a rather grim sort of way, and he was drawn to girls inappropriately young. When they met, Dorothea was, I think, a rather young 17, and he must have been 25 or 26. He was what I think we would now call a control freak and Dorothea was always on pins lest she upset him.

Quite why she agreed to marry him none of us ever knew, though it may well have been the only route she could see by which she could escape the equally oppressive regime of her stepmother. They were married and within eighteen months Dorothea was confined to the cheerless Victorian world of the local mental hospital following an appalling experience with what we now term post-natal depression.

Harry resolutely refused to have anything to do with the child, claiming that the baby was tainted with the same madness that had claimed the mother. An ignorant and cruel man, he sought and gained a transfer to a branch of the bank in the Home Counties, handing the child over to an adoption agency. What became of the baby, I have no knowledge. This far on, I am ashamed to say that neither my sister nor I can remember if the child were a boy or girl; in my sister's defence, I would say that by that time, thanks to Harry, there was little contact between her and Dorothea.

When she finally was allowed to leave the mental hospital, Dorothea was very bitter and wanted to cast her past entirely from her. My sister was saddened by this, but not surprised. We were delighted to see her rise to celebrity, though both horrified by the news of her death.

I do hope this is of some assistance. Should you wish to talk to me, you will find me in the Wakefield telephone book under my parish of St Barnabas-next-the-Wall.

With best wishes

Rev. Tom Harvey

I wasn't surprised that Gloria had called the whole sorry business tragic. I couldn't help wondering where Harry Thompson was now and what he was doing. Not to mention the mysterious baby. I kept having visions of a swaddling-wrapped infant abandoned on the doorstep of the local orphanage. I think I saw too many BBC classic serials when I was a child.

It was time for some serious digging, the kind that is well beyond my limited capabilities with electronic systems. I copied the two key e-mails to Gizmo, with a covering note explaining that I needed him to use his less advertised skills to unearth all he could about Harry Thompson and the riddle of the adopted child. Then I started accessing what legitimate data sources were available on a Sunday evening to answer the queries that had come in from the two foreign agencies.

When the doorbell rang, I exited the database I'd been in and severed my connection. Those on-line services charge by the minute and I wasn't prepared to put myself in hock if it took me five minutes to dislodge a Jehovah's Witness or a local opportunist offering to dig my car out of snow that would probably be gone by morning. To my astonishment, it was Gizmo. 'I just sent you an e-mail,' I said.

'I know, I got it.' He marched in without waiting to be asked, stamping slush into my hall carpet. On the way to the spare room that doubles as my home office, he shed a parka that looked like it had accompanied Scott to the Antarctic and had only just made it home again. By the time I'd hung it up, he was ensconced in front of my computer. 'Gotta beer?'

I was shocked. I didn't think I'd ever seen Gizmo with any kind of liquid within three feet of a keyboard. Same with food. If it wasn't for thirst and hunger and bodily functions, I've often thought he would spend twenty-four hours a day in front of a screen. 'I'll get one,' I said faintly. I raided Richard's fridge and came back with some elderberry beer made to an old English recipe, a grand cru wheat beer and a smoked rye ale. I swear to God the beer drinkers are getting even more pretentious than the winos and foodies. I mean, how can you have a grand cru beer? It's like going into McDonald's and asking for one of their gourmet burgers.

Gizmo went for the elderberry beer. Judging by the look on his face as it hit his taste buds, he'd have preferred a can of supermarket own-brand lager. I sat on the edge of the bed and sipped the Stoly and grapefruit juice I'd sensibly sorted for myself. 'You were about to tell me what was in my e-mail that made you rush round,' I lied.

Gizmo shifted in his seat and wrapped his legs around each other. I'd seen it done in cartoons, but I'd always thought until then it was artistic licence. 'I felt like some fresh air.' Lie number one. I shook my head. 'I was a bit worried about discussing hacking in e-mail that wasn't encrypted.' Lie number two. I shook my head again. 'I wanted to check what virus protection you've got running on this machine because I've not looked at it for a while and there's all sorts of clever new shit out there.'

I shook my head sadly. 'Strike three, Giz. Look, you're here now. You've made the effort. You might as well tell me what you came to tell me because we're both so busy it could be weeks before there's another window of opportunity.' I felt like a detective inspector pushing for a confession. I hoped it wasn't going to be another murder.

Gizmo ran a finger up and down the side of the beer bottle, his eyes following its movement. 'There's this . . .' He stopped. He looked up at me like dogs do when they're trying to tell you where it hurts. 'I've met . . . well, not actually met . . .'

Light dawned. 'The flowers,' I said.

The blush climbed from the polo neck of his

black sweater, rising unevenly like the level of poured champagne in a glass. He nodded.

'"www gets real." The cyberbabe,' I said, trying to sound sensitive and supportive. The effort nearly killed me.

'Don't call her that,' Gizmo said, a plea on his face. 'She's not some bimbo. And she's not a saddo Nethead who hasn't got a life. She's really interesting. I've never met a woman who can talk about computer code, politics, sociology, music, all of those things.'

All of those things I never knew Gizmo knew anything about. Except computer code, of course. 'You've never met this one,' I said drily.

'That's kind of what I wanted to talk to you about.'

'A meeting? Getting together for real?' I checked my voice for scepticism and thought I'd probably got away with it.

'What do you think?'

What did I think? What I really thought was that Gizmo was probably typical of the people who spent their nights chattering to strangers in Siberia and Sao Paolo and Salinas, weird computer geeks telling lies about themselves in a pathetic attempt to appear interesting. A blind date with Gizmo would probably have turned me celibate at sixteen. On the other hand, if I'd been a geek too – and there were one or two female nerds out there, most of them inevitably working for Microsoft – I might have been charmed, especially since my efforts at grooming had rendered Gizmo almost indistinguishable from the human species. 'Does she work for Microsoft?' I asked.

He gave me a very peculiar look. 'That's sick. That's like asking a member of CND if he fancies someone who works for MOD procurement.'

'Has she got a name?'

His smile was curiously tender. 'Jan,' he said. 'She has her own consultancy business. She does training packages for the computer industry.'

'So how did you . . . meet?'

'Remember when Gianni Versace got shot? Well, there was a lot of discussion on the Net about it, how the FBI were using the on-line community to warn people about the suspect, and how far the federal agencies should go in trying to exploit the Net to catch criminals. I was checking out one of the newsgroups and I saw Jan had said some interesting things, and we started exchanging private mail.' Oh great, I thought. A mutual interest in serial killers. Always a good place to start a relationship. 'Then we found out we both hung out in quite a few of the same newsgroups,' Gizmo continued. 'We'd just never crossed paths before.' He stopped dead and took a deep swig of beer. It was possibly the longest speech I'd heard Gizmo make.

'And?'

'And we really hit it off. Loads of stuff in common. Lately, it's been getting more and more intense between us. I . . . I don't think I've ever felt like this before,' he mumbled.

205

'And now you want to do a reality check by getting together in the flesh?'

He nodded. 'Why not? Pen friends have been doing it for years.'

This wasn't the time to remind him that pen friends had one or two little safeguards like knowing where each other lived. It also wasn't the time to remind him that it was somehow easier to lie in cyberspace than in meatspace, since right from the beginning the hackers and computer freaks who had hung out on the very first bulletin boards had always hidden behind nicknames. The first time I'd been confronted with Gizmo's real name was years into our acquaintance, when he'd signed his initial consultancy contract with Brannigan & Co. I sipped my drink and raised my eyebrows. 'And sometimes it's a big disappointment. Why is it so important that you meet? If things are so excellent between you, maybe it's better to keep it cyber.'

He squirmed in his seat. 'Sometimes it's too slow, the Net. Even in a private conference room in a newsgroup, you can still only communicate as fast as you can type, so it's never as spontaneous as conversation.'

'I thought that was the charm.'

'It is, to an extent. You can structure your dialogue much more than you can in a meatspace conversation where you tend to go off at tangents. But we've been doing this for a while now. We need to move on to the next stage, and that's got to be a face-to-face. Hasn't it?'

I wasn't cut out for this. If I'd been an agony aunt, my column would have invariably read, 'For God's sake, get a grip.' But Gizmo was more than just another contractor. Less than a friend, admittedly, but somebody I cared about, much as I'd cared about Polly the cocker spaniel I'd grown up with. So I took a deep breath and said, 'Where does she live?'

'London. But she comes up to Manchester every two or three weeks on business. I was thinking about suggesting we got together for a beer next time she's up.'

It would be a beer, too. Somehow I didn't have this woman pegged as a white-wine-spritzer drinker. 'You don't think it might destroy what you've already built up?'

He shrugged, a difficult feat given that he was impersonating a human pretzel. 'Better we find that out now, don't you think?'

'I honestly don't know. Maybe the cyber relationship is the shape of things to come. Communication with strangers, all of us hiding behind a façade, having virtual sex in front of our terminals. Not as replacement for face-to-face stuff, but as another dimension. Adultery without the guilt, maybe?' I hazarded.

'No,' Gizmo said, unravelling his limbs and straightening up. 'I think it's just another kind of courtship. If you don't take it out of virtuality into reality, it's ultimately sterile because you've no objective standards to measure it against.'

Profound stuff from a man I'd never suspected of being capable of love for a sentient being without microchips. 'Sounds to me like you've already made your decision,' I said gently.

He took a deep breath. His shoulders dropped from round his ears. 'I suppose I have.'

'So go with your instincts.'

I'd said what he wanted to hear. The relief flowed off him like radiation. 'Thanks for listening, Kate. I really appreciate it.'

'So show me how much, and dig me some dirt on Harry Thompson and the mystery baby.'

14

JUPITER TRINE SATURN

Cheerful Jupiter tempers the stern, hard-working nature of Saturn. She is a visionary, but one firmly rooted in the practicalities. She is a good organizer and seldom feels overwhelmed by her responsibilities. She is good at coordinating people to collaborate with her. She has the self-discipline to achieve her goals without getting wound up about it.

From *Written in the Stars*, by Dorothea Dawson

I'd set off early enough to follow the snow-plough down the main road from Oldham through Greenfield. Getting down Gloria's alley was out of the question, but the hacks had moved on to the next big thing, so the only threat to Gloria's wellbeing was the possibility of wet feet. I should have known better.

She emerged in knee-high snow boots and a scarlet ski suit with royal-blue chevrons and matching earmuffs. 'Hiya, chuck,' she greeted me.

'I've never been skiing in my life, but they do great gear, don't they?' she enthused. As usual, I felt underdressed. Wellies over jeans topped with my favourite leather jacket had seemed fine in Ardwick, but somehow they just didn't cut it in the country.

'Got over your hangover?'

'I'll thank you to remember it was a migraine, young lady.' She wasn't entirely joking. 'By the way,' she said as she settled into the car, 'there's been a change of schedule. Somebody got excited about the snow, so we're going to do some location shooting instead of studio filming.' Gloria explained that because of the weather, cast members involved in the location shooting had been told to go directly to Heaton Park on the outskirts of the city rather than to the NPTV compound. The park was easier to reach than the studios since it was just off the main motorway network and on a major road. There were various nearby locations that would be used in the course of the day, but we'd be based in the main car park with the catering truck, make-up and wardrobe. And the snow. I could feel myself growing almost wistful about being a lawyer, cocooned in a nice warm courtroom with nothing more taxing to do than get a client off a murder charge.

The one good thing about being away from NPTV was that we seemed to have escaped the delights of Cliff Jackson's company. According to Rita, Jackson and his team had been interviewing cast members in their homes over the weekend, but they were concentrating on office and production staff at the studios now. Also according to Rita, who had clearly elected herself gossip liaison officer, they were no closer to an arrest than they had been on Friday night. She had managed to get Linda Shaw to admit that neither Gloria nor I were serious suspects; Gloria because there were no spatters of blood on the flowing white top she'd been wearing, me because Linda thought it was one of the daftest ideas she'd ever heard. I thought she'd probably been telling the truth about me, but suspected she might have had her fingers crossed when she exonerated Gloria. In her shoes, I would have.

Gloria went off with Ted so Freddie Littlewood could work his magic on their faces. I let them go alone since I could see the short gap between the two vehicles from where I was sitting in a corner of the cast bus with Rita and Clive. I settled down, ready to soak up whatever they were prepared to spill. 'So who had it in for Dorothea?' I asked. Some people just don't respond to the subtle approach. Anyone with an Equity card, for example.

Clive looked at Rita, who shrugged like someone auditioning for 'Allo, 'Allo. 'It can't have been to do with her professional life, surely,' he said. 'Nobody murders their astrologer because they don't like what she's predicted.'

'But nobody here really knew anything about

her private life,' Rita objected. 'Out of all the cast, I was one of her first regulars, and I know almost nothing about her. I've even been to her house for a consultation, but all I found out from that was that she must have been doing very nicely. A thatched cottage between Alderley Edge and Wilmslow, if you please.'

'Did she live alone?' I asked.

'Search me,' Rita said. 'She never said a dicky bird about a boyfriend or a husband. The papers all said she lived alone, and they probably know more than the rest of us because they'll have been chatting up the locals.'

Clive scratched his chin. 'She knew a lot about us, though. I don't know if she was psychic or just bloody good at snapping up every little scrap of information she could get her hands on, but if she'd written a book about *Northerners*, it would have been dynamite. Maybe she went too far with somebody. Maybe she found something out that she wasn't prepared to keep quiet about.'

The notion that there was any secret black enough for a *Northerners* star to feel squeamish about using for publicity was hard for me to get my head round. Then I remembered Cassie. Not only what had happened to her, but what she'd said about the prospect of losing a plum role being motive enough for some desperate people. 'If that's the case, then the dark secret probably died with her,' I said despondently.

'I'm afraid so,' Clive said. 'Unless she kept the

details on her computer along with our horoscope details.'

My ears pricked up. 'You think that's likely?'

Rita's eyes were sparkling with excitement. 'That'll be why the police have taken her computer off to analyse what's on it,' she said. 'That nice Linda said they'd got someone working on it already, but they've got to call in an expert who knows about astrology because a lot of it's in symbols and abbreviations they can't make head nor tail of.'

Another alley closed off to me. Out of the corner of my eye, I saw Ted emerge from the make-up caravan. Time for action, I thought. I didn't want Gloria left alone with anybody connected to *Northerners*, even someone as seemingly innocuous as Freddie from make-up. He was just finishing off painting Gloria's lips with Brenda's trademark pillar-box-red gloss as I walked in. 'Don't say a word,' he cautioned Gloria. 'I won't be a minute,' he added, frowning as he concentrated on getting the lipline just right. I closed the door behind me and leaned against the wall. 'There,' he said with a satisfied sigh. 'All done.'

Gloria surveyed herself critically in the mirror and said, 'Bloody hell, Freddie, that's the most you've said all morning.'

'We're all a bit subdued today, Gloria,' he said, sounding exhausted. 'It's hard not to think about what happened to Dorothea.'

Gloria sighed. 'I know what you mean, chuck.'

She leaned forward and patted his hand. 'It does you credit.'

'It's scary, though,' Freddie said, turning away with a tired smile and repacking his make-up box. 'I mean, chances are it's somebody we know who killed her. Outsiders don't wander around inside the NPTV compound. It's hard to imagine any of us killing someone who was more or less one of us.'

'The trouble is,' Gloria said, getting to her feet and pulling her coat on, 'that half of us are actors. Who the hell knows what goes on in our heads?'

Neither Freddie nor I could think of anything to say to that one. I followed her out the door and caught up with her and Ted at the edge of the car park. The director was explaining how he wanted them to circle round so that they could walk down the virgin snow of the path towards the camera. It looked like they were set for a while, but I didn't want to go back to the bus and leave Gloria exposed. It wasn't as if I could prevent an attack on her; but I hoped my presence would be enough to give her menacer pause.

I walked over to the catering bus, where Ross was working with a teenage lad I'd not seen before. 'I suppose a bacon butty would be out of the question?' I asked. 'I left the house too early for breakfast.'

Ross served me himself, piling crispy rashers into a soft floury roll. 'There you go. Coffee?' I nodded and he poured me a carton. 'Mind the shop a wee minute, son,' he said, coming out of the side door and beckoning me to join him. 'You got anything for me?' he asked.

I shook my head, my mouth full of food. 'I'm working on it,' I managed to mumble. 'Irons in the fire.'

'I was doing some thinking myself. You know, nobody knows more about what goes on behind the scenes of *Northerners* than Dorothea did. She had the inside track on everybody. She'd have been perfectly placed to be the mole,' he said eagerly.

'Handy for you,' I said cynically. 'What better way to get yourself off the hook than to blame a dead woman?'

His mouth turned down at the corners and his bright blue eyes looked baffled. 'That's a wee bit uncalled for. You know I liked Dorothea fine. It's just with her being in the news this weekend, I couldn't help remembering how she always had everybody's particulars at her fingertips. And she was never backwards about taking advantage of the press for her own purposes. That's all I was getting at.'

'I'm sorry,' I said. 'You might have a point. The only problem I can see is that Dorothea didn't have access to scripts, so she wouldn't have known the details of the future storylines, would she?'

Ross looked crestfallen, his shaggy red hair falling unheeded over his forehead. 'I suppose,' he said. 'I wasn't really thinking it through. My wife says I never do.'

Before I could say anything more, the bleat of my moby vibrated in my armpit. I unzipped my jacket and pulled it out. 'Hello?'

'All right, KB? Where are you?' It was Alexis, far brighter than she had any right to be on a Monday morning when she was the co-parent of a teething baby.

'Why?'

'I'm out and about making some calls and I thought we could link up. I've got a juicy bit of info for you, and you know how insecure the airwaves are these days. We've probably got half the world's press listening in at your end and the bizzies at mine. Are you down at NPTV?' she asked, her voice all innocence.

'Security be buggered,' I said. 'You just want to get alongside the *Northerners* cast to see how many exclusives you can dig up about Dorothea.'

A throaty chuckle turned into a cough. 'You got me bang to rights. Call it the quid pro quo.'

I wiggled my fingers at Ross. He took the hint and shambled back inside. 'I'm not actually at NPTV.' I told her where to find me. 'They've got some very basic security on the main entrance, but a devious old bag like you should have no problem with that.'

'They'll be laying out the red carpet for me, girl, just you wait and see. I won't be long, I'm only down the road in Salford.'

I cut across the car park at an angle, ploughing my feet through the dirty slush. It's just as much

216

fun at thirty-one as it is at five. I ended up over near the entrance, but still in a line of sight to Gloria. I was pretty certain by now that she was at no real risk, but being visible was what I was being paid for, so visible I'd be.

Alexis was as good as her word. Within ten minutes of our phone call, she drove authoritatively into the car park. The two elderly security men made a few futile gestures in a bid to get her to stop, but it's hard to argue with something as big as the Range Rover her and Chris had bought to combat the wild weather on the Pennines. Nobody else was interested. I'd soon realized that in a TV production unit, everybody's too busy with their own job to pay attention to anything else short of a significant thermonuclear explosion. That would make Cliff Jackson's job a lot harder. I couldn't resist a shiver of *schadenfreude* at the thought.

Alexis jumped down into the slush and took a few steps towards the security men. 'I'm with her,' I heard as her arm waved in my general direction. There was nothing wrong with her eyesight. 'Brannigan and Co,' she added, veering off towards me.

'You really are a lying get,' I said when she was close enough for them not to hear.

'Only technically,' she said. 'I am, after all, here on a mission on your behalf.'

'No, you're not, you're here entirely on a fishing expedition to net you tomorrow's front page. So what's this momentous news you have to impart?'

I glanced over my shoulder to make absolutely sure we couldn't be overheard.

'Does F. Littlewood mean anything to you? F. Littlewood of fifty-nine, Hartley Grove, Chorlton?'

I tried not to show that more bells were ringing and lights flashing inside my head than on the average pinball machine. The address was unfamiliar, but I had no trouble recognizing the name. Why was Freddie Littlewood the make-up artist betraying his colleagues so viciously and comprehensively? What could he possibly have to gain? And how did he obtain the intimate details of people's past secrets? I'd already seen how casually Gloria let slip information to the charming Freddie, but I couldn't believe her fellow stars would have readily revealed most of the *Northerners* scandals. Alexis had done me a favour, but in the process she'd given me a headache.

I found a pen and notepad in my bag and got Alexis to write down Freddie's address. 'You're sure this is the mole?' I asked.

'This is the person who got paid for the story about you bodyguarding Gloria,' she said cautiously. 'More likely than not, that's your mole. I finally got my hands on the credits book this morning, and that didn't take me a whole lot further forward. What it is, you see, sometimes we need to make irregular payments to regular sources who need to be protected. So then we use code names. The very fact that this Littlewood person has a code name means he or she has done this before.'

'So how did you get from the code name to the identity?' I asked. It wasn't important, but I'm a sucker for other people's methods. I'm not such an old dog that I can't learn new tricks.

Alexis winked. 'There's this cute little baby dyke in accounts. She thinks being a reporter is seriously the business. She thinks my new haircut is really cool.'

I groaned. Forget the new tricks. 'And does she also know you're happily married?'

'Let the girl have her dreams. Besides, it made her day to tell me that The Mask is F. Littlewood. Whoever he or she is?'

I shook my head. 'That's for me to know and you to find out.'

'Oh, I will, believe me. This isn't soft news any more. It's crime, and that's my business. If the newsdesk won't share, I'll just have to help myself.' Alexis cupped her hands round a cigarette and lit it. She breathed a smoky sigh of satisfaction. 'God, I love the first cigarette of the day. If you need more leverage, by the way, we've paid F. Littlewood five times in the last year. I checked out the back numbers and they were all *Northerners* stories. I'd bet it's the same mole selling the stories to the nationals, because all the ones we've had have either been local interest only or time sensitive. Except for the one about you and Gloria, interestingly enough.' Alexis's eyes were flickering round the car park and over towards the distant shrubberies. She'd done her duty and now she was sniffing the air for her story. 'You going to tell me who this Littlewood character is?' she asked, not really expecting an answer.

'Just be grateful I've not shopped you. Thanks, Alexis.'

'No problem.' She was already on the move. 'Hang in there, KB. Jackson's so busy getting his knickers in a twist about his missus that he's not got a fucking clue who to arrest. So there's plenty of room for glory.'

I watched her trudge through the snow, the ultimate bulldog when it came to stories. Which reminded me that I had to see a woman about a dog. I checked my watch. Chances were that Ruth would be in court. I decided to call her mobile and leave a message with the answering service. 'Ruth, it's Kate,' I said. 'Can you check for me if Dennis shows any signs of having been in a ruck with Pit Bull's pit bull? Or if the pit bull shows any signs of having been in a ruck with person or persons unknown? I'm ashamed to say it was Debbie's idea rather than mine, but it's worth pursuing.'

The second call was to Detective Chief Inspector Della Prentice of the Regional Crime Squad's fraud task force. She should have been Detective Superintendent by now, but a sting I'd set up with her had gone according to someone else's script and Della was still scraping the egg off her face. I knew she didn't blame me, but if anything, that made it worse. Sometimes I looked round the table on our girls' nights out and wondered how Alexis,

Ruth, Della and two or three of the others put up with the fact that one way or another I'd exploited each and every one of them and managed to drop most of them in the shit along the way. Must be my natural charm.

I tracked her down in a building society office in Blackpool. She sounded genuinely pleased to hear me, but then she was working her way through a balance sheet at the time. 'I doubt you're having a more pleasant time than I am,' she said. 'I see from the papers that you and Cliff Jackson are too close for comfort again.'

'Being on the same land mass as Jackson is too close for comfort. Especially at the moment. Did you hear about his wife?'

'Even in Blackpool,' she said drily.

'You should rescue that Linda Shaw from his clutches. She's got the makings of a good copper, but he gives her the shit work every time and sooner or later she's going to get bored with that.'

'We'll see. My sources tell me that my promotion's likely to come through soon,' Della said. It sounded like a nonsequitur, but I figured she was trying to tell me that she was slated for a senior post in the Greater Manchester force. And that Linda might not be Jackson's gofer much longer.

'I can't tell you how relieved that makes me feel. I'm buying the champagne that night.'

'I know,' Della said without bitterness. 'So what's the favour?'

'Does there have to be a favour,' I asked, wounded.

'In working hours, yes. You never ring up for a gossip between nine and five.'

'You know about Dennis?'

'What about Dennis? I've been stuck in Blackpool since Thursday. I'm praying the snow keeps off so I can get home tonight. What's Dennis done this time?'

'For once, it's what he's not done.' I gave her a brief rundown. 'I've got a hunch that's so far off the wall I'm not even prepared to tell you what it is,' I said.

'What is it you need?'

'A look at the scene-of-crime photos. I don't know any of the team working the case, otherwise I'd ask. The boss cop's a DI Tucker.'

'I know Tucker's bagman. He did a stint with me at fraud before he was made up to sergeant. I expect I can persuade him he owes me one. I'll try and sort something out this evening, provided I can get back to Manchester,' she promised. I grovelled, she took the piss, we said goodbye.

I automatically scanned the car park, clocking Alexis over by the chuck wagon. She was leaning on the counter, steam rising from the cup of coffee in her hand, deep in conversation with Ross and a couple of the younger cast members who had braved the cold in search of a free bacon butty. I didn't envy their chances of escaping the front page of the next day's *Chronicle*.

I drifted back across the churned-up slush to where Ted and Gloria were rounding some bushes and walking into shot, their body language shouting 'argument' at the top of its voice. At the same moment, I heard a commotion behind me. I swung round to see Cliff Jackson loudly lecturing a PA that he was a police officer and this was a public car park and she was in no position to tell him where to stand.

The director's head swung round. 'Jesus Christ!' she yelled. 'And cut. Who the fuck do you think you are?' she demanded.

'Detective Chief Inspector Jackson of Greater Manchester Police. I'm here to interview Ms Gloria Kendal.'

'Are you blind? She's working.'

Nothing was calculated to make Jackson's hackles rise faster than anyone who thought the law didn't apply to them. 'You can't seriously imagine that your television programme takes precedence over a murder investigation? I need to talk to Ms Kendal, so, if you don't mind, you'll just have to rearrange your filming schedule to accommodate that.'

Gloria and Ted had reached us by now. 'Accommodate what?' she demanded crossly. She was clearly not thrilled with the prospect of shooting the snow scene again.

'As I've just explained to your director here, I'd be obliged if you would accompany me to the police station for a further interview,' Jackson barked. He clearly wasn't star struck like Linda Shaw.

Gloria gave me a panic-stricken look. 'I don't want to,' she protested.

Time for my tuppenceworth. 'You don't have to. Not unless he's arresting you. If you want him to interview you here, that's your right.'

Jackson rounded on me. 'You're still here? I thought I told you to butt out of this investigation?'

'When you pay my wages you can give me orders,' I said mutinously. 'My client does not wish to accompany you to the police station, as is her right. She is willing to talk to you here, however. Do you have a problem with that, Inspector?'

Jackson looked around him. 'There's nowhere here to conduct an interview,' he said contemptuously.

Seemingly out of nowhere, Alexis loomed up at his elbow. 'I wouldn't say that, Mr Jackson. I've been doing interviews all over the place. Is there some kind of problem here? Is somebody being arrested?'

'What the hell is the press doing here?' Jackson exploded.

'Press?' the director yelped. 'Suffering Jesus, this is supposed to be a closed set. Security!' she bellowed. She pointed at Alexis. 'You, out of here.' Then she turned to Jackson. 'The same goes for you. Look, we've got a people carrier over there.

Plenty of room in that. All of you, just fuck off out of my sight, will you?'

Gloria started walking towards the big eight-seater van as two uniformed security guards appeared to escort an unprotesting Alexis back to her car. 'Come on, Kate,' Gloria called over her shoulder. 'I'm not talking to him without you there.'

'She's got no right,' Jackson protested. 'You're not a lawyer, Brannigan.'

I shrugged. 'Looks like you get to talk to Gloria with me present, or you don't get to talk to Gloria at all. She is one determined woman, let me tell you.'

I watched Jackson's blood pressure rise. Then he turned abruptly on his heel and stalked past Gloria towards the people carrier. She followed more slowly and I brought up the rear with Linda Shaw. 'I thought Gloria was off the hook,' I said mildly.

Linda pursed her lips. Then, so quietly I could have believed I was imagining things, she said, 'That was before we knew about the motive.'

15

PLUTO IN VIRGO IN THE 5TH HOUSE

She is critical, both of herself and others. She is driven to seek the answers to the world's problems and has an analytical mind which she uses in her pitched battles against injustice. She has a great appetite for life, enjoying a vigorous lust in her sexual relationships.

From *Written in the Stars*, by Dorothea Dawson

I'd barely absorbed the impact of Linda Shaw's bombshell when she delivered the double whammy. 'Or the fingerprints on the murder weapon,' she added. There was no time for me to find out more; we'd reached the people carrier by then. Funny, I'd never suspected her of sadism before.

Gloria had already climbed into the front row of rear seats and Jackson, predictably, was in the driving seat. I went to sit next to Gloria, but Linda put a hand on my arm and motioned me into the back row before she slid into place next to my client. 'I've already told you everything I know,' Gloria started before the doors were even closed. Bad move.

'I don't think so,' Jackson said brusquely, twisting round to face us. I had a moment's satisfaction at the sight of a painful razor rash along the line of his collar. Couldn't happen to a nicer bloke.

'I didn't kill her. She was still alive when I left her.'

'You had reason to want her dead, though.' Jackson's words seemed to materialize in the cold air, hanging in front of us like a macabre mobile.

'I beg your pardon, I never did,' Gloria protested, her shoulders squaring in outrage.

Jackson nodded to Linda, who took out her notebook and flipped it open. 'We've had a statement from a Mr Tony Satterthwaite –'

'That vicious scumbag?' Gloria interrupted. 'You're not telling me you wasted your time listening to that no-good lying pig?'

'Your ex-husband has been extremely helpful,' Jackson said smoothly, nodding again at Linda.

'Mr Satterthwaite was distressed by Ms Dawson's death, not least because, according to him, it was his affair with her that precipitated the end of your marriage.'

I remembered that line about backbenchers resembling mushrooms because they get kept in the dark except when someone opens the door to shovel shit on them. I knew just how they felt. I glared at Gloria. She stared open-mouthed

227

—at Linda. It was the first time I'd ever seen her stuck for something to say.

'He suggested that you had never really forgiven Ms Dawson for the affair, and that you were, and I quote, "the sort of devious bitch who would wait years to get her own back". We'd be very interested in your comments, Ms Kendal,' Linda said coolly.

'You don't have to say a thing, Gloria,' I said hurriedly.

'What? And let them go on thinking there's a word of truth in what that money-grubbing moron says? My God,' she said, anger building in her voice, 'you lot are gullible. I dumped Tony Satterthwaite because he was an idle leech. He couldn't even be bothered to look further than his own secretary when he decided to have a bit on the side. Even though she looked like Walter Matthau. He never even met Dorothea, never mind had an affair with her. I'd kicked him out a good six months before she first turned up at *Northerners*.'

'So why would he tell us a pack of lies?' Jackson sneered.

'Because if he saw a chance to give me a bad time, he'd not let it go past him,' Gloria said bitterly. 'Especially if he could see a way of turning it into a moneyspinner. You can bet your bottom dollar that the next call he made after he spoke to you was to the *Sun* or the *Mirror*. You've been had, the both of you. What you don't realize is that if he had been having an affair with Dorothea, I'd have bought her a magnum of champagne for giving me a twenty-four-carat reason for ditching the sod. Ask my daughter. Ask anybody that was around me then. They'll tell you the same.' She snorted. 'Tony Satterthwaite and Dorothea? Don't make me laugh. Apart from anything else, Dorothea had a hell of a lot more taste than to get between the sheets with a snake like Tony.'

'You married the man,' Jackson pointed out.

'Everybody's entitled to one mistake,' Gloria snapped back. 'He were mine. Let me tell you, you'll not find a single person can back up his tale and there's a good reason for that.'

Linda and Jackson exchanged a look that said they both knew they were backing a loser here. I wasn't so sure. I'd seen how well Gloria acted off screen. But even if the tale of the affair was true, I couldn't see Gloria nursing her bitterness for all those years. She was far too upfront for that. If she'd had a bone to pick with Dorothea, it would have been lying bleached in the sun a long time since.

'At the end of the day, we don't have to prove motive in a court of law,' Jackson pointed out. 'Most people think detectives have to prove means, motive and opportunity. But we don't. All we need is evidence. And we've got evidence against you. There's circumstance – you're the last person known to have seen her alive, and more often than not the last person to see a victim alive is also the first person to see them dead.'

I opened my mouth to speak and he waved a hand at me. 'You'll get your say in a minute. Let me finish first. But we've got more than that, Gloria. We've got fingerprints. To be precise, we've got your fingerprints on the murder weapon.'

There was a long silence. Gloria stared impassively at Jackson, then lit a cigarette with a hand that showed no tremor. 'The crystal ball?' she asked.

His smile was as thin as the line of the new moon. 'The crystal ball,' he confirmed.

It was obviously my week for fingerprints. All I needed now was for one of DI Tucker's merry band to find Gloria's prints inside Dennis's shop and then I could swap client for buddy behind bars. Then something occurred to me. 'Excuse me, but I don't remember anyone taking my client's fingerprints. Where exactly has the comparison set come from?' I asked belligerently.

Linda's eyes widened and I could see her forcing her body not to react. Jackson scowled. 'That's neither here nor there. Take my word for it, the prints on the murder weapon are a perfect match for Gloria's here.'

I shook my head. 'You'll have to do better than that.' I glanced at my watch. 'Otherwise I'm going to call Ruth Hunter and get this whole shooting match on the record. And I don't have to tell you how much Ruth hates having her lunch interrupted.' I knew the last thing Jackson wanted now was to get to the 'lawyers at dawn' stage. He was relying on Gloria being confident enough to think she could handle this alone, and even with me along to stick a spoke in his wheel, he still thought he was the one holding all the cards. You'd think he'd have known by now. 'So where did you get a verified set of my client's prints?' I demanded again.

'You gave her a glass of water in the green room on Friday night when we had our initial interview,' Linda said. Jackson glared at her, but he must have known they'd reached the point of put up or shut up.

'And you helped yourself to it after we left,' I said, shaking my head in a pretence of sorrow at their deviousness. 'So how do you know it's not my prints on the murder weapon?'

Linda allowed herself a small moment of triumph. 'Because you were still wearing your leather gloves.'

OK, so I'd forgotten. I didn't think Gloria was going to sue me. At least the conversation had provided enough of a diversion for my client to pull herself together. 'Of course my fingerprints were on the crystal ball,' she said. All three of us turned to stare at her.

'Gloria,' I warned, stifling a momentary panic that she was about to confess.

'It's all right, chuck. There's a simple explanation.'

My favourite kind.

'I'd just had a consultation, hadn't I? I'd been sat opposite Dorothea, with my fingertips touching the crystal ball. That's what we always did. I suppose she did it with everybody, but she must have buffed it up between times because it was always sparkling, that crystal. She'd lay her fingertips on one side and I'd match her on the other side. To form a psychic bond,' she added, as if stating the obvious.

I grinned. Usually when I'd been present to watch Jackson get shafted, I was the one doing the shafting, which meant the pleasure was always tinged with a degree of apprehension. This time, the delight was entirely unadulterated. Jackson looked like a man whose cat just ate his prize canary.

'I bet it was just my fingertips on that crystal ball, wasn't it? Not my whole hand,' Gloria said. She sounded as if she was half teasing, half scolding a naughty schoolboy. 'You've been trying to get me going, haven't you? You've been stretching the truth to try and get me to confess.' She wagged her finger at him. 'I don't like people that think they're smart enough to get clever with me. Brenda Barrowclough might have come up the ship canal on a bike, but I'm not so daft. I'm not talking to you again, Mr Jackson, not without I've got my solicitor with me.'

'I can't believe you tried that on, Jackson,' I said. 'Wait till Ruth Hunter hears about this. You better thank your lucky stars that you didn't drag us down the nick for this bag of crap.'

Jackson turned dark red, his eyes narrowing as I'd seen them do too many times before. Just before the geyser of his rage erupted over us, the door behind him jerked open, nearly tipping him backwards towards the slushy car park.

John Turpin stepped back, not prepared to stand between Jackson and a nasty fall. At the last minute, Jackson grabbed the steering wheel and hauled himself back into the seat. 'Jesus,' he exclaimed. 'You nearly had me on the floor there, Mr Turpin.'

Turpin's broad face was wearing a scowl that matched most of the tales I'd heard about him. 'I'm very disappointed in you,' he said, his voice as sharply clipped as a topiary peacock. 'I had thought we'd reached an accommodation. We've bent over backwards for you and your team. We've given you space to work in, we've offered you full access to our site and to all NPTV staff. The one thing I asked was that you didn't disrupt filming.' He shook his head sorrowfully.

Jackson was at a major disadvantage, stuck in the van seat well below Turpin's superior height. 'I'm conducting a murder inquiry,' he retorted, pushing himself clear of the steering wheel and out into the car park. He was still four inches shorter than Turpin, but that didn't seem to worry him. 'When evidence presents itself, I have to act on it. I said we'd do our best not to disrupt your filming schedules, but as far as I'm concerned, better your film crew stands about idle than a murder suspect slips through the net.'

Turpin snorted and jerked his thumb at Gloria. 'That's your murder suspect?' he said, his voice a suppressed laugh. 'My God, man, you must be grasping at straws. This is the woman who's so timid she's hired a private detective because she's had some hysterical hate mail. Even if she had the nerve to commit murder, I don't think she'd be doing it when she's got a minder on her tail. Unless of course you think Gloria hired Brannigan and Co to commit murder for her?' I couldn't repress my smile. Linda broke into a spasm of tactical coughing, but Jackson couldn't see the funny side. He probably thought Turpin's sarcastic suggestion was a promising line of inquiry. 'It wouldn't have hurt to have waited for a natural break in filming. I mean, she's hardly dressed to go on the run, wearing Brenda Barrowclough's wig,' the TV executive continued with genial sarcasm. 'Did you think she was going to take a cameraman hostage with her handbag?'

'This is a police inquiry,' Jackson said obstinately. 'Only the case dictates the timetable I work to.'

Turpin gave Jackson a thoughtful look. When he spoke, his voice had a kindly tone at odds with his words. 'The press is always interested in anything that affects *Northerners* and this company is a notoriously leaky sieve. You might think your murder investigation is the most important thing in this city, but there are far more people interested in the outcome of Monday night's episode of *Northerners* than in who killed some stargazing charlatan. You might want to think about how dumb you could be made to look by some news-hungry journalist.'

Without waiting for a reply, Turpin bent forward, head and shoulders into the van, forcing Jackson to step hastily aside, with the cavalier lack of concern most big men display.

'Gloria, my dear,' he said coldly. 'Time to earn your grossly inflated salary. Mustn't keep Helen waiting, must we?'

Gloria squared her shoulders, gathered her coat around her and made a nimble exit. 'Ta-ra, Linda, chuck,' she said, leaning back into the van. 'I won't be talking to you again without a lawyer, but I don't hold that sneaky trick with the glass against you. You were only doing your job, and we both know what it's like to work for complete shits, don't we?'

Turpin's stare was surprisingly malevolent. 'The people you have to deal with in this job,' he sighed, including us all in his comprehensive glower.

'Never mind,' I said sweetly. 'If NPTV sell out to cable or satellite, you'll be able to retire to the South of France on your profits.'

His calculating eyes made the snow look warm and welcoming. 'You really shouldn't believe actors' gossip,' he said. He turned on his heel, brushing past Jackson, and made for the catering truck. I didn't envy Ross if the coffee was stewed.

Jackson spun round to close the door, his face still scarlet with rage. It was clear he regarded my continued existence on the planet, never mind in his eyeshot, as pure provocation. Rather than wait to be arrested for behaviour likely to cause a breach of the peace, I slid along the seat and out of the opposite side of the van. Sometimes, bottling out is the sensible course of action.

I gave the catering van a wide berth too and trudged across to the knot of people round the director. Gloria and Ted were already heading back across the snow to begin their long tracking shot again. At this rate it was going to take all day to film one scene. I didn't have to be an accountant to work out why that would piss Turpin off, especially if he was obsessed with making the balance sheet look good to possible bidders for the show.

I switched my phone to mute, not wanting to risk the rage of the director if it rang during another take. When the shot was finally in the bag, I followed Gloria back to the wardrobe truck. While she changed back into her own clothes, I checked for messages. To my surprise, Della had called back already. I found a quiet and sheltered corner behind the make-up trailer and dialled her number. 'Good news,' she said.

'I could use some.'

'I'm on my way back to Manchester now. I managed to get hold of my contact, and he's meeting me around three in La Tasca. If you want to swing by there around half past three, I should have what you need.'

'And I can buy you both some tapas?' I said with resignation.

'Just me,' she said firmly. 'I'm not having you corrupting any more police officers.'

'As if. See you.' I hung up and checked my watch. If the roads were still as clear out in Saddleworth as they'd been earlier, I could get Gloria back home and still make it to the tapas bar in time for my meeting with Della.

Forty minutes later, outside my house, I handed Gloria's car keys to a nervous Donovan. 'Do I have to stay over?' he asked, glancing apprehensively at Gloria who was giving him flirtatious waves and winks through the windscreen.

'She's got no personal appearances this evening, but she wants to visit her daughter for dinner. I'd like you to drive her there and take her home afterwards. I've told her I think she's in no danger and she should pay us off, but she's adamant that she wants us to carry on.'

'She's after my body, more like,' he grumbled.

'You should be so lucky. I think pretending she's trying to get into your knickers is a more acceptable motive to her than admitting she's scared shitless. Just because she doesn't like doing vulnerable doesn't mean she's not afraid,' I told him. 'So it might not be a bad thing if you do stay over. It also saves me having to drive to Saddleworth in arctic conditions at the crack of sparrowfart, and if

I was you, I'd be happy to store up a few Brownie points with the boss.'

He grinned. 'You going to tell my mum, then?'

Suckered again. 'I'll tell her. At least you're not going to get arrested for taking care of Gloria.'

He didn't look as if he thought it was much of a consolation. I waved them off, then walked across to Upper Brook Street and caught a bus down to Deansgate. Even public transport was better than trying to get into town and parked legally when the snow was falling three weeks before Christmas. I ducked into the steamy warmth of La Tasca with five minutes to spare. I was glad Della had suggested it; with its wood panelling, nicotine-coloured paintwork and salsa music, it feels enough like the real thing to hold a Manchester winter in abeyance.

I spotted Della right away, sitting at a round table near the back. She was sitting with a young Asian bloke who I guessed was her former colleague, now DI Tucker's bagman. I helped myself to one of the tall wooden bar stools and ordered a Corona. It came with the obligatory slice of lime, which always made me feel like an amateur teenage drinker again, fourteen and down the pub with a half of lager and lime. These days, I need all the help I can get.

Ten minutes later, her companion left and I picked up my beer and threaded my way across the room. 'You look good,' I said, meaning it. Her copper hair had started to show a few silver strands, but somehow it only made it look richer. Her skin was still glowing from the month she'd just spent in Australia; the old shadows under her eyes hadn't reasserted themselves yet. A Cambridge-educated economist, Della had one of the most devious financial minds I'd ever encountered. Way too smart for the Serious Fraud Office, she'd carved out her own niche in the north, unrivalled when it came to unravelling the sordid chicanery of the sharks in sharp suits.

'You look knackered,' she said. 'Have some chorizo. I just ordered more prawns and the aubergine with grilled cheese.'

My mouth watered and I remembered how long it had been since breakfast. As I made uncouth sandwiches with French bread and the meltingly rich sausage, I filled Della in on my day. She winced at the encounter between Turpin and Jackson. 'I wouldn't like to be Linda Shaw this afternoon,' she said. She pushed a large manila envelope towards me as I finished the last of the chorizo. 'One set of crime-scene photographs. I've had a quick look myself, and I didn't see anything to excite me. But then, murder has never interested me much.'

I didn't bother opening them. There would be a better time and place soon. Besides, food was due any minute, and I didn't want to lose my appetite. 'Thanks.'

Della smiled. 'I said it might tie in with a long firm fraud I was working on, but I didn't want to go public on it yet, hence the unofficial request. I don't think he believed me, but I don't think he much cared. So, no big deal.'

'I owe you,' I said. I meant it; but what I owed Della was nothing compared to the debt Dennis would face if my hunch worked out. I couldn't wait to see his face when I told him he was in hock to a DCI.

16

SUN CONJUNCTION WITH URANUS

She has an independent, progressive and original mind, backed with a strong and forceful personality. Individuality is important to her and she thrives on breaking patterns. She can be a breath of fresh air or a devastating tornado. In the 5th house, friends will be important in helping her to secure success.

From *Written in the Stars,* by Dorothea Dawson

The gods had finally started to smile on me, I decided when I arrived at the office to find Shelley temporarily absent from her desk. Before she could emerge from the loo, I slipped into my old office where I found Gizmo hunched over one of the computers. I recognized the program he was running, a basic template for a computer-controlled security system for a medium-sized building split into a mix of large and small rooms. It looked like one of the privately owned stately homes whose owners had turned to us after we'd scored

241

a spectacular success in closing down a ring of specialist art thieves. It was a case that I didn't like thinking about, for all sorts of reasons, so I was more than happy to have Gizmo around to take care of that end of the business.

He grunted what I interpreted as a greeting. 'I've been thinking, Giz,' I said. 'I know you probably think I'm being paranoid, but if you're going ahead with a meeting with the cyberbabe . . .' I caught his warning look and hurriedly corrected myself. 'I mean Jan, sorry. If you're going to arrange a meeting with her, you should have somebody to cover your back. Just in case she turns out to be a nutter. Or the whole thing is some terrible set-up.'

He did that thing with his mouth that people use to indicate you might just have something. 'I guess,' he said. 'It'd have to be somebody I could trust. I don't want the piss taking out of me from now till next Christmas if it's a meltdown.'

'How about me?'

'You don't mind?'

I sat down and made meaningful eye contact. 'Gizmo, you need someone who can suss this woman out at a hundred yards. Your anorak friends would be about as much use as a cardboard barbecue. Besides, this is self-interest. The last thing I need right now is the human equivalent of the Pakistani Brain Virus eating up my computer genius. Just check the date and time with me, and I'm all yours.'

'Sound,' he said, his eyes already straying back to the screen.

'There is, of course, a price to pay,' I said.

He closed his eyes and raised his face towards the ceiling. 'Suckered,' he said.

I spread out the contents of the envelope Della had given me and explained what I wanted. 'It's a freebie,' I said. 'For Dennis. Can do?'

He scratched his chin. 'It won't be easy,' he said. 'I'll have to take it home with me. I don't have the software loaded here. But yeah, it should be doable. When do you need it for?'

'The sooner the better. The longer it takes you, the longer Dennis is going to be behind bars.'

He shuffled the photographs together, giving each one a glance as he fed them back into the envelope. 'I'm still working on the Dorothea information,' he said. 'I farmed one end of it out to a lad I know who's shit hot on adoption records. But there are some more avenues I can pursue myself. Which is the priority – this stuff or the Dorothea material?'

I had to think about it. All my instincts said that I should be pulling out all the stops to help Dennis. But whoever killed Dorothea might have other victims in mind so the sooner I got to the bottom of that can of worms, the better. Besides, I was being paid for finding out who had murdered the astrologer. If there had been only me to consider, the decision would have been easy. But being the boss isn't all about strutting your stuff in jackboots, especially with wages day approaching on horseback. 'Dorothea,' I said reluctantly.

Gizmo had the look kids get when they're told they can't play with the new bike until Christmas morning. 'OK,' he said. 'By the way, I think Shell wants a word.'

I bet she did. Short of abseiling out of the window, I didn't see how I was going to be able to avoid letting her have several. I took a deep breath and walked into the outer office. Shelley was sitting behind her desk. It looked as if she was balancing the cheque book, a manoeuvre I find slightly more daunting than walking the high wire. 'Hi, Shelley,' I said breezily. 'I'm glad you're back. I wanted to tell you Donovan will be doing an overnight, so you won't have to bother cooking for him tonight.'

If glares had been wishes, the genie would have been on overtime that day. 'I've been wanting to talk to you about my son,' Shelley informed me.

The words alone might not have seemed menacing, but the tone put them on a par with, 'Has the prisoner a last request?' Ever since she had her hair cut in a Grace Jones flat top, I've been expecting her to batter me. Sometimes when I'm alone, I practise responses to the verbal challenges I know she's storing up to use against me. It doesn't help.

I smiled and said brightly, 'Don's settling in really well, isn't he? You must be well proud of him.'

Her eyes darkened. I waited for the bolts of black lightning. 'I was proud of his A level results. I was proud when he made the North West schools basketball team. I was proud when he was accepted at Manchester University. But proud is not the word for how I feel when I find out my son's been arrested twice in the space of a week.'

'Ah. That.' I tried edging towards the door, but noticed in time that she'd picked up the paperknife.

'Yes, that. Kate, I've been against this right from the start, but I gave in because Donovan wanted so badly not to be dependent on me and not to get deep into debt like most of his student friends. And because you promised me you wouldn't expose him to danger. And what happens? My son, who has managed to avoid any confrontation with the police in spite of being black and looking like he can take care of himself, gets arrested twice.' She banged her fist on the desk three times, synchronizing with her last three words. I've watched enough natural history documentaries to understand the mother's passion for her young. I wondered whether I'd make it to the door before she could rip my throat out.

'You can't hold me responsible for police racism,' I tried.

'Suddenly it's a secret that the police are racist?' Shelley said sarcastically. 'I can hold you responsible for putting him in places where he's exposed to that racism.'

'We're working on a way to deal with that,' I

said, trying for conciliation. 'And the work he's doing tonight couldn't be less risky. He's protecting Gloria Kendal against a nonexistent stalker.'

Shelley snorted. 'And you don't think that's dangerous? I've seen Gloria Kendal, remember?'

Time for a different approach. 'Gimme a break here, Shelley. People pay money in encounter groups for the sort of experience Don's getting here. He's not complaining, and he's making good money. You've done a great job with him. He's solid as a rock. He can handle himself, he knows how to take responsibility, and it's all because he's your son. You should believe in him. And it's about time you let him go. He's a man now. A lot of lads his age are fathers. He's got more sense, and it's down to the way you've brought him up.'

Shelley looked astounded. I couldn't remember the last time I'd stood up to her like that either. We faced off for a good thirty seconds that felt more like minutes. 'His name's Donovan,' she said finally. 'Not Don.'

I nodded apologetically. 'I'm going home now,' I said. 'I need to have a bath and a think. I've done some background checks for Toronto and San Juan, I'll e-mail you the billing details.' I made for the door. On my way out, I turned back and said, 'Shelley – thanks.'

She shook her head and returned to the cheque book. We hadn't actually built a bridge, but the piers were just about in place.

*　　*　　*

I got home to two messages on the answering machine. Richard had called to tell me he'd be home around nine with a Chinese takeaway, which was more warning than I usually get from him. I'd been thinking about going round to Freddie Littlewood's to ask him why he was leaking such destructive stories to the press, but just for once, I was tempted to let pleasure beat business into second place. Richard and I hadn't had much time alone together lately, and the fact that he'd taken the trouble to phone ahead with his plans indicated he was missing it as much as I was. I decided to leave Littlewood until the morning.

The second message was from Cassie, asking me to call her when I could. She sounded concerned but not panicky, so I fixed myself a drink and ran a hot bath that filled the air with the heady perfume of ylang-ylang and neroli essential oils. I was determined to make the most of a night in with Richard. I slid into the soothing water and reached for the phone. Cassie picked up on the second ring.

'Thanks for getting back to me, Kate,' she said.

I could feel the water soothing me already. 'No problem. How can I help?'

'Well . . .' She paused. 'It could be something and nothing. Just a coincidence. But I thought you might be interested.'

'Fire away,' I said. 'I'm always interested in coincidence.'

'I've just had a reporter round. A freelance that

247

does a lot for the national tabloids. She was waving the cheque book, trying to get me to dish the dirt on Dorothea and the *Northerners* cast. Scraping the bottom of the barrel, I thought, but I suppose everybody who's still on the show has closed ranks. They'll have been warned, reminded that their contracts forbid them to talk to the press without the agreement of NPTV. So the hacks have to dredge through their contacts books to see if they can find anybody who might talk.'

'And because you sold your story at the time, they think you might be tempted to spill some more beans?'

'Exactly. But I said everything I was ever going to say back then. And that's what I told this reporter. The thing is, though, I recognized her name. Tina Marshall. It's her by-line that's been on most of the really big *Northerners* scandal stories. She's obviously somebody that has a direct relationship with the mole.'

'That's certainly worth knowing,' I said, trying to sound interested. I couldn't figure out why Cassie felt the need to phone me up to tell me something I could have worked out for myself. Discovering who the mole was talking to wasn't going to get me any further forward, not even if this Tina Marshall and Alexis went way back. No journalist, especially not a freelance, was going to give up a source who was the fountainhead of her bank balance.

'But that's not all I recognized,' Cassie continued. 'I recognized her face, too. A couple of months back, a friend of mine took me to dinner at the Normandie. Do you know it?'

I knew the name. Alexis and Chris always went there for their anniversary dinners. Alexis claimed it was one of the best restaurants in the region, but I wasn't likely to be able to verify that for myself as long as I stayed with a man who believes if it hasn't come from a wok it can't be food. 'Not personally,' I sighed.

'Well, it's not cheap, that's for sure. Anyway, when I went to the loo, I noticed this woman. I didn't know then that she was Tina Marshall, of course.'

I was sceptical. A quick glance in a restaurant a couple of months previously wasn't the sort of identification I'd want to base anything on. 'Are you sure?' I asked. The fragrant warmth had clearly activated my politeness circuit.

'Oh, I'm sure. You see, the reason I noticed her in the first place was her companion. She was dining with John Turpin.' Cassie mistook my silence for incredulity rather than stupefaction. 'I wouldn't make any mistake about Turpin,' she added. 'He's the bastard who gave me the bullet, after all. So seeing him wining and dining some woman in the kind of sophisticated restaurant where he's not likely to run into *Northerners* regulars was a bit like a red rag to a bull. I paid attention to the woman he was with. When she turned up this afternoon on my doorstep, I knew her right away.'

'Turpin?' I said, puzzled. The man had no possible motive for leaking stories about *Northerners* to the press, least of all to the woman who had plastered scandal after scandal over the nation's tabloids. I pushed myself up into a sitting position, trying not to drop the phone.

'Turpin. And Tina Marshall,' Cassie confirmed.

'Unless . . . he was trying to get her to reveal her source?' I wondered.

'It didn't look like a confrontation,' Cassie said. 'It was far too relaxed for that. It didn't have the feel of a lovers' tryst, either. More businesslike than that. But friendly, familiar.'

'You got all this from a quick glimpse on the way to the loo?' I asked doubtfully.

'Oh no,' Cassie said hastily. 'Turpin had been sitting with his back to me, but once I realized it was him, I kept half an eye on their table.' She gave a rueful laugh. 'Much to the annoyance of my companion. He wasn't very pleased that I was so interested in another man, even though I explained who Turpin was.'

'Did Turpin see you?' I asked.

'I don't think so. He was far too absorbed in his conversation.'

'I'm surprised Tina Marshall didn't clock you. Women check out other women, and you must have been familiar to her,' I pointed out.

'I look very different from my Maggie Grimshaw days,' Cassie said. 'Nobody stops me in the street any more. Thank God. And like I said, the Normandie

250

isn't the sort of place you'd expect the *Northerners* cast to be eating. It's not owned by a footballer or a rock star,' she added cynically. 'So, do you think there's something going on between them?'

I groaned. 'I don't know, Cassie. Nothing makes sense to me.'

'It's very odd, though.'

I was about to tell her exactly how odd I thought it was when my doorbell rang. Not the tentative, well-mannered ring of a charity collector, but the insistent, demanding, lean-on-the-bell ring that only a close friend or someone who'd never met me would risk. 'I don't believe it,' I moaned. 'Cassie, I'm going to have to go.' I stood up. It must have sounded like a whale surfacing at the other end of the phone.

'Are you OK?' she asked anxiously.

'Somebody at the door. Sorry. I'll call you when any of this makes sense. Thanks for letting me know.' As I talked, the phone tucked awkwardly between dripping jaw and wet shoulder, I was wrapping a bath sheet round me. I switched off the phone and drizzled my way down the hall.

I yanked the door open to find Gizmo on the doorstep. 'Hiya,' he said, not appearing to notice that I was wrapped in a bath sheet, my damp hair plastered to my head.

'What is *wrong* with the telephone, Gizmo?' I demanded. Remarkably restrained in the circumstances, I thought.

He shrugged. 'I was on my way home from

the office. You know, going home to sort out Dennis's little problem? And I thought you'd like to see what I found out about Dorothea's mysterious past.'

I shivered as a blast of wintry air made it past him. There goes snug, I thought. 'Inside,' I said, stepping back to let him pass. I followed him into the living room. 'This had better be good, Giz. I'd only just got in the bath.'

'Smells nice,' he said, sounding surprised to have noticed.

'It was,' I ground out.

'Any chance of a beer?' Spoken like a man who thinks 'considerate' is a prefix for 'done'.

'Why not?' I muttered. On the way, I collected my own glass and topped it up with the Polish lemon pepper vodka. I grabbed the first bottle that came to hand and relished the look of pained disgust that flashed across Gizmo's face when his taste buds made contact with chilli beer – ice-cold liquid with the breathtaking burn of the vengeful vindaloo that curry shops serve up to Saturday-night drunks. 'You were saying?' I asked sweetly, enjoying the sudden flush on his skin and the beads of sweat that popped out across his upper lip.

'Jesus, Mary and Joseph,' he gasped. 'What in the name of God was that?'

'I didn't know you'd been brought up Catholic,' I said. That should discourage him from the space-invading that was threatening to become a habit.

'It's a beer, like you asked for. Now, what did you want to tell me about?'

He fished inside his vast parka and produced a clear plastic wallet. Wordlessly, he handed it over. I took the few sheets of paper out of the sleeve and worked my way through them. By the time I reached the end, I knew when Dorothea had been born and who her parents were, when she'd married Harry Thompson and when they'd been divorced. I knew the date of Harry's death, and I knew the date of Dorothea's release from the mental hospital.

Most importantly, I knew who the mystery baby was. And I had more than the shadow of a notion why the relationship might have led to murder.

I opened my mouth to try out my idea on Gizmo. Of course, the phone rang. 'I don't believe this,' I exploded, grabbing the handset and hitting the 'talk' button. 'Hello?' I barked.

'It's me,' the familiar voice said. 'I'm in Oldham police station. I've been arrested.'

17

MOON TRINES MERCURY

She concentrates best on matters she's emotionally involved with. She expresses herself fluently and clearly and has a quick grasp of what is being said, easily picking up facts and drawing apt conclusions. Shrewd and intuitive, she sometimes lacks a sense of direction, shooting off in different directions at the same time. She has a good memory and is naturally inquisitive.

From *Written in the Stars*, by Dorothea Dawson

The desk sergeant at Oldham police station was obviously having about as good an evening as I was. His waiting area was clogged with hacks who'd heard there had been an arrest involving Gloria Kendal. Somewhere inside the station, the three photographers and two reporters were being treated as witnesses. Somewhere else, my part-time process-server and bodyguard was under arrest for breach of the peace and

254

assault. Berserk student batters mob-handed team of journos. Yeah, right.

I pushed my way through the representatives of Her Majesty's gutter press, waving an ineffectual hand against the cigarette smoke and wondering if force of numbers was the only reason why they were allowed to ignore the 'no smoking' notices that everybody else was told to obey. 'You're holding an employee of mine,' I said to the sergeant, trying to keep my voice down. 'His solicitor is on her way. I wonder if I might have a word with the arresting officer?'

'And you are?'

'Kate Brannigan.' I pushed a business card across the counter. 'Donovan Carmichael works for me. I think we can clear all this up very easily if you could arrange for me to talk to the arresting officer.'

He picked up the card as if it contained a communicable disease. 'I don't think so,' he said dismissively. 'We're very busy tonight.'

'I was hoping to reduce the burden of work on your officers,' I said, still managing sweetness. 'I'm sure there has been some misunderstanding. I don't know about you, Sergeant, but I hate paperwork. And just thinking about the amount of paperwork that a racism case against GMP would generate gives me a headache. All I want to do is chat to the arresting officer, explain one or two elements of the background that might show the evening's events in a different light. I really don't want to spend the next two years running up legal bills that your Chief Constable will end up paying.' I could feel the smile rotting my molars. For some reason, the desk sergeant wasn't smiling.

'I'll see what I can do,' he said.

That was clearly my cue to go and sit down. I just carried on smiling and leaning on the counter. 'I'll wait,' I said.

He breathed heavily through his nose and disappeared through a door behind the counter. One of the hacks casually wandered across to me and offered his cigarettes. 'I don't do suicide,' I said. 'Quick or slow.'

'Sharp,' he said, slotting in beside me at the counter with a swagger designed to show off his narrow hips and expensive suit. 'What's a spice girl like you doing in a place like this?'

'Just a little local difficulty to sort out,' I said. 'What about you? You don't look like Oldham Man to me.'

He couldn't resist. 'I'm a reporter.'

'Ooh,' I said. 'That sounds exciting. Who do you work for?'

I got the full CV, ending with the most notorious national tabloid. He shrugged his shoulders in his jacket, just to make sure I hadn't missed how gorgeous he was. In his dreams.

'Wow,' I said. 'That's impressive. So what's the big story tonight?'

'Are you a *Northerners* fan?' I nodded. 'You'll have read about Dorothea Dawson getting murdered on the set, then?' I nodded again. 'Well, a couple of my colleagues got a tip-off from the police handling the murder inquiry that Gloria Kendal's fingerprints were plastered all over the murder weapon.'

I couldn't believe what I was hearing. I had no doubts where this particular leak had come from. That bastard Jackson was getting his own back for being made to look a pillock first by me and Gloria and then by John Turpin. 'No!' I gasped, struggling to keep up the pretence in the teeth of my anger.

'I'm telling you, that's what we heard. So we send out a pic man and a reporter to Gloria's place, out in Greenfield. She comes out in the car, and our lads are standing at the entrance to her lane, just doing their jobs, trying to get a picture or a story. Then this big black lad comes jumping out of the car and weighs into our lads. One of the reporters calls the police, Gloria shoots off God knows where in the car, and the rest is history.'

'The bodyguard started it?' I couldn't keep the scepticism out of my voice.

My new friend winked. 'Five words against one. Who do you think the cops will believe?'

Not if I had anything to do with it they wouldn't. But before I could let him know what I thought of the credibility of the press, the door to the station swung open and Ruth sailed in like a Valkyrie on ice, her blonde hair loose for once, falling in a cascade over the silver fake fur. At once, the journalist forgot all about chatting me up and scuttled towards her. 'Ruth,' came the cry from several throats. 'Tell us what's going on!'

She swept past them, a snow leopard scattering fleas in her wake. 'Later, boys and girls, later. Let me at least speak to my client. Kate,' she greeted me, putting one arm round my shoulders and turning me so that we formed an impenetrable wall of backs as she pressed the button for the desk officer. 'You know I can't take you in with me?' she said, her voice low but audible against the clamour behind us.

'I know. But I want to talk to the arresting officer first, before you all get embroiled in interviews. I want him to know that if they charge Don, I'm filing a racial harassment suit first thing in the morning. I told you about their antics last week, didn't I?'

'Oh yes. I'm sure we're not going to have a problem with them.'

'It's Jackson that's behind this.' I told her briefly what I'd just learned. There was no time to discuss it further, for the desk officer reappeared.

'I'm Ruth Hunter,' she said. 'Here to see my client, Donovan Carmichael. His employer also has some relevant information to place before the arresting officer if you would be so good as to get him here?'

The desk man nodded to a door at the side of the reception area. 'He'll be right out.'

The journalists were still hammering us with questions when the door opened moments later.

The uniformed sergeant who emerged looked harried and hassled, his short red hair sticking out at odd angles as if he'd been running a hand through it. His freckles stood out like a rash on skin pallid with tiredness. 'Ms Brannigan?' he asked, looking at Ruth.

'I'm Ruth Hunter, Donovan's solicitor,' she said. A gentle shove in the small of my back propelled me towards the door. 'This is his employer.' Ruth continued her forward movement, sweeping all three of us back through the door and neatly closing it behind us. 'A moment of your time before I see my client, Sergeant?'

He nodded and led us into an interview room that looked freshly decorated but still smelled inevitably of stale smoke, sweat and chips. I think they buy it in an aerosol spray. 'I'm Sergeant Mumby,' he said, dropping into a chair on one side of the table. 'I'm told Ms Brannigan wanted a word.'

'That's right,' I said, glad I'd had the chance to forearm myself with information from the smoothie outside. 'I don't want this to sound threatening, but if you charge Donovan tonight, Ms Hunter's firm will be making a complaint of racial harassment against GMP. He's already been arrested twice in the last week for nothing more than being black in the wrong place. Now he's facing serious charges because five white people who were blocking my client's private road wouldn't get out of the way and they didn't like being told what to do by a young black lad. That's about the size of it, isn't it?'

He sighed. 'I've got five witnesses saying he came at them like a madman, pushing them and shoving them, and that he punched one of them in the back. Believe me, I sympathize with your point of view. When we turned up, it was all over bar the shouting. But Mr Carmichael had made no effort to get away from the scene. And he's actually the only one with any visible injury.'

I caught my breath. 'What happened?'

'Just a split lip. He says one of the photographers swung his camera at him; the photographer says Mr Carmichael tried to head butt him and the camera got in the way.'

I shook my head incredulously. 'This is outrageous. Some scummy paparazzo smacks Donovan in the face with a camera then turns round and says he started on them? And Don's the one facing charges? What has Gloria got to say about all this?'

The sergeant's lips compressed in a thin line. 'We've not been able to contact her yet.'

'I bet she'll have plenty to say. Not least about the fact that this whole thing happened because one of your colleagues decided to leak confidential evidence in a murder inquiry to the press. Evidence which has already been totally discredited,' I said bitterly.

Ruth leaned forward. 'There is, of course, one way to make all of this go away. You can let my client go without charge. Give him police bail if you must. He's not going anywhere. He's a student at Manchester University, he lives at home with his mother and sister, he has no criminal record and he has a part-time job with Ms Brannigan. I'm certain that once Ms Kendal has outlined the real course of events you'll realize the only charge that should be brought is one of wasting police time, and not against my client. What do you say, Sergeant? Shall we all have an early night?'

He rubbed a hand over his chin and cocked his head on one side. 'And if I do what you suggest, it'll be all over the papers that we let a black mugger walk free.'

'Probably,' Ruth agreed. 'But that's a story that will be history by the weekend, whereas a racial harassment action will rumble on for a very long time. Especially one that's supported by Gloria Kendal.'

'And the *Manchester Evening Chronicle*,' I added. 'Donovan's mother is a very close friend of the *Chronicle*'s crime correspondent, Alexis Lee. They love a good campaign at the *Chron*.'

He smiled, a genuine look of relief in his eyes. 'You talked me into it, ladies. Between ourselves, I never saw it the way the journalists were telling it. For one thing, a lad built like your client would have done a hell of a lot more damage if he'd had a serious go. But what can you do? You've got witnesses saying one thing and not much evidence pointing the other way. At least now I can let you take Mr Carmichael home secure in the knowledge that I've got good reasons to put in front of my inspector.' He got to his feet. 'If you'd just wait there a minute, I'll get it sorted.'

He left us alone to exchange gobsmacked looks. 'I'd always heard the police out here were a law unto themselves, but I didn't think that'd ever work in my favour,' I said faintly.

'I know,' Ruth said, sounding somewhat baffled. 'I must tell all my clients to make a point of getting arrested in Oldham.'

'I can't believe that scumbag Jackson,' I said.

'You'll never nail him on it. He'll have got one of his minions to do the dirty work. Go after Jackson and you'll probably end up with Linda Shaw's head on a stick.' Ruth leaned back in her seat and lit one of her long slim cigarettes. 'By the way, I made those inquiries you suggested about Pit Bull Kelly's dog. Dennis has no marks anywhere on his body that correspond to dog bites. And the dog himself showed no signs of having been in a fight. Care to tell me where this is going?'

'I've got Gizmo working on something. An idea I had. It came from a case I read about on the Internet a while back. An American case. I'd rather wait till I've got something concrete to show you, because it sounds so totally off the wall.'

Ruth gave me the hard stare, but she could see I wasn't going to budge. 'How long?'

'Probably tomorrow? I'll need you to set up a

meeting with DI Tucker. Preferably at my office. I'll let you know when I'm ready. Is that OK?'

'The sooner the better,' Ruth said. 'Normally, Dennis takes custody in his stride, but this time he's not handling it well. Probably because he's genuinely innocent,' she added drily.

The door opened and Sergeant Mumby stuck his head into the room. 'Your client's ready to leave now. I think the back way would be better, in the circumstances.'

I left Donovan climbing reverently into the Bentley, Ruth promising to drop him at his girl-friend's so we could avoid letting his mother know about his latest brush with the law. I looked at the dashboard clock and realized there was no point in going home. Richard would have eaten the Chinese; it takes more than irritation at being stood up to disturb his appetite. Then, if habit held, he'd have decided to show me how little he needed me by jumping a taxi back into town and partying the night away. I couldn't honestly blame him.

I sat in my car and rang the number Gloria had given me for her daughter's house. The voice that answered was familiar in its inflexions, but twenty years younger in its tones. 'I'm looking for Gloria,' I said. 'Can you tell her it's Kate?'

'Hang on, love, I'll just get her.'

Moments later, I heard the real thing. 'All right, chuck?'

'I am now,' I said severely. 'Now I've got Donovan out of jail.'

She chuckled. 'That poor lad's having a proper education, working for you. I knew you'd have it sorted in no time. Whereas if I'd hung around, it would just have got more and more complicated.'

'He got a smack in the mouth from a journalist's camera,' I said coldly.

There was a short pause, then, serious, she said, 'I'm really sorry about that. Is the lad OK?'

'He'll live. But the police need a statement from you, otherwise they're going to have to believe that bunch of scumbag hacks claiming Donovan set about them without any provocation.'

She gasped. 'Is that what they're saying?'

'What else do you expect paparazzi to be saying, Gloria? The truth?' I demanded sarcastically. 'They've got bosses on the newsdesk who aren't going to be well impressed if they tell them they didn't get a story or pictures because a teenage lad told them to bugger off. If they don't get a proper story, they make one up.'

'Aye well, at least you got it sorted,' she said, sounding chastened for once.

'It'll be sorted once you've given Sergeant Mumby a statement and half his colleagues an autograph. Now, are you staying at your daughter's tonight?'

'I better had, I suppose. And I'm not filming tomorrow, so I'll probably take her shopping.'

'Not in town,' I said firmly.

'Harvey Nicks, chuck,' she said. 'In Leeds. I'll bell you in the morning once we've decided what's what. Thanks for sorting it all out, Kate.'

264

The line went dead. Nothing like a grateful client. Given that the wheels were well and truly off my evening, I figured I might as well go for broke and see what Dorothea Dawson's child had to say about her murder. It was, after all, what I was being paid for. I drove through the virtually deserted streets of Oldham, south through Ashton, Audenshaw and Denton, past rows of local shops with peeling paint, sagging strings of dirty Christmas lights, sad window displays and desperate signs trying to lure customers inside; past the narrow mouths of terraced streets where people sprawled in front of gas fires denying the winter by watching movies filled with California sunshine; past down-at-heel pubs advertising karaoke and quiz nights; past artificial Christmas trees defiant in old people's homes; past churches promising something better than all of this next time round in exchange for the abandonment of logic.

It was a relief to hit the motorway, hermetically sealed against the poverty of the lives I'd driven past. Tony Blair said a lot about new Labour giving new Britain new hope before he was elected; funny how nothing's changed now he's in power. It's still, 'get tough on single mums, strip the benefit from the long-term unemployed, close the mines and make the students pay for their education.'

I cruised past Stockport, admiring the huge glass pyramid of the Co-op Bank, glowing neon green and indigo against the looming redbrick of the old mills and factories behind it. It had stood empty for years, built on spec in the boom of the Thatcher years before the Co-op had rescued it from the indignity of emptiness. I bet they'd got a great deal on the rent; wish I'd thought of it.

I took the Princess Parkway exit, almost the only car on the road now. Anyone with any sense was behind closed doors, either home writing Christmas cards or partying till they didn't notice how cold it was outside while they waited for the taxi home. Me, I was sitting in my car opposite the other deadheads in the vast expanse of the Southern Cemetery. Only one of us was using the *A-to-Z*, though.

The street I was searching for was inevitably in the less seedy end of Chorlton, one of those pleasant streets of 1930s semis near the primary school whose main claim to fame is the number of lesbian parents whose children it educates. To live comfortably in Chorlton, you need to have a social conscience, left-of-centre politics and an unconventional relationship. Insurance salesmen married to building society clerks with two children and a Ford Mondeo are harder to find around there than hen's teeth.

The house in question was beautifully maintained. Even in the dead of winter, the garden was neat, the roses pruned into symmetrical shapes, the lawn lacking the shaggy uneven look that comes from neglecting the last cut of autumn. The stucco on the upper storey and the gable gleamed in the streetlight, and the stained glass in the top sections of the bay window was a perfect match for the panel in the door. Even the curtain linings matched. I walked up the path with a degree of reluctance, knowing only too well the kind of mayhem I was bringing to this orderliness.

Sometimes I wish I could just walk away, that I wasn't driven by this compelling desire for unpicking subterfuge and digging like an auger into people's lives. Then I realize that almost every person I care about suffers from the same affliction: Richard and Alexis are journalists, Della's a detective, Ruth's a lawyer, Gizmo's a hacker, Shelley's never taken a thing at face value in all the years I've worked with her. Even Dennis subjects the world around him to careful scrutiny before he decides how to scam it.

The need to know was obviously too deeply rooted in me to ignore. Sometimes it even seemed stronger than the urge for self-preservation. Driven as I was by the prospect of finding out what lay behind the string of recent strange events, I had to remind myself that I might be knocking on the door of a murderer. It wasn't a comfortable thought.

I took a deep breath and pressed the bell. A light went on in the hall, illuminating me with green and scarlet patterns from the stained glass. I saw a dark shape descend the stairs and loom towards me. The door opened and Dorothea Dawson's genetic inheritance stood in front of me. I should have seen it, really. The features were so similar.

'Hi,' I said. 'I've come for a chat about your mum.'

18

Freddie Littlewood blinked rapidly, dark eyes glittering. His thin lips twitched. It was hard to tell if he was furious or on the point of tears. I figured he was deciding whether to brazen it out or to deny all knowledge of what I was talking about. It was possible, after all, that I was only guessing. 'My private life is no concern of yours,' he said eventually, sitting firmly on the fence.

I sighed. 'That's where you're wrong, Freddie.

I'm very concerned with the relationship between you and Dorothea. The nature of my concern rather depends on whether you killed her or not. If you did, it puts my client in the clear and it probably means Gloria isn't the next target of a killer. If you didn't, you can probably tell me things that would help me to protect her. Either from false accusation or from murder. So my concern is legitimate.'

'I've nothing to say to you,' he said, closing the door in my face.

I hate bad manners. Especially when it's late and there are almost certainly more interesting things I could be doing with my time. I took out my mobile phone and pushed open the letterbox. 'The police don't know Dorothea was your mother.' I started to press numbers on the phone, hoping the beeping was evident on the other side of the door. 'Want me to tell them now?'

Before I could have pressed the 'send' button if I'd been serious, the door opened again. 'There's no need for this,' Freddie snapped. 'I didn't kill Dorothea. That's all you need to know. And it's all you're getting from me. I don't care if you tell the police she was my birth mother. It's not like it was news to me. I've known for ages, and I can prove it. Even the police aren't stupid enough to take that as a motive for murder.' He was probably right. The bitterness in his voice spelled motive to me, but acrimony's never been grounds for arresting someone.

I leaned against the doorjamb and smiled. 'Maybe so. But if you factor in the stories you've been selling to the papers, the picture looks very different. Intimate details that people have revealed to Dorothea, spiced with the snippets you've picked up, that's what's been tarted up in the tabloids. Maybe Dorothea decided she didn't need a partner any more?'

His eyes widened and he flashed a panicky glance to either side of me, as if checking whether I was alone. 'You're talking rubbish,' he said, his voice venomous.

I smiled. 'Have it your own way. But you didn't get paid in cash. Somewhere there's a paper trail. And one thing the stupid old plod is very good at is following a paper trail. Freddie, if what you're saying is true, and you didn't kill Dorothea, I've got no axe to grind with you. John Turpin isn't paying me to find out who the *Northerners* mole is.' I refrained from mentioning that Ross Grant might be. There was no point in complicating things that were already difficult. 'All I'm interested in is protecting Gloria. You *like* Gloria, for God's sake, I know you do. I've seen the way you are with her. Can we not just sit down and talk about this? Or do I have to blow your life out of the water with NPTV as well as the cops?'

One side of his mouth lifted in a sneer. 'Gloria said you were smart,' he said, opening the door wide enough to let me enter. He shooed me ahead of him into a small square dining room. There was an oak table with four matching chairs, all stripped back to the bare wood, oiled and polished till they gleamed in the soft glow of opalescent wall lights. A narrow sideboard in darker oak sat against the far wall. The only decoration came from the vibrant colours of the Clarice Cliff pottery ranged along a shelf that ran round the room at head height. If it was genuine, selling the collection would have bought him a year off work. Freddie waved me to a chair and sat down with his back to the door.

'How did you find out she was my birth mother?' he asked.

I raised one shoulder in a shrug. 'There's not much a good hacker can't find out these days. How did you find out?'

He ran his thumb along the sharp line of his jaw in a curious stropping gesture. 'A mixture of luck and hard work,' he said. 'The first time I got into a serious relationship, when I was in my twenties, I decided I wanted to know where I'd come from. It hadn't seemed important before, but the idea of being with someone long term, maybe even having kids with them, made me curious. I searched the records, and found out my father was already dead. Killed by a heart attack.' He gave a bitter cough of laughter. 'Not bad for a heartless bastard. I carried on looking and I discovered my mother was Dorothea Thompson, née Dawson. But the trail went cold.' His eyes were alert, never leaving my face. I suspected he was watching for any signs that he was breaking new ground, revealing things I didn't already know.

'I know about the breakdown,' I said. 'Was that where the trail petered out?'

He nodded. 'She was released from the hospital still using her married name, and she disappeared without trace. I found a cousin, the only other member of the family still alive, but he had no idea what had happened to her. The only useful thing I got from him was a copy of her wedding picture. I even hired one of your lot, but he never found her. Then one day I was sitting in the staff canteen at NPTV and Edna Mercer walked in with her latest fad. It was like someone took my stomach in their fist and squeezed it tight. I didn't need to hear her name to know who she was. That was just confirmation of what I knew the minute I saw her face. All those years later, she was still the spitting image of her wedding picture.'

'But you didn't rush across the room and reveal you were her long-lost son.'

He gave a twisted smile. 'When I started out looking for my past, I don't think I'd thought it through. In a way, it was almost a relief not to have found her. You see, I blamed her. My childhood was a nightmare. I never knew what it was to be held with love. I was bullied because I was small. I was beaten black and blue by one sadistic bitch of a foster mother because I was still wetting the bed when I was seven. I was gang-raped in a children's home when I was eleven by three older boys and

273

a so-called care worker. I never got to choose my own clothes or my own toys. I was supposed to be grateful for what I was given. I never even got to keep my own name. My father changed it by deed poll before he dumped me.' He stopped, apparently choking on the bile of memory.

I couldn't think of anything to say that wasn't offensively trite. My childhood was breathtaking in its comforting and confident normality. When I'd fallen over, there had been someone there to pick me up and stick a plaster on my knee. I'd fallen asleep with stories, not nightmares. There had always been arms to hold me and faces to reflect pride in my achievement. I could barely imagine the yawning gap of such an absence, never mind the agony of having it filled with such poisonous viciousness. 'You must have come to hate her,' I said, surprised by the huskiness of my voice.

He shifted in his chair so his face was obscured by shadow, his spiky hair emphasized in a dark fragmented halo. With his black polo neck and black trousers, he looked like a satanic ghost. 'I wanted to make her life a misery too,' he said. 'I wanted her to understand something about the pain and misery she'd given me.'

'I don't think she had a lot of choice in the matter.'

'More choice than I did,' he blazed back at me. 'She could have come looking for me. It couldn't have been that hard to find a child in care. But she made the decision to leave me in whatever hell I happened to be in.'

In the silence that swallowed his outburst, I thought of how it must have been for Dorothea. Tainted with the stigma of mental illness, abandoned by her husband, wrenched from her child, without resources. She couldn't go home for she had no home to go to. The village where she'd grown up was the one place she'd never be allowed to forget or escape. She had no formal training, no professional skills to fall back on, yet she had to find a way to scrabble together enough to live on in a town where she had not one friend to turn to. It must have taken every ounce of guts she had just to survive. She probably saw it as a kindness to her son to leave him be. 'Maybe she did try,' I suggested. 'Maybe they wouldn't give you back to her.'

'*She* tried to get me to fall for that line,' he said scornfully. 'No way. She never came after me. She left me to it. And my problem is that I'm not stupid. I know I'm fucked up. And I know exactly how and why. I'm fucked up because she left me to rot, to be abused, to be fucked over. And that's why I didn't murder her. I hated her far too much to give her the easy way out. I wanted her to go on suffering a whole lot longer. She still had years to pay for.'

Strangely, I believed him. The vitriol in his voice was the real thing, so strong it made the air tremble. 'So you didn't let on when you realized Edna Mercer's latest discovery was your mother?'

He shook his head. 'I didn't say a word. I just watched her, every chance I got. I listened to the actors talking about her when I made them up. At first, I was confused. It was like part of me desperately wanted to love her and be loved back. And another part of me wanted revenge. I just sat it out, waited to see which side would win.' Freddie shifted in his chair, folding his arms across his stomach and bending forward. Lit from above, his eyes were impenetrable pools in shadowy sockets. 'It was no contest, not really. The more they went on about how lovely she was, the more I resented what she'd deprived me of. I wanted revenge.'

'But you ended up in business with her. Earning money together,' I said, trying not to show how baffled I was by that. I suspected that he still harboured a determination not to tell me any more than I already knew.

He looked up then and stared into my face. He gave a strange barking cough of laughter. 'Don't you get it? That was my revenge. One night, I waited till her last client had gone and I walked into the van. I told her my date, time and place of birth and watched the colour drain out of her face. I didn't have to tell her who I was. Sure, she'd seen me around the place, but now it was like she was looking at me for the first time. But even then, her head was right in control of her heart. Nearly the first thing she said to me was, "Who have you told about this?"

'You see, if she revealed that I was her son, it

wouldn't just be another happy tabloid reunion story. She'd have to explain how she came to give me up in the first place. She'd have to tell the world she was a nutter. Most people find mental illness frightening. She was convinced that she'd lose her contracts, lose her clients at *Northerners* and end up back where she was all those years ago when she came out of the mental hospital. I think she was wrong, but it suited me that she believed it. That way, I had leverage. I made her tell me people's secrets and then I sold them. She had this phoney reverence thing about her psychic gift. She was always going on about being like a priest or a doctor, the repository of people's confidences.' His contemptuous impersonation was frighteningly accurate; if I'd been the superstitious type, I'd have sworn I could see Dorothea's ghost rising up before me.

'In that case, why did she tell you?'

'I was her son,' he said simply. 'She wanted to please me. It helped that she was desperate to keep our relationship secret, so she needed to keep me sweet.'

'So you put together what she winkled out from her clients with what people let slip in the make-up chair, and with the overlap between two sources you were able to expose all those people who probably think of you as a friend?' I said.

'Don't make me laugh,' he said bitterly. 'I'm not a friend to them. I'm a servant, a convenience. Oh sure, they treat me like I'm their best buddy, but if

I died tonight I doubt if more than three of them would make it to the funeral, and then only if they knew the photographers were going to be there. The programme's last publicist, he made the mistake of thinking they were his friends. He had a breakdown – too much stress. One cast member sent him a get-well card. One sent him a bunch of flowers. And that was it. He'd been working his socks off to cover their backs for the best part of five years, and the day he went sick, it was as if he'd never existed. So don't do the betrayal number on me. The only person I betrayed was my mother, and that was deliberate. And she knew it.'

'Wasn't it a bit of a risk, revealing secrets people knew they'd told Dorothea? Didn't anybody put two and two together?'

He shook his head, a smirk on his narrow mouth. 'I always waited a few months. I used the time to do a bit more digging, see if I could come up with extra information, stuff my mother hadn't been told about. Once you know where to look, it's amazing what you can find out.'

Tell me about it, I thought, feeling a strange pity for this damaged man who'd subverted the tricks of my trade and used them to generate misery. 'I suppose leaking the storylines as well helped to cover your tracks.'

He frowned. 'Storylines? That wasn't me. I never really know the storylines in advance. Just bits and pieces I pick up from what people say. I'd heard it's supposed to be somebody in the location catering company doing that. Turpin's giving them the heave, and they're getting their own back. That's what I'd heard.'

I couldn't help believing him. He'd been so honest about the other stuff, and that painted him in a far worse light. Besides, he was completely off-hand on the subject. I'd begun to realize that Freddie Littlewood was intense about the things at the heart of his life. Anything else was insignificant. 'Did you make her take some of the money too?' I asked.

'I tried. But she wouldn't cash the cheques. I even paid cash into her bank account once. The next week, she gave me a receipt from Save the Children for the exact same amount.'

It would have been so simple if I could have persuaded myself Freddie had killed his mother. All the pieces were there; a racket selling stories to the press that worked primarily because their relationship remained secret; a falling out among thieves, aggravated by the emotional charge of their relationship; a spur of the moment act of shocking violence. The only problem was that it wasn't true. And if I gave Cliff Jackson the pieces, he'd force them to fit the pattern his closed mind would impose.

But if it wasn't Freddie, who else? Who else would benefit from Dorothea's death? Whose purpose would be served? 'I don't suppose you know what was in her will?' I asked.

'I know I wasn't,' he said decisively. 'When I told her I was going to start selling the stories to the papers, she said that if I needed money, all I had to do was ask. She said that as soon as she'd satisfied herself that I really was her son, she'd changed her will in my favour. She said I might as well have the money now, while she was still alive and we could enjoy it together. I told her I didn't want her money, that wasn't the point. I wasn't selling the stories to make a few bob. I was doing it to hurt her. The money was just a bonus. She told me if I went ahead with it, she'd change her will back again and leave all her money to mental health charities.'

'I bet she didn't do it,' I said.

He moved his head almost imperceptibly from side to side, rubbing his thumb along his jaw again. 'You didn't know Dorothea. The week after the first story was published, she sent me a photocopy of her new will. Dated, signed, witnessed. Apart from a few small legacies to friends, everything she owns goes to charity.'

'It could have been a bluff. She might also have made a second will leaving it all to you.'

He shook his head. 'I don't think so. If she had, I think the police would have been round. Either that or the solicitor would have been on the phone. No, she meant it. I don't mind, you know. I've never expected anything good from life. That way, you're not disappointed.' Freddie pushed his chair back, the legs squeaking on the parquet floor.

He looked down anxiously, checking the polished surface wasn't scarred.

I stood up. 'I'm sorry,' I said.

His wary look was back. 'Why? I wasn't part of her life. I don't know who her friends were outside *Northerners*. I don't even know if she had any lovers.' He sighed. 'In all the ways that count, we were strangers, Kate.' It was the first time he'd used my name.

I followed him to the door. As we emerged into the hall, a woman was coming downstairs wrapped in a fluffy towelling dressing gown. I don't know who looked more startled, me or her. I hadn't registered any sounds to indicate there was anyone else home. She looked uncertainly from me to Freddie, her soft features concerned rather than suspicious. 'This is Kate,' Freddie said. 'She's from work. She just bobbed round to tell me about a change of schedule for tomorrow's filming. Kate, this is Stacey, my fiancée.'

I took my cue from Freddie and grinned inanely at the woman who continued down the stairs and gave me a trusting smile. She had a disturbing resemblance to Thumper the rabbit but with none of his street smarts. 'Hello and goodbye, Stacey,' I said, noticing that she looked a good ten years younger than Freddie.

'Maybe see you another time, eh?' she said, standing back to let me reach the front door.

'Maybe,' I lied, suddenly feeling claustrophobic.

I turned the knob on the lock and let the night in.
'See you, Freddie.'

'Thanks, Kate.'

I looked back once, as I turned out of the gate.
His slim frame was silhouetted dark against the
light spilling out of the hallway, Stacey a white
blob beside him. I didn't fancy her job one little bit.

My stomach hurt. Not because of the nagging
sense of failure but because it was a very long
time since I'd last eaten. I stopped at the first
chippie I came to and sat in the car eating very
fishy cod and soggy chips, watching tiny stutters
of snow struggling to turn into a blizzard. They
were getting nowhere fast, just like me. So far,
I had no idea who'd been sending hate mail to
Gloria Kendal, or why. I had no idea who had
killed Dorothea Dawson, or why, or whether
they posed a threat to Gloria or anybody else. I
couldn't even clear my sort-of other client, Ross
Grant, because the only mole I could substitute
for him in Turpin's firing line was someone who
had even more to lose. My assistant had been
arrested more times than I'd had hot dinners all
week, my computer specialist was in love with
somebody who might not even exist and one of
my best friends was in jail.

It was just as well none of the women's magazines were thinking about profiling me as an
example of Britain's thrusting new business-
women.

I scrunched up the chip papers and tossed them into the passenger footwell. I hoped I'd remember to dump them when I got home, otherwise the car would smell of fish and vinegar until the first sunroof day of spring. Home seemed even less appetizing, somehow. The idea of an empty house and an empty bed felt too much like film noir for my taste.

I had a reasonably good idea where Richard might have gone. Since he'd planned a romantic night in, he wouldn't have made any plans to listen to a live band. That meant he'd have chosen somewhere he could sit in a corner with a beer and a joint and listen to techno music so loud it would make his vertebrae do the cha-cha. I knew he wouldn't have ventured further afield than the city centre when the roads were so treacherous and there was no one to drive him home. There were only a couple of places that fitted the bill.

I gave the matter careful thought. Frash was the most likely. He'd been raving about the new midweek DJ there. The way my luck was running, that meant he was almost certainly not grooving in Frash. It had to be the O-Pit, a renovated die-cast works down by the canal that still smelled of iron filings and grease. To add insult to injury, there was a queue and I didn't have enough energy left to jump it. I leaned against the spalled brickwork, shoulders hunched, hands stuffed deep into my pockets. I might not be dressed for the club, but

I was the only one in the queue who stood a chance against hypothermia. Eventually, I made it inside.

It was wall to wall kids, fuelled with whizz and E, pale faces gleaming with sweat, clothes sticking to them so tight they appeared to be wearing body paint. I could spot the dealers, tense eyes never still, always at the heart of a tight little knot of punters. Nobody was paying them any mind, least of all the bar staff who could barely keep pace with the constant demand for carbonated pop.

I found Richard where I'd expected, in the acoustic centre of the club, the point where the music could be heard at maximum quality and volume. Unlike the dancers, he went for the drug that slowed down rather than speeded up. His eyes had the gently spaced look of the benevolently stoned. A half-litre bottle of Czech Bud hung from his right hand, a joint from his left. A copper-haired teenager wearing a lot of stripy Lycra and young enough to be his daughter was giving him covert come-on glances. I could have told her she was wasting her time. He was lost in the music.

I moved into his line of vision and tried an apologetic smile. Instead of a bollocking, he gave me that slow, cute smile that had first reeled me in, then drew me into his arms and gently kissed the top of my head. 'I love you, Brannigan,' he shouted.

Nobody but me heard. 'Let's go home,' he yelled in my ear.

I shook my head and took a long swig of his beer, leading him to the dance floor. Sometimes sex just isn't enough.

19

NEPTUNE IN SCORPIO IN THE 6TH HOUSE
She loves research and investigation, particularly if it is done secretly. She uses her discoveries to assert her power in the workplace. She is subtle, fascinated by secrets and their revelation and loves to expose hidden wickedness, especially if they feed her sense of social justice.

From *Written in the Stars*, by Dorothea Dawson

I remember a Monty Python sketch where a character complains, 'My brain hurts. I've got my head stuck in the cupboard.' I knew just how he felt when the opening chords of Free's 'All Right Now' crashed through my head. It felt like the middle of the night. It was still dark. Mind you, in Manchester in December, that could make it mid-morning. I dug Richard in the ribs. It was his house, after all. He made a noise like a sleeping triceratops, rolled over and started snoring.

I stumbled out of bed, wincing as my aching

286

feet hit the ground and gasping at the stiffness in my hips as I straightened up. Richard's 'Twenty Great Rock Riffs' doorbell blasted out again as I rubber-legged my way down the hall, wrapping my dressing gown around me, managing to tie the belt at the third fumbling attempt. I knew I shouldn't have had that last treble Polish hunter's vodka on the rocks. I yanked the door open and Gizmo practically fell in the door, accompanied by half a snowdrift.

'I've done it,' he said without preamble.

I wiggled my jaw in various directions, trying to get my mouth to work. 'Oh God,' I finally groaned through parched lips. I leaned against the wall and closed my eyes while the floor and ceiling rearranged themselves in their normal configuration.

'You look like shit,' Gizmo observed from the living-room doorway.

'Bastard,' I said, gingerly pushing myself away from the wall to test whether I could stand upright. Nothing seemed to collapse, so I put one foot in front of the other until I made it to the living room. 'My place,' I croaked, leading the way through the conservatory to the life support system in my kitchen.

'It's not that early,' Gizmo said defensively. 'You said it was important.'

The clock on the microwave said 07:49. 'Early's relative,' I told him, opening the fridge and reaching for the milk. 'So's important.' I poured a glass with shaking hand and got the vitamins out. Four grams of C, two B-complex tablets and two extra-strength paracetamol. I had a feeling it was going to be one of those days when ibuprofen and paracetamol count as two of the four main food groups. I washed the pills down with the milk, shuddered like a medieval peasant with the ague and wished I'd remembered to drink more water when we'd finally got home the wrong side of four o'clock.

'Did you come on the bus?' I asked. Gizmo has the same affection for public transport as most obsessives. He's the sort who writes to TV drama producers to complain that they had the hero catching the wrong bus on his way to his rendez-vous with the killer.

'The one-nine-two,' he said. 'Single decker.'

'Do me a favour? I left my car at the O-Pit. If you get a cab round there and pick it up for me, by the time you come back I'll be able to listen to whatever you've got to say.'

His mouth showed his discontent. 'Do I have to?' he asked like a ten-year-old.

'Yes,' I said, pointing to the door. 'Call a cab, Giz.'

Half an hour later, I'd kick-started my system with a mixture of hot and cold showers followed by four slices of peanut-buttered toast from a loaf that had been lurking in the freezer longer than I liked to think about. I even managed a smile for Gizmo when he returned twirling my car keys round his trigger finger.

'Thanks,' I said, settling us both down in my home office with a pot of coffee. 'Sorry if I was a bit off. Rough night, you know?'

'I could tell,' he said. 'You looked like you needed a new motherboard and a few more RAM chips.'

'It's not just the brain, it's the chassis,' I complained. 'This last year I've been starting to think something terrible happens to your body when you hit your thirties. I'm sure my joints never used to seize up from a night's clubbing.'

'It's downhill all the way,' he said cheerfully. 'It'll be arthritis next. And then you'll start losing nouns.'

'Losing nouns?'

'Yeah. Forgetting what things are called. You watch. Any day now, you'll start calling everything wossnames, or thingumajigs, or whatchamacallits.' He looked solemn. It took me a few seconds to realize I was experiencing what passed for a joke on his planet. I shook my head very slowly to avoid killing off any more neurones and groaned softly.

Gizmo reached past me and switched on my computer. 'You've got Video Translator on this machine, haven't you?'

'It's on the external hard disk, the E drive,' I told him.

He nodded and started doing things to my computer keyboard and peripherals too quickly for my hungover synapses to keep up. After a few minutes of tinkering and muttering, he sat back and said, 'There. It's a bit clunky in places, not enough

289

polygons in the program to keep it smooth. The rendering's definitely not going to win any awards. But it's what you asked for. I think.'

I managed to get my bleary eyes to focus on the screen. Somehow, the colours looked brighter than they had on the original crime-scene photographs. If I'd been alone, I'd have been reaching for the sunglasses, but my staff has little enough respect for me as it is. I leaned forward and concentrated on what Gizmo had put together.

We both sat in silence as his work unfolded before us. At the end, I clapped him on the shoulder. 'That's brilliant,' I enthused. 'That must have taken you hours.'

He tilted his head while shrugging, regressing to awkward adolescent. 'I started soon as I got home. I finished about two. But I did have a little break to talk to Jan. So it wasn't like I blew the whole night on it or anything.' He scuffed his feet on the carpet. 'Anyway, Dennis is your mate.'

'He owes you,' I said. 'Don't let him forget it. There must be somebody out there you want menacing.'

Gizmo looked shocked. 'I don't think so. Unless he knows where to find the moron who sent me that virus that ate all my .DLL files.'

I said nothing. It wasn't the time to point out that if the lovely Jan was a hoax, he might want Dennis's talent for terror sooner than he thought. 'I'm going to be half an hour or so on the phone. You can either wait or head on into the office.'

'I've got my Docs on. I'll walk over,' he said. 'I like it in the snow. I'll let myself out.'

I reached for the phone and called Ruth. Within ten minutes, she'd rung back to tell me she'd set up a meeting with DI Tucker at our office later that morning. 'He's not keen,' she warned me. 'I think your fame has spread before you. He did ask if you were the PI involved with the Dorothea Dawson case.'

'Did you lie?'

'No, I told him to check you out with Della. Apparently his bagman used to work for her, so it's a name that meant something to him.'

'Ah.'

'Is that a problem?'

'Not for me, but it might be for the bagman,' I said. Tucker wouldn't have to be much of a detective to work out where I'd gained my access to the crime-scene photographs. 'My fault. I should have warned you.'

'I don't like the sound of this,' Ruth said warily.

'Don't worry. I'll see you later.'

It took another twenty minutes to sort out Donovan and Gloria. We finally fixed that he would pick up her and her daughter, take them to the police station and hang on while Gloria gave the statement that would get him off the hook. Then he'd take them shopping. I hoped they'd stick to the plan of going a very long way away from anywhere policed by the Greater Manchester force. If they were going to be arrested for shoplifting, I didn't want to be involved.

I took a fresh pot of coffee out into the conservatory. The sun had come back from wherever it had been taking its winter holiday. The reflection on the snow was a killer. I fished a pair of sunglasses out of the magazine rack and stared at the blank white of the garden. Some days I could do with being a Zen master. The sound of one hand clapping was about all my tender nerve endings could cope with, but I still had a murder to solve and no apparent prospects for the role of First Murderer. Somebody must have wanted to murder Dorothea, because what had happened to her definitely hadn't been suicide. But I still couldn't figure out who or why.

I wasn't any nearer a solution by the time I had to leave for my meeting with Tucker and Ruth. Richard was still asleep, flat on his back, arms in the crucifixion position. I considered nails but settled for sticking an adhesive note to his chest suggesting lunch. When all else fails, I've found it helps to enlist another brain. Failing that, I'd make do with Richard and his hangover.

If Shelley had heard about the previous night's debacle, the atmosphere in the office was going to be frostier than it was outside. I stopped off at the florist on the way in and bought the biggest poinsettia they had. It would act both as peace offering and office decoration. There were three weeks to Christmas, and even with my chlorophyll-killer touch the plant had to stand a good chance of making it into the New Year.

I placed the poinsettia on her desk, a tentative smile nailed on. She looked up briefly, surveyed the plant and savaged me with fashion folk wisdom. 'Red and green are never seen except upon a fool,' she said. 'Gizmo was right. You do look like shit.'

'And a merry Christmas to you too, Scrooge,' I muttered.

'I don't have to work here,' she sniffed.

'Nobody else would put up with you now the war's over,' I told her sweetly and swept into my office. Gizmo had already set everything up. All I needed now was a cop with an open mind. If they could get miracles on 34th Street, I didn't see why we couldn't have them on Oxford Road.

Ruth was first to arrive. 'I hate surprises,' she grumbled, dropping her fake fur in a heap in the corner. Maybe Tucker would take it for a timber wolf and be cowed into submission.

'Nice outfit,' I said, trying to change the subject.

'Mmm,' she said, preening her perfectly proportioned but extremely large body in its tailored kingfisher-blue jacket and severe black trousers. 'You don't think it's a bit Cheshire Wife?'

'Sweetheart, you *are* a Cheshire Wife.'

She bared her teeth in a snarl. If she'd still been wearing the coat I'd have dived out of the window. 'Only geographically,' she said. 'I thought you needed me on your side this morning?'

Before we could get too deeply into the banter, the intercom buzzed. 'I have a Detective Inspector Tucker for you,' the human icicle announced. I made a big production of crossing my fingers and opened the door.

If the man standing by Shelley's desk had been any taller, we could have dipped his head in emulsion and repainted the ceiling. He was so skinny I bet he had to make a fist when he walked over cattle grids. He had a thick mop of salt and pepper hair, skin cratered from teenage acne and a thousand-watt smile that lit up the kind of grey eyes that can resemble granite or rabbit fur. 'I'm Kate Brannigan,' I said. 'Thanks for coming. Would you like to come through?'

Close up, my eyes were on a level with the breast pocket of his jacket. I flashed Ruth a 'why didn't you tell me?' look and ushered him in. He exchanged ritual greetings with Ruth and folded himself into the chair I pointed him towards. I swung the monitor screen round till it was facing them both. 'I'm sorry I was so mysterious about this,' I said. 'But if I'd told you what I had in mind, you'd have laughed in my face. You certainly wouldn't have taken it seriously enough to come and see for yourself.'

'I'm here now, so let's cut to the chase. We're all busy people,' he said, with no trace of hostility. He obviously didn't go to the same Masonic dinners as Cliff Jackson.

'It's not a long preamble, I promise you. Last

week, you found Pit Bull Kelly dead inside a shop that had previously been squatted by Dennis O'Brien. Pit Bull had told his brothers he was going down to the shop to sort Dennis out and take over the pitch for himself. Next morning, Pit Bull was found dead from a sub-arachnoid haemorrhage, an unusual injury and one that's hard to inflict. You decided, not unreasonably given what you know about Dennis, that he'd used a commando karate blow to kill Pit Bull. But given what I know about Dennis, I know it couldn't have happened like that.' I held my hands up to ward off the objection I could see Tucker about to make.

'But putting prejudice aside, there's a key piece of evidence that tells me Dennis didn't kill Pit Bull. I've known Dennis a long time, and the one thing he won't have anything to do with is guard dogs. Back when he was burgling, he'd never touch a house that had a guard dog. If Pit Bull Kelly had turned up with his dog in tow, Dennis wouldn't even have opened the door. But just supposing he had, that dog is a trained killer. He was Pit Bull Kelly's private army, according to his brothers. If Dennis had lifted his hands above waist level, the dog would have gone for him. He'd never have got as far as laying a hand on the master without the dog ripping his throat out.'

Tucker nodded sympathetically. 'I've already heard this argument from Ms Hunter. And if this crime had taken place out in the open, I might have been forced to agree. But what you tell me about O'Brien's dislike of fierce dogs doesn't mean he didn't kill Patrick Kelly. I could make the argument that the fact the dog was separated from its master by the back door of the shop lends weight to the notion that O'Brien was in fact in the shop and agreed to talk to Kelly on the sole condition that the dog stayed in the service corridor.'

'If so, how did he escape? There's no way out through the front without being filmed by security cameras and breaking through a metal grille,' I pointed out.

Tucker shrugged. 'O'Brien's a professional burglar. If he put his mind to it, I'm sure he could find a way out that neither of us would come up with in a month of Sundays.'

'That's not an argument that will carry much weight with a jury in the absence of any evidence to the contrary,' Ruth chipped in drily. Tucker's eyebrows descended and his eyes darkened.

'What I want to show you,' I interrupted before the goodwill melted, 'is an alternative hypothesis that answers all the problems this case presents. It should be relatively easy to make the forensic tests that will demonstrate if I'm right or wrong. But for now, all I want the pair of you to do is to watch.'

I tapped a couple of keys and the screen saver dissolved. The corridor behind Dennis's squat appeared. A few seconds passed, then a jerky figure with Pit Bull Kelly's face and clothes walked towards us. Even with the limited resources of time and software that Gizmo had been working with, he managed to convey that Kelly was under the influence of the drink and cannabis that, according to his brothers, he'd indulged in before he had the courage to face Dennis. Beside Kelly, a boisterous pit bull terrier lurched, its movements twitchy and not very well coordinated. Every few steps, the dog would jump up towards its master's chest and Kelly would slap it down. Gizmo had even overlaid a soundtrack of a barking dog.

'Two of his brothers confirmed that the dog was always jumping up at Pit Bull. It's still not much more than a pup. It's full of energy,' I said, forestalling any protest from Tucker when he saw where this was heading.

'It's impressive,' was all he said.

We watched Kelly and the dog arrive at the door to Dennis's squat. He reached out a hand for the doorknob and clumsily turned it. Expecting it to be locked, he stumbled as it opened under his hand. As Kelly lurched forward, the dog yanked on its leash, jerking Kelly off balance and spinning him half around so that the vulnerable angle under his jaw cracked into the doorjamb, accompanied by a thud courtesy of Gizmo.

The screen went black momentarily. Then the point of view shifted. We were inside the shop, behind the door. Again, we saw Kelly topple into the doorjamb, the dog skittering back from his master. The leash dropped from Kelly's fingers and the dog scampered back into the service corridor as Kelly collapsed sideways to the floor, the weight of his body slamming the door shut as he fell. The final scene dissolved into the starkness of the crime-scene photograph that had been the starting point for the whole process.

I heard Tucker's breath leak from him, the first sign that he'd been taking seriously what he saw. 'I suppose I'd be wasting my time if I asked you where exactly your source material came from?'

I nodded. 'I'm afraid so. All I will say is that it wasn't the obvious route,' I added in an attempt to give Della's contact a little protection.

'I take it I can expect the immediate release of my client, in the light of this?' Ruth said, leaning back expansively and lighting a cigarette. Noel Coward would have loved her.

Tucker shook his head. 'A very convincing performance, Ms Brannigan, but you know as well as I do that it doesn't change anything.'

'It should, because it explains everything a damn sight better than any hypothesis you've been able to come up with,' I said. 'The door was unlocked because Dennis didn't want to be responsible for the landlord having to cause any damage getting into the premises. Dennis's alibi holds water. It also explains why the dog didn't get into a fight with the killer, because there was no killer. I know it's bad for your clear-up statistics, but this wasn't a murder, it was the purest of accidents.'

Tucker sucked his lower lip in between his teeth.

'You make a good case. But O'Brien's wife has given him false alibis before, and he did have a strong reason for falling out with the dead man.'

'You will be running full forensic checks on the doorjamb, won't you, Inspector?' Ruth said ominously.

'I'm not sure that's justified,' Tucker said cautiously. 'Besides, the crime scene has been released.'

'Because if you don't,' Ruth continued as if he hadn't spoken, 'I will. I'll be getting my own expert witness down there this afternoon. And when he finds fragments of skin and maybe even a bit of blood with Patrick Kelly's DNA all over that doorjamb at precisely the height where his jaw would have hit it, Mr O'Brien will be suing you for false imprisonment. Won't that be fun?'

'A lovely Christmas present for the Chief Constable,' I added. I was starting to get the hang of threatening the police. I could see why Ruth got such a buzz out of her job.

Tucker sighed then chewed his lower lip some more. 'I will get someone to take a look at the door,' he eventually said. 'And I will also have a word with the pathologist.' He stood up, his long body unfolding to its unnerving height. 'It's been an interesting experience, Ms Brannigan. I'm sure we'll meet again.'

Ruth extracted a promise that he'd call her as soon as he had any information, and I shepherded him out.

'Tell me, what set you off on this train of

thought?' Ruth demanded the moment the door closed.

'I wish I could say it was some brilliant intuitive leap. But it wasn't. I'm on the Internet mailing list of a forensic pathology newsgroup,' I said, feeling slightly sheepish. 'Mostly I'm too busy to do much more than skim it, but every now and again, some bizarre detail sticks in my mind. I read about a similar case and I remembered it because the reporting pathologist described it as, "Man's best friend and worst enemy".'

If Ruth had had four paws and a tail, her ears would have pricked up. Instead, she settled for leaning forward with an intent gaze. 'You've got a copy of this?'

I shook my head. 'I don't save the digests. But I could put out a request for whoever filed the original case report to get in touch with me. I've managed to track down a couple of references to it, and that should be enough to get me heading in the right direction.'

Ruth got to her feet, stubbing out her cigarette in the soil of the dying Christmas cactus on the windowsill. 'Do it,' she said decisively, reaching for her coat. 'You did a great job there,' she added. 'I shall tell Dennis he owes his freedom entirely to you. Send me a bill, will you?'

'I thought Dennis was on Legal Aid?'

'He is.'

'But the Legal Aid Board won't pay for this,' I protested.

Ruth's smile matched the timber-wolf coat. 'No, but Dennis will. You're running a business, not a charity. There's favours for friends, and there's charges for professional services. This is one he pays for.'

'But . . .'

'No buts. You're no use to either of us if you can't make this business pay. Send me a bill.'

I would have argued. But she's bigger than me. Besides, it always takes forever to argue with a lawyer. And I had a lunch appointment.

20

She is idealistic, and enjoys discussion on a theoretical
or philosophical level. She can be excessively generous
and will go out of her way to help others. She does not
always manage to meet her own high standards.

From *Written in the Stars*, by Dorothea Dawson

The Yang Sing was Manchester's most famous
Chinese restaurant until it burned down, and it
suffered accordingly. Trying to get a table at a busy
time of day or night, especially near Christmas, was
about as rewarding as waiting for a night bus. What
the tourists didn't know was that just round the
corner is the sister restaurant, the Little Yang Sing,
where the cooking is at least as good and the decor
leans more towards the clean lines of sixties retro
than the traditional fish tanks and flock wallpaper
of most Chinese restaurants.

Richard was already there by the time I arrived.

So were a couple of bottles of Tsing Tao, a plate of salt and pepper ribs and a tidy little mound of prawn wontons. I dropped into my seat and reached for the beer. If the morning had taught me anything, it was that the only way to get through the day was going to be by topping up the alcohol level in my bloodstream at regular intervals. I didn't have time to suffer today; I'd have my hangover when I was asleep and not before.

As I swigged beer, I checked out Richard. Even allowing for the fact that he'd had four hours more sleep than me, he had no right to look so untouched by the excesses of the night before. His hazel eyes looked sleepy behind his new rimless glasses, but then they always have that fresh-from-the-bedroom look. The light dusting of stubble was sexy rather than scruffy, and his skin stretched tight over his broad cheekbones. I swear he looks no older than the night we first bumped into each other six years ago. I wish I could say the same, but one look in the mirrors that line the back wall of the restaurant and I knew it was a lie. The unforgiving light glinted on a couple of strands of what might have been silver in my dark-auburn hair. To dye or not to dye was a decision that was closer than I liked.

'How was your morning?' he asked just as I got a spare rib to my lips. Typical; he always asks questions when there's food to be fought over.

I shook my head and stripped the bone with my

teeth. 'Tough,' I said. 'But it looks as if Dennis is going to be back on the streets for Christmas.'

'That's one less thing for you to worry about, then. And Gloria? Has she had any more hate mail?'

'Nothing. I've got Donovan taking her and her daughter shopping today. I keep waiting for the phone call.'

Richard grinned. 'Switch the phone off. You need both hands for what I've ordered.'

He wasn't wrong. We ate our way through half a dozen dim sum and appetizers, a double helping of hot and sour soup and four main-course dishes. My capacity for food after a heavy night never ceases to astonish me. I'll probably need a stomach transplant when I'm forty. By then, they'll probably be able to give me one.

I picked up the last king prawn with my chopsticks then laid it regretfully back on the plate. 'I can't do it,' I said.

'Me neither,' Richard admitted. 'So where are you up to with this murder?'

I brought him up to speed on my meeting with Freddie Littlewood. It felt like half a lifetime ago, but it was only the night before. 'So I seem to have tracked down the source of most of the tabloid stories,' I said. 'At least, the ones involving personal scandal rather than storyline revelations. But I don't know how to use the information to clear Ross Grant without dropping Freddie in the shit. I don't really want to do that if I can help it, because, to be honest, he seems to have had a pretty raw deal from life anyway.'

'And you're sure he didn't kill his mother? He'd have had the opportunity, and he freely admits to hating her.'

'I just don't think he did it. Why should he? He was making a nice little earner out of their story selling, and he got the added bonus that it really upset her. Profitable revenge. There's not many of us manage that.'

Richard poured himself a cup of Chinese tea and stared into it consideringly. 'Maybe she'd had enough,' he said at last. 'Maybe she was going to blow the whistle on the whole racket and throw herself on the mercy of her clients.'

I snorted. 'She certainly wouldn't have got much change out of them. And even supposing the cast members were prepared to forgive and forget, John Turpin would never let her back on NPTV property again. Which reminds me . . .' I drifted off, remembering what Cassie had told me.

'I said,' Richard commented in the tones of a man repeating himself, 'who is John Turpin?'

'He's the Administration and Production Co-ordinator at NPTV,' I said absently. 'One of those typical telly executives. You know the kind. About as creative as a sea slug. They're great at counting beans and cutting expenses. You must have them in journalism.'

'Editorial managers,' he said glumly.

'And he's obsessed with uncovering the mole

who's leaking the *Northerners* stories. He's even threatening to end the location caterers' contract because he suspects one of them of being guilty.'

'Nice guy. So what is it about this Turpin that sent you off the air just now?' Richard asked.

'I was just remembering a conversation I had yesterday with Cassie Cliff.'

'Maggie Grimshaw as was?'

'The same.'

Richard smiled reminiscently. 'I loved Maggie Grimshaw. The woman who put the "her" in *Northerners*. The sex goddess of soap.' His smile slipped. 'Until the truth came slithering out. So what did Cassie have to say about John Turpin?'

I told him the tale about Turpin and Tina Marshall in the Normandie. 'I can't figure it out at all,' I said.

'He might have been wining and dining her on the off-chance that she'd let something slip about her mole.'

I pulled a face. 'I don't think he's that stupid.'

'He might be that vain,' Richard pointed out. 'Never underestimate a middle-aged executive's opinion of himself.'

I sighed. 'Well, if that's what he was after, he obviously didn't succeed, since he's still making a huge performance out of flushing out the mole.'

'Has he got shares in NPTV?' Richard asked.

'I think so. *Northerners* is up for contract renegotiation. One of the actors was talking about how much money Turpin would make if NPTV got into a bidding war between the terrestrial and the pay channels over *Northerners*. So I guess he must have some financial stake.'

Richard leaned back in his seat, looking pleased with himself. 'That's the answer. That's why Turpin was cosying up to Tina Marshall. John Turpin's the *Northerners* mole.' He signalled to a passing waiter that we wanted the bill.

Sometimes I wonder how someone who never listens makes such a good living as a journalist. 'Richard, pay attention. I already told you who the mole is. Freddie Littlewood was using Dorothea to dig the dirt then he was dishing it.'

'I *was* paying attention,' he said patiently. 'Freddie was pulling skeletons out of cupboards, courtesy of Dorothea's privileged information. What you didn't tell me was who's been selling out the storylines. From what you say, Turpin must have access to them.'

'But why? What does he gain by it?'

Richard shook his head in wonderment. 'I can't believe you're being so slow about this, Brannigan,' he said. 'You're normally so quick off the mark where money's concerned. It's viewing figures, isn't it? The more notorious *Northerners* becomes, the more people watch. The more people watch, the higher the value of the show when it comes to negotiating any satellite or cable deal because there are people who will shell out hundreds of pounds for satellite dishes and cable decoders and subscription charges rather than be parted from their regular fix of *Northerners*.'

'I know that,' I protested. 'But it's different with storylines that get leaked before transmission. That makes people turn off.'

The waiter dumped the bill on the table between us. Automatically, we both reached for our wallets. 'Says who?' Richard demanded as his plastic followed mine on to the plate.

'Says the actors. When the punters know what happens next, they don't mind missing it. And they get hooked on something else so they drop out altogether.'

The waiter removed the bill and the credit cards. 'Two receipts, please,' we chorused. He nodded. He'd served us enough times to know the routine of two self-employed people who liked to eat together. 'That's bollocks, you know,' Richard said. 'That might be what Turpin's telling them, but it's bollocks. If you leak upcoming storylines, what happens is you get a buzz going. First one paper breaks the story, then all the rest follow it up, then the TV magazines pick it up and run with it and before you know it, everybody's buzzing. Don't you remember the whole "Who shot JR?" thing back in the eighties? Or the furore over Deirdre Barlow and Mike Baldwin's affair on *Coronation Street*? The whole nation was watching. I bet Turpin got the idea when Freddie's exclusives started hitting the headlines and the viewing figures rose along with them.'

'He wouldn't dare,' I breathed.

'Where's the risk? He's in charge of hunting for the source of the *Northerners* stories. Turpin knows there's a real mole as well as himself, so if he does uncover anything, he can pin all the guilt on the other one. There's no way Tina Marshall is going to expose him, because he's the goose that lays the golden eggs. She's probably not even paying him much.'

I leaned across the table and thrust my hand through his thick butterscotch hair, pulling his head towards mine. I parted my lips and planted a warm kiss on his mouth. I could still taste lemon and ginger and garlic as I ran my tongue lightly between his teeth. I drew back for breath and said softly, 'Now I remember why I put up with you.'

The waiter cleared his throat. I released Richard's head and we sheepishly signed our credit card slips. Richard reached across the table and covered my hand with his. 'We've got some unfinished business from last night,' he said, his voice husky.

I ran my other thumbnail down the edge of his hand and revelled in the shiver that ran through him. 'Your place or mine?'

Just before we slipped under my duvet, I made a quick call to Gizmo, asking him to arrange for some background checks into the exact extent of John Turpin's financial involvement with NPTV. Then I switched the phone off.

Sometime afterwards, I was teetering on the edge of sleep, my face buried in the musky warmth of Richard's chest, when his voice swirled through my mind like a drift of snow. 'I'll tell you one thing, Brannigan. If a few juicy stories can push up the ratings, just think what murder must have done.'

Suddenly, I was wide awake.

Sandra McGovern, née Satterthwaite, had inherited her mother's flair for ostentation. The house where she lived with her husband Keith and their daughter Joanna had definite delusions of grandeur. Set just off Bury New Road in the smarter part of Prestwich, it looked like the one person at the party who'd been told it was fancy dress. The rest of the street consisted of plain but substantial redbrick detached houses built sometime in the 1960s. Chateau McGovern had gone for the Greek-temple makeover. The portico was supported by half a dozen ionic columns and topped with a few statues of goddesses in various stages of undress. Bas reliefs had been stuck on to the brick at regular intervals and a stucco frieze of Greek key design ran along the frontage just below the first-floor windows.

They might just have got away with it on a sunny summer day. But the McGoverns clearly took Christmas seriously. The whole house was festooned with fairy lights flashing on and off with migraine-inducing intensity. Among the Greek goddesses, Santa Claus sat in a sled behind four cavorting reindeer, all in life-size inflatable plastic. A Christmas tree had been sawn vertically in two, and each half fixed to the wall on either side of the front door, both dripping with tinsel and draped with flickering-light ropes. A vast wreath of holly garlanded the door itself. I pressed the doorbell and the chimes of 'Deck the Hall with Boughs of Holly' engulfed me. Sometimes I felt Scrooge had had a point.

There was a long silence. I was steeling myself to ring again when I saw a figure looming through the frosted glass. Then Donovan opened the door. But it was Donovan as I'd never seen him before, swathed in a plum silk kimono that reached just below his knees. A fine sheen of sweat covered his face and he looked extremely embarrassed. 'Bah, humbug,' I muttered. He seemed baffled, but what else could I expect from an engineering student?

'Hiya, Kate,' he said.

I pointed to his outfit. 'I hope this isn't what it looks like,' I said drily.

He rolled his eyes heavenwards. 'You're as bad as my mother. Give me some credit. Come on in, let me get this door shut. We're through the back,' he added, leading the way down the hall. 'You think the outside is over the top, wait till you see this.'

I waded after him through shag pile deep enough to conceal a few troops of Boy Scouts. I tried not to look too closely at the impressionistic flower paintings on the walls. At the end of the hall was a solid wooden door. Donovan opened it, then stood back to let me pass.

I walked from winter to tropical summer. Hot, green and steamy as a Hollywood rainforest, the triple-glazed extension must have occupied the same square footage as the house. Ferns and palms pushed against the glass and spilled over in cascades that overhung brick paths. Growing lamps blazed light and warmth everywhere. The air smelt of a curious mixture of humus and chlorine. Sweat popping out on my face like a rash, I followed the path through the dense undergrowth, rounded a curve and found myself facing a vast swimming pool, its shape the free form of a real pond.

'Hiya, chuck,' Gloria screeched, raucous as an Amazonian parrot.

She was stretched out on a cushion of wooden sunbed, wearing nothing but a swimsuit. Beside her, a younger version reclined on one elbow like a Roman diner, a champagne glass beaded with condensation hanging loosely from her fingers. Gloria beckoned me over, patting the lounger next to her. 'Take the weight off,' she instructed me. I sat, slipping off my leather jacket and the cotton sweater underneath. Even stripped to jeans and cotton T-shirt, I was still overheating. 'Don, sweetheart, fetch us another sunbed, there's a love,' Gloria called. 'This is our Sandra,' she continued. 'Sandra, meet Kate Brannigan, Manchester's finest private eye.'

We nodded to each other and I told a few lies about the house and swimming pool. Sandra looked pleased and Gloria proud, which was the point of the exercise. Donovan reappeared carrying a fourth lounger which he placed a little away from our grouping. Self-consciously, he peeled off the robe, revealing baggy blue trunks, and perched on the edge of the seat, his body gleaming like a Rodin bronze. 'No problems today?'

Gloria stretched voluptuously. For a woman who was fast approaching the downhill side of sixty, she was in terrific shape. It was amazing, given what I'd seen of her lifestyle. 'Not a one, chuck. Nowt but pleasure all the way. We went to Oldham police station and I spoke to a lovely young inspector who couldn't see what all the fuss last night had been about. Any road, young Don's in the clear now, so we don't have to worry about that. And then we went shopping for Christmas presents for Joanna. We had to get a robe and some trunks for Don and all, because our Keith's a tiddler next to him. We've not seen a journalist all day, and there's nobody more pleased than me about that. What about you? Any news?'

'I wanted to ask you about something,' I said, side-stepping the question. 'You remember when I came to fetch you from Dorothea's van the night she was killed? Well, I was busy wrestling with the umbrella and keeping an eye out in case anybody jumped us, so I wasn't really paying attention to individuals. Besides, I don't really know anybody at NPTV, so even if I had noticed who was around, it wouldn't mean anything to me. But you . . .'

'You want me to think about who I saw in the car park?'

'It might be important.'

Gloria leaned back, closing her eyes and massaging her temples. 'Let's see . . .' she said slowly. 'There were two women getting into a car a couple of bays down from Dorothea's. I don't know their names, but I've seen them in the accounts office . . . Valerie Brown came out of the admin block and ran across to production . . . I saw that red-haired film editor with Maurice Warner and Maurice's secretary. They were legging it for Maurice's car . . . John Turpin was standing in the doorway of the admin block, like he couldn't decide whether to make a run for it . . . Freddie and Diane and Sharon from make-up, they were getting in Sharon's car, that lot always go to the pub in town on a Friday . . . Tamsin from the press office, she came out the admin block and went across towards the security booth, but she wasn't running because of them daft shoes she wears.' She opened her eyes and sat up. 'There were one or two other folk about, but either they were too muffled up for me to see who they were or else I didn't know them. Does any of that help?'

I reached for my sweater. 'More than you can imagine, Gloria. Much more than you can imagine.'

'So what's going on?' she demanded. 'Do you know who killed Dorothea?'

'I've got an idea,' I said. 'I don't want to say too much yet. I've got stuff to check out. But if you get Donovan to bring you to the office first thing tomorrow morning, I think I might be able to give you your money's worth.'

Donovan gave me a look of resignation. 'You want me to stick with Gloria?'

'Oh, I think so,' I said. 'You make such a lovely pair.'

21

SATURN IN PISCES IN THE 11TH HOUSE

She is comfortable with her own company and works best alone. Her friends are valued as much for their experience as for their personal qualities. She has a single-minded concentration on objectives, but has a flexible and sympathetic mind. She is intuitive and imaginative. She can be moody.

From *Written in the Stars*, by Dorothea Dawson

When Freddie Littlewood got home from work, I was waiting for him. Stacey of the big eyes and trusting soul had made it back fifteen minutes ahead of him and she'd let me in without a moment's hesitation. She'd shown me into the dining room again, presumably because that was where Freddie and I had spoken before. She'd been back inside five minutes with a tray containing teapot, milk, sugar and a china mug with kittens on it.

'It can't have been easy for Freddie, the last few days,' I said sympathetically.

She gave me an odd look. 'No more than usual,' she said. 'Why would it be difficult?'

Until that moment, the idea that Freddie might not have mentioned his mother's murder to Stacey hadn't occurred to me. People have called me cold in my time, but I don't think I could plan to spend the rest of my life with someone I trusted so little. 'I meant, with the police everywhere,' I improvised hastily, remembering I was supposed to work for NPTV too. 'It's been really disruptive. They walk around as if they own the place, asking all sorts of questions. And it's not even as if Dorothea Dawson worked for NPTV.'

Seemingly satisfied, Stacey drifted off, saying she was going to get changed and get the dinner on, if I didn't mind. I also couldn't imagine marrying someone with so little curiosity about a strange woman who turned up looking for her fiancé twice in such a short space of time. I sipped my tea and wished there was a large lemon vodka in it. The sound of the front door opening and closing was immediately followed by Stacey's footsteps in the hall and the low mutter of conversation.

Freddie stepped into the doorway, looking grey-faced and exhausted. 'What's so urgent it couldn't wait for work tomorrow?' he asked brusquely. More for Stacey's benefit than mine, I suspected.

'I needed the answer to a question,' I said. 'I won't be at NPTV first thing in the morning, so I thought you wouldn't mind if I caught up with you at home.'

317

He closed the door behind him and leaned against it. 'Have you never heard of the telephone?' he said, exasperation in his voice.

'It's much harder to tell when people are lying,' I said mildly. 'Sorting out the truth is difficult enough as it is.'

Freddie folded his arms over his chest and glared. 'Since you're here, I'll answer your question. But in future, if you want to talk to me, see me at work or call me on the phone. I don't want Stacey upset by this, OK?'

'That's very chivalrous of you,' I said. 'There's not many men who are so concerned for their future wives' wellbeing that they don't even tell them their prospective mother-in-law's just been murdered.'

'What goes on between Stacey and me is none of your business. You said you had a question?'

'You told me that it wasn't you who leaked the advance storylines to the press, and I believe you,' I said. 'But somebody did. I was wondering if Dorothea had ever indicated to you that she knew who the mole was?'

He gave me a long, considering stare, running his thumb along his jaw in the unconscious gesture I'd already become familiar with. 'She once told me that it wasn't hard to work out who the mole was if you looked at the horoscopes. She said there weren't that many people connected with *Northerners* who had the right combination of features in their charts. If you excluded people who didn't really have access to advance stories, she said, it narrowed right down.'

'Did she mention anybody's name to you?'

He shook his head. 'Not then. She said she didn't seem to have much choice about passing me other people's secrets but that she wasn't going to ruin somebody when she had no evidence except her own instinct. But then later . . .' His voice tailed off.

'What happened, Freddie?' I asked urgently.

'Turpin was in make-up one day and somebody said something about one of the stories in the paper and was it true he was going to get rid of the caterers because they were the moles. Turpin said he wasn't convinced that would solve the problem. I turned round and he was staring at me. I thought maybe he suspected me. So I went round to Dorothea's house and told her. I said she'd probably be glad if Turpin did find out, because then she'd be off the hook and wouldn't have to break her precious client confidences any more.'

'She wasn't though, was she?' I said gently.

He shook his head and cleared his throat. 'No. She said she wouldn't let Turpin destroy my career. She said she was as certain as she could be that he was the storyline mole and she was going to confront him.'

'She was going to expose him?' I couldn't believe Freddie was only revealing this now.

'No, she wasn't like that. I told you, she was

obsessed with trying to do her best for me, supposedly to make up for all the bad years. No, she said she'd do a deal with Turpin. If he stopped hunting the mole, she'd keep quiet about her suspicions of him.'

'But she didn't have any evidence apart from an astrological chart,' I protested.

'She said that if she was right, there had to be evidence. All it needed was for someone to look in the right place and Turpin would realize that once she'd pointed the finger, he'd be in trouble. So he'd have to back off and leave me alone. Except of course she wasn't going to come out and say it was me, not in so many words. She was just going to tell him that she was acting on behalf of the mole.'

'When was this?' I asked, trying to keep my voice nonchalant.

Freddie shrugged. 'A couple, three weeks ago? She told me afterwards he'd agreed to the deal. That he'd seen the sense of what she was saying. You don't think that had anything to do with why she was killed, do you?'

'You don't?' I asked incredulously.

'I told you, it was weeks ago.'

I couldn't get my head round his naiveté. Then I realized he wasn't so much naive as self-obsessed. 'There's a lot at stake,' I pointed out. 'You know yourself you'd never work in TV again if I told NPTV what you've been doing. And there are a lot of people involved with *Northerners* who have a lot more to lose than you do. If somebody thought Dorothea was a threat . . .'

Freddie stared at the floor. 'It wasn't like she was blackmailing him. She was too straight for that.'

'She let you blackmail her,' I pointed out.

'That was different. That was guilt.'

'Looks like it killed her, Freddie.'

I got up and put a hand on his arm. He pulled away. 'Don't touch me! It's meaningless to you. You never knew my mother.'

There was nothing more to say. I'd got what I came for and Freddie Littlewood was determined to need nobody's sympathy for the death of a mother he'd barely come to know. I walked back to the car, glad I wasn't living inside his skin.

I'd barely closed the door when my moby rang. 'Hello?'

'Hey, Kate, I'm out!' Dennis's voice was elated.

'Free and clear?' I could hardly believe it.

'Police bail pending results from the lab. Ruth says you played a blinder! Where are you? Can I buy you some bubbly?'

If anyone deserved champagne, it was the long-suffering Debbie. But female solidarity only stretches so far, and I needed Dennis more than she did. I was glad I hadn't done as Ruth suggested and submitted a bill, because tonight I needed payment in kind. 'Never mind the bubbly,' I said. 'I need a favour. Where are you?'

'I'm in the lobby bar at the Ramada,' he

announced. 'And I've already got the bottle in front of me.'

'Take it easy. I'll be there in half an hour.' I needed to make a quick detour via a phone book. I started the engine and fishtailed away from the kerb. The roads had iced up while I'd been indoors. It was going to be another treacherous night. And I was quite sanguine about contributing to the total.

If you walk out of Strangeways Prison up towards town, the Ramada Hotel is probably the first civilized place to buy a drink. It's certainly the first where you can buy a decent bottle of champagne. Following the IRA bomb, its façade reminded me of those mechanical bingo cards you get on seaside sideshow stalls where you pull a shutter across the illuminated number after the caller shouts it out. So many of the Ramada windows were boarded up, it looked like they'd won the china tea service. I found Dennis on a bar stool, a bottle of Dom Perignon in front of him. I wondered how many 'Under a Pound' customers it had taken to pay for that.

He jumped off the stool when he saw me, pulling me into a hug with one arm and handing me a glass of champagne with the other. 'My favourite woman!' he crowed, toasting me with the drink he retrieved from the bar.

'Shame we're both spoken for,' I said, clinking my crystal against his.

'Thanks for sorting it,' he said, more serious now.

'I knew it wasn't down to you.'

'Thanks. This favour . . . we need a bit of privacy?'

I gestured towards a vacant table over in the corner. 'That'll do.' I led the way while Dennis followed, a muscular arm embracing the ice bucket where the remains of the champagne lurked. Once we were both settled, I outlined my plan.

'We know where he lives?' Dennis asked.

'There's only one in the phone book. Out the far side of Bolton. Lostock.'

He nodded. 'Sounds like the right area.'

'Why? What's it like?'

'It's where Bolton folk go when they've done what passes for making it. More money than imagination.'

'That makes sense. I looked it up on the *A-Z*. There's only houses on one side of the road. The other side's got a golf course.'

'You reckon he'll be home?'

I finished my champagne. 'Only one way to find out.' I pointed to his mobile.

'Too early for that,' Dennis said dismissively. Then he outlined his plan.

An hour later, I was lying on my stomach in a snowdrift. I never knew feet could be that cold and still work. The only way I could tell my nose was running was when the drips splashed on the snow in front of me. In spite of wearing every warm and waterproof garment I possessed, I was cold enough to sink the *Titanic*. This was our second stakeout position. The front of the house had proved useless for Dennis's purposes and now we were lying inside the fence surrounding an old people's home, staring down at the back garden of our target. 'Is it time yet?' I whimpered pathetically.

Dennis was angled along the top of the drift, a pair of lightweight black rubber binoculars pressed to his eyes. 'Looks like we got lucky,' he said.

'Do tell me how.'

'He's not bothered to pull the curtains in the kitchen. I've got a direct line of sight to the keypad that controls the burglar alarm. If he sets that when he goes out, I'll be able to see what number he taps in.'

'Does that mean we're going to do it now?' I said plaintively.

'You go back round the front. I'll give you five minutes before I make the call. Soon as he leaves, you shoot up the drive and start working on the front-door lock. I'll get to you fast as I can.' He turned and waved a dismissive hand at me. 'On your bike, then. And remember, we're dressed for the dark, not the snow. Keep in the shadows.'

That's the trouble with living in a climate where we only get snow for about ten days a year. Not even serious villains bother to invest in white camouflage. Neither Dennis's lock-up nor my wardrobe had offered much that wouldn't blend in with your average dark alley. I slunk off round the edge of the shrubbery and down the drive of the old people's home. I nipped across the road and on to the golf course, where I waded through knee-high snow until I was opposite the double-fronted detached house we were interested in. A light shone in the porch, and the ghost light from the hall cast pale oblongs on the ceilings of upstairs rooms. The rooms on either side of the front door had heavy curtains drawn.

I checked my watch. A couple of minutes before, Dennis would have rung the house and explained that there had been a break-in at the administrative core of NPTV and that the police wanted Mr Turpin to come down right away to assess the damage. A quick call to Gloria had already established that he was divorced and as far as she knew, unattached. We were taking a gamble that Turpin was alone. As I watched, the front door swung open and he appeared, shrugging into a heavy leather coat over suit trousers and a heavy knit sweater. On the still night air, I could hear the high-pitched whine of an alarm system setting itself. He pulled the door to behind himself, not bothering to double lock it, and walked briskly to his car. A security light snapped on, casting the drive into extremes of light and shade.

Ignition, headlights bouncing off the garage door, reversing lights, then the big Lexus crunched down the icy drive and swung into the road. I watched the tail lights as far as the junction, then scrambled over the banking, across the road and up Turpin's drive, dodging in and out of shadow and blinding light. The porch was brighter than my kitchen. I'd never broken the law in quite so exposed a way before. I fumbled under my jacket and fleece, fingers chill in latex probing the money belt I was wearing until they closed around my lock-picks. At least I'd be able to see what I was doing.

Oddly enough, it didn't really speed up the process. Picking a lock successfully was all about feel, not sight, and my fingers were still clumsy from the cold. Dennis was hovering impatiently by my shoulder by the time I got the right combination of metal probes, muttering, 'Come on, Kate,' in a puff of white breath.

The door opened and he was past me, running down the hall to the alarm panel, tapping in the code to stop the warning siren joining forces with the klaxon that would deafen us and, in an area like this, have the police on the doorstep within ten minutes. I let him get on with it and checked out the downstairs rooms. A living room on one side of the hall, a dining table on the other. Kitchen at the rear. I ran up the stairs. Four doors, three ajar. The first was Turpin's bedroom, an en suite bathroom opening off it. The second, closed, was the guest bathroom. Third was a characterless guest room. Last, inevitably, was the one I was looking for. As I walked in, the alarm went quiet, the silence a palpable presence.

Luckily, Turpin's study overlooked the back garden, so I felt safe enough to switch on the desk lamp. I took a quick look around. There was one wall of books, mostly military history and management texts. On the opposite wall, shelves held file boxes, stacks of bound reports and fat binders for various trade magazines. A PC squatted on the desk and I switched it on. While it booted up, I started on the drawers. None of them were locked. Either Turpin thought himself invincible here or we were doing the wrong burglary.

Suddenly, Dennis was standing next to me. 'Do you want me to do the drawers while you raid the computer?' he asked.

'I'd rather you kept an eye out the front,' I said. 'I know it should take Turpin an hour to get to NPTV and back, but I'd rather be safe than sorry.'

'You're probably right,' Dennis said. He went out as silently as he'd come in. At least now I didn't have to worry about being caught red-handed. I checked out the computer. It looked as if Turpin used Word for all his documents, which suited me perfectly. I took a CD-ROM out of my money belt and swapped it for the encyclopaedia currently residing in the drive. It had taken all my powers of persuasion to get Gizmo to lend me this disk and I hoped it had been worth it. It was a clever little piece of software that searched all Word files for particular combinations of words. I typed 'Doreen Satterthwaite', and set the program running.

Meanwhile, I started on the desk. Not surprisingly, Turpin was an orderly man. I flicked through folders of electricity bills, gas bills, council-tax bills until I found the phone bills I was looking for. Domestic and mobile were in the same file. A quick glance around revealed that I wasn't going to have to steal them. Turpin had one of those all-singing, all-dancing printers that also act as a computer scanner and a photocopier. I extracted the itemized bills for the last six months and fed them through the photocopier.

When the phone rang, I jumped. After three rings, the answering machine kicked in. A woman's voice floated eerily up from the hall. 'Hi, Johnny. It's Deirdre. I find myself unexpectedly at a loose end after all. If you get this message at a reasonable time, come over for a nightcap. And if I'm not enough to tempt you, I've got sausages from Clitheroe for breakfast. Call me.' Bleep.

I glanced at the screen and discovered that there were two files containing 'Doreen Satterthwaite'. I was about to access them when Dennis's yell made my heart jolt in my chest. 'Fuck!' he shouted. 'We're burned, Brannigan!'

22

The adrenaline surge was like being plugged into the mains. Dennis was almost screaming. 'Switch off. Spare room. Now!' No time to exit properly from Windows. I stabbed my finger at the computer power button. I grabbed the photocopies and stuffed the originals back into their folder, thrusting them into the drawer without checking I was returning them to the right place. I leapt to my feet, switching off the desk lamp.

Three paces across the room, I heard the wail of

the alarm siren as Dennis reset it. I dived across the hall and into a spare room bathed with light from the security lamps outside. I skidded round the door to stand against the wall. Seconds later I heard Dennis pounding up the stairs. Then he was beside me, his chest heaving with the effort of silent breathing. 'There's a sensor in the corner,' he said. 'Under the bed. Quick!'

I dropped to the floor and rolled, aware of him following me. As I hit the bedside table on the far side of the bed the alarm finished setting itself and silence fell once more. I heard the slam of a car door. Then the front door opened and the warning siren went off again. By now, every nerve in my body was jangling, and I suspected Dennis was no better. I was going to wake up sweating to the nightmare sound of that burglar alarm for months to come, I could tell. 'How the fuck do we get out of this?' I hissed.

'Worst comes to worst, we wait till he goes to sleep. Just relax. But not too much. Don't want you snoring,' Dennis muttered, clutching my hand in a tightly comforting grip. We endured a few more seconds of aural hell, then blessed silence apart from the thudding of two hearts under John Turpin's spare bed. If he'd had parquet floors instead of carpet, we wouldn't have stood a chance. Then a click, a bleep and a replay of Deirdre's attempt at sultry seductiveness, thankfully muffled. I heard the clatter of a handset being picked up and the electronic stutter of a number being keyed in. Amazing how certain sounds travel and others don't. At first all I could hear of Turpin's voice was a low rumble. Then, as he mounted the stairs and walked into his bedroom, I could hear every word.

'. . . halfway down the motorway when it dawned on me. When I'd asked this supposed security man if he'd called Peter Beckman, he'd said Peter was already on his way in. But Peter's taken a couple of days off this week to go to some stupid Christmas market in Germany with his wife. So I rang him on his mobile, and he's only having dinner in some floating restaurant on the bloody Rhine.' I heard the sound of shoes being kicked off.

'Well, I know,' he continued after a short pause. 'So I rang studio security and they denied any report of a break-in or any call to me . . . No, I don't think so. It'll be some bloody technicians' Christmas party, some idiot's idea of a joke, let's bugger up Turpin's evening . . .' Another pause. 'Oh, all right, I'll check, but the alarm was on . . . Yes, I'm just going to get changed, and I'll be right over. You know how I feel about Clitheroe sausages for breakfast,' he added suggestively. I was going to have serious trouble with sausages for a while, I could tell.

I strained my ears and picked up the sound of sliding doors open and close, then faint sounds like someone doing exactly what Turpin had said. I heard the bathroom door open, the sound of a light cord being pulled once, twice, and the door closing. A door moved over carpet pile, a light switch snapped twice. The study. He was checking, just like he'd told Deirdre he would. My throat constricted, my muscles went rigid. Gizmo's CD-ROM was still in Turpin's drive. Where had I left the CD I'd taken out of it? Dennis's hand clamped even tighter over mine. All round the bed was suddenly flooded with light, but only momentarily. Then twilight returned.

I felt the tension slowly leaking out of my body. We'd got away with it. Turpin was going out again. The terrible irony was that if we'd waited quarter of an hour longer before Dennis had made his hoax call, Deirdre would have saved us the trouble and I'd not have lost five years off my life expectancy. Dennis let go of my hand. I patted his arm in thanks.

Finally, the alarm was reset and the low thrum of Turpin's car engine dimmed in the distance. 'Now what?' I asked.

'He's gone for the night. You've got hours to play with,' Dennis said cheerfully.

'The alarm's on. As soon as we move out from under the bed, Lostock calls the cavalry. And for all we know, Clitheroe sausages is only a couple of hundred yards away.'

Dennis chuckled. 'The trouble with you, Kate, is you worry too much. Now me, I've got the advantage of a commando training. Cool under pressure.'

I poked him sharply in the ribs, enjoying the

squeal that accompanied the rush of air. 'You can't get the staff these days,' I said sweetly. 'I'll just lie here and meditate while you get it sorted.' It's called whistling in the dark.

In the dim gleam from the landing, I watched as Dennis rolled on to his stomach and propelled himself across the floor using toes, knees, elbows and fingers for purchase. Keeping belly to the carpet made it a slow crawl, but it was effective. The little red light on the passive infrared detector perched in the corner of the room stayed unlit. He disappeared round the corner of the door and my stomach started eating itself. I badly needed to go to the loo.

Time stretched to impossible lengths. I wondered if Dennis was going downstairs head first or feet first. I wondered whether the keypad itself was covered by an infrared detector. I wondered whether it was possible to install detectors that didn't show they'd been activated. I even wondered if Turpin was paranoid enough to have installed one of those silent alarms that rang in a remote control centre staffed by battle-hungry security guards. I wondered so much about burglar alarms that night that I was beginning to consider a new profit centre for Brannigan & Co.

Suddenly the main alarm klaxon gave a single whoop. Shocked, I cracked my head on the underside of the bed in my manic scramble to get out from under there. 'It's all right,' Dennis shouted. 'It's off.'

He found me sitting on the landing carpet gingerly fingering the egg on my forehead. 'Don't ever do that to me again,' I groaned. 'Jesus, Dennis, if I was a cat I'd be on borrowed lives after tonight.'

'Never mind whingeing, let's get done and get out of here,' he said. 'I fancy a night in with the wife.'

'I didn't realize you'd been banged up that long,' I said tartly, getting to my feet and heading back into Turpin's study, this time via the loo. I was amazed we'd got away with it; directly in the line of sight from the doorway was a CD gleaming like a beacon on Turpin's desk.

Ransacking his secrets took less time than I expected. Less time, certainly, than I deserved, given how overdrawn my luck must have been that night. We let ourselves out of the front door just after midnight. I dropped Dennis outside his front door half an hour later and drove home on freshly gritted roads. For once, Richard was home alone, awake and ardent. Unfortunately I felt older than God and about as sexy as a Barbie doll so he made me cocoa and didn't say a word against me crashing alone in my own bed. It must be love.

I think.

I was constructing the fire wall between me and the evidence when Gizmo stuck his head round my office door next morning. 'What's happening?' he asked.

'I'm trying to make this stuff look like it came

through the letterbox,' I said, waving a hand at the pile of material I'd amassed from John Turpin's office. 'It's all sorted now, except for the computer files. All I can do is enclose a floppy copy with a printed note of where to find the original files on Turpin's hard disk. But it's not conclusive.'

Gizmo sidled into the room, looking particularly smart in one of the suits I'd chosen. He'd even had a haircut. I wondered if today was the day. I'd find out soon enough, I reckoned. He placed a thin bundle of papers on the desk in front of me and said, 'I think this might be.'

The top sheet revealed John Turpin's present shareholding in NPTV as well as details of his future potential share options. I whistled softly. Even a movement in share price of a few pence could make a significant difference to Turpin's personal wealth. Next came what were clearly commercially sensitive details of NPTV's current negotiations with a cable TV company. I didn't even want to know where this stuff had come from. What was clear from the terms of the deal was that if certain levels of viewing figures were reached in the twelve months either side of the deal, senior executives of NPTV – among them John Turpin – were going to be a lot richer than they were now.

The last sheet was the killer. Somehow, Gizmo had got his sticky fingers on the details of a transaction carried out by John Turpin's stockbroker on his behalf. The order for a tranche of NPTV shares had been placed on the day of Dorothea Dawson's murder. According to the computerized time code on the order, Turpin had instructed his broker in the short space of time between Gloria and me leaving the camper van and the police arriving in response to my call.

I looked up at Gizmo. 'I suppose he thought he'd be too busy later on to get his order in. And then he'd have lost the edge that killing Dorothea had given him.'

'You mean he killed her just to push up the programme ratings and make himself richer?' Gizmo said, clearly shocked.

'I think that was just a bonus. He actually killed her because she'd sussed that he was the mole leaking the storylines to the papers. Ironically, she had powerful reasons for keeping quiet about his involvement, but he didn't believe her. He thought she was going to blackmail him or expose him, and he wasn't prepared to take that risk. He just bided his time till he found the right opportunity.'

Gizmo shook his head. 'It never ceases to amaze me, what people will do for money. People always say shit like it buys you privacy, or it lets you live the life you want. But I don't know. I've got all the privacy I need, and I'm mostly skint. But I live the life I want. I reckon most people that chase money only do it because they don't really know what it is they do want.'

Philosophy for breakfast now. It had to be better than Clitheroe sausages, I thought with a bitter smile. I hoped Turpin was making the most of it. He'd be a fair few years older before he tasted anything other than prison food. With a sigh, I picked up the phone and managed to persuade the police switchboard to connect me to Linda Shaw. 'Hi, Sergeant,' I said. 'It's Kate Brannigan.'

'Oh yes,' she said, her voice guarded.

'I've something at the office I think you might like to see,' I told her.

'Oh yes? And what would that be?' She sounded neutral. I guessed Jackson was within hearing range.

'You need to see it to get the full effect. I can promise you it'll help your clear-up rate.'

'I'd heard you've already contributed to that this week,' she said tartly. 'I can't say I'd like to share the experience.'

'This is different,' I said firmly. 'Please, Linda. I'm trying to do us both a favour here. You know and I know that if I approach Jackson his first instinct will be to rubbish what I've got. And that could mean a murderer walking. You don't want that any more than I do. So will you come round?'

'Give me an hour,' she said, a noticeable lack of enthusiasm in her voice.

It couldn't have suited me better. An hour was perfect for what I had to do.

Given the grief I'd already had over the Perfect Son, I'd expected Shelley to rip Gloria's face off and

337

send her home with it in a paper bag. Instead, Gloria got the star treatment. Apparently, according to Shelley, if her boy was with Gloria, he couldn't be getting into the kind of trouble I organized especially for him on a daily basis. But Gloria, being a mother herself, would understand Shelley's concerns. Gloria patted Shelley's hand, sympathized and told her what a credit to his mother the Perfect Son was. Donovan shifted from foot to foot, faintly embarrassed but relieved not to be on the receiving end of another maternal diatribe. Excuse me, I wanted to shout. Who's the one with frostbite and coronary heart disease and a major sleep deficit and a bump on the head the size of Rochdale as a result of this case?

Eventually, I managed to shoo Gloria into my office. She did a double take when she saw Freddie perched uncomfortably on the edge of the sofa. I'd promised him there was no reason why anyone had to know he was Dorothea's son or that he'd been the major mole, but his body language didn't actually indicate conviction. When Gloria walked in, his face spasmed in panic. 'Gloria,' he stammered, jerking to his feet and taking an involuntary sideways step away from her.

'Hiya, chuck,' she said warmly, collapsing on to the sofa. 'You another one of Kate's mystery witnesses, then?'

'Er . . . yes. She never mentioned you were coming . . .' He shot me a look that said he'd never trust a private eye again. I wouldn't have minded so much if I'd lied to him, but I hadn't. Well, not so's you'd notice.

We didn't have long to wait for Linda. She came in with more attitude than a rap band. 'This better be good,' she said even before she got across the threshold. I waved her to a chair and leaned against my desk.

'Since you're all so thrilled to be here, I'll keep it short as I can. There's been a mole at NPTV making a small fortune out of selling scandal stories and advance storylines to the press. Dorothea Dawson thought she had worked out the identity of that mole by studying her astrological charts and matching what they told her against the names of people who had access to advance stories and who were in a position to find out about the murky pasts of the cast.' I nodded towards Freddie.

'You might remember Freddie here. He works in the make-up department at *Northerners*. Freddie witnessed an encounter between Dorothea and a senior management figure at NPTV. Freddie, can you tell DS Shaw what you told me last night?'

He was so overwhelmed with relief that I hadn't after all revealed either of his secrets that he told the story we'd agreed eagerly and openly, with none of his awkward mannerisms to make Linda wonder if there was more going on than met the eye. 'Dorothea had come over to the make-up studio looking for one of the actors so she could rearrange an appointment, but she'd just missed him. Anyway, Turpin came in just as she was leaving. She asked if he was still wasting his time on the mole hunt. Then she said she had a pretty good idea who the mole was, and she'd tell him if the price was right.'

'What did Turpin say?' I asked.

'He went bright red. He told her if he wanted to waste the company's money, there were plenty of perfectly good charities. Then he just stomped out without doing whatever it was he'd come in for.'

'Turpin might well have interpreted Dorothea's comments as an indirect blackmail threat,' I pointed out.

Linda had listened with her head cocked to one side, critically appraising his words. Then she gave a slight nod. I was about to say more, but she raised one finger and made a series of notes in her pad. 'Interesting,' she said.

'There's more.'

'I'm sure,' she said.

'You've already taken a statement from Gloria about the events of the evening when Dorothea was killed. I don't know if you remember, but she had a far better opportunity than I did to take notice of who else was in and around the car park at the same time. Among the people she saw was that same NPTV executive, John Turpin. Maybe you'd like to confirm that for us, Gloria?'

My client nodded avidly. 'That's right, chuck,' she said eagerly. She was loving every minute of it, just as I'd expected. I hadn't really needed her there, but she was paying the bill, and I figured a bit of grandstanding might just be worth a Christmas bonus. 'I saw John Turpin standing in the doorway of the admin block. He looked as if he was wondering whether it was worth chancing getting his good suit wet in the sleet.'

'Thanks for confirming that, Ms Kendal. But we did know that already, Kate,' Linda pointed out, not even bothering to make a note this time.

'I'm just sketching in the background, Linda,' I said apologetically. 'I became involved in this case because Gloria here was getting death-threat letters. She hired me to take care of her.'

'Which you and yours have done admirably,' the irrepressible Gloria chipped in.

'Thank you, Gloria. I may need that testimonial before long,' I said. 'This morning, when I unlocked the office, there was a padded envelope in the mailbox.' I produced an envelope from the desk behind me.

'Inside was an assortment of papers and a floppy disk. The disk contains what I believe are the originals of the letters sent to my client. A note attached to the floppy claims that the originals are to be found on the hard disk of John Turpin's home computer. I'd have thought that might be grounds for a search warrant?'

Linda grunted noncommittally, frowning at the disk and the note I handed her. 'Why would he target you specifically, Gloria?' she asked.

'I haven't a clue, chuck,' she said. 'The only thing I can think of is that I'm the only one of the show's really big names who lives alone, so maybe he thought I'd be easiest to scare. Mind you, he's never entirely forgiven me for our Sandra giving him the elbow all those years ago.'

'What?' Linda and I chorused.

'He took our Sandra out for a few weeks, years ago now. Before she met Keith. Any road, she decided he wasn't for her and she chucked him. He wasn't best pleased. He's never had a civil word for me since.'

All I could do was stare at her and shake my head. I love clients who go out of their way to make the job easier. I just don't seem to get many. I took a deep breath while Linda took more notes.

'Also in the envelope.' I placed more papers in front of her. 'A photocopy of Turpin's phone bills, home and mobile. A photocopy of what looks like a Rolodex card, giving the number of Tina Marshall. She's the freelance journalist who broke a substantial number of the *Northerners* stories in the press. Check out the number of calls to her number. I think you'll find most of them were made a few days before a big *Northerners* story broke.'

Linda was now sitting upright, totally focused on the papers in front of her. Her finger flicked to and fro. Then she looked me straight in the eye. 'This fell through your letterbox,' she said flatly.

'That's right. It seemed to be my civic duty to pass it on to you, Sergeant.' I rummaged inside the envelope. 'There is more.' I handed her the material Gizmo had culled from his electronic sources. More for Gloria and Freddie's benefit than Linda's, I ran through the contents.

'And at the time when he placed that order for NPTV stock,' I wound up, 'only the killer could have known that the viewing figures were about to climb sky-high on the back of Dorothea Dawson's murder.'

'Hellfire, Kate, you've done wonders,' my grateful client said. 'I can sleep easy in my bed at night now.'

'I'm glad,' I said. Not least because I could get Donovan back on the work he was supposed to be doing. I turned back to Linda. 'Taken together, it's a hard conclusion to resist.'

'It'd be easier for my boss to swallow if the information came from somewhere else,' she said resignedly.

'Howsabout if it does?' I asked. 'It won't take five minutes for Gizmo to walk down to Bootle Street and leave it in an envelope at the front counter with your name on it. You can tell Jackson you've been out taking a statement from Freddie about Dorothea's conversation with Turpin and then when you got back to the office, hey presto! There it was. You can leave me out of it altogether.'

'Are you sure?' she said. I could tell she was weighing up how much my generosity might cost her in the future.

I shrugged. 'I don't need my face all over the *Chronicle* again. Besides, there is one thing you could do for me.'

Her face closed like a slammed door. 'I thought it was too good to be true.'

I held my hands up. 'It's no big deal. Just a word with your colleagues in uniform. Donovan is going to be serving process for me for at least the next eighteen months. I'd really appreciate it if you could spread the word that the big black guy on the bicycle is wearing a white hat.'

Linda grinned. 'I think I can manage that.' She got to her feet and took some folded sheets of A4 out of her shoulder bag. 'As it happens, I've got something for you too. I'll see myself out.'

Curious, I unfolded the bundle of paper. There was a Post-it stuck on one corner in Linda's handwriting. 'Printed out from Dorothea Dawson's hard disk. It gave us all a laugh.' I pulled off the note and started to read: *Written in the Stars for Kate Brannigan, private investigator.*

Born Oxford, UK, 4th September 1966.

* *Sun in Virgo in the Fifth House*
* *Moon in Taurus in the Twelfth House*
* *Mercury in Virgo in the Fifth House*
* *Venus in Leo in the Fourth House*
* *Mars in Leo in the Fourth House*
* *Jupiter in Cancer in the Third House*
* *Saturn retrograde in Pisces in the Eleventh House*
* *Uranus in Virgo in the Fifth House*
* *Neptune in Scorpio in the Sixth House*
* *Pluto in Virgo in the Fifth House*

* *Chiron in Pisces in the Eleventh House*
* *Ascendant Sign: Gemini*

Sun in Virgo in the 5th House: On the positive side, can be ingenious, verbally skilled, diplomatic, tidy, methodical, discerning and dutiful. The negatives are fussiness, a critical manner, an obsessive attention to detail and a lack of self-confidence that can disguise itself as arrogance. In the Fifth House, it indicates a player of games . . .

'What is it, chuck? You look like you've seen a ghost,' Gloria said, concern in her voice.

I shook my head, folding the papers away. 'It's nothing, Gloria. Just some sad twisted copper's idea of a joke.'

Epilogue

SATURN TRINES NEPTUNE

She loses her own apprehensions through her pro-
found and penetrating investigative interest in others.
She has a strong sense of how her life should be
arranged, often bringing order to chaos. She follows
her feelings and is sensitive to the subtext that lies
beneath the conversation and behaviour of others.
She can harness irrationality and factor it into her
decision-making.

From *Written in the Stars,* by Dorothea Dawson

If I hadn't known how thoroughly Dorothea Dawson
researched her clients, I'd probably have been
impressed with her astrological analysis of my
character. I wouldn't have minded betting that
the minute Gloria told Dorothea she'd hired me,
the astrologer had started digging. I wasn't exactly
a shrinking violet. For a start, I'd appeared in
Alexis's stories in the *Chronicle* more times than
I was entirely comfortable with. So it wouldn't

have been too hard for Dorothea to pick up a few snippets about me and weave them into an otherwise standard profile.

What she missed completely was my sense of humour. I mean, if I didn't have a world-class sense of humour, why else would I be sitting in the Costa Coffee forecourt at Piccadilly Station drinking moccachino and reading my horoscope when I could be at home, snug as a bug in a phone, working out how to solve my latest computer game with a Stoly and pink grapefruit juice on the side?

The reason why I was lurking among the sad souls condemned to travelling on Virgin Trains was shuffling from foot to foot a few yards away, like a small child who needs to go to the toilet but doesn't want to miss some crucial development in his favourite TV show. Gizmo had clearly had a hard time deciding between style and comfort and he'd ended up wearing one of the suits I'd chosen for him. The trouble was, the only outer garment that went with it was his mac, which wasn't a lot of use in the lowest December temperatures on record. Neither were the thin-soled Italian shoes. Sometimes I wonder what real Italians wear in winter.

As well as hopping from one foot to the other, Gizmo was clutching a copy of Iain M. Banks's cult sci-fi novel, *Feersum Endjin*, the agreed recognition signal. He'd arranged to meet Jan off the London train at half past eight and he'd been dancing his quaint jig since a quarter past. Imagine expecting a train to be early. I'd sat comfortably sipping my brew and dipping into Dorothea's digest of my personality.

There was an indecipherable announcement over the Tannoy and Gizmo stopped jigging. He leaned slightly forward, nose towards the platforms like a setter scenting the breeze. I followed his gaze and watched the dark-red livery of the London train easing into platform six with a rumble and a sigh. I couldn't help crossing my fingers. If this went pear-shaped, I'd get no proper work out of him for weeks.

The carriage doors were opening the length of the train and people spilled on to the platform. First past us were the smokers, carrying with them a miasma of overflowing ashtray after two and a half hours sitting in stale tobacco smoke. Then the usual Friday-night mixture of day-trip shoppers, students coming to Manchester for a groovy weekend, senior citizens exhausted from a week with the grandchildren, sales reps and educational consultants in cheap suits crumpled by the journey and, finally, the first-class passengers in sleek tailoring with their identikit suit carriers and briefcases, men and women alike.

Gizmo bobbed like a ball on the tide of humanity streaming past him, his eyes darting from side to side. The crowd swelled, then steadied, then thinned to the last stragglers. His head seemed to shrink into his shoulders like a tortoise and I saw him sigh.

Last off the train was a blond giant. His broad shoulders strained a black leather jacket that tapered to narrow hips encased in tight blue denim. They didn't leave much to the imagination, especially with his swivel-hipped walk. As he reached the end of the platform, he turned his head right, then left, a thick mane of blond hair bouncing on his collar. He looked like a Viking in the prow of a longship, deciding which direction held America.

He settled for left and moved in our direction. As he grew nearer, I could see the book clutched in the massive hand that wasn't carrying the black leather holdall. I closed my eyes momentarily. Even Dennis might have a bit of bother menacing his way out of this one. Gizmo would have no chance.

When I opened them, Jan was looming over Gizmo. 'You're Gizmo,' he boomed. I couldn't quite place the accent.

Gizmo half turned towards the café, panic in his eyes. 'I never . . . she never said anything about anybody else,' he stammered desperately.

Typical, I thought. Great with silicon, crap with carbon-based life forms. Does not compute.

Jan frowned. 'What do you mean?' I figured he wasn't sure if Gizmo had missed the point completely or if there was a language problem.

Gizmo took a hasty step backwards. 'Look, I never meant to cause any trouble, I didn't know anything about you. Whatever she's said, there's been nothing between us, this would have been the first time we'd even met,' he gabbled.

Jan looked even more puzzled. He waved the book at Gizmo. 'I brought the book. So we'd know each other,' he said in that pedantic way that Germans and Scandies have when they're not sure you've understood their impeccable English.

Gizmo swung towards me. 'Tell him, Kate. Tell him it's all a misunderstanding. She never said anything about having a bloke. I thought she was unattached.'

With a sigh, I got to my feet. 'You're Jan, right?' I said, giving the J its soft Y sound. Gizmo's mouth fell open and the Iain M. Banks tumbled to the concourse floor. Then, suddenly, he whirled round and ran for the escalator down to the tram terminus below. Jan made a half-hearted move to step around me and give chase but I blocked him. 'Leave it,' I said. 'He's not the one, Jan.'

He frowned. 'Who are you? What's going on?' He craned past me, peering anxiously towards the escalators, as if he expected Gizmo to reappear. Fat chance.

'I'm Kate. Gizmo and I work together.'

'Why has he run off? We arranged to meet,' Jan said, sounding puzzled. 'We have been e-mailing each other for months. Getting to know each other. We both figured it was time to meet.' He made the inverted commas sign in the air that pillocks use to indicate they're quoting. '"Time to take things further," Gizmo said.'

'Don't you think it might have been sensible to mention that you were a bloke?' I said, unable to keep the sarcasm out of my voice. 'He thought you were a woman. Jan with a J, not Jan with a Y.'

Jan's fair skin flushed scarlet. 'What does that matter? I'm still the same person. Because I am a man suddenly it's different?'

'Of course it's different,' I protested. His disingenuousness was really winding me up. 'He's not gay, for one thing. I can't believe you never made it clear you're a man. It can't be the first time someone's made that mistake.'

He glared at me. 'Why should I? I'm not responsible for someone else's assumptions. You British are so terrified of anything that is different, that challenges your sad little conventions.'

By now, the entire coffee shop was enthralled, waiting for my response. 'Bollocks,' I said contemptuously. 'Tell that to Julian Clary. Don't try and pretend that deceiving Gizmo was some kind of heroic act of sexual liberation. It was cowardice, that's what it was. You were scared to admit you were a man because you thought Gizmo would end your cyber-relationship.'

'And I was right,' he shouted.

'No, you were wrong,' I said quietly. 'He might have rejected you as a lover, but he would still have been your friend. And I've got good cause to know just how much that signifies.' Three women sitting round a table in the coffee shop gave me a ragged round of applause.

351

Jan's laugh was harsh. 'In cyberspace, he didn't need a woman to fight his battles.' Then he turned on his heel and stalked off towards the taxi rank.

I gave the women a sardonic bow and walked out into a heavy drizzle. Underneath the entrance canopy, the Salvation Army band was playing 'In the Bleak Midwinter'. A beggar with a dog on a string was trying to sell the *Big Issue* to people with a train to catch. A traffic warden was writing a ticket to stick on some poor sucker's windscreen.

I couldn't see Gizmo turning up for work on Monday morning as if nothing had happened. It looked like Brannigan & Co had just lost their computer expert. And when I got back to my car, the back tyre was flatter than my spirits.

If this was what was written in the stars, there was a scriptwriter somewhere who'd better watch his back.